By Clark Thomas Carlton

THE PROPHET
OF THE
TERMITE GOD

The Prophet of the Termite God

Prophets of the Ghost Ants

THE PROPHET OF THE TERMITE GOD

Book Two of the Antasy Series

CLARK THOMAS CARLTON

HARPER

VOYAGER

IMPULSE

An Imprint of HarperCollinsPublishers

THE PROPHET OF THE TERMITE GOD. Copyright © 2019 by Clark Thomas Carlton. All rights reserved. Printed in the United States of America. No part of this book may be used or reproduced in any manner whatsoever without written permission except in the case of brief quotations embodied in critical articles and reviews. For information, address HarperCollins Publishers, 195 Broadway, New York, NY 10007.

Digital Edition APRIL 2019 ISBN: 978-0-06-242976-6
Print Edition ISBN: 978-0-06-242977-3

Cover design by Guido Caroti
Cover art by Daniel Liang

Harper Voyager, the Harper Voyager logo, and Harper Voyager Impulse are trademarks of HarperCollins Publishers.

HarperCollins is a registered trademark of HarperCollins Publishers in the United States of America and other countries.

FIRST EDITION

19 20 21 22 23   OPM   10 9 8 7 6 5 4 3 2 1

In memory of Caren Bohrman
Friend, Fighter, Goddess of Laughter

THE PROPHET
OF THE
TERMITE GOD

CONTENTS

on the conquest of the Slope and the extermination of its millions. I cannot exaggerate the threat that was the Hulkrites and the extent of their crimes, all of which were justified as the demand of their termite deity in order to create a singular, universal religion. As greed is never satisfied, the Hulkrites would have used the Slope as the base for their next conquest: our Dranverite Collective Nations. The first of the prophet-commanders was Tahn, a capable warrior utterly convinced of himself as the Warrior Prophet of Hulkro. Tahn's rise from poverty to power was in the chance discovery of an ant queen landed from her nuptial flight. Her progeny, the ghost ants of Hulkren, were supreme mounts in war as well as providers of food in a desolate land of the starving. Part of Tahn's plan for conquest of all the Known Sand was the domestication of leaf-cutter ants in order to provide mushrooms for his women and make them as fertile as Slopeites. He abducted a leaf-cutter egg-layer as well as a Slopeish royal, Queen Polexima, to serve as his urine sorceress and protect the fungus farms from the Yellow Mold. When it was learned that Polexima's urine had no powers without the consumption of roach eggs, a clan of my Britasyte people and their roaches were abducted and imprisoned in Hulkren. With that clan was my beloved, Daveena, who has since become my wife.

In the attempt to rescue my people, I posed as a defector from a fictional nation to become a Hulkrish warrior. I learned their ways and witnessed their conquests. I freely admit that when I had my chance, I slaughtered Tahn and over a hundred of his highest-ranking officers. I am grieved over their deaths and their misspent lives, but I suffer no guilt for my actions as each of them was a killer, a rapist, and an enslaver. I freed my roach people as well as Queen Polexima. We escaped being killed by Tahn's successor, Commander Pleckoo, the Second Prophet. I knew Pleckoo's next mission would be the gathering of his armies for the complete destruction of the people of the Slope—for I knew and understood Pleckoo all too well.

On my return to the Slope, I posed as the Dranverite commander Vof Quegdoth, and with Polexima's support, we raised and trained a people's army with the promise of creating a new and just nation. Our victory was a narrow one, made possible by the use of aerial warfare at night. This was conducted on the backs of night wasps—yes, night wasps—which we managed to harness and pilot with the help of an ally, King Medinwoe and the Grass Men of Dneep. They are a roach people who seek to relocate their nation to the Weedlands on our southern border as their Promised Clearing.

I fully admit that on the War of One Night I used a fire effigy as a means of terrifying our enemy and confusing their ants with enemy kin-scent. The Hulkrites outnumbered us with millions of ghost ants and skilled soldiers with the most lethal of weapons.

The risk of igniting a wildfire with our effigy was not great, but I understand now that fire in warfare must never be risked, that it is better to lose a war than to ignite a holocaust. For this, I apologize to you and to all people on the Sand.

Since the war, I have made a political marriage with a Slopeish royal in hopes of preserving a truce between Bee-Jor and the Old Slope. Princess Trellana, the daughter of Poleximα, is a woman whose first misfortune was to rule briefly over the lost colony in Dranveria. Trellana's most recent misfortune is to be married to me.

Dwan, I have succeeded in winning a war and creating a new nation, but now I am like some spiderling who has captured a hundred lethal hornets with the first web it has ever spun. Bee-Jor struggles to establish itself while the Old Slope plots to retake us. In the East, the Seed Eaters are likely planning to attack our young and vulnerable nation and retake its stolen mounds. In the West, the Carpenter Nation are already at war with the old and crippled Slope and they have likely set their next sights on Bee-Jor. And as for the South, in what was Hulkren, a thousand other threats are hatching in the chaos of a land whose masters are dead or hiding. My greatest fear is that Commander Pleckoo, my cousin, is very much alive and his greatest passion is to destroy me and all I have won.

I have no choice but to rule as best as I can with

CHAPTER 1

THE DREAM HATER

Pleckoo was in the softest bed, licking honey off
the nipples of a sweet-smelling beauty as her fingers scratched through his fresh-washed scalp. He
looked into her face with its parted lips and violet
eyes and he saw her pure desire for him. She kissed
his mouth, then rubbed the delicate tip of her nose
against his. Startled, he reached for the center of his
face, and instead of finding a rough cavity he felt a
warm tip.

"A mirror!" he shouted, and turned to the wall
where a sheet of polished obsidian stood like the
portal to another world. He walked towards his reflection and saw it, a perfect nose on the handsomest

face with skin that had somehow lightened. Laughing with relief, he rubbed this nose to make sure it wouldn't fall off when the mirror trembled, opened like a mouth, then sucked him in with a moist tongue. Passing down the wetness of a pulsing tube, he found himself squeezed into the palm of a great and glowing hand. Pleckoo looked up at the full moon face of Hulkro, in his aspect of Lord Termite of the Night Sky. Crawling to the edge of his god's sixth hand, Pleckoo gaped in fright at the distant sand below when the Termite inhaled and blew him out of His palm. Screaming as his body spun, he plummeted over a parade of ghost ants marching back to their mound. He landed, knees first, on the natural saddle of an ant's head where he collapsed and blacked out.

When Pleckoo roused from a swirling darkness, he probed his face and did not find a nose, but the usual bone jutting from a jagged hole. "I hate dreams!" he said to himself, realizing he had fallen asleep on his mount. He looked around, wondered where he was, and realized days had passed since he had climbed on the ant's head at the Brackish Lake. She had found a trunk trail where her sisters were returning with bits of digger wasps as well as the cicada grubs with which they had provisioned their burrows. The morning sun was illuminating a human-inhabited ant mound in Hulkren—but which one? Near the first ring in a clearing he saw hundreds of women in hooded shrouds, gathered at an outdoor shrine and kneeling before a slice of wood with a gallery track. Looking down at himself, Pleckoo realized he was completely naked.

Intensely thirsty, Pleckoo slid over the ant's head to her mandibles and jumped off them when he reached a clump of barley grass. He used his sword to saw off a central stalk and then sucked up the water that welled at its top. To cover the hole in his face, he made a sash from a grass blade, then tied it around his head with its stringy vein. Before approaching the women, he turned his sword belt so that the hilt fell over his genitals. The women turned and saw him, a nude man whose skin was a bizarre mottle of green pond scum, white paint, and lake mud. As he walked towards them, his sword bobbled between his legs and the sight made them giggle.

"Do you know who you laugh at?" Pleckoo snarled. The women turned away from him and back to their shrine. "I asked you a question!" he said, kicking at their backs until one stood tall to face him.

"Good Hulkrite, we not here for laughing," said the woman in broken Hulkrish. Her face was shadowed by her shroud. "For victory, we pray here."

"I heard them laugh!" Pleckoo said, hitting the side of her head with his fist. The woman peeled back her hood. She was a great beauty with thick, sensuous features, tawny skin, and massive braids of dark orange hair that had softened his blow. Her

"You ask too many questions, woman. Send food and drink to the throne room in your husband's palace."

The woman's slave returned with a plain tunic of chewed eggshell and a simple pair of antennae. After dressing, Pleckoo walked back to the trunk trail and antennated a ghost ant that had squirming clover mites visible in its abdomen. After climbing atop the ant, he rode it to the mound's top, where hobbled man-slaves dangled from ropes to rub dust and grime from the translucent walls of the crystal palaces. Looking down through the different levels of the mound, he saw slaves going about the usual labors of dew delivery and carrying off trash. Below, in the riding fields, Fadthan youths were riding atop ghost ant minims and at play in mock battles with blunted weapons. A field over, younger boys were involved in the same activity with stick ants between their legs. The women at the shrine had turned from worship to the stringing of dried flower petals for victory wreaths and garlands.

Pulling himself through a portal flap, Pleckoo entered the throne room of the largest palace, where a wealth of treasures bulged from boxes and barrels. The glittering jewels hurt his eyes, as the light flooding in made them all too beautiful. He looked up the flight of steps, which in ancient times had been peaked with thrones for Slopeish royals. Now they were topped with a pedestal bearing the usual lump of rough wood and a single termite track.

Drawn to a pile of human-hair rugs, Pleckoo collapsed into their softness and felt all the aches of riding for days on an ant. He wanted to sleep, but when he closed his eyes, he saw it again, that monstrous image: a rising effigy of the Roach God, blazing with fire and falling to blind and burn His men. After ripping away the tatter of grass around his face, he shouted up the steps to the block of termite-ravaged wood. "Wake me from this dream, Termite! Show me that all was not lost, I beg You!"

Hulkro did not crawl out of the wood to perch upon it and offer a comforting message.

Knowing he was alone, Pleckoo fell to his hands and knees and wailed. He choked on his own sobbing, hoping to cough out the hundred thousand demons that warred inside him. Dizzy with convulsions, he looked up to see several figures in the shadowy distance rising from amber loungers. Sleepy or drunk or both, they stood on unsure legs as they left their silky cushions.

"Who makes such unmanly noise?" shouted one, with a harsh and gravelly voice, in Hulkrish. The men fumbled for their swords and stumbled towards Pleckoo as he reached for the handle of his own. He stood slowly, his head down as he retied his face sash, and the strangers faced him in a half-circle. Their feet and legs were coated in a filth-spattered white paint—Hulkrish warriors. But what were they doing here?

"Forgive me, Good Hulkrites," said Pleckoo. "I am a wood brother too."

"Oh, wood brother, you are?" said Gravel Voice as he curled his lip. Pleckoo raised his eyes to look at them, his nose hidden. The men were naked, reeking of grass liquor, and their lips and teeth were stained with green. Gravel Voice was large and hairy, and his front teeth looked to have recently been knocked from his bloody gums. His chest was matted with drying blood from recent cuts.

"Not from this mound, you are?" asked Gravel Voice. Pleckoo guessed from his orange pubic hair and his accent, like Muti's, that he had been a Seed Eater.

"I am from Zarren," Pleckoo said.

"Zarren-dozh," said the man next to him, who scratched inside his ear with his thumb. He had thumbs and pinkies but his other fingers were missing and the stumps of them were covered with leaking scabs. He struggled to grip his sword as he squinted at Pleckoo. "Was it not Zarren where righteous Second Prophet foresaw greatest victory of Hulkrish army?"

"What great victory it was," said the third man, who tilted to one side. Between his ribs was a length of a Seed Eater's arrow with its four-pronged arrowhead buried inside him, too deadly to remove.

"Hulkro tests the faithful," Pleckoo said.

"No more talk like that," said Gravel Voice. "We tested Hulkro and found Him failing."

"Do not speak that way—about the One True God."

"One True God is true shit who led hundreds of thousands of followers to slaughter."

"They're martyrs!" Pleckoo shouted. "They went straight to the Promised World!"

"Followers went straight to shit after carrion beetles ate corpses, and got squeezed out as dry little turds."

Pleckoo blinked in silence. "H-how did you get h-here?" he stuttered. "Did you desert?"

"Not desert," said Fingerless. "We fought. We believed—until we believed no more. When old country joined battle we saved ourselves instead of waste our lives. You, wood brother, why you not up in Promised World eating honey while angel-girls gobble on knob?"

"I . . . I survived," Pleckoo said. "A ghost ant took me here."

"Me too," said Leans to One Side. "Survivor. Deserter not. Smart enough to get ride on ants who knew it was over too. No shame in it . . . . wood brother."

They were quiet a moment, studying Pleckoo, then looking into each other's faces to confirm a mutual suspicion.

"From where you . . . from where before, brother?" asked Gravel Voice. "Before you wear white paint?"

"I was . . . was . . ."

"Ear is clipped."

"Yes."

"From Slope, are you? Mushroom Eater?"

"I was."

"Should hate you for that . . . since we are Seed Eaters, what you call us. People of Barley Lands."

"Best maybe you move on to Urtkess-dozh," said Fingerless. "Heard other mushies make it back there. You like own kind to be with, yes?"

"All men are my kind," Pleckoo said. "We are all brothers, created by the One True . . ."

"Stop!" said Gravel Voice. "No mention of *Blind One* again—if you want to keep own eyes."

Pleckoo blinked. A silence passed in which all he heard was his breathing and his thumping heart.

"Why you hide face?" said Leans to One Side as he stepped in for a closer look.

"I was . . . I was wounded too."

"Let us see if wound you have is as bad as ones we have," said Fingerless as he extended his sword slowly to Pleckoo's face. "As we Barley people say, problem shared is half a problem."

Fingerless snapped the grass sash which revealed the hole in Pleckoo's face.

"How you lose nose, brother?" asked Gravel Voice.

"Wound not looking fresh," said Leans.

"We heard tale," said Fingerless, "that before he wandered into Hulkren, Commander General Pleckoo was noseless slave in Slopeish midden."

"Right. Cleaned shit pots is what heard we," said

Gravel Voice through a chuckle that revealed his bleeding gums.

Pleckoo suddenly straightened at the mention of his old life at the midden of Cajoria. A bolt of anger had pierced him and radiated through every limb.

"It is true," Pleckoo said, his voice reverberating through the palace as his eyes opened and glittered. "Pleckoo was a nothing, a no one on the Slope, where the Wood Eater's shrines had been desecrated with idols. But Hulkro loves the humble and brings them to the greatest heights. The more we give to Him, the more He gives to us. And you, survivors, are about to receive His greatest gift."

Captured by his sonorous voice, the three looked stunned, then soothed, by Pleckoo's conviction. They were not ready for the moment he swung out with his black glass sword, which cut sharp and clean through Gravel Voice's right wrist and then down through his ankle. His severed hand landed on his severed foot as he fell on his back and twitched.

Pleckoo turned to see Leans to One Side swing his blade up and lunge, but his movements were lame. His sword came down, slow and wobbling, dragging him forward. Pleckoo stepped out of the way, then raised his own blade to slice down on the open neck. The man's head fell, but dangled from a hinge of flesh before his body slumped to the tiles.

Fingerless was at Pleckoo now, using both his mutilated hands to clutch his sword. As their blades clashed, Fingerless whimpered. Each swing was growing weaker as his hands bled over his handle. Pleckoo pulled back, dangling his blade like bait that he then whisked away, teasing. Fingerless dropped his weapon and fell to his knees, breathing hard as he looked up with pleading eyes.

"Pick it up," said Pleckoo.

"Cannot," said Fingerless.

"I said pick it up!" Pleckoo roared. "No Hulkrite ever abandons his weapon."

Fingerless reached for his sword as globs of blood grew from his finger stumps. His thumbs and pinkies wrapped around the grip. He strained to raise it up when it fell to rest on his shoulder.

"Kill me," he said. "No life here but liquor grass. Cannot go home."

"Are there others?" Pleckoo asked.

"Others?"

"Hulkrites. Deserters."

"Yes. Spread through palaces. Most out now in local weeds for gathering honey grass for ferment."

"How many?"

"Eighty, ninety, maybe one hundred. Will be back before nightfall."

"What did they tell the women they were doing here?"

"Following orders is what we told Fadtha's wife, Muti—sent back here to protect mound in case Barley people attack."

Pleckoo shook his head. *A hundred deserters? I can't stay here.*

"Commander . . . what you do with me?" Fingerless asked.

"I told you . . . I will fulfill Hulkro's greatest gift. Do you accept Him as the One True God?"

"I . . . I do, Prophet."

"Then join Him in the Promised World."

Pleckoo gripped his sword with both hands and drove it up and into the man's chin until the tip scraped the ceiling of his skull. After withdrawing his sword, Pleckoo looked at the blood and brains that clung to its blade. He walked towards Gravel Voice, who suddenly flattened to offer his chest. "Do it," he said, but Pleckoo, infuriated, screamed and grunted and hacked at the man's face, slicing away his nose before plunging his sword into the open throat.

Pleckoo walked to the loungers and found the men had made a makeshift altar to a Seed Eaters' deity woven from barley fibers—perhaps a grain goddess with the leafy wings of a katydid. They had offered Her a bowl of their green spirit, which they surely drank a moment later. He kicked the idol off its pedestal and it landed near the piles of the men's armor, which he went to and sorted through to find pieces that fit him. In Fadtha's garment room he found riding gloves with fresh scents, a gossamer cape, a captain's helmet, a full-length mirror, and a sealed barrel of fine white paint and brushes.

After he scraped himself clean and coated himself in fresh paint, Pleckoo looked in the mirror and was reminded that he was a noseless monster. He searched with fury through the chamber's treasure barrels, kicking them over, scattering their contents, and trampling through a fortune of jewels and carvings until something that didn't glimmer caught his eye—a mask facing down. He turned it over to see that the mask was inlaid with slices of orange onyx and veins of black obsidian in a pattern that resembled the wings of a milkweed butterfly. It was a Britasyte bauble and likely worn by a woman in their scandalous dancing spectacles—but the straps were intact and he tied it on.

Pleckoo heard the rustling flaps of the portal as Muti and other women pushed in, panicked and out of breath from riding up the mound. They halted before the corpses, shocked, it seemed, for a second time, and stared at Pleckoo.

"Did you ride an ant up here?" he asked. "That's forbidden to a woman."

"Did not steer. Only rode."

"What's wrong?" he asked.

"Look out window."

He threw aside the curtain of a quartz-slice window and saw that the ghost ants had left their parades and were scattered in panic throughout the humans' shelters as they raced to the mound's peak. Above him he heard the clamor of their claws on the chamber's roof as they raced over the palace, then under the rain shield to retreat down their tunnels.

Looking out to the distance, he wondered what made the ants flee instead of fight, when something appeared on the distant sand: a moving arrow-shaped mass of crawlers hauling sand-sleds. He knew what they were: roaches. *The ants of Cajoria hid like this when the Britasytes were passing through,* he thought. *Has Anand found me?* He saw that the roaches had halted in unison, controlled by the men who rode them.

"What happened to these men?" Muti shouted, her eyes darting over the corpses.

"What?" Pleckoo said through a gasp, barely able to turn from the window.

"Heard me, you did! These men have been killed—by you!"

"Hulkro wanted them dead," Pleckoo answered decisively.

"Why?"

"They blasphemed against the Termite and returned to their idols. They're cowards who ran from the war."

"How you know this?"

Pleckoo turned to her and the other women as sunlight from the window radiated through his cape and shone on the fresh paint of his skin. The mask he wore was orange, like the rising sun, and he imagined they saw it as bright and warm.

"You have kept faith, Muti. You and these women,"

he said in his richest voice as he felt his connection with the divine. "Hulkro has told me of your attentions at His shrine, of your thousands of prayers which rise like a perfume to please Him."

"Who are you?" Muti asked.

"Don't you recognize the Second Prophet?"

She gasped and blinked.

"I did not, Commander. Forgive," she said, and fell to her knees. The other women followed her example.

"You are forgiven. Rise." Pleckoo opened his arms and Muti walked towards him and into his embrace.

"The Termite has chosen you, Muti. You must protect this mound, protect the ghost ants that live here during this time of . . . uncertainty."

"Chosen me?" Muti said.

"Yes," said Pleckoo. "Don't you feel it? You are His Entrusted."

He pulled away from her, looked in her eyes. She began to shake, her eyes filling with tears as she stumbled from a faint.

"You have been reborn in the spirit of the Termite. Look to Him, seek His counsel. He will advise you until my return. Now, let us go and see what mischief these infidels on the backs of roaches have brought to our Holy Land."

With no ants to ride, it was a long walk before Pleckoo and the women, slowed by their jewels and shrouds, reached the clearing where the roaches had rested. Under a cluster of yellowing barley clumps,

Pleckoo sighted a large, squat barrel, the lid of which was missing to reveal a yellow goop that smelled of honey and insect fat. The young boys riding stick ants were gathered around it, staring.

"Who left this here?" Pleckoo shouted.

"Yellow men," said the oldest boy.

"Did you talk to them?"

"Shouted at us, but not our tongue. Made gestures we should not eat this. Maybe it makes us itchy?"

"Itchy?"

"Yes. Yellow men scratched a lot. In pain. Legs covered in big red bumps."

Pleckoo pondered that as he walked towards the barrel when he realized the ghost ants were reemerging from the mound. They were back on the downward trail to a food find, and several smaller ants had detected the barrel and raced to gather and slurp from it. "No!" shouted Pleckoo as he used his sword to stab through the ants' eyes and through to their brains. "Wrap up that barrel now!" he shouted, and both boys and the women obeyed by pulling over a wax-embedded tent canvas with attached ropes. "Let no one, ant or human, eat from this barrel. Gather the slaves, now, and make a deep pit to bury it—and these dead ants! Don't let them leave here or get eaten by their sisters."

"What is it?" Muti asked.

"Poison," Pleckoo answered, not completely sure. "A slow-acting poison."

CHAPTER 2

FILTHY SQUIRTERS

The men standing before Pleckoo were wobbling from drunkenness. Some had grins on their faces, others looked sleepy or irritated. A tall, muscular man with an eyepatch looked deeply angry. He shouted at Pleckoo in the Seed Eaters' tongue.

"Do you speak Hulkrish, brother?" Pleckoo asked.

"Brother?" said the man in slurred Hulkrish. "Bledtha is my name. Dead is my brother Fadtha. Who is it who wears my brother's cape and helmet?"

Muti, standing nearby, stepped forward. "He is . . ."

"Keep quiet, woman," said Bledtha. "I ask him, not you."

"I am a Good Hulkrite, brother," Pleckoo answered, looking at Muti as she lowered her head and stepped back.

"You wear Britasyte mask—why? You some lovely roach-girl come to dance for us while we jerk our pissers?"

The others laughed as Pleckoo knelt, lowered his head.

"Forgive my trespass, brother Bledtha. I am just a wayward warrior. On the night of the battle for the Slope, my mount fled in fright from a tree-tall roach wrapped in fire—my ant was uncontrollable. I fell asleep on her head and days later woke up to see she had returned to this mound. If you are the ruler here, all I request is that you let me go."

"From curl of your tongue I guess you are Slopeite."

"I was. I seek Urtkess-dozh, west of here, which I am told is a refuge for Slopeites in Hulkren. If you will excuse me, brother, I was leaving."

"Not yet. Leave behind stolen things."

"I . . . I will."

"And then dance for us."

The men laughed.

"Dance? I don't . . ."

"Sure can you. Do us squirmy little roach dance and shake your rump."

Pleckoo stood, raised his obsidian sword. "A Hulkrite does not dance," he said. "And not for other men."

"No Hulkrites left," said Bledtha. "Hulkro is dead, Tahn is dead. For all I know and hope, Pleckoo dead too."

"Pleckoo not dead!" Muti shouted. "He stands there now—behind that orange mask!"

Bledtha turned his head to look at Muti. He seemed unaware, a moment later, that a sharp, thin blade had cut through his neck until his head slid off his body. Pleckoo spun, whirling his blade through the men who fell or scattered. He reached the leg of a trucking ant and climbed up its spikes. Using his sword, he severed the ropes that bound the ant to a cart and then mounted her head. "Help me, Hulkro," he said aloud, and pressed the index finger of his gloved hand near the root of her antenna. The ant jolted off into a spiral and outraced the men running after her. After Pleckoo sheathed his sword, he prodded both antennae to achieve a straight, swift crawl to the outer weeds of the mound.

Muti felt numb, and then a growing rage. She was unsure if she was walking towards another cluster of corpses or if it was her ghost who had left her body to take a look. She became aware that other women had joined her, wailing as they searched the faces of the dead. One of them, barely a woman, screamed and began to wail. "Husband!" she cried out in Hulkrish. "Killed by that Slopeite!"

"He is not a Slopeite," Muti answered in the old language. "That was the Second Prophet. He has blessed us with a visit."

Muti walked towards one of the drunkards who had crawled into the shade of some grass to nap, too drunk to acknowledge or care that his kinsmen were dead. She picked up his sawing-scythe, pressed the sharp end of its hook under his neck, and kicked him.

"Ow!" he screamed. "I was sleeping, woman!"

"Tell me the truth," she said, stepping on his chest and gouging him with the hook. "Are you a deserter?"

"Get off me, witch! I know what you were in the old country—why you had to take up in Huikren."

"I have never been a witch. The Second Prophet has left me in charge. He has seen my connection, a divine tunnel, to Lord Termite."

"The Second Prophet? More like Big Impostor. Pleckoo prophesied a great victory against the Slope, something he would achieve in one night's battle!"

"You are from Durxict," she said, "judging from your accent."

He shrugged.

"What's your name?"

"Suck me," he said.

She was breathing hard. "Suck Me, is it? Are you a deserter, Suck Me? Did you run from the war?" She pressed the hook in deeper, drawing blood.

"Don't you understand, flea-spawn? We lost the war. It was *over* in a night. Our old country entered the war. The Hulkrites battling in the East were unprepared, without breathing masks, for one thing and they choked on the harvester ants' toxins. Some of us who grew up in the Barley Lands survived—the ones who were used to their poisons."

"And in the West?"

"They lost too. From what we heard it was even worse—slaughtered by the Beetle Riders in the Pine Lands."

"So all of you, you *men*, have been lying to us."

"We've been protecting you from the truth. You'd know that—if the Termite really spoke to you."

Protected from the truth! She had an urge to kill this man, to jerk the blade up his chin and rip his jaw out. For a moment, she felt the urge to kill *all* men, these hairy monsters that were always beating them and inserting their squirting, filthy parts before putting them to work. And now it was *men* who were *lying* to them, hiding that they had failed in their only real task: to protect them from enemy nations. *And those are nations with their own men*, she thought, *who would treat us even worse.*

She looked down at Suck Me, who was heaving and frightened but failing to hide his contempt for her. *Just what do I do with this one?* she was asking herself when he kicked out the scythe from her hand, grabbed her ankle, and yanked her to the ground. She punched at his face as he crawled on top of her, attempting to grab her neck.

"Kick him!" she shouted to the other women, who hesitated as his thumbs gouged into her throat. "Kick him, before he kills me!" she wheezed.

The women circled the two of them. The first kicks were weak and tentative. Suck Me growled and grabbed one woman's leg and bit deep into her ankle. She screamed, then retaliated with a sharp kick to his nose. The others followed her lead, kicking the man's ears, his neck, his ribs.

"You bloody slits!" he shouted as the foot bashing continued. He was unable to move, and they heard the sound of his ribs cracking with the crash of their feet.

"Stop!" Muti shouted. "Turn him over."

The women obeyed, pushing him onto his stomach as Muti retrieved her scythe.

"You may have your uses yet, Suck Me," she said, and gouged below his calf with the scythe to snap his tendons. She scraped the blood off the blade, raised it up, and looked around to find the women and the boys were staring at her, frozen in fear and awaiting her next order.

crenate, kidney-shaped leaves were yellowing at the ends of stems that still held some green. Pleckoo urged the ant over the jagged sand to enter into the plant's shade, then tied the ant's hauling rope to a stalk as a tether. After dropping to the ground, Pleckoo thrust his sword into the base of the plant and twisted it in hope that a bead of sweet water might bloom from the cut.

But nothing came. He searched through the leaves in hope that one of them might be moist enough to chew for its water, but their undersides were speckled with the bright orange of a poisonous rust. *I'm defeated . . . again,* he thought as he felt his dry tongue, trapped inside his drier mouth, and tasted its own bitterness.

Defeated—the word echoed in his brain. He fell to his knees on the flat of some sand grains and felt an unbearable heaviness, as if he carried a boulder of the Great Jag on his back. He hesitated to lie down, thinking he might never get up again, then willed himself to kneel for a moment longer to pray. He looked up between the spaces of the leaves to the sun-bleached sky above and the promise of an evening moon.

Hulkro, Your ways are mysterious, but if ever You loved me, I ask You to send water, then show me the way. Pleckoo removed the sweaty mask from his face, then gathered bits of crumbled leaves around him to use as a crunchy pillow. After closing his eyes he chanted the round of Hulkro's names until he fell asleep, hoping he would not wake before morning, with its blessing of a quenching dew.

Sometime later, Pleckoo woke and looked through the leaves to see a graying sky. As the sun was dying in the West, the tattered phantoms of rain clouds thickened into a dark and soggy blanket. A moist breeze gently tossed the mallow's leaves and then there was the sharp, fresh aroma of a coming storm.

It can't be rain! Pleckoo thought. *Too soon in the autumn for that.* Then he heard it—the soft plop of a drop. He left the shelter of the mallow to see a dome of water on a sand grain that had broken into smaller beads that shrank as they seeped into the ground. He went to lick what he could when a second drop fell and sent up a brief crater bursting with tiny tendrils of smaller drops. He ran towards the flattening moisture when a great drop landed on a fallen leaf and broke into domes that held their shape. He approached the closest drop, puckered his lips, and sucked. It was sweeter than aphid syrup, a taste of the Promised World. More rain was falling, creating a broken maze of crystal domes that shrank before they disappeared. Returning to the protection of the mallow plant, he saw the ant had roused and widened its mandibles to suck in a drop that suddenly doubled when it combined with one nearby.

Pleckoo's stomach was full and his head was clearing, but his panic spiraled as the sand's grains upended and shifted in a fierce downpour. Soon, a thick layer of water was over the ground. As he paced, the moisture was sucking at his boots and his cape grew heavy as it soaked up water. He had no shelter with a pitched roof he could retreat into: he could only look up at the stems of the mallow as its leaves bobbed in the pelting rain and hope it was enough to protect him. Climbing up and into the plant, he looked down at the ant as she strained against the rope that bound her. As the water rose, the ant's legs paddled above the sand as she drifted left and right on her tether.

Pleckoo coughed as he shook himself free from water that beaded and bunched on his head and shoulders. He needed to climb higher, but his feet slipped in the crook of the stems as his armor and clothing grew weighty with dampness. Going higher, he sheltered under a leaf that filled with rain, then lowered over his head like the heaviest hat before it spilled out its load, then shot back up. The sky was turning black and promising a long, dank night of struggling for breath and staying aloft. He sat in a crook of the plant's stems and slumped against one, using his legs and arms to grip it as rain collected on him in an enveloping sphere, drowning him as he fought to break through its surface tension. Dizzy and panting, he was stunned when violent flashes of lightning broke through the leaves and were followed by a shocking burst of thunder.

Hulkro is angry! Pleckoo thought. *He's destroying the world and starting it over!*

A second flash of lightning showed him the fast-rising water. The ant was not dead but twisting and turning on her rope as the rain splashed thicker and harder. Pleckoo's heart thumped in fear as water enclosed his head again. He shook himself hard to break free and breathe.

A sharp and howling blast of wind came up and he felt the tilt of the plant as the gusts tore off its dying leaves, then blew him out of its slippery stems. As he scrambled to climb back up the plant, the wind-driven rain hurled down with a renewed violence. He pulled himself back into the tangle of stems when the wind smacked him out and down, smashing him into an upended sand grain that gouged his forehead and bloodied the hole of what had been his nose. Pain radiated in unbearable throbs through his head when he fell facedown and plummeted into a depth of water as deep and as black and as unending as death . . .

I've drowned! I'm dead! he thought as he sank deeper and deeper into the depths of some sudden lake. He hit its silty bottom when the water vanished and left him on a dry land of black sand and weeds that screamed in a freezing wind. He sat up and looked at Demoness Lair Spider, pushing up from the Trap Door to the Netherworld.

"Worm awaits you," she said from the mouths of both her heads, "and will judge your duties to caste."

Lair Spider snatched him with the web between her claws and spun him into a capsule before she retreated with him down a tunnel that went deep and cold and darker. She slipped through the portal of a vast palace with black crystal walls, then crawled with Pleckoo, rocking between her fore-claws, through an immense chamber lit by fungus torches. He looked out of the webbing when Lair Spider reached a long, crooked spiral of stairs and began a nauseating descent. Pleckoo bobbed in the tangled hammock, paralyzed with fear, when he was set before the muck-covered throne of Judge Worm, who coiled up and out from His loam-filled seat. Stretching His segmented body, He bent down His tapered end to nuzzle and sniff Pleckoo, who squirmed in the webbing.

"Pleckoo," Worm said from the tiny opening at the end of His undulating body. "You are dead now, your soul before me. Have you been dutiful to your caste?"

"I have no caste!" Pleckoo shouted.

"What? No caste?" He said through a chuckle. "Everyone has a caste."

Worm's chuckle turned into a hissing laugh. Pleckoo could see that in the back of His throne were two portals, one that seeped a bright, yellow light and the sweet scents of sage and primrose. On the other side was a dark portal whose flap muffled the howls and sobbing of a trillion tormented souls.

An angel appeared from the glowing portal, wearing a black-and-orange mask like the one Pleckoo had adopted. On his back were the wings of a milkweed butterfly. He unmasked and revealed the mirror image of Pleckoo when he was younger and at his handsomest, with a winsome and upturned nose. Pleckoo gasped as he watched the angel take flight, twirling as he flew up, then hovered over the throne. Worm bent His end to hear the angel's whispers, then shook it in deepest disapproval. The angel lowered slowly to stand before the portal to the World of Rewards, his arms folded under a somber face.

The other portal opened. A black mist seeped out and filled the palace with the sour stench of maggots feasting on human flesh. Pleckoo held his breath and tried not to inhale, but the stink of the World of Eternal Punishment was deep inside his nose and left it chafed and bleeding. A winged demon stepped out of the portal with skin of chitinous black and garish indigo stripes. On his back were the fiery orange wings of a night wasp. Pleckoo looked at the demon's face and saw his mirror reflection with its missing nose, but as if it had been freshly ripped off with dripping blood. The demon buzzed its wings and flew up to Worm's end to whisper its report. Pleckoo watched as Worm wriggled in the loam of His throne, then suddenly rose up and lashed like a great, thick whip at him. His blob-shaped head burst from out of its end and revealed its circular mouth of razor-teeth.

"Pleckoo," Worm said in a throaty hiss. "You defected from your mound. You wandered south into the Dustlands to worship Hulkro. You abandoned the duties of your caste."

"It is true," Pleckoo said, his body shaking in the webbing.

"But Hulkro does not rule the Netherworld. I do. Where is Little Termite now?"

"High above, in the night sky, where He rules over all."

"You have said He is the only god—yet here I am, deciding your fate for eternity."

"You are nothing more than a dream I will wake from at any moment."

Worm's hissing laughter filled the palace.

"Pleckoo of Cajoria, of the midden caste. You stand before me as the greatest of all transgressors of the Divine Laws. Not even your commander, this Tahn of Hulkren, was as great a sinner, for his people had become ignorant to the One Great Truth. But you were born a son of the Slope, a descendent of Ant Queen, and given the honor to serve Her. Yet you turned against your goddess, the one whose drop of blood is carried in your most humble veins. You warred on Her descendants and murdered hundreds of thousands of them defending Her Slope."

"I . . . will . . . wake from this dream!" Pleckoo shouted.

"You are not dreaming. You are most dead. And you are being judged."

"When I die, I will not face You," shouted Pleckoo. "I will rise to the World Above Clouds, to the Battlefield of Stars, and see the face of the One True God. I will join the First Prophet where we will feast and drink and battle through eternity."

"You mean Tahn, the false prophet, the lunatic worshipper of Termite as Moon."

"Hulkro exists . . . and is the only god."

"My cousin Hulkro exists. But He was thrown out of the Tree Palace of Ganilta, never to dwell there again."

"You are an illusion spewing lies!" said Pleckoo.

"You lie to yourself, Termite worshipper. Tahn does not feast and drink in a Realm of Stars with endless concubines. He is here. With me. Would you like to see him?"

The flying demon flew through the stinking portal. A moment later, it split open and a massive ball of buzzing night wasps rolled out of it. The wasps untangled, flying up to reveal a man who screamed on the floor and gasped for breath as his body lay in paralysis.

"Pleckoo!" wheezed Tahn, who barely raised his head. "Renounce me, renounce Hulkro! Save yourself from this!"

Smaller night wasps dropped down from their larger, hovering sisters to cover Tahn's naked body. They sank the hooks of their mandibles into his skin, cut it into patches, and then ripped it off to expose his muscles and organs as he screamed in agony. One wasp severed his liver and kidneys and tossed them up to her larger sisters to swallow. A second wasp crawled towards Tahn's face and yanked out his eyeballs with the spikes of her claws. His screaming diminished by half as one lung was plucked from inside his rib cage, and he was silenced with the removal of the other. Blood flowed from his dissected body as his heart beat inside the emptied rib cage. Pleckoo spasmed in shock to see that Tahn was still alive, still twitching, as his muscles were severed, then stripped from the bones of his arms and legs. Finally, a wasp broke open the rib cage to gobble down the heart. The skeleton went still as the rest of the wasps lowered to the floor, and gathered in a disc to march over the bones. The wasps spun away from each other, flying up to reveal Tahn, completely intact and ready for another destruction.

"Pleckoo, renounce me!" Tahn screeched as the smaller wasps converged on him, ripping open his abdomen and yanking out his intestines. The wasps used his guts as ropes to wrap around his feet and hands, then lifted him to fly through the portal. As it opened, the agonizing screams of the Trillion Damned filled the palace.

Pleckoo wanted to muffle his ears, but his arms could not rise. Worm stretched over him, looking down at his face with invisible eyes. "Renounce Tahn. Renounce Hulkro," He murmured with a genuine kindness. Pleckoo felt something moist and warm as

Worm's end kissed his ear, then whispered inside it. "The gods are merciful, Pleckoo. Renounce the Termite and save yourself."

"No!" screamed Pleckoo. "I am a warrior for the One True God!"

Worm whipped away as the dark portal's slit parted again. The night wasps crawled out of it, marching towards Pleckoo with their mandibles scissoring, their antennae lashing, and with wings of actual fire that turned the palace into a scalding kiln. Two wasps cut through the threads of the capsule, then grabbed Pleckoo by each ankle. He saw his reflection in their massive eyes as they crawled backwards, hauling him up the stairs, and bouncing him over its rough steps and through to the Place of Endless Suffering. His first breath inside was a painful intake of a poisoned air that scorched his nostrils and burned his lungs. His back roasted on the scalding sand and he felt a thousand blisters bubbling and popping.

"Save me!" he screamed as his agony intensified. "Save me, Hulkro!" But his words had become flames that scorched his throat. Strange, knotted antennae were probing his face when he realized a roach was behind him. Sitting on the roach's head and driving it was his Demon Twin and Eternal Tormentor. The roach clamped its mouth over Pleckoo's head as it pinned down his arms with its front claws. A swarm of smaller roaches scurried over Pleckoo's naked body and stripped off his skin in ribbons. As his blood cooked on the sands, Pleckoo convulsed in an expanding agony. He felt his head being chewed off his neck.

Blackness, then silence.

Pleckoo felt himself reforming, his hearing returning, and realized he was kneeling on the saddle of an insect crawling on fine, golden sand. Around him was a meadow of dew-spattered clover and fragrant poppies that swayed overhead. In the air he sniffed the bright scent of honeyed turpentine. The insect halted, rose up, and Pleckoo slid off its back. The sky turned a rich and deep violet, and a billion stars popped and glittered from its vault.

Pleckoo got to his knees to look at the insect that had rescued him. It was a termite with lacy wings twice as long as its body. As it climbed up a stone, it glowed warmly when it reached the top and splayed its wings. Its head took on a human aspect.

"Pleckoo," said Hulkro in the voice of a gentle father. "You have been tested and won. Never forget these visions. Be haunted by them, always, as they haunt all on the Slope and keep them in poverty, and in endless labor and as prisoners of their castes."

"Great Wood Eater," Pleckoo whispered. "Why must you always test me?"

"It is a privilege to be tested."

"Will You test me again?"

"You shall be so fortunate."

Pleckoo was quiet.

"Lord . . . have I seen the worst of it?"

"Certainly not."

Pleckoo slumped.

"You will fall even further and see much worse . . . before you fulfill your destiny as my Most Favored Son and Holy Emperor of All the Sand."

Pleckoo watched as the Termite grew and grew, His glow becoming brighter and blinding. He flew from the pebble and flapped his way up to fix Himself in the night sky. A cloud like a soft mattress floated over His face as He transformed into the Waxing Moon, the symbol of Holy Promise to the Faithful. A figure rose from the mists of the cloud, clad in a golden armor. Pleckoo wept to see Tahn, raising his hand and warmly smiling.

"Go forth now, Pleckoo, and fulfill your destiny," Tahn said.

"Why did we lose the war?" Pleckoo asked.

"You lost a battle. You will win the Holy War. You, Pleckoo, will bring the truth of the One and Only God to *all* peoples on the Sand, to the Seed Eaters, the Beetle people, and this benighted Dranveria and beyond, where millions are condemned by ignorance."

"And the Slope?"

"The Slope must be destroyed. To make way for the Pure Land."

"I will go forth," said Pleckoo as tears flowed in a

stream from his eyes. "My God and my Prophet have not abandoned me."

"We have not. Never forget that, no matter your hardships."

The cloud curled around the moon and Tahn disappeared.

Pleckoo's relief brought a gush of tears that thickened and turned into a rising dome around him. He was drowning, trying to break out of the water, when he coughed so hard the dome burst and he fell facedown in its puddle . . .

Pleckoo rose up out of the receding water, gasping for breath. He felt a throbbing, bleeding bump on his forehead. Looking around him in the darkness, he realized he was back on the Sand, under the mallow plant where the ant, maybe alive, was still tethered. A crack of thunder warned him of continuing rain.

"I have not been abandoned," he said to himself as he climbed back into the mallow plant, smiling as he recalled his vision and Hulkro's words. *You will fall even further and see much worse . . . . before you fulfill your destiny as my Most Favored Son and Holy Emperor of All the Sand.*

sunshine faintly glimmered on the wet sand, he felt a little bit of hope. Turning to the ant, he saw a weak twitching of its antennae at the roots. She was alive, and somehow, so was he. After another long and rainy night he was strangely wracked with thirst, and fell to his knees to suck up some water trapped between sand grains. Next he wondered what he might eat to fill his grumbling stomach. "Feed me, Lord Termite," he prayed aloud. Looking back at the ant, he wondered if he might be able to ride her; then he looked at his ragged steering gloves, which were stained with the green of the mallow's stalk. He sniffed his fingers to find only the plant's musky stink.

Slowly, he approached his mount, which lowered her antennae after she found an oily remnant of kin-scent. He climbed to the top of her skull and probed the roots of the antennae with the shreds of his gloves. No response. *I will have to sit here and wait until the sand dries, and see if she can sniff out a trunk trail,* he thought. *But which direction would she take me? Or will she wander off on a food find?* Using his sword, he cut the tethers to the mallow and resumed chanting.

Pleckoo drifted into a light sleep when he woke to the ant's stirring. He was woozy as he clutched at the antennae, which were active, probing, and he fought to stay seated. The ant crawled, but her path was erratic, zigging this way, then zagging the other as she searched for a trunk trail that had been scattered by the storm. Pleckoo realized she was not taking him east to Urtkess, but back to Fadtha. "Shit, shit, shit!" he shouted.

Balancing himself, he stood on the ant's skull, raised his sword high, then thrust it through her brain. After he pulled the sword out, he licked the nourishing goop off it and felt his hunger ease. He slid down the ant's face to the ground, then used his blade to cut through the chitin of her abdomen. The ant-flesh was thick and pleasantly tart. With his strength returning, he made packages of it with a sectioned mallow leaf to feed and water him on his foot journey. Fashioning his cape into a crude backsack, he loaded it with his packages and tied it around his neck. He scooped out more ant-lymph and sucked as much as his stomach could keep down.

"Thank you, Lord Termite," he said, bowing to express his gratitude, when he saw the mask he had taken from Fadtha-dozh. Moisture had swelled its wood and its inlays of minerals had fallen out or were loose. As he walked, he scraped out the rest of the bright jewels and pocketed them, knowing that a gaudy mask would draw too much attention.

The morning's journey east was a perilous one as he slid and slipped over mud-smeared sand grains, some of which were so large he had to crawl or pull himself over their sharp ends. He veered around clusters of weeds that portended dangerous mud pools, and lost his bearings when clouds obscured the sun. It was almost evening when he reached an open place where a cluster of worms had surfaced, then died from sun exposure—a rich feast for hundreds. *But why haven't the ghost ants come to devour these? Or the Hulkrish foragers that ride them?* He gorged on the worm flesh, which made him sleepy, almost content, then fell into a deep and dreamless sleep on a bed of grass cut from a cluster of fescue.

The following day, as the sun brightened the world, he sighted what he hoped was Urtkess-dozh. As he hiked, the sand grains got smaller, were easier to walk over, and the weeds thickened. Something glinted mildly in the distance, and as he got closer he saw it was a ghost ant, dead and tucked into a bank of sand grains. A short distance away was another ant, lying on its back and exposing its last meal of what might have been the yellowish pulp of a dead leaf-cutter ant. *Anand!* he thought. *Has he killed all our holy ghost ants?*

More ant corpses crowded the path ahead of him. Around one with punctures in its abdomen was a scattering of human corpses. They were Hulkrish soldiers, stiffened now, with their white paint breaking into crackle patterns and their armor gouging into their dead flesh.

As he got closer to the weeds of the mound's outer rings, he heard snoring, and then found a circle of men. They were Hulkrites of Slopeish stock, lying on filthy beds of pulped honey grass that had stained their skin and clothing green. All had abandoned their armor, likely left in the nearby watchtower they had slept in to avoid drowning in the rain. Near them was a nutshell basin, stained with the liquor that had fermented inside it as well as the pestles they had used to grind the grass.

"Drinking during the day!" Pleckoo blurted out, scolding them. One of them roused, a man whose upper teeth were at an extreme angle and gave his mouth a bizarre overbite, made stranger still with his green-stained lips.

"What's that you say?" said Overbite in Slopeish.

"I s-s-said . . ." Pleckoo stuttered in a higher pitch to hide his identity, "that I'm . . . I'm thirsty, would like a d-drink . . . today."

"Didn't leave you none. Go harvest some grass for tomorrow's drink and we'll help with the pulping. Looks to be some good stands out there, some sprouts from the rain, just a bit west of here. All the ants are dead, so you'll have to haul it yourself." He nodded towards a travois.

"I'll . . . I'll do that," Pleckoo said.

"What mound were you from?"

"What? Oh . . . Venaris."

"Venaris? With all them awful priests sticking their pricks where they don't belong? No wonder you left."

"H-how many Hulkrites are here?"

"None."

"None?"

"You heard me. One, maybe—if that's what you're calling *your*self—but I wouldn't advise it. We're Hulkrites no more. Not Slopeites neither, since they aren't likely to take us back as anything other than offerings to Mantis at the next assembly."

Pleckoo gulped, looked into the distance, and then hung his head as once again the gloom of defeat descended on him in dark, heavy waves. He slumped, wondering if it was possible that grief could kill, for surely he had to be dying.

"Aww," said Overbite with a grin. "Even sadder than the rest of us, are you? Take this."

Overbite lifted a squeeze bag from his side that was a third full of drink.

"You honor me, brother," Pleckoo said, and surprised himself when he grabbed the bag and drained it of its acrid goop. He felt only a mild effect from the fermentation, and strangely, it deepened his despair. Looking up at the sky, at Hulkro, he said, "Forward," to himself, then trudged to the distant shelters where he might find an empty hovel and collapse on something soft. The mound itself was still and quiet—not a single living ant was crawling up or down its arteries.

The path ahead of him was becoming a meandering snarl of dead ghost ants when he saw the first women of Urtkess, who were walking in clusters. A few appeared to be of Slopeish stock—women abducted from Palzhad—who had divided into their old castes as they walked. Another cluster of women were yellow-skinned natives of Hulkren in rich dress, and another group was of varying complexions: assorted, beautiful prizes stolen from conquered lands. All of them were heading north, wearing their clothing in layers and dragging sacks behind them bound to poles or with baskets they balanced on their heads.

"Where are you going?" Pleckoo shouted at one group, led by a woman with a scowl on her brown Slopeish face.

"What business is that of yours?" she asked, and then reached for the handle of the sword tucked into her waist sash. Pleckoo noticed all these women had swords or daggers at their sides. *Impudence!* he thought. *Women carrying weapons! They have lost all respect for men!*

Breathing heavily, he blinked, made a humbling nod.

"I am sorry, sister. I am just a stranger to this mound who no longer recognizes Hulkren. I'm lost . . . in many ways."

"Lost is the right word," said Scowl, avoiding his eyes and continuing her march. "There is no Hulkren anymore. These are just the Dustlands."

Pleckoo could not imagine hurting any deeper, but the woman's words cut a new wound.

When he reached the first of the pitched shelters on the flats, he was pained to hear a baby's screams. He looked up at the huts on their wobbling rain stilts and crawled up the ladder of one as the crying got louder. Pulling himself through the shelter's flap, he found not one but two babies, completely naked, lying on the rough floor. One boy was dead, the other was soaking in his own urine.

Hulkrish babies abandoned! And sons! He heard screams from yet another baby in a neighboring hut. When he looked out the flap and down, he saw a cluster of light-skinned Slopeish women heading north. With them were freckled women of the servant caste who had resumed their old ways and carried their mistresses' burdens.

"You! Woman!" he shouted at one, a beauty with long, wobbling earlobes that had once held a fortune in jewels. "There are babies up here, Hulkrish babies, that are starving and thirsty!"

"So?" said Earlobes.

"So? So they need your help!"

"Not my problem," she said.

"But they are boys!"

"Exactly."

"But their fathers are Hulkrites!"

"Sorry," she said with an angry grin. "But I don't have time to strangle any Hulkrish babies." This was followed by a chuckle from the others and then looks of open contempt for Pleckoo. He looked down at the infant before him, who cried but had no tears to shed.

The baby was not pretty but was snub-nosed with long, thin nostrils. Pleckoo felt a strange mix of love and pity, which surprised him because all his life he had hated babies as noisy, needy little grubs.

After unfastening his cape, he reached for one of his lymph packages and bit its corner to make an opening and then pressed it into the baby's open mouth. The baby sucked from it and was pacified, and was quickly asleep. Pleckoo envied the baby and felt a sudden over-whelming drowsiness. "Sleep again?" he said to no one at all as he resisted lying down. *I could sleep the rest of my life away.*

Determined to stay awake, he picked up the baby, wrapped it in a filthy blanket, and tied it over his shoulders before descending down the shelter's ladder. He made his way up the rings and to the main artery and looked up at the mound's peak. Something, per-haps the invisible hand of Hulkro, was pushing him towards the crystal palaces; perhaps he would find a reserve of Hulkrish soldiers who would greet him as their Prophet Commander. It would be a strenuous climb to the top without an ant to ride. And as for the ants, they were all too abundant—abundantly dead and crowding his path, which grew steeper.

Standing before the slitted portal of the main palace, Pleckoo was unsure about entering. The translucent sand grains allowed him some vision of the chambers' interior and he saw movement within of what had to be men. But what kind of men? They appeared to be dressed in warriors' whites! He slipped through the wax-embedded cloth to a short tunnel and heard muffled voices. Taking a deep breath, he pushed through the second slit and into the throne room and gasped to see hundreds of Hulkrites dressed in the White Robes of Pure Faith.

But something was wrong.

Only a few of these men were wearing armor under their robes, and none were coated with the White Paint of Submission. They pointed at Pleckoo and murmured as they took in his muddied officer's clothing, his damaged mask, and the sling that held a baby. He looked over the men's heads and up the long flight of stairs where he expected to see a relic of Sacred Wood with a termite track. Instead he saw distant figures sitting on grimy amber thrones. The vast room went quiet when a man of forty or so summers rose from the central throne to stand on unsure feet. The chamber went quiet, and Pleckoo felt heat and sweat from under his mask.

Using a jewel-encrusted rod, the man made a painstaking descent to the middle of the stairs. Pleckoo thought from the man's white complexion that he might be a faithful Hulkrite wearing the Paint of Submission. Without thinking, Pleckoo bowed his head, as if he were back in Cajoria and standing before someone of higher caste. The man shouted at him in a tongue he did not know.

"Do you speak Hulkrish, sir?" Pleckoo asked.

"I do not," said the man. "But I can if I need to. Who has dared to enter our palace?"

The man descended further, ever so slowly, down the next of the 123 steps. As he got closer, Pleckoo saw he was not wearing white paint but had a complexion that was so pale it revealed the red of his blood. He had been a slave who was hobbled, likely with a cut to the tendons in his heel. Now he stood before Pleckoo as a king of some kind.

"What is your name, masked one?"

"I have no name," Pleckoo said. "I was known as Come Here."

Slave King smiled, almost laughed. "Come Here, yes, a very common name among us. Where were you from before you were enslaved?"

"I . . . I don't know. I never knew my mother."

"But you speak Hulkrish with a Slopeish accent."

Pleckoo hesitated—aware that he was blinking too much in the holes of the mask.

"My . . . my master was a Slopeite before he wore the white paint."

"But now you want to be with us."

"Yes. I heard Slopeites are allowed here."

"As our slaves, yes. Why do you wear a mask?"

"You would not want to see what my master did to my face."

Slave King came closer, looking at the baby in Pleckoo's chest-sling as the crowd's whispers turned to louder murmurs. Women appeared from the kitchen with rolled-up leaf platters of food, hobbling in with the usual pained expression.

"Have you brought us a gift?" asked Slave King.

Pleckoo blinked. "A gift, sir?"

"The baby. Is it for us?"

"Y-yes. It is, sir."

"Let me see."

Pleckoo pulled back the cloth of the sling and revealed the baby's face, which was peaceful and sweetly yawning.

"Too ugly to raise," said Slave King as he reached for it, signaling to the kitchen women. "But I'm sure he'll taste as good as any other."

"No!" said Pleckoo, who yanked the baby away and backed into the portal. As he squeezed through the slit of its cloth he felt hands grasping at his ankles, trying to pull him back. Once he made it out, he ran down the main artery, weaving between ant corpses as the baby woke and cried in his arms. An arrow flew over his head and he knew the men in the palace were outside and chasing him.

As he neared the flats, Pleckoo's lungs were bursting and his legs were wobbling. When he could run no more, he veered off the route into a thicket of finger grass where he found an upright pebble he could lean against to hide. He collapsed against the pebble and then coughed and wheezed until eventually he caught his breath. As the baby cried, Pleckoo rocked him while singing the Termite's different names as a lullaby. Just as the baby quieted, he heard the louder screaming of women.

Setting down the baby, he peered over the pebble and through the grass to see two women with the black-purple skin and the bright green eyes of the Meat Ant tribe of Ledack. They watched as their sand-sled was hauled away by several yellow-skinned women who had assumed its reins.

"What's happened here?" Pleckoo asked the Ledackis as he stepped out.

"They're stealing our sled!" said the taller of the two.

"It's our sled now," shouted one of the yellow-skinned women in polished purple silks. She turned and thrust out a costly sword made from a serrated queen-bee mandible rooted in an amber handle. The woman snarled and buzzed as she used her sword to cut the air, her companions following her example.

"Drop those reins!" Pleckoo shouted, rushing to them, raising up his own sword.

"I am a witch-daughter of Hulkra-tash," said the woman in purple silks, spitting at Pleckoo over her extended blade. "My spit will sicken and kill you!"

"I'll risk it. You took this sled from her?" he asked in Hulkrish.

"She's as black as a lair spider," said Spit Witch in unaccented Hulkrish.

"No one's skin color gives them the right to steal

from another Hulkrite," he said. "Drop those reins and keep walking . . . if you want to keep your limbs."

Spit Witch and the other two made buzzing sounds through their clenched teeth as the three of them raised their heavy swords. *Silly women*, Pleckoo thought. Using his own sword he knocked their blades out of their hands and they flew into a grass cluster.

"Run! Before I cut all your clothes off," Pleckoo said. Silently, the women walked backwards, then turned and ran. He looked at the Ledacki women, who met his eyes in an immodest way.

"Thank you, Good Hulkrite," said the older and taller of the women. "If there is such a thing as a *good* Hulkrite." Her companion nodded at Pleckoo. Both were dressed in a faded finery of painted egg-cloth but they wore it in the Ledack style, as a loose wrap that started at the head. He looked at their small and filthy hauling-sled and its cargo box filled with crude jars and rough sacks and hopefully . . . food. The sled's runners had worn and missing scales, and its twigs were graying and riddled with holes.

"Where are you going?" Pleckoo asked.

"To Bee-Jor, of course," said the taller one.

"Bee-Jor?" he repeated in disbelief.

"Yes. A land of endless honey, where the ants bring sweets and roasted meats to hammocks in the shade, where no one has to work and . . ."

"Yes, yes, yes . . . I know what Bee-Jor is. And just where do you think you will find it?"

"To the North somewhere, in the land of leaf-cutter ants. Locust the Sky God has put his son on the Slopeish throne and brought paradise to the Sand."

"Who told you this?" he asked, slowly aware that he was speaking to a woman of remarkable beauty with a long, slender neck and high, arching eyebrows. Her eyes were as bright and green as a new caterpillar.

"Everyone knows . . . just as everyone knows the Hulkrites were defeated by Vof Quegdoth, the Son of Locust, who has given a powerful magic to the Grass Men of Dneep to kill the ghost ants of Hulkren."

Pleckoo was stunned, breathing hard, feeling as if a wasp was inside him and about to rip from his stomach.

"Were you in the battle?" the tall woman asked.

Pleckoo hung his head, slumped.

"Do not be ashamed. If you did not fight, then you were wise . . . you are alive."

"I fought!" Pleckoo shouted, and then looked abashed when he saw fright in their widening eyes. "I'm sorry," he said, lowering his voice. "Are you not Hulkrish women? Wood sisters?" he asked.

"We are *not!* We were captives of the Hulkrites! Thrown into bags when they raided our country. Ledack is no more. Our Meat Ants are no more."

"How do you know you'll be welcome in . . . Bee-Jor?"

"All who worship Bee and submit to the Son of Locust are welcomed in Bee-Jor," said the shorter woman. "It's a place where anyone can start over . . . maybe even a Hulkrite." Pleckoo thought her no less appealing with her long-lashed eyes and her thick-lipped mouth in a tight and perpetual smirk. Her tighter wrap hinted at a voluptuous figure. A new wave of dark emotions silenced Pleckoo, made him slump.

"Why do you speak through that mask?" the taller woman asked.

"I am hiding my wounds," Pleckoo said. "They are sickening to look upon."

"You should go to Bee-Jor," said the younger woman. "The Son of Locust is a great healer who has married the Mushroom Eaters' sorceress queen. Together they have a godly magic that can restore eyesight to the blind and hearing to the deaf."

"And grow new limbs for the crippled," said the older one. "Slaves can stand straight again after bathing in the queen's magic urine."

"The Son of Locust," Pleckoo said as he felt pangs of what he had to admit was a bitter, thickening envy. "If Locust is this man's father, then who is his mother?"

"A human woman: the Empress Quegdoth of the Red Ant people."

"Empress Quegdoth?"

"Yes, she's a direct descendant of Goddess Bee. Her son, known as Vof, is the Glorious Founder on his divine mission to unite all peoples of the Sand and bring the Thousand Year Peace."

Pleckoo tried to control his breathing. Rage and fear and envy had replaced his blood, his breath, his very being. *How has this ridiculous story, this heresy, come into existence?*

"Are you all right?" the woman asked.

"No, I . . ."

Pleckoo fell to the sand and bawled like a battered child. *Anand sits on a throne in a Slopeish palace and is worshipped as a god!* Pleckoo was filled with shame when he looked up to see the women staring at him. They watched him in disgust as he stood, picked up a disc-like sand grain, and rotated his entire body to hurl it. The grain ricocheted off a dried grass blade and hit his mask, dazing him. He spasmed, then dropped and let out a harsh mewl of pain.

"Let's go," said the taller woman to her companion, and the two resumed the reins of their sled.

"Wait," Pleckoo said, struggling to rise. "I'm sorry. I was—I was taken over by some ill spirit. It's left me."

The two were quiet, ignoring him, and kept trudging.

"Please," he said. "Let me accompany you. Women should not be alone on journeys. Not in these . . . . Dustlands."

"So says the Hulkrish warrior," said the taller woman, turning in contempt.

"I will protect you," he said, crossing his chest with his sword where it caught the light and glimmered. "I am good with this."

She stopped and stared at him, looked at his deadly and beautiful blade. "Have you a name?" she asked.

"A Hulkrish name—one I will no longer use."

"Black sword," she said. "*Khali talavar* in my old language."

"Khali Talavar," Pleckoo said. "And your name?"

"Jakhuma Samra, Modee Kee Ladack, formally."

"What does that mean?" he asked.

"It means First Princess of the Central Kingdom," said the younger woman, bowing. "My name is Kula Priya. It means beloved servant."

"You may call me Jakhuma," said the princess to Pleckoo.

"Jakhuma. Let's gather the swords of that Hulkrish spit-witch and her friends," said Pleckoo. "And someday, I will teach you how to use them."

The two women looked at each other.

"We should like to learn," said Jakhuma.

"Wait one moment," Pleckoo said, and ran into the finger grass. He returned with a bundle in his arms.

"What is *that*?" Jakhuma asked.

"Not what. Who," said Pleckoo, looking deeply into the woman's eyes.

"A Hulkrish bastard," said the princess. "The

offspring of some Termite-worshipping rapist. It will only slow us down. Is it yours?"

Pleckoo seethed and bit his tongue with his molars before speaking.

"No. But he's a baby," he said. "If we leave him here, he'll be eaten."

"All the Hulkrites' bastards are being abandoned," said Jakhuma. "Why do you care about this one?"

"I would bring them all if I could," said Pleckoo. "They did not ask to be born. Shouldn't everyone be allowed a chance to live in Bee-Jor? Especially an innocent baby?"

Jakhuma was silent.

"We have no milk to nurse it. But we'll carry it a ways. Take these reins, and start pulling, Khali Talavar, but before you do . . ."

She went to the sand-sled and returned with a jar of soap weed unguent and a thorn brush with harsh bristles. "You are not going anywhere with us until you remove what remains of your *white paint*."

Pleckoo looked at his arms and legs and saw a patchwork of peeling white flakes. He stepped away from the women, hid behind a grass clump, and removed the paint with the unguent, wiping his skin clean with his cape. He was naked and drying when Kula approached him with a garment painted with swirls of red and yellow.

"Put this on," she said. Pleckoo froze, his hand covering his face.

"I cannot. That is a woman's garment."

"It is a man's garment if you wear it. You can't go to Bee-Jor dressed as an armored Hulkrite."

Pleckoo took the garment, which would cover his head as well as his body, and pulled it on. Underneath it, he could at least wear the back and chest plates of his armor. The garment had openings in its sides to leave his arms free for use of his sword, and he could adjust the cowl to cover his lower face and be free of the mask that scratched his skin. When he emerged from the grass in his new guise, the women approved even as they heard the squeak of his armor when he walked.

"Now pick up those reins and pull," Jakhuma said, and Pleckoo obeyed, feeling humiliated and strangely comfortable at the same time. It felt familiar to be someone's submissive again, but peculiar to take orders from a woman, especially one with darker skin than his own. *Bide your time, Khali Talavar,* he thought as he tucked the ropes under his armpits and let them press against his chest plate. He peered sideways at the suddenly haughty First Princess of the Central Kingdom of Ladack as she strode forward, her servant a few steps ahead to help her mistress over the rougher sand grains.

As Pleckoo lugged the cargo-sled, his anguish gave way to anger and put strength in his arms and legs. He was not trekking to this so-called Bee-Jor ruled by the Son of Locust—he was going to the place where his half-breed cousin sat on a Slopeish throne. And Cousin Anand's blood would spatter that throne once his head had been whacked off his neck. As Pleckoo marched, he turned to an inward chanting of Hulkro's names to soothe himself but another name kept working its way into the order—a name he could not dispel.

Anand, Anand, kill little Cousin Anand.

place where his half-breed cousin sat on a Slopeish
throne. And Cousin Anand's blood would spatter
that throne once his head had been whacked off his
neck. As Pleckoo marched, he turned to an inward
chanting of Hulkro's names to soothe himself but

Anand, Anand, kill little Cousin Anand.

CHAPTER 5

THE BEE PEOPLE

Daveena worked with the roach wranglers in detaching her sand-sled from the ailing insect that could no longer pull it. It was the second roach to have died on this journey, even though they were less than three moons old. Perhaps its breathing ventricles were blocked with mud from the recent rain, or it ailed from some poison in the Hulkrish dust; the wranglers were unsure. This was the first time the Entrevean clan had traveled in Hulkren, which some were already calling the Dustlands again.

She bowed to Madricanth in prayer as the roach was freed. "Thank You, Sweet Roach Lord, for lending us Your offspring," said Punshu, her sled's driver, as he wrenched the saddle from the insect's thorax and dropped it to the ground. He was a fierce-looking boy of twelve, with long hair in ringlets that covered most of his back. Punshu was glowing with pride that he had been reassigned to drive the sled that carried the wife of Anand the Wasp Rider, Commander General of Glorious Bee-Jor. He watched with Daveena as the freed roach revived for a moment, its antennae weakly twirling, before it crawled off slowly, like a sleepy baby, to die. The wranglers returned with a fresh roach from the pack at the caravan's tail and fitted it to the sled's reins.

"We'll help you with that," said a wrangler as Punshu hoisted up the saddle.

"It's all mine," said Punshu, who looked determined to show his clan he was as strong and capable as any adult. He set the saddle's under-cord around his neck to free his arms, then climbed the rope ladder attached to the roach's thorax. The wranglers held the ends of the roach's antennae to steady it as Punshu slipped the saddle on the end of the thorax and secured it with its over-cord. Seating himself, he pulled back the antennae until he found the sensors that allowed him to guide it. Daveena noticed this new roach was larger and stronger than the last and she admired its chitin, which glistened like wet lacquer. She realized from the insect's size that it must have recently feasted on dead ghost ants and, from its fetid meaty smell, the carcasses of Hulkrish men.

After Daveena checked the tethers, Punshu prodded the roach's initial steps to test the harnessing. "Ready!" he cried, and his signal was passed up to the caravan's head. Thagdag, the Entrevean's chieftain, appeared atop the lead sled, with his long, waxed mustache rising up like roach antennae from his lips to his ears. He sounded his thorn horn twice, and the sleds resumed what had been an unnerving journey.

Daveena looked at her copy of the simple map Anand had drawn into some scratching paper. It was mostly accurate and included landmarks like tree stumps and prominent rocks, but it did not predict the puddles and mud traps they had to veer around after heavy rains, nor the weeds that had expanded to block them. The worst obstacles were some nearly impassable gullies they had to bridge with planks that needed to be reset every forty roach steps.

Daveena almost welcomed these challenges since they took her mind off her husband and his own uncountable adversities. It had not occurred to him or to her just how complicated and perilous a trip into a newly liberated Hulkren might be, especially after a long and unseasonable rainstorm. As for these bee people of Bulkoko, would they willingly follow a band of roach people to a strange land? Anand had told her, "They hated their masters in Bulkoko, I am sure they hated the Hulkrites more. I believe they will welcome the chance to live among us."

"But everything has been upended," she had countered. "How can we be sure this is a safe place for them—for anyone? And what do you know about these Bulkokans? They could be vicious cannibals or complete degenerates. You're inviting strangers to a disordered mess—with angry enemies on every side."

"Uncertainty is the only certainty in life," he had said—and ended the conversation.

Anand, Anand, Anand, she thought to herself in her lonely sand-sled, and felt sadness, irritation, and then an irrepressible longing for this *boy* who refused to live an ordinary life. And for the fifth or sixth time that day, she felt a bodily hunger for him, yearning to push her hands inside his garments and shuck them. How much she wanted to see his dark and glistening eyes as they stared into hers with his fiery want, to feel his arms as they yanked her down to their mattress and wrapped around her waist, to feel the hardness of his muscles under his hot skin as his ankles wrapped around her own. Breathing quickly, she remembered the feel of his lips on hers, of his hot tongue in her mouth, as his fingers probed and readied her to the point where she ached for his blissful onslaught. His first thrust always brought relief, and then led to a spiraling ecstasy that forced her to close her eyes. Whenever she opened them, she saw him looking at her, pleasuring in giving her the deepest fulfillment.

She shook her head, rousing herself from her reverie. *We have a mission. And I am pregnant,* she thought as she watched Punshu bob on the saddle.

"Punshu, it looks like a very good hauling roach," she said to make conversation.

"It is a fine roach, Madame Anand," he said over his shoulder. "The antennae are a little spiky to hold but they respond well."

When the caravan reached the peak of a stony grade with few plants, Daveena climbed up the storage chest to raise the roof-flap for a good view of what had to be Halk-Oktish. Anand had described it to her as a larger but shorter mound with a modest collection of palaces at its peak, most of them in ruins. *Anand*, she thought again, and her longing was renewed and made her feel weak and a little ashamed. She returned to the hollowing of beads to string them, and realized she had accomplished but a few bracelets and the beginnings of a necklace on this journey. It was late afternoon and the clan would need a place to camp before darkness descended.

The caravan halted when they sighted a lush cluster of weeds that could hide the sand-sleds in their depths. Several scouts donned camouflage of baby roach costumes and crawled in a scattered band, imitating the erratic, circular path of roaches. They entered the weeds to see if they were free of Hulkrites or other human enemies as well as predatory insects, spiders, mites, and ticks. As they waited for the scouts to return, Daveena heard the buzz of honeybees and looked up to see some flying overhead. The sacks on their hind legs were not yellow with pollen, but with the dark brown propolis they mixed with their wax to make a glue to build or repair their dwellings. The bees turned south, then dropped over what was likely a hive tended by the mysterious Bulkokans.

"Daveena," shouted Worela, wife of the chieftain, her abundant jewelry shaking like a bead-chain drum as she walked. "You speak the Seed Eaters' tongue, yes?"

"I do."

"Thagdag wants you and the other two-tongued to approach these bee people and see if we can find a common tongue."

"These are an eastern people. I don't know that they will know *Yatchmin*," she said, using the Seed Eaters' word for their language.

After the sand-sleds were set in a circle under the weeds, the clan's children were gathered in its center. The girls were handed materials for making jewelry and the boys were set to music practice on drums and other instruments. A contingent of men was left behind to guard the children as the roaches were released from the sand-sleds' tethers.

The beehive was approached with the women riding atop the roaches and the men alongside on foot as their protectors. An increasing number of bees, making their way home at the end of the day's foraging, were a helpful guide. The women steered the roaches through a winding path between towering stalks of dying sun daisies with hairy, brown leaves and limp flowers that resembled murdered spiders at the end of spikes. As the men of the clan walked, the light armor they had taken to wearing rattled under their loose clothes. They had bows at the ready, quivers full of arrows, and swords at their sides—weapons they were allowed to display in Bee-Jor as well as in this strange land. Some men at the tail of the procession walked backwards, anticipating the appearance of hidden aggressors. Here and there were dead ghost ants, testament that the Dneepers had done their job and left an effective poison.

As the bees increased in number above them, the parade continued up a path that revealed the strange sight of a towering cube composed of thirteen sheets of interlocking wood. As they got closer, they saw that between the sheets were massive discs of six-walled cells of wax. Masses of bees were climbing over these cells and engaging in a variety of activities. The bees bent their heads, either to deposit something, take something out, or feed something in a cell. The sight got even stranger when a cluster of bees from the middle crawled backwards down a series of ladders.

Daveena realized these backwards crawlers were not insects, but humans disguised as bees. Their costumes had black and ocher bands on their baggy trousers and had jackets of bee fuzz as their tops. On their backs were pairs of wings and on their heads were short antennae, which bent at the pedicle. The roach people advanced until they reached open ground to see that the hive was built atop a large and sturdy cage that housed a few hundred people. The Bulkokans on the ground were excited, shouting and buzzing among themselves, as the hive workers hurried their descent. The captives gathered at the bars of the cage, standing on each other's shoulders to see the visitors. Daveena gasped when she saw that within the cage there were grass roaches, identical to their own. Some roaches were crawling at the top of the cage's bars and others were on the ground, bearing roachlings on their backs as well as human children.

So it is true! she thought to herself. *Bees and roaches have no quarrel and can live with each other. This is what kept the ghost ants from attacking and eating the bees.* The roach Daveena was riding, a female, was raising its wings and exuding its bright, sharp perfume in flirtation with the males in the cage. One of them was interested and responded by raising its own wings and then pivoting backwards to display its abdominal spikes. *It's a good sign!* Daveena thought as she raised her hands up the antennae and pulled to keep the roach from assuming the mating position.

The Bulkokans were clamoring now, shouting to the roach people in an unknown tongue, when two little Hulkrites in transparent armor emerged from a nearby twig-and-leaf hut. They were without the white paint—too young for it, perhaps—and looked groggy and roused from a spirit-induced nap. They shouted at the Bulkokans, it seemed, for disturbing their sleep. A moment later the little Hulkrites jumped in shock to realize a mass of visitors on the backs of roaches had gathered behind them. They responded by reaching into their quivers to nock their bows, then realized they had no arrows. They raised little swords against a sizable army whose arrowheads glistened with a dark poison.

Those are just children, Daveena thought of the Hulkrites as she dismounted and joined the other two-tongued women. They were Queestra and Ulatha, who worked in the jewelry markets as fortune-tellers, and wore necklaces that held a seer's orb as their pendants. Queestra spoke the Carpenters' tongue and Ulatha spoke the best Slopeish.

The little Hulkrites were shaking as they attempted to look fierce. They did not respond to Slopeish or the Carpenters' tongue. Daveena noticed that one boy had reddish hair edging out from his helmet and the orange-tinged skin of the Barley people. "Can you understand my words?" she shouted. Behind him, the Bulkokans were watching, loudly whispering in their own language, which was thick with the vibrational sound of bees. The boy was quiet, then lowered his sword, vaguely nodding.

"You are from the Barley Lands?" Daveena asked. He wanted to answer her, but he looked at the other boy, a pale yellow Hulkrish native, for permission.

"Go ahead. Speak with me, little sir. No one else

will understand," Daveena said, kindness entering her voice.

"I am from the Barley Lands," he said, affecting some bluster. He had dark scattered spots across his broad nose and the round eyes and overbite typical of the working castes of the eastern nation. "But I am a Hulkrite who worships the One True God. Praise Lord Termite."

They were quiet for a moment, averting each other's eyes. "You should leave," the boy said. "We have orders to destroy roach people on sight. Your corpses are worth a thousand pieces of gold pyrite and two thousand of silver."

"That's not likely to happen," said Daveena. "The Hulkrites . . ."

"At any moment our warriors will be returning," he interrupted. "The Second Prophet has no tolerance for you and your stinking insects. You will all be buried in a pit."

"The Hulkrites will not be returning," Daveena said. "I'm afraid that most of them are as dead as your ghost ants."

"Our Holy Warriors are returning as soon as they slaughter every last idolater on the Slope. And we'll bring a new egg-layer to this mound just as soon as they do. Our ghost ants will thrive, once again, in service to Lord Termite."

Daveena sighed, shook her head. "The Hulkrites have lost the war. Few of them survive. The ghost ants have been poisoned here and at all the other mounds. Their corpses litter Hulkren."

The boy trembled and struggled to find his voice. "You lie!" he said, his voice cracking. "You lie! You lie! You lie!"

The Hulkrish boy demanded a translation from his orange-haired companion. He relayed Daveena's words in Hulkrish, his knees buckling and the words sticking in his throat to choke him. Both boys were sobbing, turning away in shame to hide their watering eyes, when they fell to the sand and shook. Daveena had no love for Hulkrites, but she looked at these boys in pity. She did not see them as rapists, looters, and killers, but as little boys leaking tears. The Hulkrish boy struggled to his feet and stumbled off in the direction of the mound. The red-haired boy looked up at her with his wet eyes.

"Why are you here?" he asked Daveena.

"I will tell you if you tell me your name."

"Odwaznee," he said, and Daveena smiled, for the name meant *brave*.

"I am Daveena," she said.

"My mother told me never to talk to a roach woman."

"I mean you no harm. And I am part Yatchminish, like you. We have come to invite these bee people and their insects to live in Bee-Jor."

"*Bee-Jor*? Bee-Jor is not real. The prophets have

made this clear. The only Promised Land is the one that a faithful Hulkrite goes to after his death."

"We are making a Bee-Jor, which will need bees and their honey. You could live there too. You can't go back to *Yatchmina Nyatsay*."

"How do you speak my old tongue?"

"I learned it from my grandfather. He was like you, a villager in the Barley Lands who was forced all his life to the same dull tasks. His fate was to die as a sacrifice to the Mantis Riding Moon God. My grandmother, a roach woman, thought him clever and handsome and invited him to her parents' sand-sled. His days were spent traveling and trading until he was seventy."

"And just where is this Bee-Jor?" Odwaznee asked as he dried his eyes with the back of his hands. "Do you climb the tallest oak, then ride on a cloud of sugar-fluff for forty days to the west?"

"No. Our Bee-Jor is in what used to be *Grizhabev Grizaboff*," she said, using the Yatchminish name for "Land of Mushroom Eaters." She saw him wince.

"Why would anyone live among leaf-cutter ants?" he asked. "They are filthier than your roaches."

"It is not a perfect place. But you could live there in honor—as the boy who brought the honey-makers."

"I am a man," he said.

"Well, certainly . . . you almost are."

The Bulkokans had been quiet, but now they were

buzzing again. Odwaznee turned and yelled at them, his mouth making the long vibrations that emulated the sound of bee wings.

"So you speak their tongue," Daveena said.

"It is something like my own," he said. "Barley and bee people are cousins. We share the same color hair and skin."

Daveena looked over at Queestra and Ulatha, who were near the cage, crying out to the Bulkokans in the Slopeish and Carpenter tongues.

"What are those women doing?" Odwaznee shouted. "Tell them to get back!"

Daveena saw that Ulatha had entered into conversation with several of the bee people. She turned to the clan. "Some of them know the Carpenters' tongue! They have traded with them!" Ulatha shouted into the cage in her loudest voice. When she finished speaking, the Bulkokans who understood burst into what sounded like cheers and then spread her words.

"What is she telling them?" Odwaznee shouted at Daveena.

"That we are freeing them, opening their cage, taking them to Bee-Jor."

"No!" he shouted. "Those are infidels! They are servants to Hulkro! Their honey is only for the True Believers!"

The Bulkokans ran for the ladders in their cages and then slid them between its bars. The roach-men set the ladders against the cage's door and climbed to its heavy rope-lock. Using the toothed sides of their daggers, they cut the lock's intricate knot, then dropped its ropes to the men on the floor. The cage's door was pulled open as the Bulkokans cheered and sang what had to be a buzz-filled prayer of thanks as they looked to the sky. They poured out of the cage and ran into the arms of their roach-riding rescuers.

Odwaznee shook with anger as he watched. He walked towards Daveena, who stepped back and reached for her dagger. The boy hung his head and dropped his sword.

"I'll be killed," he said, looking up and into her eyes. "For letting this happen."

"Come with us," she said. "We'll protect you."

Freed Bulkokan women were coming towards Daveena, their arms open, their mouths curling with little smiles. Daveena saw that these were a chubby people and their mouths were full of rotting teeth—if they had any teeth at all. *Too much honey!* she thought as they took turns embracing her.

After hugging Daveena, the Bulkokan women gathered together, whispered among themselves, then turned on the boy who had been their warden. Like a swarm of bees, their mouths buzzed as they surrounded Odwaznee and pulled daggers of bee stingers from their jackets' pouches. "No!" Daveena screamed, and attempted to tear him away as they stabbed the boy in his arms, his legs, his face, and neck.

CHAPTER 6

MONSTERS BIG AND SMALL

"No," said Anand, again scratching at the exposed part of his thighs, which were raw and moist. "We are not sitting on the Mushroom Thrones."

"Why not?" Trellana asked. "They are perfectly comfortable."

"For one thing, they're at the top of one hundred and twenty-three stairs."

"We can sit on litters and be brought up to them. That's how it's always been done."

"That will require the labor of four men."

"What else have *they* got to do?" said Trellana, using her chin to point at Anand's guards. "And why are you all scratching yourselves?" she asked as she watched them claw at their legs. "That is something to be done in private if it cannot be done discreetly."

"We are so sorry to offend," said Anand, who restrained himself from scraping again at something that moved in slow, agonizing circles under his skin. He wished he were alone for a moment to be able to use his dagger to excise whatever had taken up house inside him. Just how and when had he been infected?

"*Creet-creet*," called Polexima as she and Terraclon entered her old palace reception chamber through the flaps of the portal. As Terraclon helped her through the portal's slits, Anand could see she was wearing the braces that strengthened her legs and straightened her back. No longer leaning on crutches, she clutched a staff topped with the carved knob of a cricket's head. Her shin-length robe of woven grass fibers was painted a deep blue, and spattered with swirls of yellow stars to suggest the night sky. As she walked she rustled like a leaf in the wind and her second pair of antennae, twice the length of her body, floated like frail, thin pennants in a breeze.

Terraclon plodded behind her, like an upright caterpillar, in a striped robe of yellow and purple. He had tailored it to hide his meager frame and sewn an excess of cloth to the back as a train, which made him lean forward, as if walking into the wind. His dark face was caked and stiff with yellow pollen on one side, a thick red paint on the right, while his brown complexion was left to shine in the middle. Over his hood were purple antennae spangled with flecks of amethyst.

Emerging more slowly from the portal flaps was Pious Dolgeeno, dressed in a similar garment, but resembling a floating tent as his robe bloomed outwards in its unfolding. Under his eyes were drooping bags of a muddy purple that looked darker against his sallow complexion. Behind him were guards with sharpened pikes that seemed at the ready to prod the Ultimate Holy's behind if he slowed or veered off path.

"You look absolutely interesting, Mother," said Trellana with a smirk as Polexima pulled back her hood to reset her antennae over her shaved head. "A bit on the dark side for morning, but, well, most daring."

"The compliments go to Terraclon," said Polexima. "Perhaps he can come up with a few things for you . . . something more suitable to the new era."

"I wouldn't dare to put him to the trouble."

"You might find what he makes very comfortable."

"I am not so interested in being comfortable. I am interested in being beautifully dressed."

"Something dark might suit you quite well," said Terraclon. "Black can be *so* slimming, did you know?"

Trellana glared at Terraclon in silence. Anand tried not to grin. "Well, Ter, congratulations. I believe that was your first understated riposte."

"It is not my last," he said, and glared at Trellana. "As I am terribly inspired."

"Speaking of comfort," Trellana said, turning to Anand. "I am sure my mother would enjoy sitting on a nice, comfortable throne this morning instead of some wretched stool."

"I don't know that I'm up for a climb," said Polexima, looking up the long flight of steps. "And I wouldn't impose on anyone to bring me up there."

"Agreed," said Anand with a smile. "And we don't want people having to shout up to us—as if we were the gods in the Heavenly Treetop. Let's have a throne for all of us, but bring them down here."

Anand gave orders to his men in the dialect of his old caste, which he knew Trellana found both hard to understand and harsh to the ear. She wandered over to the large quartz viewing window and looked in disdain at dark-skinned children riding on ants. She gasped with disgust when some held tight to their saddle-knobs and crawled up the window to block her view.

"What are you staring at, Trelly?" Polexima asked.

"Why are children, and these kind of children, riding ants?"

"It's permitted now," said Anand. "Anyone may ride an ant."

"Shouldn't they be at work?" asked Trellana.

"Every eighth day is a time to rest now—and to have a bit of fun."

"In a time of mourning? Should anyone be having *fun*?"

"Children, especially, should have a little fun. We've all been shut up inside due to the rains, and should all be enjoying some sunshine."

"More of your charming notions from Dranveria, I presume. Remind me again, please, just who it is we're receiving today."

"Our fellow *citizens*," said Anand, "with grievances against fellow citizens that our government might correct."

"Citizen. This is a Dranverish word."

"Yes, a citizen is anyone who owes allegiance to our nation and benefits from its laws and protections."

"Are you telling me that just anyone can come in here? Anyone with an accusation?"

"Not just anyone," said Anand. "Citizens of Bee-Jor. We will adjudicate as best we can in hopes of retaining order in our new nation." Trellana turned from the window with a sour, then a bored, look on her face.

"Let us welcome our first plaintiffs," said Anand after the thrones were set in a semicircle. "Dolgeeno, will you be so kind as to record for us?"

"I don't believe I have a choice," said the high priest, who turned to see Polexima's son, Pious Nuvao, walking towards him with a cylinder of scratching paper and an implement and brush to sweep the scrapings. One of Polexima's Cricket acolytes, a young woman in the same priestly dress, laid a writing plank over the armrests of Dolgeeno's throne. He began scratch-

ing furiously, and Anand wondered if he might be
drawing more than writing.

The guards escorted in two dark-skinned and
heavyset men, who brought with them the familiar
stink of the midden. They were followed by two other
middenites, a meek-looking married couple who had
dressed in simple but clean garments. As the first two
approached, Anand stiffened with shock, then hatred.
He looked to Terraclon, who was gripping the armrests of his throne and gritting his teeth. Here in the
palace were Keel and his son, Tal. Neither of them
had a shred of humility, but looked menacing as they
strutted their bulk. Both wore quilted silk tunics that
were stretched to the point of ripping, but indicated
their new wealth as operators of the midden with
rights to sell its salvage. When they reached the reception area, Tal used his thumb to pull his greasy
locks over his ear to reveal its clipped lobe.

"Well," said Terraclon, loud enough so that all
could hear him. "It looks like someone is even better
fed these days."

"Well, Terraclon. Looks like you're doing all right
for yourself too," said Tal.

Anand looked from Keel and Tal to the married
couple, whom he recognized as his distant kin from
the midden, some fourth or fifth cousins. The husband had worked at trash- and corpse-sorting with
Yormu, his father. He made the traditional bow

before the royals by showing hands empty of weapons, followed by a deep lowering of the head, while his wife attempted a curtsy as she raised the cloth of an imaginary gown.

"It is proper to bow before your queen and your highest priest," said Dolgeeno to Keel and Tal.

"Is it now? We thought those ways was over, Your Holiness," said Keel.

"They are not," shouted Trellana, not looking at them, but at Anand. "These are middenites!" she said in something between a shriek and a whisper. "Here, in my *palace*, speaking in their filthy voices to royals!"

"Pardon me, Your Majesty," said Tal with a mock curtsy. "But we thought you was married to a middenite. Why, I believe that *two* of their dirty asses are mucking up your thrones at the moment."

Anand leapt up at the same instant the pain in his thighs became unbearable. He could not help but scratch himself as he spoke. "We will all speak in a respectful way to each other. Good Bee-Jorites, who has the grievance?"

"The grievance is ours, Commander," said the salvager. "I am Gelk, and this is my wife, Canathy. I fought the night of the war against the Hulkrites, in the second division, protecting the tunnel to Gagumji."

Gelk turned his leg to show how most of his left calf had been sliced away by a Hulkrish arrow. "As was promised me, I moved my family up to the black-sand barracks and into the house of a dead Slopeish soldier. We'd made ourselves a nice home, but when we got back one night, our chambers was taken over by Keel and his son here, and all their family. He said as foreman of our caste, it was his right to take our place and that we should move elsewhere. They grabbed my little sons by the throats and threatened to snap their heads off their necks if we didn't leave."

"We did no such thing," said Tal. "He's lying!"

"The house is ours!" blasted Keel. "Didn't Vof Quegdoth, the Son of Locust hisself, promise that all who fought in the war could move up the mound to a soldier's quarters?"

Anand squinted at his old nemeses. "I thank you for your service, Good Bee-Jorites, but . . . I do not recognize you as having been among our Laborers' Army."

"We was there—among the hundreds of thousands," said Tal through his thin and almost lipless mouth. "Fought bravely, we did, and even coated ourselves in roach muck."

"What division were you in?" asked Terraclon.

"We was both in the Twenty-ninth," said Keel. "Joined right up after you and Yormu left for the border. Took us days to walk there since they wouldn't let us ride on speed ants or fly us on a locust."

Yormu! Anand thought, and his heart quickened. *Where is my father?* "And where was the Twenty-ninth posted?" he asked, shaking himself out of his worry.

"I dunno," said Keel. "Where they put us. Somewhere before the Tar Marsh."

"Who was your captain?" Anand pressed.

"Some yellow fellow. I don't remember his name and I couldn't pronounce it if I did. Killed, he was, by Hulkrish arrows—the big ones, missiles."

"Who else fought with you and will vouch for your honor?"

"Half of us in our division died that night," said Tal. "We hid in the marsh grass and climbed up in the punk weeds after retreat was called. The others that survived were men from different mounds. Never saw 'em again."

Anand stared at Keel and Tal, then looked to Terraclon for confirmation of his doubts. Terraclon faintly shook his head.

"Your caste's idols keeper will know where you were before the war and the night of it," said Anand. "He is bound by his oaths to the gods to speak the truth before his queen and highest priest. Shall we send for him . . . for Reverend Glurmu the Floppy-Eared?"

"Glurmu told us not to go—he said the Son of Locust was none other than a fraud, a false prophet, and if we joined up with him we'd be betraying the duties of our caste."

"But he'd know how many days you were gone or not," said Anand, "and whether you had left for the border in time to train for the battle."

Tal and Keel were all too silent.

"We fought for Bee-Jor!" Keel finally blurted. "Are

you saying our service meant nothing? That we should go back to our shacks at the midden?"

Anand stared at Keel and churned with rage as he remembered a long chain of his cruelties. In his mind he heard the snap of Keel's thorn-laced whip on his father's back as it sent bits of his flesh flying. *I should have never allowed him to remain as foreman,* Anand scolded himself. In the silence, Anand could hear himself breathe . . . as well as the movement of the tiny monsters spinning under his skin.

"Either go back to the midden, Good Bee-Jorites," he finally said, "or we could escort you to the western border to join the Slopeites in their own country, where you can live in the old ways. Surely they could use your bravery in their battle with the Beetle Riders preparing to attack their mounds."

Keel and Tal looked at each other, then grimaced at Anand. "Excuse us, Your Majesties and . . . others," said Keel. "We don't want to upset the shit-cart, as it were. Thanks for hearing us out . . . Anand. Perhaps we could move up when a place becomes available. You never know when someone might, you know, get killed."

"Do . . . not . . . make . . . threats!" said Anand, blasting each word.

"Why, Commander. You've misunderstood us. No threats here. Just respect and reverence."

Anand's nostrils quivered with rage as he turned

to his guards. "Accompany this valiant defender, Citizen Gelk, and his wife, Citizen Canathy, back to the chamber they were granted," commanded Anand. "And make sure it is empty of all but their own family before they resume it." He turned to the father and son.

"Do not test me, Keel. Do not."

"Test you? Why, we are mighty proud of you, Anand. Saved us from your cousin Pleckoo and the Hulkrites, you did."

"Leave. Now."

Keel and Tal gave with a low, grunting laughter, then lumbered out as guards escorted in the next group. The plaintiffs were a married couple with dark brown skin who clutched babies in swaddling to their chests. Behind them was their daughter, her face to the floor, who had just reached womanhood. She was clutching a third baby. The women sobbed as they stood before the thrones, waiting for the accused to join them. They were three upper-caste women in lacy widows' whites with two-tailed trains and layers of underskirts. The guards behind them used the sharp ends of spears to prod them into keeping pace. The oldest and stoutest of them came to a halt and turned on the guards just as they reached the thrones. "If you poke me with that spear again, you dark, brazen trash, I'll strangle your children too!" she screeched.

The lush costumes of the three were so thick that

they bunched up against each other as they stood before Anand. He was amused, for a moment, by the lower portion of their gowns, which were in the shapes of three-tiered pyramids, but his inner state had gone from anger to alarm. The accused curtsied gracefully before Polexima and Trellana, who appeared to know them. They turned to Dolgeeno, fell on their knees, and then rose while rubbing their palms and cocking their heads in imitation of Mantis.

"What are your names?" asked Anand, gesturing to the sobbing family. He heard the gasps of the accused—they were offended he had not addressed them first.

"Klurteth," said the man. "And my wife is Adelica. Our daughter is Ensay."

"They can answer for themselves," said Polexima.

"My daughter cannot," said Klurteth. "She has lost her speech."

"What caste are you from?" asked Trellana.

"We don't ask that question anymore," snapped Anand. "What is your work?"

"We work at the sun-kilns, baking and roasting— some distilling with those in the fermenters' caste. I fought in the war," said the man as he turned his head to show where an arrow of Foondathan obsidian had removed a patch of his hair.

"Thank you for your service in feeding the people of our mound," said Polexima, "and for your defense against the Hulkrites."

"What is your grievance?" asked Anand.

"Our babies were killed!" screamed Adelica before she fell into sobbing. "Killed, by those women there!" The kiln workers approached Anand, and set down and unwrapped their bundles to reveal the corpses of infants. Anand gritted his teeth in rage.

"How many children do you have?" asked Polexima over the sobbing.

"We had twenty-seven. We have twenty-one now," said the man.

Twenty-seven children, Anand thought. *We must end the eating of mushrooms.*

"As was my right, I moved my family up the mound and into the black-sand dwelling of a Cajorite captain who died in the war," said Klurteth. "Three of my eldest sons died in the battle and the house was our reward for my family's sacrifice. We came home from the kilns one night and found our eldest daughter here, beaten and bloody, with the corpses of our triplets at her feet. She told us these women from the neighboring dwelling came in, beat her with a spiked mace, and left her for dead before strangling our babies. They said they would come back to kill the rest of our children until we left what had been their house."

"Is that true?" Anand asked the silent daughter. She nodded her head through her sobbing.

Anand turned to the widows, who stood with their chins raised in defiance. "You stand accused of the murder of infants and the attempted murder of this young woman," he said. "Who are you?"

"I am the Widow Gafrexa Chando," said the stout woman. "And this is Entath and Namity, sisters of my husband, Lieutenant General Chando, who gave his life to defeat the Termite worshippers." On her forehead as well as those of her sisters-in-law, Anand saw a weaving of widow's marks they had painted with their own blood. The largest mark was a horizontal slash for her husband; the vertical marks were for sons, and the diagonals were for fathers and brothers.

"My sympathies to you," said Anand, "and our thanks for their sacrifice. Do you deny these charges against you?"

"We do."

"You did not kill these babies?"

"We did. But we are guilty of no crime."

"How can you say that?" shouted Polexima.

"Your Majesties, Polexima and Trellana. We request that you rescind the orders of this Dranverish alien and allow us to return to our rightful home with our children. We reject the ridiculous proclamation of this filthy outsider that allows these feculent lice to displace us from our homes merely because they survived the Hulkrish attack."

"The defenders did more than survive," said Anand through a tightening mouth. "They *fought* . . . and not in some useless, prideful way but in a way that actually won us the war."

"How dare you!" Gafrexa screeched. "Are you suggesting my husband wasted his life? Our Holy Slopeish Armies sacrificed themselves to destroy the Hulkrites so that your rabble—coated in roach grease—could run over their corpses and steal their glory."

"I reject your account," shouted Anand through teeth that were grinding. "And warn you to be cautious with your words."

"If you have no husband, the edict is that you are to consolidate your household with your siblings," said Polexima. "I remember you well . . . I reviewed your situation and ordered your evacuation. Your sister is Vereetha, widow of Lieutenant General Gambo. Her chambers are spacious and should be quite accommodating for all your family."

"Majesty—with all due respect—this Dranverish alien has poisoned your mind," the Widow Chando shouted. "I will not impose on my sister and her family, as they are dealing with their own grief. My chambers have been in my family since the founding of Cajoria. And I will remain in them with *all* my family . . . and I will kill anyone who attempts to take them from us, as well as their *screaming babies*."

Anand burned with a pulsing anger at the same moment a patch of skin on his thigh bubbled up and sent out a sharp pain that stabbed through his entire leg, then throbbed through his body. He looked down to see the sharp-edged jaws of something tear through the skin of his blister and reveal itself as an eight-legged creature crawling out of the rupture. He chased it with his hand as it scooted over his thigh, then under it where it jabbed into his skin with its clamping jaws. He stood, clenched his teeth, then tore out the mite and ripped it in two. The widows failed to hold back sniggers. Trellana looked amused. A moment later a second blister was rising, leaking fluid.

Terraclon jumped up and untied his heavy robe to step out of it. He was naked but for a loincloth and the holster for his dagger as he grabbed Anand's arm. "Let's go," he said. "We're cutting those things out *now*."

"No. Others are waiting for justice," said Anand. "How many seek an audience?" he asked the closest guard who wriggled in pain from his own infestation.

"Commander, we have lost count. There are hundreds, perhaps thousands, waiting to see you. Some have arrived from neighboring mounds."

Anand scraped at his legs as he walked to the window. He saw a loose queue of scuffling, screaming people threatening each other with blades and blow-darts as guards threatened a greater violence to keep them all in line. At the head of the queue were well-dressed merchants defending themselves with walking sticks tipped with wasp stingers, which they thrust in the faces of their accusers. One merchant's stinger connected with the cheek of a dark-skinned man who fell to the ground, screaming and clutching his eye. A moment later, all the merchants were on the ground, targeted with darts and twitching and spitting up foam. The accusers were rushing over to strip the merchants of their clothing and possessions, and getting in kicks to their cheeks. Anand was about to run out and call for order when another bubble at the back of his thigh ripped open and a mite crawled up his buttock to sink its jaws.

"Excuse me, Commander," shouted the Widow Gafrexa at Anand as Terraclon tried to drag him away. "But we should like to return to our home now. Perhaps these people will listen to *you* when you tell them to get out of our house."

"You will not return to your old dwelling," Anand shouted. "But you *will* pay for your crimes." He turned to his guards. "Cage these women. Put them on display before the palace entry, near the royal dew station, and guard them day and night. Spread the word that they are baby-killers and will be dealt with accordingly." He turned towards Polexima.

"Polly, I need your help."

"Yes," she said, rising.

"Step outside and tell the people that we cannot address their grievances as long as they are attacking each other. Tell them we will have a compulsory assembly in three days' time. Until then, order *will* be kept in Bee-Jor, and anyone who violates the peace will be severely punished."

"Of course," she said, and left with her acolytes.

Terraclon stood next to Anand, tugging his arm, as they watched the violence outside the window.

"Why an assembly?" Terraclon asked. "What will you announce?"

"I don't really know, Ter," he said as he clenched his teeth to keep from screaming, and failed when he heard another rip of his skin.

"Of course", she said, and left with her acolytes.
Terraclon stood next to Anand, tugging his arm
as they watched the violence outside the window.
"Why an assembly," Terraclon asked, "What will
his teeth to keep from screaming, and failed when he
heard another rip of his skin.

CHAPTER 7

A TIME TO GET DRUNK

Anand and Terraclon raced into Trellana's chambers, where thirteen maidservants washed and scrubbed surfaces that needed no cleaning. "Please leave," Anand said, and it seemed like forever as the women gathered up their polishing cloths, brushes, and pods of cleaning potions, then joined in a ritual formation to exit in a slow, grave march. Anand ran to a clay barrel, flung off the top, and dunked his head inside it to suck up what remained of some aphid-milk liquor. He fell to the floor, writhed, and removed his clothes as Terraclon came closer. "All right, cut them out," Anand shouted. "Start with the one on my right foot.

Pry up the skin, then scrape and smash every little fucker!"

"Get rags and mallets," Terraclon shouted to the nearest guards, who were confused, wondering why their commander was stripping to submit to some strange procedure.

"Do what he said," Anand shouted, and the guards obeyed. "Dip the knife in liquor first," he said to Terraclon, who was checking the sharpness of his quartz blade.

"Why?"

"To reduce other infections."

"Infections of what?"

"Of even smaller parasites. Creatures you can't see. It's something I learned in Dranveria."

"Creatures you can't see . . . really."

Terraclon dipped his knife in the liquor, then went to work on a welt on Anand's foot. He sliced around the raised skin, then peeled it off to reveal a mite that swiveled in the clear liquid. Inside its transparent body, he saw what looked like dark clusters of tiny waving fingers.

"Holy Mother Ant!" Terraclon whispered as he prodded the creature. Anand gasped in deeper pain as the mite sank its fangs into his flesh, injecting venom as it anchored itself. Terraclon slipped his dagger under the creature and jerked it up, then set it on the floor tile where it spun to dry itself before its legs extended to crawl away. Chasing after it, he stabbed it with his knife, then held up its corpse to the light to examine it. "Eight legs," he said.

"Yes, it's a mite. But I've never known of mites that live *under* the skin of men until they're fully grown," said Anand. "Just how and when did they get inside me?"

The guards returned with rags and mallets.

"Hamlutz," Anand said to his head guard, a tall and strong young man with dark skin and large, black eyes. "Tell all the men who are infected as I am that they are to report to me now, in the ballroom of this palace. Summon the cutters of the blinders' caste and ask them to bring their sharpest blades. Tell the brewing caste to bring every available barrel of distillate."

"Yes, Commander," Hamlutz answered before he scratched at his own legs.

Anand tore cloth from his tunic and rolled it up into a wad to clench with his molars to keep from screaming. His legs became a grotesquery of wounds as Terraclon continued the extractions. "I need more drink," Anand shouted over the cloth. A guard rolled over an ornately carved keg of nut liquor and turned the spigot-bladder to Anand's mouth. He sucked down its thick, sweet contents, then felt the shocking nausea of too much drink. A moment later, he had an inner floating sensation, and some small relief from the torment of the surgery.

Terraclon made faces as his hands and neck grew stiff with fatigue. He looked surprised when he felt something brush the back of his feet and turned to see Trellana, whose voluminous gowns had grazed him. She looked down at his naked back between Anand's parted thighs with the latter's genitals on full display.

"Well. It is just as I suspected," she said. "Commander Quegdoth, vanquisher of the Termite worshippers, likes to get drunk, then fellated by fay young men."

"Help or get out," Terraclon said.

"Do not speak that way to me. Not in my chambers. Why are you in here?"

"Because this is where the liquor is," said Anand.

Trellana blinked, ever so slowly. "Will this take long?" she asked. "I'm tired and I want to go back to bed."

"I'm sorry you've had such a long, difficult morning—having to get dressed and eat breakfast and other taxing labors," said Terraclon. "But you might have noticed your husband is in agony and in need of your bed."

"He will not be getting into my bed to muck it up with his bleeding legs."

"He can't walk at the moment."

"Then pick him up and drag him out."

"You stinking flea-anus," said Terraclon.

"You scum-eating deviant. Get out!" shouted Trellana, pointing to the hall.

"*You* get out!" Terraclon shouted, and flung the goop on his knife in her face.

"How dare you!" she shouted, then screamed in pain when her ear was smacked by the heavy end of a staff.

"How dare *you*!" shouted Polexima from behind her daughter. Trellana, wincing, turned to face her mother, only to receive a second smack from her staff to her cheek. Stunned and bleeding from punctures to her face, she dropped to kneel in the mass of her gowns.

"Father," she whispered through her sobs as she stared at the blood that spotted her hand. "I want my father."

"Then go to him," Polexima shouted, pulling the staff back for another blow. "Get on your own two feet and walk to his chambers."

"You are the cruelest people on the Sand," Trellana screeched.

"Get out of here *now*," Polexima shouted, flipping her staff to use the sharp end as a threat.

Trellana tried to back away, lost in the thickness of her costume, falling again and again until the guards lifted her. "Don't touch me," she screamed at them. "Mother, tell these dark wretches to stop clawing me!"

"Take her out of here," Polexima commanded the guards. "Drag her by her hair if you need to."

Polexima came closer to Anand, and failed to hide her pity when she saw the sickening array of his wounds. "The crowd outside has dispersed. How can I help here?"

Good, he thought. *They still obey her as queen.*

"Get long strips of cloth and soak them in the purest distillate of fermentation we have," he whispered as the guards set him in bed. "Then wrap them around my legs. And later, I'm going to need some crutches." A moment after that, his pain increased to something so unbearable all he could do was shake and shut his eyes. *I accept this pain,* he shouted inside himself, then felt a strange and sudden relief, followed by a flash of ecstasy. He was plunging into a sweet darkness as sleep fell on him like a heavy rock.

When Anand woke, he saw the brighter light of the noon sun coming through the windows. A pair of fine crutches fashioned from grasshopper femurs had been set by the bed. His legs had been wrapped in lengths of cloth stained with the light brown of a barley liquor. He rose gingerly, his legs throbbing with pain as he took up the crutches to hobble out to a hubbub coming from the ballroom. When he entered the vast chambers, he saw hundreds of his defenders scratching and scraping at their infected legs. They turned towards him, saw his bandages, and quieted to slap their chests and dip their heads.

"Defenders," he shouted, sighting the delivered barrels of spirits. "Relief is on its way. In the meantime, get very well drunk—as you have never drunk before." As casks and barrels and kegs were opened, the men of the blinders' caste arrived in their stiff rags, crusty with dried green muck. Many of them squinted—unused to daylight—and soon they were taking in the magnificence of the crystal palace's ballroom.

"Men of the blinders' caste," Anand shouted as Terraclon and Polexima joined him. "Welcome and thanks for your help today. Our defenders need your skills. You must cut out the mites under our fighters' skin with the same delicacy you use to cut out the eyes of the ant hatchlings." The blinders looked surprised and proud to take up this task. "Defenders, can I get a volunteer?" Anand said, turning to the infested. "Who will go first?"

A man stepped towards Anand with a square jaw and squarish nose that he recognized.

"You, Good Defender, were a wasp rider, yes?"

"I was, Commander Quegdoth. I am Hwagol."

"Bring Hwagol a keg," Anand said, "and a blanket to lie on. Pious Terraclon, show our good blinders how this is done."

Terraclon, now dressed in a simple tunic, dipped his knife in the keg before the rest was handed to Hwagol to drink. The blinders watched as Terraclon delicately cut around the raised flesh, then peeled it back to reveal its living inhabitants in different stages of development. Some mites were large and dark and immediately active. Others were smaller and pale and showed little life. Anand looked around at all the infected men whose faces were a mix of hope, dread,

and agony. He gasped when he realized that all of
them, all those infected, had been pilots. A moment
later, he realized they weren't just locust pilots—all
these men were riders of night wasps.

The mites came from infected night wasps!

Sweat beaded on Anand's brow, and his throat felt
like it was twisting shut. *Medinwoe and the Dneepers*, he
thought. *Out there in Hulkren! All of them wasp riders!
They must be in agony!*

Polexima supervised the palace servants as they
spread through the ballroom laying out blankets, cushions, cloth, and old clothes—whatever could be used
as bedding. Men quickly fell to the floor as the blinders set to a task only mildly more gruesome than their
usual work. Screams of pain echoed around the vast
chambers as skin was cut open, with mites injecting
their venomous fangs in an attempt to stay fastened.
Terraclon continued the surgeries, with Polexima
joining him as his executioner, smashing the mites
into a blood-soaked mush with a mallet. Around the
ballroom, piles of the dead mites were shoveled up and
into the painted and ornate trash bins that palace servants usually hauled through festive evenings.

Anand tried not to cringe as he listened to the
splash, the *splat*, and the wet *rip* of the tiny monsters
as they were excised and killed. *I am responsible for this*,
he thought as the men's screams and calls for mercy
to the gods pierced his ear. *But why wasn't I infected the
first time I rode a wasp?*

"Messenger," he shouted to the first of the long-legged young runners. They waited attentively at the main entrance, their hands clasped behind their backs as they stared at the gore. The first of them trotted to Anand and turned his right ear after a shallow bow. "Yes, Commander Quegdoth."

"Get a speed ant and go to the locust cages. Summon the foreman who tends them and have him alert the locust pilots that they are needed. Tell him it's urgent—hundreds of lives are at stake."

As the messenger sped off, Pious Nuvao walked swiftly towards Anand, his face puckered in disgust as he took in the carnage. "Anand," he said. "These men should be ingesting something more than spirits right now. We can end their suffering in moments. If *you* are still in pain you should drink *this*."

From under his cloaked arm, Nuvao lifted a seed canteen and pulled out the stoppers on both ends. He took a light suck of it, then handed it to Anand, who drank the rest. It was a sweet, floral liquor but something musty and bitter was in it, burning his throat. The taste that lingered on his tongue was vaguely familiar, and so were the sudden, beautiful sensations that made his insides feel like a rushing brook.

"The black mildew," he said. He looked out the window and saw that the cage he had ordered had been placed by the dew station. Guards were forcing the Widow Gafrexa and her sisters-in-law into it as they screamed and fought and spit. The guards responded by hurling them in. They tumbled, then stood and rearranged the lacy coverings that fell down the tiers of their pyramidal gowns. Anand gasped. "That's it!" he said aloud, and laughed. He turned and saw Nuvao next to Terraclon, comforting him as he rested and offering a drink of water from a nearby basin. Anand kept laughing as he walked towards them, which he knew seemed strange given the present circumstances.

"Just what's gotten into you . . . Quegdoth?" Terraclon asked.

"I've seen something, a vision, for the assembly—what we need to do! Nuvao, where is it the priests keep their scrolls? In the storage room? Let's have Pious Dolgeeno meet us there."

"He will be there late in the afternoon to bless the day's recordings. But none but priests have ever been allowed in the storage rooms," said Nuvao.

"Then it's best we surprise him."

CHAPTER 8

THE HEAVENLY FIELD
AT THE FEET OF GRASSHOPPER

As he looked at his fingers wet with his own blood and pus, King Medinwoe knew they could go no further than the mound of Ashkad-dozh.

The return to Dneep, through a devastated Hulkren, had been a delight of open spaces as he surveyed the sprawl of this sun-drenched land. Now the mission to destroy the ghost ants and free the Hulkrites' slaves and captives was not only incomplete; it was ending in humiliation and insufferable pain. The Dneepers' roach caravan halted, once again, to rest the ailing roaches which suffered in this place.

This also allowed his men ample time to deal with the deepening irritation in their legs. Now with each scratching, the agony only got worse; just touching the welts prompted the creatures within to pump out more of some excruciating poison. Medinwoe could barely look at his men, who were palsied and wailing as they attempted to claw or cut out the tiny monsters. And now he realized he could no longer ride or walk himself. His body spasmed so violently that his hands could barely hold, much less prod, the antennae of his roach. The last of the men to stay mounted, he fell off his saddle and dropped to the sand.

"Good Dneepers," he shouted to his men as they writhed on the ground. "We may die here—might be eaten from the inside out by these demons in our legs. But we must try and cut them out, whatever they are. Take your knives and daggers and work on each other . . . you cannot cut them out of yourself, I have tried."

As he looked at his men, he knew most had only half-heard him. Some made the attempt to unsheathe their knives, and a few could at least hold if not grip them. Medinwoe was distracted by a fresh pain in his inner thigh, when a reddening welt popped of its own accord. Something was pushing out, and when it emerged it spun left, then right, as it extended its eight legs to shake off moisture. He grabbed at it to fling away when it scurried down his leg and clamped in his ankle with a sharp bite. The mite swelled and reddened as a second one near his knee emerged in a slow burst of pus and blood.

Medinwoe took his knife, made from a roachling's pincer, and scraped up the mite from his ankle. It swung on the blade with its fore-claws before it fell, then scampered off. He grabbed the second mite with his hands, then regretted it when it sank its fangs into his fingers and pumped its venom. His hand stiffened with aches as the poison spread, and he writhed on his back and bit his tongue to stop himself from the indignity of screaming. Around him, the roaches were shifting, colliding with each other, stretching the tethers that bound them as a team. *They've picked up the scent of something,* the king realized as he sniffed the air. *But what? Ants? Beetles? Hulkrites?*

He turned to the man closest to him and saw it was his young nephew, Prince Tappenwoe, whose wisp of a yellow beard was wet with sweat and snot and tears. "Uncle, please, try and cut them out," he said, "or at least cut off my legs!"

"Men!" he shouted. "We will survive this! These creatures want out of us—if we can't cut them out first, they will leave on their own!"

Tappenwoe set his head against an upended sand grain and braced himself. The king attempted to use his clumsy left hand to make an incision and open a welt on his nephew's shin, but he could not control his fingers. He tried making a shallow stab to kill the mite; this seemed to work, and the blister stopped its throbbing. Stabbing at all his nephew's blisters, each jab ended with the boy's yelps of pain. The king stopped when he felt a different, deeper pain at the back of his thigh and turned to see that a Hulkrish arrow had pierced him. Another flew past his arm and entered his nephew's shoulder.

"Hulkrites!" he shouted as arrows skidded over the hard and greasy chitin of the roaches or found their targets in the Grass Men's flesh. The roaches, excited by the smell of advancing predators, were whipping their antennae in a fury. They bashed into each other as the cargo-sleds were bandied about, shaking out their contents as they teetered. As the roaches pulled away, the rudders of the sleds ran over the Dneepers, grinding and spreading them over the rough sand and leaving them exposed.

Medinwoe used the last of his strength to push up a long, flat sand grain to use as a shield. He looked through its cloudy glass to see an army of hobbled men—and perhaps some women—advancing towards them. None in this army were covered in white paint. They wore rags and the salvaged armor and the ill-fitting boots of Hulkrites, but they were not warriors for the Termite. Some raised broken swords or bows and mismatched arrows as they grunted and screamed threats in a jumble of tongues. They ran, as best as they could, not towards the Dneepers, but to the carts in back of their thrashing roaches.

The raiders helped each other climb up to the rattling wagon beds, where they took their contents and tossed them into the arms of their fellows. They unwrapped the bundles of flattened ant eggs, worm jerky, and cured cricket and cicada meats, and stuffed them into their mouths. The clay jars of aphid and barley syrup were broken open, and they scooped out and ate their oozing contents and licked it off the shards. Some raiders climbed up to the other carts, where they found the squat barrels full of insect fat and arsenic, and greedily ate it because it was sweet and rich.

When all the wagon beds were emptied, the raiders stood in a circle and stared at the squirming, screaming roach riders, who were unable to rise and fight and reclaim their goods. A few raiders stepped closer to the Dneepers and used rapiers to cut off their tunics for a closer look at their exotic wounds. They stripped Tappenwoe of all his clothes, then pulled him over a barrel to stare at his crawling skin, which brought gasps followed by giggles, then a startled silence when a mite erupted. When it spun out of its messy liquid and scooted away, the raiders cheered. Their children chased after the mite until one stabbed it with his pike, then held it aloft in triumph.

The cheering came to an end when the raiders' leader, a man who looked like his ears had been chewed off, shouted his orders, then pointed his bow and arrow down at the fallen Dneepers. The other bowmen followed Chewed Ears's example, and they spread through the shaking, spastic Grass Men, examining each one and shouting foreign words that were a threat of some kind.

Medinwoe did not understand much of what they shouted at him. From their gestures he realized the raiders wanted his fine sword, his finer dagger, and the jeweled medallion around his neck. He looked over at Tappenwoe, who gave forth with a piercing shriek as yet another mite ripped out from the side of his thigh. Chewed Ears came over and shouted at the prince, annoyed by his screaming, and stuck his heel in the prince's mouth to quiet him. In his torment, Tappenwoe could not control himself, convulsing as he choked. Chewed Ears screamed in pain when the prince bit through his boot and into his foot. "I can't breathe!" the prince shouted.

"Please! We've done nothing to you! What's ours is yours!" Medinwoe shouted. Chewed Ears was coming towards him, nocking an arrow, as Medinwoe mumbled his prayers to the Heavenly Field. "Save us, Great Grasshopper!" he repeated, until he sank into a trance, down to a place where the world was smaller and quiet. He was resigning himself to dying when he saw a circle of turquoise blurs overhead, and heard the buzz of beating wings.

The raiders were falling, pierced by darts and arrows, or they were running for their lives. Medinwoe could make out men and their weapons on the backs of the locusts, and smelled drops of the brown sludge that sprayed from the insects' mouths when they spiraled. The hobbled attackers disappeared into the sparse weeds, but some who had eaten the poisoned insect fat fell from a sudden illness. They were on their knees, clutching their stomachs as their contents erupted with violence. Some fell facedown in their own vomit to suffocate quickly, while others twitched in violent spasms before going stiff and dying.

The blue locusts landed, making awkward and jarring descents. Medinwoe smiled to recognize them as men of Bee-Jor. Behind each pilot was a bowman with a readied arrow, or else a dark-skinned rider dressed in stiff rags with a long, thin knife at his side. These men in rags looked both exhilarated and airsick by what had to be their first flight.

The leader of the pilots jumped from his locust and ran towards Medinwoe. He appeared to be a young, yellow-skinned Slopeite, perhaps a defector from his upper caste, and he spoke to the Dneepers' king in their similar tongue. "Commander Quegdoth sends his deepest apologies," he said, and bowed his head. "I am Captain Dziddens of Mound Cajoria of Bee-Jor. Our commander wants you to drink this before submitting to the blades of these skillful Bee-Jorites. They have come to cut the wasp-mites from your legs."

Wasp-mites! So that's where they came from, Medinwoe thought. The captain and other locust pilots pulled hollowed seed canteens from their backsacks. "These are from the secret hordes of the Slopeish priests," said the captain as he unstoppered the canteen.

Medinwoe and the others sucked the liquid out of the seeds. He tasted the nectar of honeysuckle, but then his tongue sensed something bitter that irritated his throat. The king sucked his canteen dry, and a moment later, the pains in his legs felt like something almost pleasant. The Bee-Jorites and their locusts, the cloudy sky above, the wailing of the defeated raiders hiding in the weeds all seemed beautifully, strangely hilarious—and so did the darkly ugly, knife-bearing Slopeite coming towards him to cut out the parasites under his skin. Medinwoe smiled when he realized he wanted to talk to one of these wasp-mites, wanted to question and sympathize with it, as well as examine it for its strange beauty. *I want to forgive it for having been born with such a difficult nature*, he thought. The only pain the king felt now was from his mouth, which was stretched too wide in a grin.

Whatever he had drunk, he must drink it again. He must have this every day and share it with all Dneepers. The knife cutting into his legs was painful at first, but then felt like the tongue of the most skillful concubine making her way up his thighs. This coarse, night-dark Slopeite in his awful rags had taken on the appearance of a heavenly slave. After he skillfully cut around each welt and plucked out the mite by its safer end, he handed them to the handsome, well-born Captain Dziddens, who skewered them on his rapier. And all of this was happening under a soft shower of the tiniest gold flakes that sprinkled from the sun—overwhelmingly gorgeous. When all the mites had been removed, Medinwoe's body turned as light as milkweed fluff. A wind picked him up and he floated and rocked on warm currents until he reached the pristine blue of the sky . . .

Medinwoe reached a cloud with the beautiful face of a woman, who sang a welcome to him in the sweetest voice and urged him to climb on her back. He sat atop a soft bulge on the cloud-woman's back to ride under the great blue dome. They flew in an instant to a distant place, beyond the known world. The king looked down on a vast, open place which he knew immediately as the Heavenly Field at the Feet of Grasshopper.

Soft, fluffy hands in the cloud reached for him and set him on the ground. He looked up to see Lord Grasshopper, as tall as a tree, and seated on His crystal throne. All six of His hands were petting His worshippers, who queued up, patiently waiting their turn to adore Him and to be adored. Across the plain was a gently glittering, multicolored sand that was fine and soft to the touch, and warmed Medinwoe's feet. Fragrant flowers, changing their colors through the rainbow's spectrum, were softly waving on their stems. One flower above him dipped its petals, then shook out a shower of caterpillar custards rolled in glistening honey crystals.

As Medinwoe feasted on the sweet meats, a choir of thousands sang the sweetest music from clouds that spiraled above. He watched hundreds of thousands of men, women, and children join hands in a circular dance around the towering Lord Grasshopper. A few of His worshippers stopped dancing when they noticed Medinwoe, and rushed towards him with the most joyful expressions. Sweet-tasting tears streamed from the king's eyes when he recognized his father, his mother, and his grandparents, all restored to their youthful beauty. He fell into laughter-filled embraces with each one, then followed them into the dance, where his ecstasy increased with each kick and step. It was then that he noticed that all in this promised world had yellow skin—skin as bright and yellow as the mustard blossom.

Where are the dark-skinned dead? he wondered. *The brown- and black- and tawny-skinned of other nations?*

At that moment, Grasshopper looked at Medinwoe, and spoke directly to him as he fell away from the dance.

"The dark-skinned have their own paradise," He said in a loud but sweetly pleasant voice. "Their promised lands are provided for them by my cousin, Locust, my sister, Milkweed Butterfly, and my aunt, Cricket, where they can be among their own for eternity. You, King Medinwoe, were chosen by me to lead my Chosen People, my greatest creation, out of the grass of Dneep and back into the Promised Clearing, to make it the Pure and Yellow Nation."

Grasshopper smiled at Medinwoe, who felt his skin transforming into something warm and shining. He looked at his arms and legs and feet, and saw that his skin had turned from yellow into a pure golden light, as if dipped into a sunbeam. He was floating again, rising to join his god, who reached into His chest, opened it, and allowed Medinwoe to enter, where the two became one.

"I must rid the Promised Clearing of all but yellow people," said Medinwoe/Grasshopper to himself as he accepted what he had always known: that he was the direct descendant of Lord Grasshopper, who by divine right would occupy the weeds on the edges of the place known as Hulkren and purge it of all its impure beings.

CHAPTER 9

A QUARTER MOON
SPITTING OUT STARS

The priests quieted when Nuvao entered the antechamber of the storage rooms, where they were cataloguing their depleted stocks of potions and their ingredients.

"Is his Most Pious in the back?" Nuvao asked of Frinbo, who sat at his carved desk, with its inlays of opalescent beetle chitin. Before him was a coarse sheet made from a sun-dried ant's egg and next to that was a pen in a pod of wasp-gall ink.

Pious Frinbo frowned as he rose, froze, and then grimaced when six of the Dranverite's armed guards entered—then parted to reveal Anand on crutches. Terraclon followed after him.

"I suppose it would be pointless to tell you this place is forbidden," said Frinbo, "to all but ordained priests."

"It would be," Anand said.

"Even the royals are not allowed here," said Frinbo.

"If they had been, they'd have known how you concoct all your so-called potions."

"I'll permit *you*, Commander," Frinbo said, then pointed with his chin at the guards. "But not those dark things, with their weapons at the ready."

"You will permit us all. To ensure my safety."

"Would you have Pious Dolgeeno come and meet us?" said Terraclon. "Please."

"Well, I believe we've had a little miracle," said Frinbo. "A request ending with a 'please.'"

"Yes. *Please* have him join us," said Terraclon. "Unless he's defecating, or otherwise engaged in something that stimulates that particular orifice."

Frinbo struggled to look indignant, but couldn't help smirking. "And why, if I may ask?"

"We are requesting a tour," Anand said. "Of your . . . your . . ."

"Of what?" Frinbo said, looking very much annoyed.

"Of our records," said Nuvao. "Of all that has been written down."

"And the ingredients in the potions—what we call *formulas* in Dranveria. All this knowledge should belong to all people."

"Commander Quegdoth," said Frinbo, raising his chin. "Would you want *all* people, even the lowest-born and the steadfastly stupid, to have access to the most dangerous information?"

"Dangerous to whom?"

Frinbo was quiet, then turned to Nuvao. "What else have you been sharing with the commander, Nuvao? His eyes are dilated."

"I gave him the mildew," said Nuvao. "Combined with an extraction of claw root for his pains. He was suffering. Terribly suffering."

"I would say he is doing much better," said Frinbo.

"It's not my first time," Anand said.

Nuvao smiled to see that Anand was giddy, and leaking little chuckles as he looked around the bright, cheerful chamber with its walls of pink crystals on one side, and its shelves full of scrolls on the other. Anand delighted in looking at the old, round priests, who glared at him as he took in their elaborate necklaces and the shifting sheen of their polished silk garments. He was fascinated by the individual hairs of their long eyebrows, which they had taken pains to curl into little knots at their ends. One priest recoiled from Anand as he fingered his dangling earrings, crafted from blue scorpion shells, all while attempting to hide his writing with the drape of his sleeves. Nuvao could not help but laugh, which he muffled with his own sleeves.

"What can you bring me that is something like a primer?" Anand asked, then sharply clapped his hands—a happy sound that the priests did not care for at all.

"A primer?" asked Frinbo.

"Yes," Anand said with a radiant grin. "A scroll for beginners who are just learning to read and write."

"I can help with that," said Nuvao as he searched among the shelves. Anand looked lovingly out the windows and at the pink quartz walls, and burst into his happiest smile. "This rosy light coming in through the walls reminds me of Dranveria," he said.

"They have rose quartz in Dranveria?" asked Terraclon.

"They have entire buildings made of it . . . including the Hall of Peace in the capital. And so are the university palaces, which are set atop the mound."

"A what? A university?"

"A place of high learning. They have many rooms like this, full of scrolls where histories and ideas and stories are written down. You'd like the scrolls about clothing and its history."

"Clothing has a history?"

"Yes. It's called *fashion*. They have rooms full of scrolls with colorful pictures that are dedicated to documenting its changes over the centuries. You could lose yourself for days, Ter."

Nuvao stepped down from a ladder with a scroll and pulled out its pages. "This is typical of the first scroll anyone will see first when being initiated into what we call record-keeping . . . or *writing*, to use the forbidden word."

Anand looked at the pages and took in their rows of tiny yet elaborate drawings. "These are not simplified *letters*," he said, using a Dranverish word. "These are pictures, I assume, that stand for sounds, and sometimes look like the objects they represent."

"Exactly," said Nuvao. Grabbing Frinbo's ink pen, he dipped it in the funnel of the pod to wet it. "Here is how you write your name," he said, replicating five of the page's drawings, repeating two. One drawing looked like rows of teeth inside a circle, two were like worms tied into knots, one resembled a quarter moon spitting out stars, and the other was a human foot with a swollen big toe. It took multiple dippings of the implement before Nuvao was finished.

"That is . . . very time-taking," Anand said. "Now I understand why Dolgeeno was working so furiously."

"How do you write your name in Dranverish?" Nuvao asked.

Anand dipped the pen and rendered the five simple letters of the Dranverish phonetic system that spelled his name in the time between two heartbeats. Nuvao was stunned.

"That's it? Those little scrawls?"

"Yes. Here is how you write 'Nuvao,'" he said, and completed it just as quickly.

"And my name?" Terraclon asked.

they were tiny babies, blinking at the world in both fear and delight. Back then, they were as hungry for physical warmth as they were for food. She could barely remember them as they got older and were formally distanced from the company of women. After a certain age, she only saw her boys at functions and ceremonies where they treated her courteously, awaiting the moment they could break away and indulge in drink with other men. Watching them from a distance in the ballroom and the feasting hall, she saw that they spoke with the same voice, wore the same uniform, and laughed in the same way at jokes whispered in a tightening circle.

Her mind, beyond her control, repeated her sons' names in the order in which they were born. She remembered, as if it were a moon ago, when each of them was wrapped by the priests in a yellow blanket and handed to her as a set of twins or triplets, as she was mourning for their tinier sisters who were dead from injections of a wasp's venom. Now she was wishing that all her sons, like Nuvao, had chosen the little idol of Ant Queen over the toy sword when it was offered to them by Dolgeeno in the ritual of the Third Age Chit. Her pain deepened further when her mind turned to other dead relatives killed by Hulkrites: her father, her brothers, the sister she barely knew, and innumerable cousins, nephews, and uncles. "Peace is their greatest passion," she said aloud to herself, repeating something she had heard Anand say about his adopted land of Dranveria. How she longed to experience this place he had told her about, where war was never glorified and avoided when possible.

After scolding herself for her indulgent sadness, she pulled herself up from her bed and nodded to the idol of Cricket that was dark and glossy with a fresh staining of berry juice and set at the front of her chamber's altar. "Hail to Cricket, Defender of Peace," she said three times, and then promised her goddess that before her reign was over she would place the idols of Her at the forefront of every altar in Bee-Jor. For now, it was time to return to Anand and to duty. He was expecting her in his chambers near day's end to discuss his plans for the assembly and the restoration of order in Bee-Jor. *Just how could he manage that?*

"I'd like to walk by myself," she said to her Cricket novitiates, who nodded as they helped her through the flaps to the outside walking ring. As she walked, she saw something like normal life as the ring emptied of its tradespeople, merchants, and servants with their empty baskets or carts or barrels. Those who passed her were still not used to the sight of their once majestic queen, who dressed now in the plain guise of a priestess to a neglected deity. They thought it odd to see her walking by herself in a slow but steady way, instead of riding atop a bangled carrier ant with an entourage of gaudy priests. Still, the people stopped and bowed, and allowed her to pass before proceeding on their own way. Some even walked backwards so as not to show her their offending backsides.

I am still their queen, she thought, and felt something like a smile on her lips. The people were also doing something new: smiling back and meeting her eyes. Some of it, she was sure, was out of derision for her strange, self-humbling appearance. But it seemed for the greater part that they smiled out of warmth and appreciation, perhaps a real love instead of a fearful respect. They knew that their queen had suffered as a captive in Hulkren, then done what she could to save them from extermination by Hulkrites. *But the Cajorites seem less sure about this process to bring them— all of them—into something uncertain called the New Way.*

The same warm reactions were not coming when she reached the war widows in their bright white gowns at the decks of Sun and Moon worship. The widows had been gathering there to wait for the divine moment that both the lunar and solar deities might be visible in the sky, to allow a glimpse of their loved ones in the World Beyond Stars. When they were soldier-wives, the women would have stopped and pulled to the side, bowing gracefully for the passage of Queen Polexima. Now they gave her the sideways glare and pretended not to see her. *News has spread that I sided with the Dranverite and the untouchables against their cousin-women,* she thought. *Good!*

Polexima halted for a moment in order to look at the widows and challenged them to acknowledge her. "Good afternoon . . . Bee-Jorites," she shouted at them, and allowed herself the smug satisfaction of seeing them bristle. A few took awkward and shallow bows. From out of the middle of them, she noticed three women wearing disguises from some long-ago masquerade ball. A woman dressed in the imported robes of a Seed Eater queen came towards her, followed by a woman in something that a seamstress imagined was a Britasyte costume. She was followed by a third woman, dressed in the tunic, antennae, and leggings of a little boy with a stick ant between his legs. The three stood as a wall to block Polexima, folding their arms under their masked faces.

"Good evening . . . all," Polexima said, mildly alarmed. "What charming costumes. Is there a ball tonight?"

"We are not Bee-Jorites, and it is not a good evening at all," said the woman dressed as a Seed Eater from under a ropy, orange wig. "But it's about to get worse for you, Your Majesty." Polexima was trying to determine who the woman was from her voice when she felt a blow to each of her cheeks from the other two. As Polexima reeled, the Seed Eater impersonator shot out her fist to land on Polexima's nose, and drew blood. Polexima gripped her staff harder and attempted to swing it at her assailants when they grabbed it from her. The Britasyte imposter knocked the queen to the ground and raised the staff's pointed end to jab through her robe.

"They're attacking the queen!" shouted a passing worm monger and her mud-covered daughters. As the worm monger pulled Polexima to safety, her assailants were attacked by rough laboring women. These were no strangers to violence. The worm daughters were a noisy mass of aggression, and took running leaps at the costumed widows, knocking them down, beating their faces with grubby fists, and scratching with their filthy nails. A one-armed daughter used her dark, dirty head to smash in the face of the widow dressed as a boy, then clamped her teeth around the woman's nose.

The war widows advanced into the fray when Terraclon arrived, foot guards at his back. "This ends now!" he shouted as the guards raised their blowguns and threatened the darts. The widows backed off, and the attackers were arrested. The masks were ripped from their faces as their hands were tied behind their backs. Terraclon went to Polexima and pulled her to her feet as she took in the faces of her attackers. She knew each of them, second and third cousins, who glared at her in rage before they were dragged off to a cage, cursing her to an eternity of torture as they went.

"No more walking alone for you, Majesty," said Terraclon as he examined her robe for damage.

"I suppose not," Polexima managed to respond.

"First time you were ever in a fight, I imagine."

"You imagine right. But I am sure it is not my last."

"Something you need to know, then," he said, reverting back to his laborer's accent. "Next time, when you know you're going to be attacked, you throw the first punch. Even if it's three of 'em. Should have punched 'em one, two, three—square in the nose. While they're stunned, you kick them—where it hurts, if they're men."

"I could not possibly do that. That is most . . . unseemly."

"Majesty, it's stupid not to defend yourself," Terraclon said, and he handed the queen her staff before they resumed walking. "Let's get a sharper point on the end of this staff, and some side blades. Next time you're threatened, you jam it through their guts."

When they entered Anand's chamber, Polexima saw that he was lying at the edge of his bed so he could be close to his visitors. Terraclon helped Polexima reach the bed as Anand flipped through a series of renderings made on scratch paper. Standing near his bedside and looking impatient were Pious Frinbo and other priests, as well as the foremen from the builders' and stonecutters' castes.

"Polexima!" Anand shouted when he realized she was beside him. As she got closer, he gasped with alarm to see her nose was bleeding.

"What's happened to you?"

"I have learned an important lesson today," she said. "And I have been a bit stupid. I am wiser now and will not allow you or anyone else to spend one more moment on this minor incident."

"All right, then. Someone, please, get a chair for Her Majesty," said Anand. "You've arrived at a good time. We are finalizing our plans for the assembly."

"Something tells me this will not be the usual ceremony," Polexima said.

"No," said Anand. "But it will be the same in one way: we will use it to set an example. Murder must never be tolerated."

"Agreed. Nor even the threat of murder—like from those two louts from the midden we heard from today."

Anand was quiet, his eyes looking left, then right, when he suddenly gasped. "Dad! My dad!" he said aloud to himself. "Messenger!" he shouted across the room to the young men waiting near the door. "Ride a speed ant down to the midden, and summon Yormu the Mute and return him here."

"To the *midden*, sir?"

"Yes, that's where you'll find him. He is a celebrated veteran of the War of Hulkrish Aggression. Treat him with all due honor."

Polexima saw worry in Anand's shifting eyes. "I'm sorry, Polly. It's my father—I'm worried what those miserable shits might have done to him."

She watched Anand as he panted, then steadied himself, before he picked up two of the drawings, considered them, then proceeded to draw some more, finalizing a vision of the structure he had in mind. He was finishing the final sketch and explaining his vision to Polexima just as daylight was ending. She was stunned by the simplicity of his plan. Why had it never occurred to her or anyone else on the Slope to do this? How much simpler it would have made things!

The torch-making caste entered with a few lights made from the last of the lightning-fly eggs, but most of their torches were chips from glowing bark fungus and had a weaker light. As they set up the torches in the wall holsters, the messenger reappeared through the portal, looking panicked and out of breath. Polexima looked at Anand as he tamped down his alarm.

"Did you find Defender Yormu?" he asked.

"I did, Commander. But he is unable to travel here. It's best you go to him, sir. Some speed ants are docked outside the portal."

"Excuse me, Polexima," Anand said, and left as quickly as his wounded legs would let him.

Anand and his guards leapt off the ants that had brought them swiftly to the emptier hovels of the midden. It felt strange and haunting to walk under and through the lightless dwellings of his childhood. They had the familiar sounds of noisy family arguments, and the wailing, always, of someone being beaten. *One more thing to outlaw,* he thought to himself. He reached the hovel he had grown up in, and looked up its ladder for signs that his father was inside it, when he heard raspy breathing at the ladder's base. Under a low-growing cluster of purslane, he saw his father's legs. Anand moved the leaves back, took his fungus torch, and held it to his father's head. He saw that his face was a bloody pulp with one eye so badly swollen he could not open it.

"Dad! What's happened?"

Yormu grimaced as his hands showed Anand where his rib cage had been throttled, and its bones fractured.

"Dad . . . this was no accident! Who did this to you? Was it Keel? Tal?"

Yormu shrugged.

"You don't know?"

Yormu nodded. Though it pained him, he took the rag from his tool pouch and placed it over his face.

"They were disguised?" Anand asked. Yormu nodded.

"But we know who it was," Anand said, looking in the distance towards Keel's own hovel, where they had likely returned for the night. It was the largest in the midden and the only one with a light in its window. "You can't live here anymore, Dad. You're staying with me. You have no choice in it! We'll find you other things to do."

Anand turned to his guard. "Good Defenders,

I need you to find or fashion a stretcher and gently bring this brave veteran up to my chambers where he will stay until he recovers."

"Are you thirsty, Dad?"

Yormu nodded.

"We need water!" Anand shouted to some passing middenites. They came closer and he recognized them as Zlok and Wartra, the parents of Terraclon, coming from the dew station with water bladders. They were still dressed in rags of filthy eggshell cloth and their feet were strapped with sandals of straw.

"Why should we share our water with you?" said Zlok.

"Water belongs to all," said Anand. "My father needs some. Now."

"We needs all we got," said Wartra, contempt in her words as she glared at Anand.

"And just what have I done to offend you?" Anand asked, rising.

"What haven't you done? You've turned our lives downside up. We was fine in the old way, as good as anybody else in the midden. Now we got shit and trash workers who think they're better than us, coming down here to work from some fine house in their fancy clothes."

"Our life's gotten harder, Roach Boy," said Zlok. "You took our son from us; he hasn't set foot here since you made him a priest. He was supposed to take care of us when we get older. Last time he was here, he looked at us like we was something he scraped out of a chamber pot."

"Maybe you shouldn't have beaten his ass every day," said Anand. "And he'd want to take care of you."

The three were silent, staring at each other. *Never forget, Anand,* he told himself, *some will choose the same misery over the promise of change.* Anand walked towards them, and grabbed a bladder from Zlok. "I'll return this," he said. "Thank you."

As Anand held the bladder and squeezed its water for his father, he looked up at the shelters at Keel's hovel and imagined he might have seen his shadowy figure looking out its window.

I'm not sure how or when, he thought, *but someday, I will have just cause to tear your spine out of your back, Keel, and use it to whip your sons to death.*

foraging, where they had gathered bundles of grass shoots and clover that held beads of dew, something to both water and feed the locusts. These men were followed by a hunting party, who sang happily as they returned with bits of a slaughtered ghost ant, a little food scout. The scout was a reminder that at least one of Hulkren's southern mounds had yet to be exterminated. The hunters cut up the abdomen and made crude plates of its transparent chitin to portion out its watery flesh.

Captain Dziddens noticed Medinwoe was leaning on his arms to raise his head as he yawned. The captain walked towards the king with a plate of the fresh goo that sparkled in the brightening sun. "Can you eat, Your Highness?"

"Please," said Medinwoe. "But I am more thirsty. If you've scraped some dew this morning, I would gladly drink it."

Dziddens shouted in Low Slopeish to the other pilots, who rolled over the lidded barrel that contained the morning's dew, then cut into the water with the attached trowel and offered a drop to Medinwoe. As the king's head cleared, he remembered the day before: the unbearable itch, the erupting mites, the attack of some degenerate army . . . and then the rescue by the locust pilots. A deeper, richer memory overwhelmed him when he remembered the dark, fungal liquor he was given to drink. This concoction had turned the day's suffering into a delicious feast for all five senses, and then brought him his divine revelation. Medinwoe was deep in the memory of his vision when he felt his shoulder being shaken and realized the captain was speaking to him.

"King Medinwoe," he heard. "Are you all right?"

"Yes, yes, excuse me, Captain Dziddens. I . . . I was lost in thought. What did you ask me?"

"We want to know when you might be ready to ride and return to Bee-Jor. It will take a full day, if the South wind is not too strong, to reach the border. We will likely have to spend the night there before flying to Cajoria in the morning."

"Help me stand, please," the king said, and he extended his arm. As Dziddens helped him rise, he felt painful flares over his legs, as if his wounds were all attacking each other. It could only get worse to sit in back of a pilot during a long and bumpy flight. "Before we fly, Captain, it might help if we had more of that liquor you gave us before the surgery. What was that?"

"It is called, I believe, the Holy Mildew. It is said to be a gift from the gods to the Slopeish priests."

"Holy, yes. Indeed."

"We were told not to drink it ourselves—that it would be dangerous to fly under its influence."

"Would you have any more of it?"

"I . . . I believe so, sir."

"Then bring it right here. And I will rouse the men and tell them we are flying out today."

Dziddens hesitated. "As . . . as you like, sir. Commander Quegdoth instructed us to do our very best to serve you."

As Captain Dziddens had predicted, the South wind slowed the return to Bee-Jor. Locusts were difficult if not impossible to fly in formation, but could be coaxed into something like a chevron. On the flight back, they frequently overtook each other as leader, or would suddenly drop for water or rest and had to be prodded back into the air. Two stubborn ones remained behind, and their pilots had to be moved to other locusts. The pilots clung uncomfortably as trios on the saddles for two, and slowed the locusts with their added weight.

Medinwoe, seated behind Dziddens, was for the second time savoring the thrilling intoxication of the Holy Mildew. The delights of flight enhanced by this drink were impossibly beautiful, and chills ran down his spine. The locust, of its own accord, dropped out of formation and landed in a patch of thriving weeds including clover, dandelions, and newly sprouted mallows with yellow-green leaves.

As the locust munched on a sun-spattered salad, the king felt an inner mounting ecstasy as he considered this extraordinary country, his Promised Clearing, bequeathed to his people and to him as king. He laughed without restraint when Dziddens prodded the sated locust back into the air, where it fought to fly in the strengthening wind. Dziddens struggled to steady himself when the locust was flipped by a sudden gust. For a moment, Medinwoe fell out of the saddle and dangled from its tethers before he pulled himself back to his seat. The look on Dziddens's face was both frightening and funny as he looked over his shoulder, all wide eyes and gaping mouth with its veiny red insides and wagging uvula. All of this made the king laugh harder once they righted.

The sun was sinking above the ledge of earth when they neared the borders of Bee-Jor and, further east, those of its crippled mother country, the Holy Slope. But something else, something strange and shifting and stinking, had infiltrated the Promised Clearing—an infestation of some kind.

"What wild thing are we seeing down there, within those weeds?" Medinwoe shouted. "It's an invasion of some kind."

"I'm not sure, sir, but it looks like. . . . people. Let's take a look before the sun gets swallowed. We have to land soon—this locust already senses the dark and resists my prods."

Dziddens prodded the left antenna forward and the right to the side, which sent the locust into a jerky spiral over the weeds. Medinwoe's ecstasy turned to a sudden and intense rage as he realized that tens of thousands—perhaps hundreds of thousands—of refugees fleeing Hulkren were squatting in his new land. *Why are they coming here?* he asked himself. *Instead of returning to their old countries?*

The captain steered the locust up and south, to land in a sandy patch that had been powdered with a ring of marigold dust as their place to spend the night. The king and captain dismounted to find a squadron of pilots had already prepared a camp and were hooding the locusts' heads as others scavenged for an evening meal.

Medinwoe looked into the distance and felt anger storming inside him, as if his eyes and ears were leaking lightning. In the near distance he sighted more of these raggedy refugees trudging to Bee-Jor's borders. He got a closer look when Dziddens tethered his locust to stalks of cup grass, and roused a napping trio of dark-skinned women in colorful wraps. The three stood and stared in a frightened silence at the red-cloaked pilot and his blue locust. With no words between them, the refugees knew it was time to go. They piled their possessions back into their cargo-sled as a baby in swaddling started bawling.

Medinwoe struggled to step forward and stare at the three, these blackish figures who had brought their spawn into his Promised Clearing. The tallest of them had broad shoulders and piercing, hate-filled eyes and her—maybe *his*—lower face was covered with a cowl.

That one is trouble.

Pleckoo had been napping, but now he was awake and alarmed to see men landing in the nearby clearing on flying insects, and shouting to each other in Slopeish. At first look, he thought the insects might be night wasps, but then realized it was still daylight. As more of the insects landed, he saw that they were mottled blue locusts.

They fly wasps at night and locusts during the day!

One of these locusts was coming near him led by a yellow-skinned Slopeite in a red tunic; it was an obscene and offensive crimson that Hulkro would detest. Just behind him was a struggling old Dneeper who stared at Pleckoo and the Ledacki women with an open hatred. The women were still tired and had a pained look on their faces.

"We must find someplace else to spend the night," Pleckoo said to Jakhuma and Kula Priya. "These people don't want us here."

The three looked up to see the last of some locusts and their riders almost fall from the sky, landing at their camp's center and sending up a yellow powder. This flying army of Slopeites was a combination of dark and light faces, and some he recognized as men of the blinders' caste in their crusty rags. At least half of them, the crippled ones, were the hated Dneepers— those yellow-skinned grass people who had repelled him in his hunt for Anand. *How has my unholy cousin managed to ally with them? Then again, they are a roach people too.*

Anand. The hunt for him was showing promise. Pleckoo could taste Anand's blood in his mouth . . . then realized he had bitten into his own lip.

"Just why did you pick this baby?" asked Jakhuma.

"Yes, why? He is kind of ugly. Snub-nosed," said Kula.

"As I have told you, I would have rescued them all if I could have," Pleckoo said, then realized, with a faint shock, why this baby had aroused his pity. *Snub-nosed!*

"You'll be glad to know this one's got a good appetite. He's gotten heavier since I started breastfeeding him."

"You have milk?" Pleckoo said.

"It came last night and he latched right away. Maybe Goddess Meat Ant wants him to live."

"Maybe it's the grace of the Son of Locust as we get closer," said Jakhuma.

Goddess Meat Ant! Son of Locust! Heresies! he thought to himself, and regretted he could not scream it aloud. For a moment he thought about forcing the women to pick up the reins by threatening his sword's sharp end . . . but now was not the time.

A darkly sweet and oily smell was in the air as they neared the Tar Marsh in the East. In the distance he could see the shadowy rise of the Great Jag's boulders in the West. They had reached the southern end of the Petiole and were close to that wretched place he hated most, the Slope—now known as Bee-Jor. *What a ridiculous name for a nation!* Pushed to the sides of the channel were the ravaged corpses of ghost ants, all of them broken into pieces, drained of their lymph and robbed of the contents of their abdomens. Their legs, antennae, and shattered chitin were strewn like so much garbage. The sight of dead ghost ants made walking even harder for Pleckoo, as each corpse was a reminder of the Night That Had Gone So Wrong. He had traveled up this channel, so sure of victory, and a short time later he had been forced to retreat down it in utter defeat.

Sweat was stinging his eyes when he sighted Mound Palzhad, rising above yellowing weeds that were taller over new, green plants thriving for the moment in rain-dampened soil. As they got closer, the spectacle of the palaces dazzled him as they glinted atop the ancient mound in the golden sunshine of the afternoon. The beauty of it was taunting; Palzhad should have been his prize possession, the first of the Slopeish mounds annexed by the Holy Hulkrish Empire. The more he looked at the palaces, the more it felt like he was lying under them, crushed into a puddle of flesh and blood. "Hulkro tests the faithful," he said aloud to himself.

"Khali Talavar!" he heard from behind him. Jakhuma and Kula had stopped walking, and were staring at him, startled.

"Yes?"

"What did you say?"

"I said nothing," Pleckoo said.

"We both heard you," said Kula. "You muttered the name of the . . ."

"Termite God," whispered Jakhuma.

"Did I?" said Pleckoo. "Force of habit."

"We will not hear it again," said Jakhuma. She cocked her head quizzically as she looked up at the mound. "Bee-Jor is an *old* place," she said. "It looks like it could belong in Hulkren."

"That is not Bee-Jor," said Pleckoo. "That is Mound Palzhad. It was the southernmost mound of the Slopeites. And all mounds in Hulkren once belonged to the United Queendoms."

"All mounds? Really?" she asked. "And how do you know this?"

"Everyone knows this," Pleckoo said. "Didn't you?"

Pleckoo looked left, then right, and saw tattered bands of refugees coming up behind them from the East and West. He turned and looked in back of him, and saw even more from the direct south. Most he recognized as slaves of Hulkren in their rags of grass fibers or chewed egg-cloth, but some of the women wore the castoffs of their former mistresses. Nearly all these refugees were hobbled at an ankle or hamstrung above the calf, and all looked weak from hunger and overwork. As the mound got closer and glimmered with promise, they tripped as they walked, drunk with hope, looking up instead of ahead at what they thought was an abode of the gods.

How sickeningly foolish, Pleckoo thought. He remembered how he had been taught to worship Sahdrin and Polexima and their horde of sallow, overfed children—these supposed descendants of the gods who did nothing but eat, drink, and dress up in their dwellings constructed by slaves. And each day Pleckoo was forced by the midden's idols keeper to nod towards these palaces in a prayer of thanks after receiving his meager mushroom ration. *But are the Sallows still in charge here?* Pleckoo wondered. *Or has Anand bathed them all for execution and put his roach people on the thrones?*

"Khali Talavar!" Jakhuma shouted at him. "Why have you halted?"

Pleckoo had not realized he had stopped; he was paralyzed for the moment with the old hatreds as he pondered his former life in Cajoria's midden. He resumed dragging the sand-sled forward and somehow, through his fatigue, they reached the Petiole's end and the broad expanse of the border weeds. Ahead of them was a density of camps that filled the air with the stenches of humans. Refugees were interspersed through the weeds, which they had cut down or uprooted or trimmed for materials to make shelters. Some of the hungriest were eating the weeds to fill their stomachs, or chewing on their roots for some starch and a little bit of water. All in the camps looked bored, exhausted, and then nervous with suspicion as they sighted an onslaught of new arrivals.

Pleckoo pulled up, then halted behind a camp that was a mix of youths of different races, just sprouting beards, and all of them wearing the rags of slaves. They were looking over their shoulders as they divvied up the lymph from a hairy rain beetle, whose misfortune was to emerge from its burrow in the middle of their camp.

"Get back," said a tall and spindly young man in Hulkrish, after he licked lymph off the back of his arm. "This is our place. We've nothing to share with you." Pleckoo could see that the surrounding camps were looking at these boys and their feast with envy. He could see that beyond these camps were many, many more refugees crowding the weeds, and some were drifting forward in hopes of sharing in something to eat.

"All right," Pleckoo said, dropping the reins of the sled. "That's your place. This is ours."

"When are they letting us in?" shouted Jakhuma to the boys, stepping forward as she pulled back the hood of her garment.

"No one knows," said Tall and Spindly.

"How many have they let in?" she asked.

"We don't know that they have let anyone in. Yet."

"You don't know," said Pleckoo with contempt. "Who would know?"

The youths shrugged and returned to their eating. Pleckoo's despair was giving way to the sweet rage that sharpened his mind and strengthened his limbs. He inhaled deeply, then yanked up his sword to reveal its dark, lethal blade. "Out of my way!" he shouted, his blade whistling as he brandished it at the refugees. They fell away to make a path for him.

"Where are you going?" Jakhuma shouted over the baby in her arms. "You can't leave us alone!"

"Don't move from there," Pleckoo spat, turning to face her.

"But if you leave us, we . . ."

"I said *don't move!*" he shouted in his natural voice, and the force of his words shocked her as he pointed his sword. She lowered her head, and he disappeared into the parting crowd.

The mass of refugees grew thicker as Pleckoo ventured deeper. These first arrivals looked even weaker from hunger, mute with it, and he saw resentment in their eyes as he stomped through their camps. It was twilight when he reached an encampment of what looked like pubescent Hulkrites, lying on rag-sacks. He brazenly stepped into the middle of their gathering and they stood, circling him, as they reached for weapons in their loose tunics of filthy silk.

"You are in our place," said the largest and oldest of them. He stared at Pleckoo from under a thick mass of spiraling, yellow curls.

"Your place, yes," said Pleckoo after a silence. He lowered his sword.

"What do you want?" asked Curls in a voice on the verge of deepening.

"Only to pass," said Pleckoo, resuming his higher pitch in case they might recognize his voice.

"I wouldn't go any further," said Curls. "It's dangerous. Do you have any food?"

Pleckoo was wondering who these yellow-skinned boys were. Curls spoke Hulkrish without an accent. He was likely the son of a native Hulkrite, perhaps even a relative of Tahn.

"I might have some food. Have you seen any Slopeites?" Pleckoo asked. "Have they come here? Passed any messages?"

"There are no Slopeites just beyond," said the boy. "The Slopeites' country is further west. Those are Bee-Jorites on that mound, called Palzhad."

Slopeites in the West? So the Slope has been split in two!

"When are they letting us in?"

"We don't know if they are."

"Then why are you here?"

"Why are *you* here?" said Curls. "And where are *you* from? And why do you carry a black glass sword from Foondatha and ask so many questions?"

Pleckoo was quiet. All he could guess was that these boys had escaped from a mound in Hulkren where the Faithful to Termite were no longer welcome.

"Let us say I found this sword," Pleckoo said. "And that all of us left Hulkren to seek a new life in Bee-Jor." Pleckoo made the slightest bow of his head. "I'm going to see what's beyond. And find out when they are letting us in."

"Don't go too far," said Curls. "Unless you've got some leaf-cutter kin-scent."

Curls and the others stepped aside, and Pleckoo entered into narrow paths that wound between grass stalks until he reached a place of low-lying plants he had to crawl under. Leaves of the plants ruffled up with a breeze from the south-blowing wind. *Maybe the leaf-cutter ants won't catch my scent,* he thought.

He walked up a grade to a clearing between mallow plants where he could look down and see the border wall, constructed by ants of their dung and reinforced by humans with a barrier of piled sand grains. As he walked towards the wall, he hoped the ants were distracted so that he could climb over it, and find a workman's site or an outcastes' settlement— and a tub full of leaf-cutter kin-scent. The quiet and darkness emboldened him until he saw the slightest wave of antennae and then the head of a sentry ant above the wall. When the ant crawled to the top of the barrier, he could see it was without a human sentry on its back.

The ant's antennae whirred into a blur and its body shook to release *recruit-scent.* In a moment she was joined by a stream of sentry ants, some of which carried human riders. Pleckoo was unsure of what he was seeing in the dark; the riders did not look like yellow-skinned sentries from the military caste, but were darker and wearing what looked like red quilting over crude armor.

"Get back!" shouted one ant rider in common Slopeish. "Get back or die!"

"When are they letting us in?" Pleckoo shouted through his cupped hands.

"Get back!" shouted the ant rider as a burst of ants poured up and over the wall and sped towards Pleckoo. He turned and raced back to the weeds when he heard ant-steps closing in and felt antennae brushing his neck. Around his waist he felt the tips of an ant's mandibles, and then heard the rip of his robe as he escaped the ant's grasp.

A cluster of dried barley stalks was ahead of him. He dove through a narrow opening inside the stalks, then stood and pushed into their center with all his strength. The retracting stalks made a cage around him as he worked through them to their other side. The ants climbed up the stalks and over each other as Pleckoo pushed out of the barley. He ran, crawled, and climbed over a rough patch of sand, turning for a moment. *No ants! They lost my scent,* he thought as he entered a thickness of protecting weeds on the edge of the camps. *Praise Hulkro!*

When he found his way back to the camp of the Hulkrish boys, the cloth around his face was clinging to his sweaty skin. Dizzy and out of breath, he fell to the ground on his knees.

"We told you not to go," said Curls. The boys behind him were laughing, something that increased as Pleckoo pivoted in their circle.

"What's so funny?"

"Nothing. It's just that someone looks like a whore trolling for customers—with her dark little rump on display. Does it cost extra to take the back entry?"

"Don't speak like that to me!" said Pleckoo, reaching behind him to feel the rip that exposed his backside. He reached for his sword and took the crouching position.

"We'll speak any way we want," said Curls. "We've got our own swords."

The boys stood and extended their blades towards his chin. Pleckoo looked around at them and then rapidly blinked. He was feeling strangely empty, then utterly depleted, when he became mindful of something that had climbed up his legs.

"No need for that . . . brothers," he barely managed to say. "We could and *should* help each other."

Something sharp entered his calf. He suppressed his urge to scream and fell to the thin coat of loam on the sand. Picking up the hem of his garment, he saw chubby little creatures that had clamped on each of his calves—grass ticks! He reached for one and felt the double-sided saw of its mouth tearing his flesh out as he pulled. As Pleckoo wrenched out the other, Curls used the end of his sword to stab the tick through its belly as it wobbled on its back and waved its skinny legs. The stabbing ache of the wounds rolled up Pleckoo's legs and through his torso and he fainted. When he came to, he was looking up at the young Hulkrites standing around him, chewing and slurping in indifference. He tried to rise and could not, as if his legs had turned to stone, and fell hard on his naked bottom.

"I can't walk," said Pleckoo. "Can I stay here until morning?"

"You can," said Curls. "You said you might have some food. And you did."

Pleckoo looked to the left of him and saw the legs and the mouth-saws of the grass ticks and realized that the rest of them were being devoured by the Hulkrish boys. He looked at the punctures in his legs and saw no bleeding, courtesy of the ticks' styptic potions. Crawling to the camp's edge, he reached a dying dandelion and pulled down one of its leaves to lay on as his bed. *Wake me from this nightmare, Lord Termite*, he prayed, then fell into a fragile sleep.

Pleckoo was dreaming of drowning in a pit filling with rain when he woke with a start to find his face covered with the morning's dew. He shook loose from the water and gasped for breath. It was still dark, with the sun on the verge of rising. Now was a better time to make his way back to the women—they had food. He slid down the leaf, which soaked his garment and shocked the skin of his exposed behind.

The trek back was nerve-wracking as he tiptoed through the sprawl of refugees in the dark. They were asleep under camouflaging leaves or blades of grass that blended all too well with the ground. He stepped on more than a few sleepers, who roused to grab or even bite his ankles, then got lost as he made his way south, having to weave through the camps to find the Ledackis. It was late afternoon when at last he heard their wailing near the wreck of their sand-sled. All its contents were gone. Jakhuma wiped at her tears with the back of one hand as Kula held the other.

"Who did this?" Pleckoo asked.

"We forgot to ask their names," spat Kula.

"I'll kill them! I'll cut their heads off and hang them in the weeds!"

"Very brave of you."

"Where's the baby?" he asked. Jakhuma pointed to a bundle under the sand-sled. "They tried to take him too," she said.

"Why?"

"Why do you think?" she said, and then made a gnawing motion with her mouth.

"What did they look like?"

"Like anyone who hides his face in a sack."

"You let this happen," said Kula as she rose. "You left us—two women and a baby—alone among all this human garbage. You're useless!"

Pleckoo froze, then quaked with rage.

"I'll make you useful," he said, then punched her in the eye. She buckled, gasping as he raised up his sword. "I'll kill you and feed you to the starving."

"Get away from her!" Jakhuma shouted. A piercing scream erupted from her as she leapt on Pleckoo, toppling him. He grabbed her with both arms, rolling her over, then knelt on her chest as she struggled for breath. He reached for his sword and raised it over her throat, then felt something piercing his back.

"Drop that blade unless you want this one to sever your spine," said a man behind him. Over his shoulder was a young and muscular Ledacki, whose black face was scarred from too many beatings.

"Cut me and I'll kill her!" shouted Pleckoo.

"Get off her and I might let you live."

Pleckoo felt the sword point leave his back. He rolled away, springing up with his sword to face a Ledacki of only eighteen summers. His blade was crude—an ant mandible with a handle of twine—but he held it with the skill of a trained soldier.

"You'll leave these women now," said the man in Hulkrish. "You'll leave this *place* now." Other Ledackis with black skin and green eyes were coming up behind him with pikes and knives in their hands. Pleckoo backed away and heard the giggles of onlookers, realizing his buttocks were still on display. He pushed and slid and stumbled through the crowd when he toppled into a clearing near an upright pebble in a pit being used as a latrine. After gathering the loose cloth behind him, he tied it into a knot, then crawled up the pebble. He looked south, back to Hulkren, over the heads of a lake of refugees, in search of a truly empty place—a place where he could hide from everyone and pray to his god and hope for a sign of where to go next.

CHAPTER 13

THE FIRST ASSEMBLY OF BEE-JOR

The beauty of Britasyte music was never soothing to Anand but it transfixed him. Much of it was sweetly sad, but lots of it expressed astonishment and a touch of fear—so much like the life of his wandering tribe. At the moment, his people's music was making him anxious, because it kept turning his mind to the one person whose existence was forever linked with his own. Anand chided himself for asking his clan of Entreveans to venture into a defeated Hulkren to invite the bee people of Bulkoko to join them in his fledgling nation. And under the pretense of being the best, most loyal Britasyte wife, Daveena, his goddess, the gorgeous thing that completed him, had joined the caravan. Now the Entreveans were making their way through territory where surviving Hulkrites were a possible threat, as well as their freed slaves and captives, many of which were not returning to their home nations but were gathering as refugees in the Weedlands near Palzhad.

Anand looked out the window of the stadium's tent, where they had completed preparations for the assembly's spectacle. The Fallogeth clan of Britasytes was playing for their largest audience ever, behind an array of amplifying-cones that brought their music to the back of the stadium. Behind the musicians was the tall and mysterious structure that Anand had ordered constructed and then wrapped in a patchwork of red canvas to conceal it.

The Cajorites, sitting for the most part in stands assigned to their old castes, were quiet before the wanderers' music. The look on their faces showed that many were ill at ease with roach people and their strange clothing and stranger performance. But many of the men knew this music and were captured by it; they bobbed and wobbled their heads as they entered a trance induced by its frantic and multiple rhythms. The music was completely alien to women, only a few of whom might have heard strains of it when they hid in the weeds near the Britasytes' shows to catch glimpses of their forbidden carnivals.

The roach women were not dancing on a platform

above their men as usual, but Anand could see they were straining with the urge. "It would not be seemly to dance," he had to tell them, "on what will be a somber day. Dancing will excite the Cajorite men and rouse the envy of their women. They will want your jewelry and resent you for your beauty and talents." The women were doing as Anand had instructed them, sitting to the side of the men and clicking finger drums as they swayed and chanted a rhythmic prayer to Lord/Lady Roach.

Terraclon approached Anand in a simple and somber cassock dyed with a concentrate of small-leaved indigo, red clay, and a concentrate of green acorns for a deeply black effect. In his arms were the three pieces of Anand's costume for the day, which included his turquoise tunic and matching trousers, the latter of which had to be let out to make room for the thick bandages wrapped around his swollen legs. "Thanks, Ter," said Anand as he pulled off the loose garment he was wearing, and so revealed his Dran-verish under-armor in all its interlocking intricacy—a sight that always dazzled Terraclon.

"Thanks? After you see what I've made you, I'm going to need a little more than 'thanks,'" said Terraclon.

"You look a little somber today," said Anand as he pulled on the trousers. "That cloth is blacker than tar."

"Didn't you say it was a serious occasion? I'm wearing something as dark as death—the lightless night that knows no end."

"It does set a tone."

The third piece of Anand's ensemble was the cape, which looked all the more red in Terraclon's arms against the black of his cassock. "I've been working on this for a while . . . and I'm going to miss it after I give it to you," he said. He took the garment by its collar straps and unfolded it with a quick snap of his wrists, so that it flew up, then fluttered down. Anand grabbed his chin and looked doubtful as Polexima struggled towards them to have a look at the brilliant thing that was sparkling on the floor. The cape's red had been amplified with a spatter of shimmering discs cut from the chitin of the scarlet lily beetle.

"You don't like it?" asked Terraclon.

"I . . . I love it. It's just a bit . . . much."

"*Much?* Much too what?"

Polexima was taking it in, clearly captivated. "It's very beautifully done," she said. "But perhaps a bit too . . . showy . . . for today."

"And for the New Way," said Anand.

"But you asked for something very red!"

"I did. But it's envy-making," Anand said. "Too beautiful to belong to just one person."

Terraclon gulped and Anand realized he had hurt his friend.

"Here," said Anand. "All I need to do is wear it this way."

Anand tied on the cape so that the plainer side of it was on the outside.

"Yes," said Polexima. "Understated now. Just a hint of sparkles that are glimpsed when it moves . . . intriguing."

The three of them smiled, the tension released, as Polexima's acolyte unboxed, then handed her, a pair of her old antennae. It was a pair she had worn at her first assembly in Cajoria as the arriving princess from Palzhad. They were large and opulent and encrusted with a spectrum of glittering minerals. "Speaking of showy, I suppose this tells them I am still their queen," she said as she clipped them to her head. Anand could see it was a struggle to keep her neck erect from the weight of the headpiece, which was in jarring contrast to the severity of her priestess robes. Her acolytes brought her a two-sided ladder and helped her climb to the saddle on a royal carrier ant. The ant had been painted with a light coating of sap, then dusted with patterns in powdered gold and silver pyrite. The thorax was draped with a tasseled red cloth banner instead of the old royal yellow, and the ant's legs were clasped with brown, red, and yellow bangles. Once Polexima was atop the ant, she raised her chin, and looked modestly royal as she waited to enter the arena.

Anand had wanted to fly in on a blue locust before

giving his speech, but the attempt to ride one was still painful for his scabbed-over legs. With his guards' help, he was pulled onto the saddle of a large soldier-ant that had been roused from dormancy, dusted with red powder, and outfitted with the saddle and solemn decorations of the old military. He was practicing riding the ant in a circle by using the Slopeites' traditional lure as Dolgeeno and his priests arrived in their new black frocks and simple boots with thin soles. Without their stilts or elevating shoes, they looked all the shorter, plumper and . . . more human. They lined up behind Terraclon for their part in the procession, and looked more dutiful than inspired.

"Is everyone in their seats?" Anand asked as Terraclon peeked out of the tent at the stands.

"Everyone but the war widows," said Terraclon.

"They will be here soon enough," Dolgeeno said in what sounded like a moan. "But not because they want to be."

In the distance, Anand heard what he thought might be the sound of flying locusts. He stepped out of the tent and looked up to the sky and saw the squadron he had ordered into Hulkren to rescue the Dneepers was returning—one less worry, perhaps, or one more new one.

A moment later, the war widows entered the stadium as if they were prisoners being herded by the Bee-Jorite People's Guard. Not one of them was dressed in widow's whites, but all had dressed in their gold-colored finery and they flaunted their best jewelry, as if attending a victory ball in the old nation. Their voluminous gowns swayed from side to side, making gentle collisions as they daintily rocked on platform shoes with their chins held high in defiance.

"They're wearing yellow," said Terraclon. "Royal yellow. It's a slap to your mud-brown face, Commander."

"This is a free nation where anyone can wear any color they want," said Anand. He watched as the war widows were pressed into what had been the right half of their comfortable boxes, which had once held chairs and servants to fan them on hot days. Now they were forced to share this space with prominent widows of the Laborers' Army, who had gathered in the left of the boxes with only a rope barrier between them. The Laborers' widows looked as if they had dressed to compete with the war widows, and wore many-layered gowns that were a coarse approximation of upper-caste dress. Instead of gold, they had used berry and hymen-fruit dyes for different shades of pink but few had achieved a true red. The widows in yellow pretended not to see these other women, and looked away from them while sometimes holding their noses against an imaginary stink.

Inside the tent, Anand raised a red flag, and the Fallogeths concluded their music, then picked up thorn horns and commenced the ceremony. An expanded guard on ants and on foot surrounded Anand and his mount as he entered. As the roach people played something danceable that vaguely resembled Slopeish sacred music, Anand guided his ant to the structure. He dismounted, and muttered, "Shit," under his breath when he landed hard and felt the scabs of his legs break open. He set his face in a look of indifference as he climbed the flight of stairs built into the side of his mysterious structure. Each step was more painful than the last, and he felt the wetness of his own blood.

Polexima followed after him on her ant, her acolytes aiding her in her dismount and then in her long climb to the top of the structure. She stood atop it, her antennae glittering prettily in the sunlight as she took in the crowd from left to right while smiling in approval. They stood and cheered her, and she looked warmed by their adoration. An acolyte handed her a cricket harp with a wing stretched inside its frame. She stroked the teeth-like tabs at the wing's bottom with a plectrum to make chirps as she shouted her prayer. "Mother Cricket, bless this assembly at Cajoria," she shouted, "and all who reside in Bee-Jor."

Terraclon and Dolgeeno were last to ascend, with the thin young man helping the weighty old one until they stood atop the structure's platform and faced the crowd. Eleven other priests positioned themselves at the base of the structure, spaced at intervals. Anand signaled to the thorn blowers for a final blast for silence, which left only the sound of the wind rippling through his loose garments. He slowly opened his cape to reveal its sparkling insides, as a host of trucking ants hauled out a cage on a sand-sled covered in a rough yellow canvas.

Everyone knew the cage housed the war widows who had boasted of killing dark-skinned babies before the queen and her commander—and everyone knew these widows would be punished today. *I had to do this,* Anand thought, *but I take no pleasure in what I am about to reveal.* An amplifying-cone on a pole was set before him, its smaller end framing his face in a circle. He shouted his words in Common Slopeish, which he tinged with a Dranverish accent.

"Bee-Jorites, we stand before you today, Your Commander Quegdoth, Your Queen Polexima, and Their Piouses Terraclon and Dolgeeno, to dedicate this First Monument to Law and Order in Bee-Jor."

Anand nodded to the priests below, who grabbed the quilted cover by its hem and pulled it away to reveal the structure, a pyramid-shaped monument with a flattened top. A murmur spread through the crowd as they took in its alien decorations. Anand looked at his own Britasytes, who ignored the jumble of wriggling shapes, like jumping worms at the top of the structure, and the crude drawings etched into its middle band. They were taken with the skillfully etched pictures at the bottom third, which started with an index finger tilted up to signify "No" or "Forbidden."

"These are the eight essential laws of Bee-Jor from which all other laws will descend," shouted Anand. "All citizens and other inhabitants of our nation must obey them, no matter what position they hold. What you see on this monument is something called *writing*, a way in which words are drawn. To look at written words and understand them is called *reading*."

The crowd murmured.

"At the top of the pyramid is the Dranverish way of writing," Anand continued. "In the middle band is the Slopeish way of your priests. And underneath that are pictures that show the eight laws. Monuments to Law and Order will be built everywhere in Bee-Jor, and each morning our priests will stand atop them and recite the eight laws."

Anand stepped away from the cone, allowing Dolgeeno to take his place. Terraclon pulled out a scroll on two rollers from underneath his cassock and unfurled it. Below, the priests prepared to point with their staffs to the illustrations of the new laws as each one was announced.

"Law One," Dolgeeno shouted in his melodic cant, stretching the vowels within each syllable. "No human being shall ever kill another human being *unless in self-defense*. No human may ever sacrifice the life of another human, including those of alien nations, to a god or gods."

Dolgeeno stepped aside and Terraclon took the cone. "Law Two. No human being will ever harm another's body," he shouted, using his natural laborer's accent. "This includes any physical attack on another such as punching or kicking, as well as stabbing, whipping, or using any other object to hurt another. This includes the use of any creature-derived poisons such as alien kin-scent, spider, scorpion or insect venoms, or toxins derived from plants such as poison oak or from mushrooms such as the death cap."

Terraclon yielded to Polexima. Though her gait was unsteady, her expression was resolute. "Law Three," she shouted in her surest voice. "No human being may rape another human being. Rape is defined as a sexual act forced on to an unwilling victim. All women and all girls will have the right to refuse sexual acts from *any* man including her *husband* and including *men of royal ancestry*."

A murmur went up in the crowd as husbands and wives looked at each other in discomfort. Anand knew that with this law he had offended men who believed in their gods-given right to engage in intercourse with their wives at any time. Polexima shouted over the murmuring. "And all *men* and all *boys* will have the same right to refuse sexual acts from any man, regardless of his position as a holy person."

The crowd went silent, embarrassed to confront in public the ugliest rumor about its priesthood. "And anyone who forces him or herself sexually on a child," shouted Polexima, the words catching in her throat, "will be considered among the worst of criminals and will be punished most severely."

"Law Four," said Dolgeeno, resuming the cone in the chilly quiet. "No human being shall ever steal from another human being. This includes sacrifices of food and other items brought to idols keepers who must distribute these items to those in need and not consume for themselves."

"Law Five," said Queen Polexima, anger rising in her voice as she returned to the cone again. Anand could see her struggling with her personal memories before she spoke. "No human being may ever own another human, or force another human to work for him or her without that person's consent, or without the offer of a fair compensation. No human may ever sell another human to another, including his or her own children or other relatives. Those who engage in these crimes will be known as *enslavers* and their victims known as *slaves*."

A murmur went up again. Anand knew the masses still considered themselves to be the property of their superiors.

"Law Six," said Terraclon. "No human being will ever lie about another human being in such a way as to harm another by damaging his or her reputation or endangering that person's life or body."

"Law Seven," said Anand. "All members of the nation of Bee-Jor are entitled to an *education*," he said, using a Dranverish word, "or the right to acquire the same knowledge as any other human, including priests and royalty. All citizens are encouraged to learn to read and write and their children will be instructed from the age of four in general knowledge in places called *schools*."

"Law Eight," said Terraclon, returning to the cone with a broad smile. "Beginning today, every eighth day will be a time of rest, of release from work, in which citizens choose how to spend their time. Those who choose to work may do so."

The scroll was rerolled and Anand resumed the cone. "These are the beginnings of our laws," he said. "And from these eight, other laws with their particulars will unfold. Laws are to benefit all citizens of Bee-Jor and make justice and fairness available to all."

Anand moved aside so that Polexima could return to speak through the cone. "We ask that all of you, all citizens of Cajoria and Bee-Jor," she shouted, "treat others as you would have them treat you. As you would not want your food stolen from you, do not steal food from others. As you would not want your children to be killed . . ." Polexima paused and fixed her gaze on the war widows ". . . do not kill the children of others!"

A murmur went up from the widows that turned to jeers. They stood on their side of the boxes, shaking their fists. "Heresy! Heresy!" they shouted.

"Sit down! Shut your yapping head slits!" shouted the women in pink over the rope barriers. When the widows in yellow refused to seat themselves, the crowd pelted them with food. Some threw their opened bladders of drinking water, dousing the widows. The widows responded by baring their daggers and threatening those around them. Confined by their gowns and wobbling on their shoes, this only brought the crowd's laughter.

"We will have quiet! Quiet and order!" shouted Polexima, and the crowd was silenced. "As for the killing of children," she continued. "This crime was committed by three women who admitted to it before myself, your priests, and Commander Quegdoth."

Pious Frinbo ascended the steps. His black cassock made his face an unpleasant yellow. With hatred, he eyed Anand, who suspected that the priest resented him for revealing the secrets of writing. In Frinbo's hands was the document of scratching paper with characters inscribed by Dolgeeno that recorded the grievances of the low-caste kiln workers. Frinbo held the document above his head as he shouted through the cone. "The confession of the murder of three infants and the attempted murder of their older sister by the Widow Gafrexa Chando and her sisters-in-law Entatha and Namity is recorded on this document," said Frinbo. He yielded to Anand.

"These criminals will not be executed by bathing and exposure to the ants for that is a cruel and unnecessary punishment," Anand said. "Remove the cloth!" he shouted to the guards at the cage.

The guards pulled away the cloth to reveal the three women still dressed in their widows' whites, their heads slumping forward. They had been raised up, then tied to the bars of the cage's back panel in a display. Their arms and legs were stiff, and indicated they had been dead for days. The crowd murmured in disappointment; gone were their hopes for some exciting torture followed by a bloody and protracted execution.

"These women have been executed by poison, which they drank of their own free will," said Anand. "They showed no respect for the lives of other humans—for helpless *babies* at the beginning of their lives. They showed no remorse for their crimes and boasted that they would kill again. We regret that they could not live as lawful citizens of Bee-Jor. Let their deaths be a lesson to all."

A long, low rumble spread over the stands and yielded to the piercing keening of the widows in yellow. "Infidel!" shouted some of them, "Alien!" shouted others. "Traitor queen!" shouted another widow near the rope barrier as an accusation against Polexima.

"Shut your ugly yellow hole," shouted a widow in pink next to the rope. "If you want to keep your teeth!"

"I'll cut your tongue out!" was the response she got from the widow who brandished her knife. Her kinswomen in yellow followed her lead and threatened with their own blades. They were unprepared when the widows in pink reached for their long-daggers and made the hissing sounds of bark beetles. A shrieking brawl erupted as the widows in yellow and pink slashed at each other, their dresses spotting with bloodstains. Surrounding war veterans raised their blowguns and targeted the widows in yellow. The darts sent them into spastic fits, and they foamed at the mouth as they fell on each other and out of the box. Their bodies, like worms writhing in lace, were picked up and passed through the stands. The harsh laughter of the crowd rolled through the stadium as, at last, they got their spectacle.

"Guards, soldiers!" Anand shouted. "Arrest every one of those women in yellow and cage them, in the weeds near the midden. For their own protection!"

Anand's own guard as well as the veterans in the stands gathered up the war widows and dragged them out of the stadium as they twitched. Some of them lost control of their bladders. The laughter continued until they were pulled to safety inside the tent.

"This assembly is dismissed!" shouted Anand. He stood with Polexima and the high priests atop the monument, monitoring the dispersal. The crowd began the usual and orderly exit from their rows.

"And I thought it would be boring," said Terraclon.

"The war widows will never make good citizens," said Polexima. "This will be a problem."

Anand was about to agree with her when he noticed a messenger boy panting at the base of the monument.

"Commander," the boy shouted as he regained his breath. "The Dneepers have returned. King Medinwoe requests an audience at the palace. He wants you to know that tens of thousands, perhaps hundreds of thousands, of dangerous refugees have gathered on the edge of the Dustlands and are filling the Petiole."

Anand was worried by the news, and then alarmed. *From tens of thousands to hundreds of thousands? Shit! And the Entreveans are about to return through the Petiole!*

"Daveena!" he said aloud to himself, and knew what he must do. "Tell the Dneepers they must wait!" He ran for the nearest speed ant, ignoring the agony of his wounds bleeding anew.

CHAPTER 14

HUNGER

Daveena sat by the young Seed-Eater-turned-Hulkrish-recruit as he lay on the silk cocoon mattress that had been a wedding present to her and Anand. She was sure that under its sheet of roach egg-cloth that the cushion was soaked, stained, sticky, and stinking, and would likely need to be abandoned after its occupant was removed. Days after he had been stabbed with bee stingers, Odwaznee was still rasping as he breathed. Remnants of bee venom in the Bulkokans' daggers had sent him into shock, followed by a day of spasms and a bloating so extreme he had become a captive of his own stiff skin; all his limbs could do was jerk. When his fingers could move it had been in a futile attempt to scratch himself. Daveena did this for him with an itch-comb made from the valve of a cricket spiracle. The boy's tongue was still so thick in his mouth that it almost plugged it, and made speech impossible. The punctures where he had been stabbed had whitened around the hardening scabs, and gave her hope that he might survive.

She lifted him to squeeze watered honey, then lymph, down his throat from bladder-bags. The lymph was from a slaughtered bee, one of the many that hovered noisily above them in a constant swarm as a second aerial caravan. The bees could not help but accompany their queen and mother once she had been extracted from her nest, then caged by her human parasites for a new destiny. The bee cage was at the end of the caravan, just behind Daveena's sled, which was slowing again for the third time that day. She went to the back of the cabin and opened its back hatch to see that the draw-roaches had once again broken their front legs. The bees above were always alighting on the cage, attempting a union with their queen, which made the sled heavy to haul and strained the roaches. The Bulkokans riding atop the cage waved the bees away with fans of dried mint leaves with their weak repellant, but it was just a short time before the daughters were lured back to their mother and her irresistible *queen-scent*.

The cage had also been wearing to the humans. Both the Bulkokans and the Britasytes had to take up harnesses and join the roach team in lugging the cage through the difficult, upward passages. The cage was cumbersome, as the queen inside it was the largest of all the bees. She had several daughter bees as her attendants who paced around the cage and shifted its weight. Also in the cage were some human attendants, whose job was making sure the bees had abundant sugar water and other nourishments, and that they remained free of the honey-mites that mysteriously appeared and affixed themselves to the queen's underside. Once discovered, the women in the cage would bite the honey-mites' heads off, and then eat or toss them in a pile for later consumption.

After the procession resumed, Daveena saw that several roaches from the front sleds had also been replaced. The released draw-roaches crawled off slowly into the wilds, but one just sat and waited to die. "Punshu," Daveena shouted to her driver. "As soon as we get to Palzhad, I believe we will need to contact the Pleps and get their help to replenish our roaches."

"They are good and quick at that," the boy shouted as the buzzing of the bees grew louder. "As long as they can find a warm, sunny place and gorge them on some good and oily amaranth."

She looked out at the mixed weeds in the orange sunshine of the late afternoon as they neared the mouth of the Petiole. In the North, she saw what might be a loose formation of blue locusts, plummeting just south of Palzhad. It made her think of Anand—as so many things did—and her longing for him renewed with a bittersweet ache.

"I'm bored, Punshu. Come sit with our convalescing guest and let me drive awhile."

Punshu looked over his shoulder and gave her a hard gaze. "Madame Anand, with all due reverence, you should not be roach-guiding. Especially not in these dangerous lands . . . and not when you carry the commander's children."

How did he know she carried twins? Daveena asked herself—not as if she expected privacy anymore. As she looked out, she noticed the roach's second, smaller pair of antennae were drawing back, then darting and whipping.

"What's the roach picked up?" she asked.

"I'm not sure, Madame. The stroke of the left would indicate . . . people."

"People. In the Petiole? From where?"

All the caravan's roaches had become alert and energized. In the distance, Daveena could see vague figures wandering out of the thickening weeds to make their way up the Petiole's channel of clear-sand leading to Mound Palzhad. The darkly sweet smell of the Tar Marsh came from the East. Further ahead she saw the masses of rock piles on the channels' west side, which led to the boulders of the Great Jag.

"Those *are* people out there, without ants," Daveena said, making out a mixed group of wanderers from the Southwest. In back of them appeared to be a larger group of men from the direct south, and an even larger group of women and children coming out of the Southeast.

"Who are they? Where are they coming from?" Punshu said.

"They look to be from all over Hulkren—captives, I think, as we were."

The roach caravan reached the Petiole's mouth and entered. Daveena wondered why there wasn't a single leaf-cutter ant returning up the clear-sand with bits of shredded leaves or grass for the mushroom gardens of Palzhad. In the distance, she heard the murmur of what sounded like a large human settlement on a market day. As the caravan got further north, she smelled the odors of humans, and then she saw them: masses of refugees. She knew the caravan could not stop, that they must proceed, though the people ahead were likely to panic when they saw a train of roaches, with a swarm of bees overhead with stingers gyrating at the ends of their abdomens.

The roaches were picking up speed, excited by the rich smells ahead. The buzzing of the bees increased as they flew faster and faster within their loose sphere. Now it was Daveena who was scared. Punshu looked fearful as well, judging from his silence and dilated eyes when he turned to check for her safety. She felt her body vibrating with the bees' increasing noise and then felt short, rough blasts of wind from their wings as they hovered lower. The drivers of all the sand-sleds struggled to keep their roaches in formation. The queen bee's wings buzzed angrily in her cage as it tottered on its scale-lined runners and jolted over ridges in the sand.

From the height of her sled, Daveena saw the Petiole had filled with humans who were waiting for them—either to greet or confront them—and standing as a dense wall. Some had weapons at the ready. At the same time, she could see that behind this wall were other humans who had panicked. They were fleeing from the bizarre invasion of a bee swarm partnered with a roach intrusion. The frightened were slipping down the channel's edges to wait in the shallow waters of the Tar Marsh, or they were going left to climb and hide within the jagged rocks.

As they got closer, Daveena knew from their rags that these people had been Hulkrish slaves. The men standing bravely as a wall wore ill-fitting Hulkrish armor and helmets. Some had rough pikes thrust out before them, while a few held up Hulkrish swords. They seemed unafraid of the advancing roaches but cautiously eyed the striped and noisy flyers above whose single sting could kill a human. Daveena's sled pulled out of formation as its roach lurched to the side.

"Slow the roach!" she commanded Punshu.

"I can't!" he shouted. "There's thousands of people out there—stinking of ghost ants!"

Daveena watched as Punshu flattened himself

over the saddle, straining as the roach raced to the wall of steadfast humans. They did not disperse until it was too late; the sleds of the caravan crashed into these men and sent them falling, flying, and felling the others behind them. The pikes were useless against the roaches' hard chitin, and soon their antennae were lashing and the hooks of their legs were catching and gouging the men stinking of ghost ants. Some men of this army fell under the sleds' runners, which scraped over their skin and bloodied it. Others crawled and trampled over their fellows to the channel's edge to slide and slap through the mud of the marsh and collide with its globs of floating tar. The caravan came to a complete halt when the sleds collided and jammed each other.

At the back of her cabin, Daveena opened her wedding chest to remove a battle-axe with an amethyst blade and rope hook. She climbed on top of the cabin and spun the axe over her head as a warning. Looking to her left she saw that the cage with the queen bee had fallen on its side. The bee was alive, but buzzing her wings in a rage as her daughter-attendants crawled protectively over her, spraying a bitter odor of *warning-scent*.

Looking north, then south, Daveena saw masses of refugees coming up on all sides of the crashed caravan, even at the back of it. Hungry, emaciated people were returning from out of the mud in the East and climbing down from the rocks in the West.

They gathered in an eerie silence around the glittering wreck, and stared at the bejeweled Roach Clan in their brilliant colors and at the honey-plumped bee people in their striped and fuzzy garb. Some of the refugees glanced up in fright at the bees, a few of which made alarming dives. One refugee stepped closer to Daveena, an older man wearing a Hulkrish helmet too large and loose for his head. He shouted at her in an unknown tongue. Others followed his lead, shouting at the other Britasytes until the cacophony was earsplitting.

"What are they screaming?" Punshu asked Daveena.

"I am sure they want food," she said.

Men wearing a mishmash of Hulkrish military gear were pushing their way through the crowd. None of them wore the white paint. Some raised worn and broken swords, and others aimed thick Hulkrish arrows poised in bows of ghost ant jaws.

"What do we do?" Punshu asked. "There're thousands of them!"

Chieftain Thagdag, atop his sand-sled, turned to face his clan and shouted through the amplifying-cone on its roof. "They're hungry!" Thagdag shouted. "Throw them your food!"

Daveena and Punshu went inside the cabin and retrieved their sacks of flattened and sugared aphids, the berry leathers and root chews, the cricket brickle, and the dried and shredded puffball mushrooms. They dropped the food over the side of the sled, and the refugees pressed in to fight over it. Shadowy flickers from overhead increased as the bees dropped, angrily grazing humans who got too close to their mother in her cage.

Punshu and Daveena gasped when the hungry pressed in further, chasing the puffball mushrooms, which had scattered and rolled to the queen bee's cage. The bee swarm dropped on these men and women, landing on their heads and blinding them with their claws. As the humans spun or fell, the bees stung them in their chests and backs. The attacked were instantly dead, their eyes bulging from their sockets. As some bees pulled away, they left behind their stingers and the sack of poison that ripped out of their abdomens. Other bees were stuck, pivoting in circles on the chests or backs of the dead, attempting to extricate their stingers to keep their lives. Refugees with bows and arrows aimed at the bees and felled a few—which only incited the rest to attack.

"Get away!" Daveena shouted to the bowmen in the Seed Eaters' tongue. "You're making it worse!"

The refugees ignored or did not understand her and continued shooting. The bees fell in a heavy rain of black and yellow. No sooner had they fallen than the refugees descended upon their corpses, rolling them onto their backs to haul away to butcher and eat. More refugees converged on the caravan, angrily shouting at the Britasytes to surrender the rest of their food. Daveena noticed a strange-looking person among them—a large woman or perhaps a man, wearing a brightly painted garment that hid part of his or her face. The person rushed towards her, screaming in Slopeish, attempting to climb up and into the sled. "Give us your food. We know there is more!" screamed the attacker while raising a black glass sword.

"We have no more!" she shouted as she raised up her axe. Punshu crouched before Daveena, defending her with his short sword as a new front of men with bows and arrows burst through the chaos. One of them, a gawky, limping giant with red hair, was shouting in the Seed Eaters' tongue.

"There's more bees inside that cage!" he shouted to his men. "Break it open! Kill them!"

"Noooooo!" Daveena shouted. "Don't go near that cage!"

"Who are you to give orders?" he shouted back.

"I am the wife of Commander Quegdoth, ruler of Bee-Jor!"

The giant laughed. "The god-king of Bee-Jor is married to a roach woman?" He turned to the ragged and snarling men behind him. "Kill that woman, then kill those bees."

As arrows flew at them, Daveena and Punshu scrambled to the back of the cabin and yanked up the panel to the hiding place below its floor. Punshu gasped when his shoulder was grazed by an arrow-head that broke open his skin. *Save us, Mighty Crawler!* Daveena prayed.

A loud flutter of wings fell over the sled. They heard refugees screaming, then running in fear. Darts, thin and whistling, could be heard pouring down from above. Daveena peeked outside to see that hundreds had fallen to the darts, twitching as they entered into fits. Some refugees were running back to the Tar Marsh and sliding in its mud, while others dispersed through the maze of rough rocks in the West.

"Daveena!" she heard from outside the cabin. "Daveena! Come out here—it's safe!" The voice she heard both soothed and excited her. She and Punshu edged out of the cabin's riding ledge to see Anand seated behind a pilot on the back of a locust, his dart gun at the ready. Hovering above him was his swirl-ing air force on a few hundred locusts. The refugees further north were scattering, getting out of the way of the Bee-Jorite People's Army of Palzhad as they marched up the Petiole with their grass shields pro-tecting them.

"Surround and protect!" Anand shouted when the army reached the caravan. The foot soldiers made a protective circle, four-deep, around the sand-sleds. The outer circle joined their long shields together as a barrier.

"Good travels, beautiful wanderers!" Anand shouted

in Britasyte, and his tribesmen reappeared from out of the wreck. "Right these sleds!" he commanded, and roach and bee people set about making repairs, assessing damage and gathering up their fallen possessions as the roaches were reset to their harnesses. Daveena walked Punshu to the sled of the Two Spirit to treat his wound and then—heaving with joy and relief—she ran to Anand, climbed up the locust's leg, and hugged and kissed her husband as his pilot dutifully looked away. She was intoxicated as she fell into his arms, love-blind, as the world around her turned into a warm, black mist. All she could see for the moment was her husband's shining and beautiful face. A moment later, she burst into tears, sure that she would lose him soon in their increasingly dangerous world.

CHAPTER 15

THE PASSENGER

Pleckoo was out of breath, in that dizzied, panicked place that had become so familiar to him as he escaped another danger. *Where am I? I must clear my head.* He remembered he was under a roach-sled that he had come to raid in an attempt to find food.

Looking out from under the sled he saw the fallen bodies of other refugees. They were not dead, but were twitching, breathing in short gasps with their tongues licking the air. He jolted when he saw the darts in their chests—Anand and his terrible darts! He was immersed in *that* agony again—the moon-long living death—when he noticed the bright blue legs of sky locusts near the sled. Crawling on his stomach over the sand grains, he looked out and saw the pregnant roach woman who had threatened him with her battle-axe. Now she was in the arms of a man seated atop a locust. Other locusts were landing now—locusts and their human riders. They were reporting to the man holding the roach woman in his arms.

Pleckoo's shock turned to bitter rage when he heard the man speak in Slopeish. "I'll ride back with the caravan," he heard the man shouting to fellow locust riders as they dropped from the sky. "It will soon be too dark to fly."

The Roach Boy! Pleckoo thought. *In my sights already. Thank You, Hulkro.*

He knew he had little time before he was discovered. At the moment, Anand was lost in some disgusting reunion with one of his filthy roach-whores. Looking up at the sled's underside, he saw what had to be a hatch into the sled's cabin. He searched for his sword, found it was nearby, and used the sharp end to push up the panel. Pulling himself up quietly, he saw he was not in the cabin, but just below it in some kind of secret compartment that had air vents. He raised his head quickly and bumped it against the low ceiling. In the darkness he searched with his fingers, and found sacks full of dried food and maybe jewels and other goods tied to the walls. At the back of his head was a bedroll. The sled jerked and soon he was a captive, riding inside it. Feeling the scrape of the scale-lined runners as they slid over the sand of the Petiole, he knew he was in for a rough ride. In the confines, he managed to unravel the bedroll under his body, and it was almost comfortable.

This caravan is returning to the Slope! he realized. *And it's going to take me with it!* For the first time in a fortnight, he smiled, which felt a little strange. *Thank You, Hulkro. Something has gone my way.* Then he remembered that once he was back on the Slope—or this so-called Bee-Jor—that he would need leaf-cutter kin-scent and soon.

Through the walls, Pleckoo could hear the foot army marching alongside the procession, and further off he heard the scrambling and shouting of refugees as they cleared the camps that clogged the Petiole. They were shouting at Anand, begging for food or entry to Bee-Jor, he thought; but then he heard cheers. "Quegdoth, Quegdoth, Quegdoth!" they chanted.

Forgive them, Hulkro, for they know not what they say.

As he lay on his back, he probed the compartment's ceiling and found the hatch to the entry of the sled's cabin. He heard the muffled sounds of Anand and the woman speaking in their ugly tongue, with its clicks and pops and irritating melodies. He knew their backs would be to him if he gambled a peek. Perhaps he could sneak up on them and slay one, if not both.

After gently pushing up the lid he peered out and

took in the cabin's rich interior. Moonlight poured in through a slice of clear quartz in the ceiling and illuminated a wealth of gold and silver pyrite, as well as discs of sliced amber embedded in chests and drawers and secured in the walls. To the right was an idol of the Roach God standing in front of an enormous faceted stone, perhaps a red opal, which had been cut to increase its brilliance.

Raising his head higher, Pleckoo saw his cousin's back. Anand wore a cape that looked the color of dried blood in the moonlight and he had wrapped it around the shoulders of his woman. They snuggled, their heads tilted into each other, as they chatted. Pleckoo clutched the handle of his sword—*yes!* He could crawl out and slice through Anand's neck before he had time to turn and recognize his attacker. *That's what Hulkro wants me to do,* he thought—when he noticed a silk cocoon mattress to his left. On top of it was some bloated Seed Eater boy whose eyes popped when he noticed Pleckoo. He could see the boy's tongue was swollen and stopping up his mouth. The boy's nose made a faint whistle, followed by quiet snorts, which drew attention. Pleckoo dropped below and let the hatch's lid fall quietly back into place.

Below in the compartment, he pondered slipping out the floor hatch to escape and blend in with the refugees. But in back of the sled was an even larger one, carrying a cage of bees that might run over him. Surrounding it all was the army on foot, marching beside the caravan as a moving fortress. And what would he do once they had crossed into leaf-cutter territory? He would be vulnerable to ant attacks after he distanced himself from the stinking roaches. He closed his eyes and waited for guidance from the Great Wood Eater. Until he received his message, he decided he must pray.

Anand watched as the sled's young driver turned over his shoulder from time to time to check on him and Daveena as they huddled behind a grass shield. Punshu's wound was healing under a purple splash of styptic paint, and he looked even prouder now that he was in service to both the Master of Night Wasps as well as to his wife and the mother of his offspring.

Up high in their cushioned seats, Anand and Daveena leaned against each other, savoring each other's warmth; but both were disquieted as they looked over the shield at the startling sight of countless refugees. The masses surrounding them had heard that the Commander of Bee-Jor was parading through them, and they cheered him, shouting, "Quegdoth!" Many of them bowed as he passed, extending the flats of their palms. Others prayed to Anand, their hands clasped upright. The foot soldiers, grass shields at their sides, stayed on high alert as they marched beside their commander with dart guns at the ready.

They were stacked at their thickest alongside the queen bee's cage, to protect her as the future provider of honey to Bee-Jor. The queen bee was calmer for the moment, and even her attendants seemed soothed as they rode atop her, one of them nestled in the fuzz on her back. In back of this sled were the Bulkokans, uncomfortably stuffed into Hulkrish cargo-sleds, pulled by the roaches they were found with in their prison.

The shouts of "Quegdoth!" subsided as they neared Palzhad's border walls and the camps whose refugees had been among the first to arrive. Some hailed Anand, but others were pleading with him. "Feed us!" and "We are dying!" shouted women, clutching skeletal babies or the thin wrists of children whose bellies were swollen after eating nothing but roots and leaves. Anand gulped.

"Why have they all come here?" Daveena asked. "Instead of going home?"

"Likely they have no home to go to," Anand answered.

The crowd's shouting increased as the sleds approached the border wall. "Let us in! Let us in!" they chanted in Hulkrish. In the near distance, Anand saw patrolling leaf-cutter ants crawling up and down the length of the border, one dropping off a dung pellet to reinforce their scent-wall. Men of the Palzhanite building caste disassembled the humans' wall of loose sand-bricks to let the caravan enter. Alerted to the roaches, the ants' antennae flew up and twitched, and they scattered back and up to the mound in a frenzy, leaving *retreat-scent* in the air.

As the sleds and roaches passed through the wall's opening, the chants of "Let us in" faded; but inside his head, Anand heard them just as loudly. Clouds blew over the moon, and a chill crept in on a breeze turning into a wind. The sudden quiet of Palzhad's outer, abandoned rings disturbed Anand, and he was strangely overcome with dread. Daveena, seeing this, pressed the warm back of her hand to his cheek.

"You're worried," she said.

"Always." He sighed. "Those people back there are starving. But we can't just let them in. We can barely govern the ones that live here."

"Perhaps we can at least feed them . . . until you decide what to do."

"At the moment, I'm sure they're tearing up the locusts we left behind." He smiled at her, touched by her compassion for outsiders. "I missed you, Daveena. Felt like half of myself went missing."

"I missed you too," she said, and took his hand. "Like the bees miss flowers." Their mouths meshed in a bloom of warmth as they gave in to each other's pull and felt the whirl of the evening's stars around them.

Per Anand's instructions, the caravan arrived at its usual clearing in Palzhad's northern weeds, where Britasytes conducted their markets and staged their carnivals. The sleds pulled into their customary circle, but set the cage with the queen bee into its center. The exhausted Bulkokans left the discomfort of the Hulkrish cargo wagons and surrounded the cage of their queen bee, but they were too tired to gather any bedding from the nearby weeds. Anand ordered the foot soldiers to gather grass and mallows and shred them for the Bulkokans. They fell on the shreddings in silence, and showed little interest in the food and water that passed through their camps. All they craved was rest after being dragged over the long passage of sand. When the camp quieted, Anand returned to his sled, where Punshu waited below with its draw-roach, guarding Daveena as she grated some dark amaranth seeds she had gathered from the nearby growth.

"Are you hungry?" she asked as she lifted the grater to reveal the coarse powder she would soak with some syrup.

"Not for that," he said with the most appealing smirk.

"It's been a while," she said as he pressed next to her.

"Far too long," he answered. They smiled as their breathing quickened. "Punshu, we're going to need a little privacy," he shouted down to the boy.

Punshu looked up at Anand with a grin. "Privacy? Why, whatever for?"

"Can you sit up here, guard the sled for a bit?"

Punshu climbed to the seat of the riding ledge as Anand was closing the shutters to the cabin. Inside the cabin, he turned and saw the stiff and bloated body of a strange boy lying on his matrimonial bed. And the cabin didn't smell so good.

"I forgot we have a guest," Anand said. "And just who is he?"

"He was guarding the Bulkokan's cage—a Seed Eater before he took up with Hulkro. The bee people weren't so happy with him. They attacked him with venom-daggers when they got the chance."

"Why is he with us?"

"I felt sorry for him. And he speaks the Bulkokans' language."

"I'm sorry for him too. But he is on our bed."

"We have other places to make love," she said, and pointed with her chin to the floor hatch.

"You'll have to be on top," he said through a smile.

"Why?"

"My legs are awfully stiff at the moment," he said as he undressed. "You don't want to know why. And I don't want to discuss it."

Pleckoo's heart raced as he listened to the voices and the footsteps above him. He heard Anand detaching his armor, and the rattle when it dropped to the floor. Anand was going to be naked—completely vulnerable! Pleckoo heard the sweet murmuring of the woman as she was undressed. He would wait for the moment they were lost in pleasure, then crawl out to sever their heads.

The hatch was lifting above him. His heart thumped. *Shit, they're coming down here!* He saw a strange thickness wrapped around Anand's legs as they dangled in the portal. Pleckoo pulled up his own feet before they made contact. From above, he heard the mangled grunting of the boy on the bed—he was emitting short blasts of muffled screams—trying to warn them! "Anand! Someone's down there," the roach woman shouted.

At least I'll get his foot, Pleckoo thought, and positioned his sword with his right hand as he readied to lift the escape hatch with his left. He would have to make a sure, hard stroke, given the confines. He held his breath, swiped, then scrambled out of the sled's bottom as he listened to Anand howl.

From between the rudders, Pleckoo saw the legs of Anand's guards as they converged on the sled, climbing up its sides as it rocked. When Pleckoo saw an opening, he crawled, then ran, to a thicket of nearby weeds. He heard shouting, knew he had been sighted, and heard the *whoosh* of arrows and the vague whistle of darts aimed at his back. Zigzagging, he ran through the weeds and up to the outer rings of Palzhad's shelters. He entered an area of what looked like the laborers' slums; but it was abandoned, quiet, with shelters that slumped on splintering rain poles.

Exhausted and out of breath, he heard the shouts of guards behind him and ran to the sturdiest shelter, found its ladder. As he crawled up its fragile rungs, they broke under his feet. He climbed the rest of the way using only his arms. After pulling himself inside the decrepit hovel, he felt it wobble from his weight. Catching his breath, he looked through gaps in the floor planks to see guards passing under him, arrows at the ready. He muffled his breathing, waited.

Thirst returned, as well as a sharp ache in his stomach and lungs. He had counted five soldiers in search for him, and four of them had given up and were returning. He waited until the fifth returned before he began his descent. The ladder's splinters pierced his hands, and then it snapped and he fell into a thin cushion of crumbled leaves. After a look around the darkness, he continued his hike up the neglected rings when he had a new worry: he heard the sound of marching ants. *They've smelled me! I've got to get kin-scent or they'll tear me to shreds!*

As ant steps grew louder, Pleckoo ran faster up the rings. At the next few levels were large wooden houses, shellacked and sitting on raised platforms of chiseled stone; but these areas were abandoned too. Up he went through weeds to the next ring. He felt hope when he emerged from stands of hairy fleabane to see houses of sand and tar atop pebble platforms, where the Palzhanite midden caste was living in a relative splendor. In the midst of the houses, in their outdoor common space, was a torch of glow-fungus that illuminated an altar as well as the nearby vats of a dew station. Next to these were scenting tubs covered with waxed canvas to prevent their content's evaporation.

Pleckoo heard the voices of the houses' inhabitants, and strangely, their singing, as he skulked to the dew station. A woman with a baby in a backsack was cutting a slice of water from a barrel to scrape into her seed-basin. Pleckoo remembered he was a stranger, dressed in a strange garment, and it would frighten her if he approached. He hid behind an altar full of Slopeish idols, even as that repulsed him. After waiting for the woman to leave, he quietly approached the dew barrels. Just as he peeled back the lid of a barrel and inserted his sword to lick a drop, they appeared— sentry ants!

I should have bathed first! he scolded himself as he looked at the ants with their thorny, heart-shaped skulls and whirring antennae. He knew if he had a chance that he should not run from them, but into them.

CHAPTER 16

FAMILY

Pleckoo ran towards the first sentry ant and ducked under its pulsing, sawtooth mandibles. The ant's antennae were searching downwards as she pivoted, unable to snatch the intruder beneath her. He scrambled to stay under her, away from her mouth, as he was bandied between her forelegs. Other sentry ants converged on the both of them, and he felt a soft whipping from their antennae as they probed him, piled on, pressed in. The air around him grew poisonous as he looked out from under the ant at dark walls of angry, scissoring mouths. *What can I do?*

The ant he was trapped under was immobile in the thickness of converging sentry ants that crowded and crawled on her. He felt her lowering, crushing him as his neck and arms were pierced by the thin, hairy spikes of her undercarriage. Struggling to breathe, Pleckoo worked his sword up the segment that connected her head to her thorax. Screaming in fear and panic he sawed back and forth in his confines, his arms aching, until the head was severed and broke away. When he looked up the opening he saw a dark mass of ants crawling over the severed pieces. The only place to hide now was under the sundered head—he slithered and pushed himself beneath it, and felt the lash of antennae on his legs before he could pull them in.

The sand felt rough against his chest plate as he pushed out from under the head to grab a breath. An antenna from the largest of sentry ants brushed his face. She lunged for Pleckoo, and her force pushed the severed head away, exposing him to the mass of excited ants. He crawled towards, then under, this new attacker, when he felt the ends of her mandibles as they scraped at his armor's back plate. One mandible snipped off the bottom of his garment and the other hooked into its top. He was yanked up, and shook back and forth in her jaws when he noticed he was above a scenting tub.

Raising his arms, he slipped out of the garment and fell on the tub's edge sealed with a waxed canvas. The tub's canvas was too taut—he did not sink into its water. Antennae probed his face as he bounced on his knees, broke through the canvas, and sank into the doming water. Though the water was cool, the sudden sensation of suspension was soothing. A mass of hostile ants surrounded him, but here, for a moment, he was back in the womb, and innocent to a world of pain. *I could stay here forever,* he thought—until the moment he needed to breathe. Panic grew inside him but so did the pull to some other place, as a pleasurable delirium set in. *I'm happy here,* he thought. *I never want to leave—even if I am dying.*

But leave he did, when he felt a firm grip around both his ankles. He was pulled out of the water and over the tub's edge, to land on his back. As he gasped for air in the spreading water, he saw human legs. Through them he saw that the ants had moved on. Slopeish faces were peering down at him, faces that looked as dark as his own. "Can you hear me, cousin?" he heard a man say in what sounded like laborers' Slopeish.

Pleckoo rose on his elbows and looked around. Though it was dark, he could see that the man who spoke to him had two clipped earlobes, one of which marked him as an outcaste, and the other which distinguished him as the midden's foreman. Strangely, he was well dressed. His garment was made from dyed cloth and had neatly cut and stitched openings for his arms and head, and his antennae were not the usual straw but were well-fashioned carvings with intricate designs. Standing next to him was the caste's chubby idols keeper, who held a fungus torch. He was wearing the yellow sash that conferred his status, but it was tied around what looked to be a blue tunic of very fine making.

Torches for middenites? Fine clothing? Behind these men stood other members of the caste, including mothers holding babies as well as a few children who stared at Pleckoo, curious about him. These women, as well as the children, were not poorly dressed either, but were wearing an abundance of draped cloth as well as beaded necklaces and chitin bangles. Somehow they had all gotten hold of combs and head-soap and turned the masses of tangled filth on their heads into hair. The men were holding a strange tube near their mouths; Pleckoo guessed these were the dart shooters.

"Can you hear me, cousin?" the man repeated, and Pleckoo realized his black glass sword was in the man's grip.

"Why do you call me 'cousin'?" Pleckoo responded in Slopeish.

"Your ear is clipped. You're a middenite, right?"

"Yes," Pleckoo said, and realized his wet hair had exposed him.

"What mound are you from?" asked the idols keeper. Both these men spoke in the slower, softer Palzhanite way, out of the right side of the mouth.

Pleckoo hesitated. "Gagumji," he said.

"Gagumji? So you've escaped."

"Escaped?"

"Yes, left the No Longer Great Nor Holy Slope."

"Right," Pleckoo said, still catching his breath, "to come and live in Bee-Jor." *So it's for certain: the Slope has been divided into two nations.* The men behind him relaxed, lowered their tubes. "Who . . . who rules here?"

"Commander Vof Quegdoth, the Son of Locust, rules all of Bee-Jor," said the foreman. "But the Widow Queen Clugna sits on the throne of Palzhad. Who rules now in Gagumji?"

"I no longer know," said Pleckoo, who had never known the names of that mound's king and queen. "I just knew I had to leave."

"How did you lose your kin-scent?" asked the idols keeper.

"And what strange garment is this you were wearing?" said the foreman as he picked up the torn pieces of the Ledacki frock with the end of Pleckoo's sword.

"I . . . I don't want to speak the truth," he said.

"Why not?"

"It might offend you . . . you'll consider me polluted."

"Our worry is that you are a loyal Slopeite," said the idols keeper. "How did you get here?"

Pleckoo decided the best thing was to tell as much of the truth as possible.

"I asked a caravan of roach people to bring me here. They said they couldn't, that I was the property of the royals of Gagumji and they would be forced to surrender their treasures, even their lives, if they were caught smuggling human cargo. I offered them all I had if they would hide me in their caravan and take me to Palzhad."

"And what did you—a poor middenite—have that the Britasytes wanted?" asked the idols keeper with a furrowed brow.

"Weapons. Fine swords, taken from Hulkrish corpses on the edge of the Dustlands . . . as well as their armor, boots, and the like."

"Like this sword?" said the foreman as he raised up Pleckoo's blade.

"Like that one," Pleckoo said. "To ride in their caravan, I had to remove my midden rags and take on roach-scent. Before I left their caravan, I bathed that stench from my skin. I bought that Ledacki garment from a Britasyte trader who said it was soaked in leaf-cutter-scent. I didn't realize it carried a foreign kin-scent until it alarmed the sentry ants of Palzhad. I should have remembered not to trust Britasytes."

"Do not speak poorly of roach people in Bee-Jor," said the foreman.

Do not speak poorly of roach people?

"How could you ride with the Britasytes?" asked the idols keeper. "If Slopeish sheriffs had seen you traveling with them, you would have been killed for escaping."

"I rode for days hidden in a secret compartment.

They got one under each of their sand-sleds—a place they hide themselves when under attack. It's where they hide their goods."

The foreman and the idols keeper looked at each other.

"You've come a long way," the foreman said, and extended a hand, which Pleckoo used to pull himself up. Wobbling on his feet, he felt faint from hunger.

"I would be in your debt if you could spare me a mushroom," Pleckoo said.

"Don't know about that," said the foreman. "Can you walk?"

"I can."

"You are immodest," said the idols keeper, who signaled to a woman near him to surrender her shawl. Pleckoo realized he was naked from the waist down before a group of strangers. All he had on his chest and back were remnants of Hulkrish armor. He wrapped the shawl around him, then followed the foreman into a house among the cluster on the ring.

The foreman's house was larger than the others and its sand-grain walls bound with tar were stained with a wash of blue that was brightened by the light within it. They entered through a flap to a room that was luxurious by midden standards, and very well lit. On one side of the wall was a large piece of decomposing bark that was moistened to sustain a healthy growth of scaly glow-fungus, and it illuminated the opening to a second room. Pleckoo looked around at the foreman's vast family, seated on a comfortable floor of fine grass shavings. They looked at him with almost no expression, just a mild curiosity. The family included a number of adult men and women, as well as children and elders. All were seated around a fresh basil leaf piled high with a variety of foods. Against the walls, he saw twig structures stacked three high, which supported hammocks. On the wall next to the glow-fungus was a fine piece of embroidered cloth draped to cover a household shrine—something that was likely filled with Slopeish idols.

"Sit. We were just starting supper when you came," said the foreman, and his children made a space for Pleckoo. They were quiet as they stole glances at the hole in the middle of his face, but strangely, did not seem frightened by it.

"I am Glip," said the foreman. Your name?"

"Vleeg," said Pleckoo, giving the name of the eldest of his dead brothers.

"How did you lose your nose?" Glip asked. Pleckoo covered his face with his hand as, once again, he was reminded of the most painful moment of his life. He worried they might judge him as a thief.

"There's no shame in it, Vleeg. Unless you did it to yourself."

"In truth, my nose was taken from me. By a sheriff."

"Were you stealing?"

"A mushroom. A single rotting mushroom that someone threw in a trash heap for return to the ants. I was starving."

"Those days are over," said Glip. "The Savior-Commander has ended these kinds of cruel punishments."

The Savior-Commander!

"Welcome, brother," said a man across the way. "I am Brother Kelvap, escaped from Mound Ensmut."

"Welcome, Vleeg," said the man at the leaf's point. "I am Brother Mlor, escaped from Mound Kwatgray."

Pleckoo looked at both men, and gulped as they lifted up loose kerchiefs tied around their heads to show him they both were noseless—victims of some sheriff's vicious whim. Next to them was a third man, also wearing a face kerchief that had a fine embroidery of crickets eating a cannabis leaf. He did not lift his kerchief, but nodded at Pleckoo, who wondered what deformity he was hiding; perhaps something to do with his mouth since he did not speak.

"We are not offended by your face," said Glip. "But if you would like a kerchief to cover your wound, my wife can get you one."

"Yes," said Pleckoo, and Glip's wife went into the other room and returned with a square of fine cloth with hemmed edges.

"It is permitted to hide one's face now?" Pleckoo

asked. "The sheriffs at my old mound would have punished me a second time for hiding the mark of my crime."

"It is allowed now," said Glip. Pleckoo folded the scarf in half and tied it just above his ears so that the front was a loose half that would allow him to eat and breathe.

"We have no mushrooms tonight," said Glip's wife through a giggle as she and her daughters set down glazed bowls in the middle of the leaf. "We have better food."

She speaks poorly of the sacred mushroom. Interesting.

Pleckoo looked sideways at her face, which was decorated with thin blue stripes. On top of her black and lustrous hair was a clip fashioned from blue beetle chitin in the shape of some insect—a locust? Looking at the spread of food, he recognized that the largest bowl had reconstituted curds of ant lymph mixed with a minced onion shoot; the lymph might have been from Hulkren's ghost ants. Around the lymph curds were piles of neatly cut winter pickles, including burdock root, asparagus stalks, green mustard seeds, and strips of sour purslane, all with the aroma of garlic and barley vinegar and sprinkled with flecks of dried chili. One of the offerings was a dried aphid that had been coated and preserved in its own sticky sweetness. Also present were fresh meats of roasted ringtailed earwigs and the tender abdomen of a freshly emerged autumn cicada.

"How . . . how did you come on such bounty? Have the middenites of Palzhad always eaten this way?"

"No, Vleeg. We have always eaten better than others on the Slope, but this is the New Way. We don't rely on royals anymore to give us what they will of their mushrooms. You'll see tomorrow—if you want to join us at work. Let's give thanks to the Lord."

The family joined hands. Pleckoo was startled when his left hand was taken by the young boy on his left while an old woman on his other side searched for his right. He took her hand and glanced at her face, which bore a small and constant smile below her cloudy eyes; she was blind! Why was she allowed to live if she could contribute nothing? He felt the dry, scaly skin of her hand in his, but felt a warmth coming from it. Warmth seemed to flow from everyone in this room.

"Lord, thank You for all Your blessings and for this new one today: for Your beloved son, Vleeg of Gagumji, has escaped the cruelty of the Slope and come to join our family."

Pleckoo glanced around at all the faces as they looked up and regarded him, not with fear or disgust, but with something he could not quite identify. What was it?

"Welcome, Brother Vleeg," Glip said. "You have come home."

Pleckoo was trembling, and felt a tightness in his throat. He willed himself to stillness, breathed deeply, and held his head erect. *I must take control of myself,* he repeated in his mind. Attempting to look fierce, he sat erect and remembered he was a man, someone who never gave into mawkishness when an explosion of feelings overtook him. He bent his head to hide his watering eyes. Shaking and weeping before this circle of strangers, he experienced something so rare in his life that he was uncertain of the word for it. Then it came to him: it was *kindness.*

"These are not tears," Pleckoo said as he sobbed. "This is not weeping I bring to disgrace your dinner leaf."

"No," said Glip. "Those *are* tears, and they are sweet and quenching like the first rains of autumn. Your weeping is a sweet song of sadness that we all hear, that we sing as a single family. Be not ashamed, brother, to show us your feelings. We have endured your sadness too, and are honored by your tears."

"Thank you, for your welcome and your . . . kindness," he said, and felt his shoulders shaking from an unstoppable sobbing.

Glip nodded. "Before we eat, let us offer our food to the One who guides us, protects us, who saved us and provides for us. He is forever invited to all our feasts."

Pleckoo watched as the others picked up whatever food was before them and held it up to the covered shrine. The silent man with the cricket kerchief went to the shrine's curtain and rolled up the embroidery to reveal the idols. Pleckoo's vision blurred before he could make sense of the carved deities. In the greenish light he saw vivid orange wings, a long and black body with indigo stripes, a head with bulging eyes—a night wasp. Riding on its back was a carving of a dark-faced man in blue-green robes who held a bow and arrow. In the back of this idol, the shrine's wall was painted like the night sky with spatters of six-pointed stars. Glued in the middle of this sky was a second idol of a human-faced, blue locust with its wings/hands spread in the protective mode. To the side of this shrine were two smaller ones that contained idols of Madricanth, Bee, Cricket, and Mite.

"We offer our obeisances and our food to you, Vof Quegdoth, who sits in bliss at the locust feet of Father Sky, and readies to fulfill his promise to end the Great Trial of the True People of the Slope."

Pleckoo stopped breathing. At first he felt a sudden rage, and then a crushing sadness. *Vof Quegdoth, the Son of Locust? Vof Quegdoth is Anand the Roach Boy! His father is Yormu the Mute! And Anand will end the Great Trial? The Hulkrites endured the Great Trial, not these stupid Slopeish slaves of Ant Queen!*

As Pleckoo looked at the idols, the sound of a swarm of night wasps was in his ears and he tried to shake it out of his head. Darkness fell on him, like an errant acorn that conked his head and laid him flat. Once again, he was falling, falling, until he landed with a painful splat on the roasting sands of the Netherworld. Night wasps had lined up in an eternal queue to sting him in his eyes, his ears, on his lips and tongue, until he could bear consciousness no more.

It was black inside the house when Pleckoo awoke. He gasped, looked around the darkened room. Light was leaking from a sheet over the wall fungus and he remembered where he was: among the midden caste of Palzhad in their foreman's house. *I must have fainted*, he thought. His body was gently swinging when he realized they had set him in a hammock. They had removed his boots and underneath him was a soft cushion and over his chest was a softer blanket. Lying back, he remembered his shock and his disappointment that these people who had clothed him and shared their supper were worshipping his unholy cousin as a god. *But as the Prophet Tahn has spoken, "The unbelieving should never be hated for their ignorance, only for their blasphemy."*

He quietly rolled out of the hammock, and thought of sweeping up some of the jewels in the shrines before running off—an idea that seemed completely foolish a moment later. An even more foolish notion was that he could stay in Palzhad and hope his true identity was never discovered. Where had they put his boots? His sword? Below the hammocks he saw the middenites' footwear—boots, not sandals!—and sighted a pair that would fit him under

As Pleckoo wandered back from the weeds, part of him was still tempted to run—but to where? To Cajoria, where everyone in the midden knew him? Just the idea of another journey was exhausting. *I'll stay here a bit and get strong,* he thought, *or until Hulkro shows me otherwise.*

Sometime later, sunlight made a soft entry through the translucence of the house's sand grains. Pleckoo expected to hear the *glok-glok-glok* of the idols keeper sounding the wooden bell to summon the midden to the dawn prayer, but it never came. Instead, Glip's family got up slowly, stretching and yawning before they wandered outside to begin their morning ablutions. "Blessed day," they said to each other, and also to Pleckoo. They returned at a leisurely pace to dress, and then used blue paint sticks made from beeswax to decorate their arms and faces. The silent man with the cricket kerchief returned with a fresh mint leaf rolled up under his arm, which he unfurled as a platter for the breakfast.

"Eat," said Glip's wife to Pleckoo after he returned from a trip to the nearby weeds, pointing to the leftovers from the previous night's feast. He was relieved to see that the idols in the shrine were covered up again, so he wouldn't have to offer them his food before eating it himself. As he finished his breakfast, Glip's wife came to him with a pair of sturdy but broken-in boots and a used tunic suitable to a tradesman. The garment was stained and a bit worn, but as Pleckoo pulled it on he still thought it too fine a thing to wear while cleaning chamber pots. Glip entered the house and nodded at Pleckoo before speaking. "We are leaving for work now, Vleeg. Grab your breakfast and join us, if you will."

If you will? He's giving me a choice!

Pleckoo emerged from the house to find a crowd of men from the other houses talking quietly among themselves. They were not dreading the day ahead but seemed willing to begin it. The men had travoises and sand-sleds full of empty clay jars, as well as hollowed wood barrels and nutshell and seed basins. Hung around their necks were tubes for the blow-darts. At their sides were crude swords made from mandibles of ants and other insects, which they wore openly, proudly, and without fear of punishment. When the men saw their foreman approach, they acknowledged him with nods. The idols keeper stood nearby, and opened his arms and looked to the clouds. "Praise Father Sky," he said, "the Lord Creator, for the gift of another day."

No prayer to Ant Queen or Mantis, Pleckoo thought as the men looked to the heavens and repeated the blessing. Glip stepped forward and the rest followed him out, then down the mound's main artery. Pleckoo followed at the back as they passed through at least twenty uninhabited rings on the mound's elevation, and then nine more through its flats. They continued through Palzhad's infamous overgrowth of weeds until they reached the ghostly ruins of what had to be the home of the middenites, when Palzhad had been a crowded mound in the center of the Slope. In the daylight, Pleckoo looked up at the remnants of shacks on their rain poles, including the one he had hidden in, and then at a grime-covered whipping pebble in what had once been a common area. He winced as he remembered his life in Cajoria, and felt the nettles in his back from the merciless whippings of Pictolo, the foreman, and later those of his nephew, Keel. From behind him, Pleckoo heard the steps of ants in a downward parade. He turned to see several midden ants of different sizes carrying a variety of refuse in their mandibles.

The men traveled along with the ants to a clearing where they entered the true, working midden. On its edge were sturdy worktables chiseled from flat rocks. Across the midden were the usual piles of ant dung, a scattering of termite and other wings, insect legs and corpses, as well as spent substrate from the mushroom chambers.

The midden ants dropped off their trash and Glip looked satisfied with the arrival of some newly dead leaf-cutter ants that could be salvaged for food. The men were set to work on their dissection in the shade, and Pleckoo was given a short saw of serrated quartz. He was assigned to split open the ants' abdomens and then scrape out the paste of partially digested mushrooms. The paste was to be pressed into basins, which were sealed with a cutting of waxy purslane to keep it moist. As he worked, he wondered where the chamber pots were cleaned; was there a separate midden for them? He assumed that task was how they were ending the day.

Working alongside him was Glip's son of eleven summers, Moosak, who Pleckoo thought of as Little Grinner. Moosak used a small, lacquered mandible knife to cut the purslane leaves into lids to seal the basin's contents. Always grinning, he scooped up some of the paste to eat and encouraged Pleckoo to do the same. Pleckoo looked around—where was Glip? Surely he would take out his taloned whip and punish them for stealing.

"It's all right," said Moosak. "We eat when we're hungry." And then Pleckoo remembered: he had not seen a whip at Glip's side. Pleckoo ate some of the mushroom paste, which had taken on a richer, earthy taste. It was good—like so much of what he had experienced in Palzhad. *It's not life in palaces or fighting for glory on ghost ants, but it's not the old way.* At the other tables, the men were scooping out ant lymph and packing it in barrels, or kneading it with paddles in the sun to coagulate for curds.

"Why are we doing the salvagers' work?" Pleckoo asked Moosak.

"We *are* salvagers," Moosak said. "And middenites—and hunters or defenders too. No set castes anymore."

"When do we clean the chamber pots?"

"Never."

"Never?"

"Everyone cleans their own chamber pot—if they use one."

Pleckoo was ready to ask more questions when he saw something strange and frightening making its way to the midden. The leaf-cutter ants had made chains of themselves to tug the corpse of a red-banded millipede into the midden. The men got out of the way of the ants, and when they released the corpse it uncoiled stiffly.

"This is a good day," said Glip. "We'll need the masks and the dried milkweed."

At that, some of the boys ran off. Half of them returned a short time later with the breathing masks that Slopeish soldiers wore when battling the Seed Eaters and their poison-spewing harvester ants. Pleckoo was astonished—breathing masks for middenites? And why wasn't the millipede being turned over to the priests so they could extract its poisons and other potions? Moosak and the rest of the boys returned with bundles of dried milkweed stems in their travoises. The men used their smallest, finest knives to cut the milkweed into short, exact slivers. After donning the breathing masks, they took the slivers to the millipede's corpse and inserted them into the small pores above its legs, to soak their ends in a clear poison, a substance which had a strangely sweet and fruity scent. At the same time, Glip worked carefully to remove the more poisonous claws from inside the millipede's mouth, which held a thicker liquid. The slivers he inserted into this poison were marked with a bit of berry dye as something more lethal.

The slivers dried quickly in the sun, and were being carefully wrapped in eggshell paper, when something bright and glinting made its way into the midden. The men cheered to see the ants pulling a gold-and-crystal beetle towards them. Its legs had been sheared away but its little antennae were waving, indicating it was still alive. The last time Pleckoo had seen one of these beetles was several summers past, in the Cajorian midden. He was captivated then by its strange beauty, and just as entranced now. The elytra were like great, oversized shields of quartz, which sparkled with a richness of gold from underneath. "This is a very good day, thank Locust," Glip said while looking at Pleckoo. "Vleeg has brought us these blessings. We must dissect this beetle carefully and coat its parts quickly with the preserving potions."

A tall, sinewy middenite with a quartz knife took on the task of making exact cuts, separating the elytra and the head, and then he carefully lifted the parts away to be gently coated with a clear gel of resin and ant vinegar to preserve their inner gold. Once the pieces dried, they were wrapped in thin sheets, then coarse, ugly blankets as if to disguise their beauty. "We will wait for the Britasytes to pass before selling this treasure," Glip said, then looked to the sky and the sun's position to see that it was late morning. "To the stadium," he said, and men and boys packed up all they had salvaged that day, loaded up their carriers, and made their way on a path to the shady side of the mound.

To the stadium? For an assembly? Pleckoo wondered.

As they made their way through a thicket of browning ranunculus plants and new green seedlings, Pleckoo picked up the faint odors of humans in the weeds south of the border. He thought of Jakhuma and Kula and the snub-nosed baby he had saved from death, and felt vaguely hurt by their last confrontation. *Why all these womanly feelings?* he thought, scolding himself when they reached the mound's stadium. The stands were empty but the arena was milling with people. As they got closer, Pleckoo realized this was a market. He recognized different castes of people at stalls or on plots, offering certain goods or services associated with what had been their station in life.

Glip led them to the market's edge where they unfurled leaves on the fine, worn sand, then laid out their morning's work under a stall they pitched and covered with canvas for shade. Near them were mushroom workers who traded fresh piles of capped, thin-stemmed fungus from inside the mound. The blinders' caste, in their crusty rags, had troughs full of damp ant eyes, as well as stacks of the eggshells from which new ants had emerged. The blinders' biggest prize, being haggled over at the moment, was a tender, leaf-wrapped nymph that had been born with wings—a potential rival to the ant queen, but also something good to eat. The sun-kiln workers had brought one of their crystal ovens with them and were accepting mushroom doughs, raw seeds, midges, and other captured game to roast, then return for a share. Further down were cloth makers next to tailors and then there were the craftsmen offering sitting stools, baskets, rugs, and hammocks.

"This food is ours to sell?" Pleckoo asked Moosak as they set out their bowls of mushroom paste.

"Yes," he said with his grin turning to a prideful smile. "If it ends up in the midden, it belongs to us. We can keep or trade."

"Who decided this?"

"Vof Quegdoth, of course. It started with his arrival as commander of the People's Army when all the old rules were set aside for the war effort. Since then it's been sanctioned, part of the New Way. What one worked at in the old way is now one's to sell, the Great Redistribution."

Pleckoo noticed that many of the people who were buying appeared to be the yellow-skinned widows and children of the vanquished military, while some were palace and priestly servants. Moosak opened one of the basins of mushroom paste, and its scent filled the air and attracted passersby. A woman with yellow skin wearing widow's whites stood with a tired and stooped servant who was ordered to approach Moosak. The servant's skin was richly wrinkled. She glanced briefly at Pleckoo, winced at the scarf over his face, then turned to Moosak.

"How fresh is this paste?" she asked.

"From this morning," Moosak said. "Sample."

The woman dipped in her finger and licked it, then turned to the widow, who nodded. "My mistress wants the basin."

"What have you?"

The servant pulled up her basket whose top was covered with used clothing, most of which was threadbare and dirty. Moosak shook his head as she pulled out a series of garments before reaching a man's fine sleeping tunic and a pair of loose trousers made of a dyed yellow silk and polished to a sheen.

Moosak shook his head. "No. No yellow."

The woman pulled up more yellow garments before reaching the bottom of her basket, which had a cluster of jewelry and a few loose but precious mineral bits. She held up a small but perfect cube of gold-colored pyrite. Moosak could see she had others like it.

"Need three," Moosak said, and Pleckoo was surprised. *Pyrite traded for a bowl of mushroom paste?* They were settling on two cubes when an argument broke out at the nearby stall of the mite-scrapers' caste. The chubby, eight-legged parasites they had scraped from the leaf-cutter ants were in three piles, which included plain, sugared, and powdered scallion. A scraper woman was on her feet and using the sharp flat trowel around her neck to threaten a young man with yellowish skin and a shaved head. Pleckoo recognized him as a priestly novitiate.

"I saw you!" said the scraper woman as the wattles under her chin quivered with her rage. "You slipped extra ones under your cloak!"

"I did no such thing!" the young priest yelled back at her, haughtily lifting his chin as he backed away. Pleckoo detested him immediately for the way he spoke, as if he was clenching a stick at the back of his teeth. He was a pampered little mite himself, soft looking, with a belly under his yellow garment. When he walked, he wobbled atop his platform sandals and his toes were adorned with rings and their nails were long, polished, and filed into spikes. Pleckoo had never been so close to a priest. It was one more mild shock in his day to find one doing his own marketing.

"Just what has it come to!" the young priest was shouting, holding up a stinger-ended walking stick with his free hand. "When a holy man must endure the insults of a low-bred scraper . . . and a female at that!"

"Here's how it goes, you sallow bloodsucker," the woman shouted as her kinsmen joined her. "You'll gimme those mites back, or you'll pay for 'em." The priest, gritting his teeth, clumsily attempted to poke her with his stick, but her kin were exhaling through their dart guns. The priest fell, spasmed, and his belly shook as his basket spilled and his stick rolled away. The mite-scrapers pulled off his cloak and searched through its inner pockets until they produced the mites he had stolen. The priest lay naked before the crowd except for a swaddling of cloth around his middle. Sentry ants arrived with men in sheriffs' armor on their saddles. Before they dropped to the ground, they threw their saddle ropes to Moosak and Pleckoo to tether their rides. Pleckoo lowered his face, but peeped up to see that these were not yellow-skinned elites from the military caste but men with skin as dark as his own.

"Who witnessed this crime?" the first of them asked, and a number of people raised their hands. Pleckoo broke out in a sweat. As much as he hated priests, Pleckoo feared this one was about to lose his nose.

"One moon in a cage," said the sheriff to the priest.

"B-b-but I'm a priest!" shouted the holy man, trying to regain control of his tongue.

"And I'm the peoples's sheriff. Resist and it will be two moons." The sheriffs grabbed the priest, bound his wrists together, then remounted their ants, forcing the priest to walk behind them on a rope leash. Moosak and others ran out and grabbed the items the priest had dropped. They did not keep them for themselves but ran after the sheriffs to return the articles. *That's the strangest thing yet,* thought Pleckoo. He turned to see that the mite-scrapers were walking towards the midden's stall with skewers of mites in all three flavors. They were not looking to trade for food, but were very interested in the wrapped packages that contained the morning's darts.

The lower castes are no longer powerless, Pleckoo thought, *nor poor nor starving.*

Moosak returned to the stall with his irrepressible grin and a toasted, sliced pine nut under his arm. He set the nut on their leaf, cut the string that bound it together, and let it fall into neat slices before handing a bit to Pleckoo to savor.

A very strange feeling came over Pleckoo: he liked it here in Palzhad. *In Bee-Jor.* From above, he saw a blue locust flying north with its legs trailing a yellow ribbon.

"What's the yellow mean?" he asked Moosak.

"That's a message from the palace," said the boy as his grin took leave. "Someone must have died."

CHAPTER 18

INGRATITUDE

"Thank Madricanth you were wearing these bandages," Daveena said as she unwrapped them from Anand's ankle.

"Madricanth had nothing to do with it," he said. In the early sunlight, they looked at the scabbed-over gash made with a fine and sharp blade. The attack of a mysterious assassin from the safety compartment was disturbing enough but Anand was tormented as he considered the elegance of the attacker's weapon. Was this just some random refugee striking out in fear or hunger? Or was it a Hulkrite who had known him in the Dustlands and was seeking revenge for the Termite God?

"How is our guest?" Anand asked. "Maybe when he gets his tongue back he can tell us about our other visitor."

"Odwaznee's swelling has gone down," said Daveena. "I thanked him for you—let him know he saved your life. But you might do it yourself."

Do-Tma, the Entrevean's Two Spirit, arrived in a cloud of heavy perfume. The initial scent was pleasant, but a moment later Anand felt a mild nausea. Do-Tma climbed up the sled's ladder to check on the wound he/she had painted with a styptic derived from root-borer beetles, and then wrapped with strands of spider-webbing.

"It is healing well," he/she said. "The thick white pus is the good milk of the Roach Lord's healing spirit. He/She was with you as you slept, Anand. Blessings of Madricanth on your ankle. You should toss Him/Her some of your grated amaranth as an offering."

"Blessings of Madricanth," Daveena repeated. She looked at Anand as he remained silent. The Two Spirit stood over them, making the motion of the six claws of the Roach to complete his/her blessing before he/she left.

"That perfume he/she wears is sickening," Anand said.

"Sickening? It's the Holy Scent of our Roach Lord."

"It's like being buried under flower petals. It makes me queasy and gives me a headache."

"You have my sympathies. Why didn't you echo his/her blessing?" she asked, sharpness in her voice.

"In Dranveria, we do not consider it wise to mix worship and healing."

"Why not?"

"Because the outcome of someone's condition has nothing to do with gods or spirits. Do-Tma's potion keeps a wound from festering because of its ingredients, not because of any magic."

"Are you saying he/she is a fraud?"

"A fraud knows when he is deceiving others. I believe the Two Spirits are sincere. They are just wrong . . . often enough."

"So he/she is ignorant?" said Daveena as she filled an offering bowl with the grated amaranth.

"The Dranverish word is *superstitious*. It means to believe in something not rooted in reason or knowledge."

She put the bowl under her arm and glared at him as she went to the ladder.

"Don't throw away our amaranth," he said. "It's wasteful."

She gasped, dropped the bowl.

"What's wrong?"

"You're scaring me," she said from behind her sleeve.

"*Scaring* you?"

"Yes, Commander Quegdoth. It scares people when they are told that everything they believe in is a lie. Next you'll be telling me that Madricanth is dead, killed by some Dranverish god."

He sighed. "I don't know that Madricanth ever existed to be killed by some other god. I think . . ."

She put her hands over her ears. "I don't want to hear what you think," she shouted. The both of them realized that Britasytes, Bee-Jorites, and Bulkokans were turning from their morning tasks to watch the commander argue with his wife.

"Know this, Daveena," Anand said as he took her trembling hand. "You always have my love and protection—if not that of the Roach God."

The priests of Palzhad approached Anand and Daveena's sled, a mere seven men. They reminded Anand that Palzhad was an emptying mound, further diminished by the war and the raid that had brought Polexima into Hulkren. Three of the priests were quite old and struggled as they walked in their beaded but shabby robes. Behind them were some stronger acolytes with shaved heads who carried a long stoppered vase on their shoulders. In back of them were men of the barrel makers' caste who hauled nutshell tubs on runners.

"Per your request, Commander," said Pious Ejolta, who wobbled on his box-sandals. He looked pained, as if the events of the last seasons had broken his bones into sharp sticks that cut him from the inside. "We may not have enough kin-scent for the new arrivals."

"Not enough?"

"This war with the Hulkrites has depleted all our potions as well as our ants and supplies. It will be moons before we can replace everything."

"Thank you, Pious," Anand said, falling into his refined Slopeish. "The Roach Clan has been gathering dew all morning for our beekeeper guests. Please prepare the baths and we will do what we can."

Anand watched as the priests went through their ritual of blessing the leaf-cutter kin-scent as it was scraped into the tubs. As the acolytes did the physical work, the elders did a slow and crooked whirl around the tubs while chanting the ancient words.

Punshu arrived, escorting Ulatha, the Britasyte fortune-teller who could speak with the Bulkokans in the Carpenters' words. Daveena joined Anand as they approached the bee people, in hopes she could learn some of their strange and buzzy tongue. As for the Bulkokans, many of them were still asleep. A few of them rose, turned to the queen bee in her cage, and made a shallow bow before they tore apart some roach eggs to eat as their breakfast.

"Now that is a strange sight," said Anand as he and Daveena watched someone other than Britasytes eating such a reviled food. The bee people buzzed quietly among their own, glancing at Anand with indifference as he stood nearby with his interpreters and his ever-present guards. Annoyed by their refusal to acknowledge him, he wondered what justified their arrogance.

"Peace and bounty upon you," Anand finally shouted to their turned backs. "Is there a leader among you? Someone I should address first?"

After the words were translated, a few Bulko-kans spoke among themselves before one of them finally rose, looked annoyed with Anand, then slowly weaved into the center of their camp. Six of the tallest Bulkokan men rose from the center and stood with banded staffs. They walked slowly to Anand, their kinsmen pulling aside to let them pass. Inside this circle of men, he could see a seventh person who struggled to keep apace. When this odd grouping stood before Anand, he made a shallow bow. The men had orange-brown skin, ginger hair, and dark green eyes with a fold over the upper eyelid. Their lower faces were strangely heavy and their lips were stiffened to give them a haughty air.

"Welcome to Bee-Jor," Anand said. "I am Vof Quegdoth, the military commander of our new nation. Who am I addressing? And by what title?"

The men with staffs stepped aside to reveal a short and very round woman. She was dressed, like the others, in the usual bee camouflage, but her hair was thickened with a pale yellow paste, perhaps royal jelly, and piled in a mass of stiff curls above her head. She did not look at all like a royal personage except for the upward tilt of her nose and something like a scepter she cradled in her right arm. Nodding at Anand, she spoke in a sure but soft voice that resembled the humming of bee wings, as she used the words of the Carpenter Nation.

"I am zaz-Ladeekuz," said Ulatha, interpreting her words. "Of the Bulkokan Nation. These are my husbands: zuz-En, zuz-Andozep, zuz-Hoknayz, zuz-Opz, zuz-Spurjen and zuz-Mantaz."

"What does *zaz* and *zuz* mean?" Anand asked. "This must be a title of some kind."

Ulatha spoke with the woman, who nodded her head, confirming terms. "You are correct, Anand. *Zaz* is queen, *zuz* is king."

Anand bowed.

"Only six kings?" Daveena whispered.

"Bow, please, everyone," Anand commanded, trying not to smirk. "These are royalty, and will be treated as such."

Ladeekuz nodded, apparently satisfied by the acknowledgment of her status.

"Your Highness, we are honored that you have accepted our invitation to live in our nation as a free people," said Anand. "But we do need to discuss the place where you will establish your residence."

Ladeekuz frowned, pointed to the trees that were visible in the near north. "We cannot live here," she said through the interpreter. "Those trees are sick and ugly. We want a strong and beautiful tree, one that is mature but not too old, and close to other good trees to expand our nation."

"Those are but a few of the trees in Bee-Jor. This

mound of Palzhad is one of fifty-one. You could live on one of our mounds, near a tree. To live under one is unwise. Falling acorns might kill your people, and fallen leaves will smother their homes."

Ladeekuz and her husbands shook their heads, then spat when Ulatha finished her translation.

"We are not ground dwellers! We are tree people! And we would never live near an ant mound, much less on one."

"But from what I know of you, some Bulkokans lived on the ground and others lived in a tree above them—near your beehive—before you were taken as slaves into Hulkren."

"The Icanthix lived in the tree!"

"The Icanthix?"

"Our enslavers, our captors—the ones who forced us out of our tree palaces and down to the ground. We were grateful to the Hulkrites when they destroyed the Icanthix—grateful until the Termite worshippers forced us into a cage and informed us their Blind One had enslaved Goddess Bee and killed her consort, Grass Roach."

Anand was quiet as he watched Ladeekuz and her husbands relay the indignity of their history with faces both angry and sad.

"For how long were you under the rule of the Icanthix?"

"Two thousand four hundred and thirty-seven summers, and the sixteen days of autumn. Many more of us, deeper in Bulkoko, remain under Icanthic occupation. We will liberate all my subjects when the time is right."

Anand was quiet again. "Ulatha, let's please get a clarification. That seems an awfully long time."

Anand listened as Ladeekuz answered a series of short questions and then the two conferred over some counting beads on the chain around Ulatha's neck.

"Yes," said Ulatha, "she meant to say exactly that. For thousands of years, they have counted every day of their enslavement."

Anand was marveling at these people. Had he underestimated them? If what Ladeekuz said was true, they had sustained a tribal identity as captives of another culture for twenty-four centuries.

"Who are the Icanthix?" Anand asked.

"They resemble the Carpenter people with their greenish-brown skin and black hair. All of them are ignorant thieves, descended from primitive ant peoples—like these disgusting people who live among leaf-cutter ants and eat their awful mushrooms."

Anand watched as Ladeekuz pointed and scowled at the Palzhanites.

"Respectfully," Anand said. "Your Highness should know there are many kinds of ant peoples. Some of them are quite respectable."

Ladeekuz and her husbands had a good chuckle. "There are no respectable ant people," she said. "The rightful place of our tribe is in the trees that Goddess Bee gave to her Bulkokan people."

Anand thought a moment.

"Perhaps Your Highness and her people would wish to live in the northern part of our country, near our capital, Cajoria. We have trees just beyond that are strong and tall and younger than here in the South."

"Perhaps," said the queen, nodding.

"How long will your queen bee survive in that cage? It will be a journey of many days to arrive at Cajoria."

"As long as our egg-layer is tended to, she could survive for a moon or longer."

Anand turned over his shoulder and saw that the Palzhad caste of garment workers had arrived with sand-sleds full of proper, well-made tunics and gowns suitable to the merchants' castes.

"Very well," Anand said. "In order to journey through these lands, you will need to change your kin-scent. Our priests are preparing the baths. The garment makers of Palzhad have arrived with clothing we hope you will find comfortable and attractive."

Queen Ladeekuz made a sour face, conferred with her husbands.

"We will not wear the kin-scent of an ant."

"Well, of course you would need to," said Anand, frowning. "You cannot travel safely in leaf-cutter territory without adopting their kin-scent."

"We would sooner bathe in our own vomit than wear any ant's kin-scent."

"Madame," Anand said, then started over. "Your Majesty. Sand-coaches will be arriving shortly, drawn by leaf-cutter haulers, to bring you safely to your new home in comfort. But unless you are wearing leaf-cutter kin-scent, the hauling ants will slice you into pieces with the sharpest, most powerful mandibles of any ant on the Sand."

Ladeekuz conferred with her husbands again.

"We will never agree to this. What we will do is adopt roach-scent to repel these gruesome ants. This roach caravan will continue to haul us to our new home in the North."

Anand was quietly burning inside as he turned to Daveena. "I suppose we could contact the Pleps, who are at Mound Smax. With fresh roaches, the Pleps could take the Bulkokans north."

"Or we could call them out for the rude, arrogant bee-shits they are and kick their ample bottoms back into the Dustlands," whispered Daveena.

"Tempting," Anand whispered. "But Bee-Jor must have bee people."

Anand stood his tallest and managed a forced smile as he clasped his hands behind his back.

"Very well, Majesty. We will summon our Two Spirit, and bathe your people in as much roach-scent as we can gather today. It will help to abandon your clothing, as its hive-scent may be overwhelming and attract . . . night wasps and fleas. As well as ants."

"Agreed," said Ladeekuz. "But we will wear nothing derived from ants. I like what you're wearing, this cape of yours. You should give that to me. And we like these dyed and polished silks your roach people are wearing under their capes. We've heard you have a store of robes and skirts and jackets in your sleds' compartments to sell in the Seed Eaters' markets. We'll dress in those until you can make something specific for each of us. You can tell these ant people to take their filthy, polluted rags back to their wretched mound."

Anand's teeth were gritting as the translation was completed. "That's it!" he said, shouting. "All of these people—these *ant* people—have come here to welcome you, to see to your comfort!" Anand made a sweeping point to the Britasytes, to the Bee-Jorite guards, the priests of Palzhad, and the laborers who focused on him as his fury exploded. "These *ant* people—as *I* am also an ant person—defeated the Hulkrites and helped to free *you*. So at this time *you* and *your* people need to say something to *me* and to all of the roach and *ant people* here before we go one step further!"

Ladeekuz and her husbands stiffened in a fearful awe as the translation was completed. A squeak passed from her trembling lips as she shrugged her shoulders.

"What? What do you expect me to say?"

"You are going to say 'thank you.'"

Ladeekuz and her men looked to have been punched in the face by invisible hands.

"THANK YOU!" Anand shouted, which Ulatha shouted in turn. "You and all your people are going to *stand* and thank everyone here who risked their lives and shared their food and came to *your* aid—who welcomed *strangers* into *our* land. And if that doesn't interest you, you can walk back to Hulkren with my boot in your buttocks!"

The husband-kings huddled and whispered around Ladeekuz, who sobbed, shook her head, and had difficulty breathing. She signaled with the scepter in her chubby little hand to all her people that they were to rise. The Bulkokans were on their feet, looking humbled, and repeating, "Thank you," in their tongue as they nodded to the strangers around them. At that moment, a locust fell from the sky, landing nearby on a dead ranunculus flower. As the pilot patted the locust's head to keep it from flying off, a boy dressed in a messenger's tunic climbed out of the saddle and down the flower's stem to run towards Anand.

"Commander Quegdoth," he said, and bowed. "King Medinwoe anxiously awaits your return and relays his displeasure. He has summoned you and says it is best you return immediately to the capital, that it is urgent."

"Summoned me?" said Anand, feeling new flashes

of anger rolling up his spine to explode in his head. "Just what is his displeasure?"

"He did not relay it, Commander. He asked that you replace me as the rider on this locust if none were available—so that you could make haste."

"Please tell the king I . . . I am attending my own urgent business," Anand shouted, stifling his rage. "And I will join him at my earliest convenience." The messenger bowed, then climbed up the ranunculus to fly away.

"What's this urgent business of yours?" Daveena asked Anand with a whisper.

"Spending time with my wife."

Daveena smiled, squeezed his hand. He looked at her and was soothed but a moment later he noticed Queen Ladeekuz giving him a sideways stare as she muttered to her husbands.

"This all might have been a mistake," he said to Daveena.

CHAPTER 19

NEGOTIATIONS

Anand spent the afternoon with his wife in the privacy of the chieftain's sled where they engaged in lovemaking that was both tender and tentative. He had to lie on his back, and Daveena worked with the heaviness of her pregnancy. As mild as they had been with each other, he still endured the reopening of leg wounds. Once the caravan was ready, the two rode with Thagdag at the front of his sled to Mound Smax, where the Pleps were camped before their autumn venture to the mounds of the crippled Slope.

"The Pleps won't like being redirected back to Cajoria's north," said Daveena.

"I would rather they *were* venturing into the Slope—to be my eyes and ears," said Anand.

"How do you think it goes for the *sedites* in the West?" Thagdag asked. "Any signs they plan to conquer and reunite the Slope?"

"Not while they are taking back Gagumji from the Carpenter Nation," said Anand. "If the Beetle people know the Slopeish army is made up of old men, boys, and drunkards, they are planning on grabbing it all."

"If the Carpenters take over the Slope, Bee-Jor would be next," said Daveena.

"At some point we'll make it plain to the king in Gemurfa that a war on the Slope is a war on Bee-Jor," said Anand.

The moon was getting low and orange in the sky when the caravan reached Smax. Anand remembered it was somewhat more populated than Palzhad and more prosperous, with a deposit of green clay near its mound. He remembered his mother's treasured green bowls and jars from Smax, which were durable and decorated with the grooves from a craftsman's stylus. Lights were visible in the windows of the mound's lower rings, a heartening sign that commerce was expanding for all.

As the Entreveans approached the south end of the clearing set aside for Britasytes, they found the Pleps in the midst of a performance. Anand could see the spectacle was well attended, but something about the crowd was different. As the roach wranglers herded the insects into their pens for the night, he and Daveena pulled on hooded capes to hide themselves, and ventured towards the Pleps' stage.

"I know what's different," Daveena said, smiling as she sniffed the air. "Can you smell it?"

"Oh. Yes," said Anand, feeling surprised and a little worried. As they got closer to the crowd, they saw what their noses suspected: half the people, maybe more, were *women* and they were doused in too much perfume, a substance no longer forbidden to them. Unlike the men, the women had not come to the Britasytes' camp in disguise. Their faces were exposed and they were flaunting their new, if used, finery. All of them were entranced by the spectacle, but a few were in jealous contempt, folding their arms and frowning as they compared themselves to the women onstage. The happy ones were not just watching, but moving to the music and yelping, an indication that they had drunk the phantom-berry punch and were delirious from its touch of the Holy Mildew.

Jalinget, the clan's famed singer, belted out a new song that praised the Dawning of the Age of Locust as the dancers stripped their costumes to reveal skin covered in glow-paint. Anand was surprised when some women in the crowd imitated them and went as far as to remove the tops of their own clothes to shake their breasts. This angered, shocked, and intrigued the men nearby. Brothers, fathers, and caste kin turned on these women, shouting their reprimands and demanding modesty.

"This is what happens when we allow women out of the shelters at night," said an angry father when he saw his daughter. She was smiling, oblivious to his scolding as she danced. "Do you think we can find you a husband now that everyone has seen your nipples?"

"I think now you can find me a thousand husbands," she said before her father grabbed her ear and dragged her away.

The show neared its end when a large and ornate puppet of Locust the Sky God was pushed onstage. Some dancers climbed onto the puppet's back, and others grabbed handles on its massive rear legs. Tugging at a network of cords, the dancers made the effigy's wings spread and flap while the legs in the back were pumped up and down. Naked and bobbing atop the puppet, the women waved farewells, as mild explosions filled the stage with a sweet, thick mist that cleared to reveal an empty platform. Applause and cheers went on and on as the Britasyte merchants moved the stage's lights to the market stalls and the roach-drawn rides. A few lights went into the Tent of Forbiddens where the dancing beauties entered through the back to climb atop ladders and stand out of reach of admiring men. A few women of Smax, infected with curiosity, attempted to enter the tent, but were blocked by roach-men who refused their money.

Anand had only ever seen men browsing the night markets to find a trinket or some cloth to return home with; but now it was women who jammed the stalls, excitedly buzzing at their first opportunity to purchase these goods for themselves. "Just look at them," Daveena said as the women pressed in to the jewelry stalls, noisily shoving and snipping at each other. "Like a horde of locusts ravaging the barley." The jewelry sellers went on the defense, pulling away their trays of bangles and necklaces and shouting at the women to stand back. As the supply of jewelry grew smaller, the last few items were held overhead and auctioned to buyers shouting their bids. The rug weavers, cloth salesmen, and boot makers were almost as mobbed, and the sellers of honey and aphid crystals ran out of stock in an instant.

Anand's attention was drawn back to the Tent of Forbiddens when he saw some bee people, not quite bravely, making their way through the grounds. The eyes of the young Britasytes guarding the tent went wide with astonishment to see these chubby people dressed in stripes and fuzz jackets, clinging to each other as they took in their first carnival. They attempted to follow the Smaxans into the Tent of Forbiddens without paying. When they were rejected in a language they did not understand, they buzzed angrily, in their foreign tongue, but soon moved on to gape at the roach-drawn rides. They were most entranced to see people seated in little carriages rise up on the fungus-lit Pleasure Wheel, then dip back down.

Once Anand was sure a crisis had been averted, he and Daveena pushed through the mob to reach Chieftain Zedral inside his sled. "Permission to enter, Good Traveler," shouted Daveena at the curtained opening.

"Enter," said Zedral, and the two slipped through the curtains to see overflowing barrels of gold and silver pyrite, as well as chips of rose quartz. Much of the treasure had spilled onto the floor. The chieftain should have looked ecstatic to be surrounded by a wealth that could not be contained but his long, wrinkled face was as droopy as his mustache. To Anand, Zedral looked little different from when he had been rescued from Hulkren. He might never be plump and jolly again.

"Chieftain Zedral. You are rich for life," Anand said through a polite grin as he and Daveena removed their hoods.

"Anand! Good Roach Lord! We are honored. But surprised."

Daveena bowed her head to Zedral and, sensing his aches and pains, helped him to fill his barrels and then some buckets in the light of the cabin's torch.

"We should hide most of this treasure," the chieftain said. "Since we will have to rely on savings for the days ahead."

"Why do you say that, Chieftain? It should only get better," said Anand.

"Not for everyone. This edict of yours, allowing Slopeish laborers to make and trade their own goods, has been a boon for them. But now that they conduct their own markets, they will have no need for ours. It won't be long before they have instruments to make their own music, and before their women will dance in their own shows. Their craftsmen are already making their own jewelry—copies of ours."

Anand was quiet. What Zedral said stirred up worries.

"They can't craft like we can," said Daveena to fill the silence. "And we still have markets in the pine and barley countries."

"Perhaps. But the sedites have less fear and awe of us. We are losing our . . . our . . ."

"Mystery," Anand said.

"They are still quite in awe of my husband," said Daveena.

"This man they think of as a demigod," said Zedral. "Someday they'll know he is just a boy from a wandering roach tribe."

"Permission to enter," said a voice outside, and Anand and Daveena resumed their hoods as the chieftain's nephews entered the sled. "Do we have any more sweets?"

Zedral went to the wall chest at the back of the sled and took out some net-bags full of amber-colored crystals.

"This is the last of the dried honey," he said. "And

we've no more aphid sugar. I'll keep this last bag for ourselves."

The boys disappeared with the bags. Outside the sled, Anand heard the clamor of the crowd. Another auction began and the crowd shouted what they would pay or trade for the crystalized honey.

"I think that for some of us," Zedral said, "our days as wanderers may be at an end. That someday, we too will want to live in houses and be . . ."

"Sedites?" Daveena said, not hiding her disgust.

"Settled," said Zedral. "Able to wander, yes, but able to live in a house among . . . settled people." Zedral looked at them under heavy lids and they heard his breathing. "I must admit . . . I am weary of journeys. Shouldn't the Britasytes who fought in the war have the chance to live in a house on a mound, safe from the rains, with rooms warmed by the sun in winter?"

"If such houses were available to them," said Anand, after giving it some thought. He imagined Britasytes becoming neighbors to Slopeites, a people who had feared and hated them for centuries. A wave of apprehensions soured his stomach.

"Perhaps some Britasytes might settle in Palzhad, which is still so empty," Anand said.

"What would you do for work?" asked Daveena.

"Whatever ant people do—or perhaps, what they *don't* want to do. Like raise roaches, whose products they need."

The three of them were silent. Anand imagined

that Daveena and Zedral, like he himself, were pondering a future where Britasytes no longer roamed. It was a thought that was bright and hopeful, and at the same time saddening.

"You have come here for a reason," said the chieftain to Anand.

"I am asking your clan to go north with the bee people, and help them establish a new tree-home."

"Anand . . . we were headed to the mounds of the Old Slope where their priests and merchants are anxious for our goods. If the Entreveans have brought these bee people this far, they should continue with them."

"The Entreveans are depleted. Many of their roaches died in Hulkren—in what is becoming the Dustlands again," said Anand.

"We have always known the Dustlands are not good for our insects," said Zedral. "Something in that dust sickens them."

"When they recover, the Entreveans can assume your route in the Slope. In the meantime, we need to establish these Bulkokans . . . . if we are to have honey in a country called Bee-Jor."

Zedral was quiet, then stroked his mustache in thought. He looked at the last bag of honey crystals.

"How do these Bulkokans expect to build a home at the top of a tree?"

"I don't know. But perhaps by summer we will have some honey. Cheap honey."

Zedral was quiet again, his eyes darting back and forth.

"If it is our labor that brings these bee people to the North and helps them build their home, are we not—under your edict—entitled to the fruits of that labor?"

Anand exhaled loudly through his nose. "It would be the Bulkokans' honey."

"And their wax and propolis and bee-meat and eggs," said Daveena.

"But we would be entitled to their products' second sale and have exclusive rights to their transport across Bee-Jor," said Zedral. "And the other lands."

"Yes."

"And we would have a right to occupy homes on Mound Palzhad."

"Abandoned homes, yes."

"And on Cajoria—if we are to be near these bee people."

Anand hesitated. *Cajoria has enough housing disputes.*

"Ten homes on Cajoria."

"Fifty."

"Fifteen."

"Twenty-five."

"Twenty. No more."

"Twenty, it is. By Madricanth, I swear to uphold these terms," said Zedral.

"As do I," said Anand, "by Madricanth."

The two used their hands to make the sign of the Roach's six legs before rubbing their antennae to secure the agreement.

He thinks he got the better end of that deal, thought Anand. *But he's yet to meet the Bulkokans.*

When Anand and Daveena stepped outside, they saw that the crowd had turned away from the stalls and the tent. The Smaxans were staring at the bizarre sight of exotic beings in bee garb spinning on the Pleasure Wheel. The Bulkokans were utterly quiet, intrigued yet frightened, dizzy and sick as they went around and around . . . which is exactly how Anand felt at the moment.

This is a mistake. I'm not sure how. But I shouldn't have brought these bee people here.

chambers at night—so he has one less worry while he governs this mess."

"I can't live in that palace. Not if *she's* there."

"There are four palaces. You would never have to see her. Think about it. I have to fly home and figure out the next five hundred crises."

Anand went to hug and kiss her, but she felt stiff in his arms and would not pucker her pouting mouth. He stepped out of the sled to find his guards waiting for him on the ground below, when Daveena burst through the curtains and yanked him back to become a shaking, bawling mess in his arms. "I'm going west with the Entreveans," she managed to say. "After we trade at Venaris."

"Well, of course you are," he said and sighed.

The guards below looked away as the two rocked in each other's arms. "Come, men," Anand finally said, pulling away from her. "Let's fly home."

That afternoon, Anand did not fly directly to the top of Mound Cajoria, then rush to meet Medinwoe. He ordered the pilot to land at the locust cages on the mound's outskirts, where they could return the insect to be fed and watered for later use. After that, he took a leisurely bath to get rid of some roach-scent, and it was evening when he and his guard finally took an ant train up the main artery. Instead of going straight to the throne room, he went to his bedchamber to check on his father. A messenger was waiting at the door.

"Commander, you are expected in the throne room. Queen Polexima is there with King Medinwoe. They have been waiting."

"Please tell the king he is invited here, to my bed-chamber, where he and Polexima may join me for dinner. Let them know I am looking after my father."

The messenger nodded and ran off. Anand went to Yormu, who was sitting up in a bed positioned to give him a view down the mound through the quartz window.

"How are you, Dad?" Anand asked. Yormu smiled, then bobbed his head from side to side—his way of saying he could not complain.

"Healing up all right?"

Yormu nodded.

"You must be bored," Anand said, and Yormu bobbed his head again.

"I wish you could tell me how I might better help," Anand said. Then he was struck with a thought.

"Messenger!" he called to the runners waiting near the door. The first in the queue trotted up. "Go to the stores of the priests and ask one for a dust-box and a stylus. Please."

Polexima and her acolytes arrived at Anand's bed-chamber at the moment the torch makers were leaving after lighting the room, and the kitchen workers had arrived to set out the evening meal. She saw

Anand seated next to a dark-skinned man on a raised bed with a dust-box on his lap.

"Now you try," Anand said, and gave the man the stylus. As Polexima came nearer, she saw Anand had drawn his Dranverish letters into the dust. He was expecting the man in bed to replicate the simple drawings in the space below, but he set the stylus down when he noticed Polexima. He dropped his head, went suddenly still.

"Polly, good to see you," Anand said.

"I am glad for your safe return, Anand."

"This is my father, Yormu."

Yormu did not look at her.

"He is not rude," Anand said. "One sheriff took his teeth. Another took his tongue. Together they took his speech."

Polexima shook her head and felt shame. "And why would they do that?"

"I have never known. It happened before he met my mother. But perhaps one day, through writing, he might be able to tell us."

At that, Yormu raised his head to look at Anand and seemed intrigued. He turned to the dust-box, picked up the stylus, and replicated the figures.

"What does that say?" Polexima asked.

"It spells his name."

"Yormu," she said. "I am pleased to meet you, Yormu. You must be very proud of your son."

Yormu nodded his head, kept his eyes, which she could see were watering, down.

"Dad, you should meet her eyes, please," said Anand. "It is rude not to look someone in the face when you speak to them. Even your queen."

Yormu lifted his face and looked at Polexima and nodded. She saw that his earlobe was clipped, and felt the mild wave of revulsion she had felt all her life when encountering dark-skinned workers. *I must overcome this,* she scolded herself. *For this man's son is no one's inferior.*

"Here's how you write 'Polexima,'" Anand said, taking the box to scratch eight simple figures in its fine powder. He extended the box and the stylus to her where she attempted to re-create the scratchings.

"When do Dranverites learn to read?" she asked when she finished.

"When they are children."

"Children!"

"Yes. Children don't work in Dranveria. They learn all day, and read books in buildings called schools."

"They must have many eunuchs."

"None whatsoever. They are called *teachers* and they are the most valued members of Dranverish society. All of them wear purple robes and live in fine houses. Half of them are women."

"How would we get schools here?"

"Schools are the easy part. The real trouble is finding the teachers."

"King Medinwoe has arrived," shouted one of the guards, and the Dneepers' leader entered with several of his men, bowlegged from the bandages around their legs. Anand stood. Medinwoe used a cane as he limped towards Anand, averting his eyes. His nephew, Prince Tappenwoe, was hobbling in on crutches and openly scowling. As Polexima turned to greet them, they bowed towards her as deeply as was possible.

"King Medinwoe. Our sympathies . . . for your suffering," she said. "We believe we have determined the source of these insidious mites."

"Thank you, Majesty," Medinwoe said. "Night wasps are to be avoided at all costs for several reasons. But I must state plainly that we should have been informed about this possibility."

"You should have," Anand said. "But we did not know this *was* a possibility."

"But *you* had ridden on a night wasp before," said the king. "*You* who taught us."

"I did. And I did not get infested my first time. You have my deepest apologies," Anand said. "And I am deeply sorry about this attack on your men in the Dustlands. Please let us know what we can do to aid your recovery and it will be done."

"There is something," said Medinwoe.

"I'm listening. Have a seat, please," said Anand,

pointing to a table and chairs. "I believe all of us will be more comfortable seated upright at a table."

"We are not eating," Medinwoe said.

"King Medinwoe," said Polexima. "I think all of us with our weak legs should take a chair."

"We are comfortable standing, if you please."

She noticed that he made eye contact with her but not with Anand. They had completely ignored Yormu.

"All right," said Anand. "Let's speak plainly. What is it we can do for you?"

"The Promised Clearing. *Our* Promised Clearing, south of Palzhad, is occupied by Hulkrites."

"It is occupied by refugees from what was Hulkren," Anand said. "Few, if any of them, would call themselves Hulkrites."

"He is right," said Polexima. "Nearly all of them were slaves or captives—as I myself was a captive slave in Hulkren."

"Whoever they are, they are occupying the land you promised us. And from what we have seen of them, many, if not most, are impure."

"Impure?" said Anand, bristling.

"At least half of them are dark-skinned, some so dark they reflect the blue of the sky. People of Ledack, Sathrevo, Pellicosta, and elsewhere."

Polexima looked at Anand as his eyes slitted and his nostrils flared.

"They may be dark or light," said Polexima, "but all of them suffered under the Hulkrites."

"These people are here because of the mission *that one* sent us on," said Medinwoe, pointing at Anand. "A mission that endangered our lives and turned these slaves into starving derelicts after we killed their food source—the ghost ants and their regurgitation. It is good we never completed this mission, or even more of these refugees would be swarming here from even further south."

"Would you rather these refugees remained in Hulkren, to suffer and die?" Polexima asked.

"Would they suffer and die? From what we saw, the ghost ants provided everything for them," said the king. "They are coming here because they think this place is a land of leisure, drink, and honey."

"The refugees are coming here because they can't go home or have no home left," said Anand. "And if left with colonies of living ghost ants, *these people* of the Dustlands would build new armies to start new wars."

Medinwoe was quiet. "Your Bee-Jor is a place for people of any color," he finally said in Anand's direction. "Am I correct?"

"You are," said Anand.

"If you can't send these people back to where they came from, then let them settle here."

"We can't possibly accept them all," said Anand.

"What *we* will not accept is letting *these people* squat on our land, which has been set aside for the yellow-skinned. You made us a promise, Commander

Quegdoth. We have sacrificed much and expect as much."

Polexima looked at Anand and saw a mirror of her growing rage. "So I would be welcomed to visit your Promised Clearing," she said.

"Of course, Majesty."

"But Commander Quegdoth would not be."

"Why would he want to come there? The descendants of Locust have their own land, a place where the dark-skinned can be among their own kind."

"Regardless of their skin color, all men and women are my own kind," said Anand.

"Then you will gladly welcome in these refugees."

"King, there is plentiful open space south of the border weeds," said Anand. "You could have all of that land and more."

"You know and I know that the lands you speak of are the Dustlands. And as we have learned, they are not hospitable to our roaches."

"Medinwoe . . . we are a new nation, struggling at the moment," said Polexima. "We are not ready to absorb uncountable people who do not speak our language or know our ways."

"Understood. Then send them back or put them somewhere. Or put them out of their misery. If you like, we can drive them back."

Polexima gritted her teeth as she gripped her staff and willed herself not to use its blunt end to fracture Medinwoe's skull. Anand no longer attempted to hide his feelings, and his face was tightened with rage.

"We are awaiting a response," said Medinwoe as a messenger arrived, waited to be acknowledged.

"You agreed to exterminate all the ghost ants of Hulkren at all their mounds," said Polexima. "Did you not?"

Medinwoe hesitated.

"We did, Your Majesty."

"And you also promised me the safe return of my babies left in Dneep."

Medinwoe was quiet. "Yes."

"Your bravery is celebrated and your dutifulness is admirable," said Polexima. "And much appreciated by me. You will have your Promised Clearing and Commander Quegdoth will have his extermination of the ghost ants. And I will have the return of my babies, which, I am sure, are being well taken care of."

Medinwoe looked at her and then Anand, a quizzical look on his face.

"We assume you will resume these missions when you have recovered," Polexima added. "After that we will have a more substantive conversation about your compensation."

"How many mounds in the Dustlands have active ghost ants?" Anand asked Medinwoe.

"From the map you drew for us, I remember there were two, maybe three, we did not reach in the extremes of the South. We left our roaches there, to die. We will need new ones."

"Roaches are something I can provide," said Anand.

"Your Majesty," said the messenger boy, bowing to Polexima as he gingerly came closer. "I bring you sad news from Palzhad. Your mother, Queen Clugna, is very ill. The priests do not believe she will be with us much longer. If she is still with us."

"Good gods," said Polexima, and her legs turned to water.

"I'm so sorry, Polly," Anand whispered.

"So am I," said Polexima. "Commander Quegdoth, I'm afraid this means we've got another problem on our southern borders—a very great problem."

CHAPTER 21

A DAY OF ECSTASY

A few days after his arrival, Pleckoo awoke to find the Palzhanites even slower to leave their hammocks. The women were humming or singing to themselves as they laid out the most elaborate breakfast yet, which included a barrel-jar marked with a crisscross of grooves to indicate its contents.

"Fermentation? At breakfast?" he said to Glip's wife, then regretted the scolding tone in his voice.

"It's a day off," she said.

"Off of what?"

"From work. Good eighth."

"Good . . . eighth."

"You can call me Naloti."

"But you are another man's wife."

"I didn't say I would sleep with you. I said you could call me by my name."

Pleckoo was astonished by her good-natured rudeness, and even more so by this idea of a "day off" as he pulled himself out of his hammock. When he went outside, he saw others in the dew-spattered weeds, where they gathered drinking water, washed their faces and hands, and happily chatted. "Good eighth," they wished him, and smiled.

When he stepped back into the house, he saw honey crystals at each setting on the perimeter of the breakfast leaf. The wall shrines were opened and glittering with new encrustations of the jewels traded at the markets. The statue of Anand on his wasp had been given a little necklace of chunky jewels, which Pleckoo thought made him look both effeminate and ill-prepared for war—and it made Pleckoo smile. He was tying on his face kerchief when Moosak approached him with a stick of skin paint, and he felt circles being drawn on his forehead. When he went to the little clip of a silver beetle wing the family had for a mirror, he saw a pattern that reminded him of rain ripples in a puddle. He folded the kerchief to hide only his nose so that others could see his smile.

As the family took its seats, Naloti and Glip used little scrapers to dip into the barrel-jar, and then inserted a drop under the tongues of all the adults. Pleckoo received his drop and felt a minor irritation as he let the liquor linger on the floor of his mouth. From the grassy taste, he worried this was an infusion of cannabis, an herb that the Prophet Tahn forbade as it made a warrior passive and stupid.

"*Creet-creet,*" someone shouted through the door, and Pleckoo saw men outside the house hauling a sand-sled that carried a little sun-kiln. Naloti reached into the side of her garment and took out a thin rectangle of rose quartz, then went out the door and returned with a loaf of fresh mushroom bread wrapped in a basil leaf. "Eat while it's warm," she said, and all tore into it. Pleckoo tasted a mix of mushrooms in the rich, bubbly paste, and thought it the best thing he had ever eaten until he sampled the other foods before him. The fermentation was having a quick effect, but something else was flowing through him and freeing him, finally, from the crushing pains of the Great Loss. He closed his eyes for a moment to experience a moment of purest bliss. He did not see darkness, but a living weaving of worms that unraveled to reveal a crimson sky, where jewel-colored moons bounced on the horizon. Ants, beetles, and humans were all crawling to the moons, and when they captured them, they sat on top of them to bounce up to star nymphs that reached out with sparkling hands to catch and tickle the riders in the ribs.

Pleckoo opened his eyes and laughed. At first, the laugher hurt, and he slapped his chest as if to dislodge something trapped for ages inside it. Around the leaf, the others were looking at him, smiling in approval, some echoing his laughter.

"Must be his first time," said Glip.

"But not his last," said Naloti, and everyone laughed. Pleckoo looked around the leaf as the family smiled at each other, touching each other's arms or legs as they commented on the food and the drink. He was fascinated by the hands and nails of the old woman across from him, which had a delightful way of flaring outwards as she picked up her food. The sleeves of her garment contained a world of beauty within them, including the fibers of the material as well as the variations of their dyes. The movement of her arm to her mouth was captivating, as well as the rolling motion of her lips as she chewed.

Returning to his food, Pleckoo picked up a honey crystal and looked inside it to see brilliant lights racing inside its facets, like the play of children. The crystal, he was sure, had dropped from the sun into his hands, and felt warm and comforting and pleasantly sticky. Inside of his mouth, he felt a lake of cool water and as he extended his tongue to lick the crystal; it felt like some great, happy grub reaching out of the earth to savor the sunshine.

When his tongue and the crystal connected, the sweetness was so intense it left him shaking. He closed his eyes and found himself on the back of a bee, on a saddle between its four wings. It flew him to a vast, globe-shaped hive where honey makers with stripes in rainbow colors marched in circles to make a living tapestry. The hive's six-sided cells overflowed with honey, which fell in soft drops to the mouths of a throng of fervent worshippers who dance-prayed on the ground below. The hives' layers unfolded to reveal the Bee Goddess, who shone bright, then brighter until She had become the Rising Sun.

Pleckoo opened his eyes and the vision was gone; but the crystal was still in his hand. He looked around to see others were biting their honey, crunching it with their back teeth, and making sounds that were almost sexual as they acknowledged the extreme pleasure. Part of him wanted to go off on his own with his sweets and lick them in solitude, to devote the rest of his life to this one activity. When he realized this would never be possible, it struck him as enormously funny that he could not eat sweets all day, and he laughed without constraint. As his diaphragm ached from laughing too hard, he looked from side to side and saw that no one was offended or even thought it strange.

The conversation and the laughter was growing louder, and as he looked at everyone's faces, their eyes seemed larger and brighter and deeply beautiful. Daring, for the first time, he looked directly on the faces of the women. Never before had he seen middenites who were so thoroughly adorned; but never before had he realized the physical beauty of his own caste. Under their wraps of bright cloth, he could see the studs of jewels the women wore in their ears and noses, and could glimpse the hair they had washed, perfumed, and parted in the middle. He imagined the loose wave of this hair when it was freed to swing over their lithe, arching backs, and then he imagined the rest of their bodies, which had to be taut and firm from heavy labors.

An old curiosity was roused: what did low-caste Slopeish women look like when they were naked? He should have known since he was born from one, but nudity was forbidden on the Slope. He imagined their breasts were perfectly orb-like and had thick, up-turned nipples. He wanted to know, then felt like he *had* to know, as he imagined their chests tapering to thin wasp waists with sweet navels, where he could insert a pinky, and below that would be a soft, fragrant patch of fine, curly hair and, under it, the trench of sweet fire.

His mind turned to that sweetness—to the hot and wet sensation of a woman who wanted a man inside her. He felt a climbing under his tunic and realized he had an erection, the first he had experienced in so many sexless days. His elbow dropped to conceal his arousal when Glip clapped his hands and stood as a sign that they were leaving. The men exited first, followed by the boys.

As Pleckoo stepped out the door he took a slow, shy glance at the women behind him, including Glip's daughters. Both were of marrying age and they chatted and giggled as they rolled up the leaf. Being noseless at Cajoria meant a life on the outskirts of the midden as a pitiable bachelor. Was it the same in Palzhad, or would these women overlook it? So many of these men had been deformed by violence, some recently in their war with the Hulkrites. Glip's oldest daughter was a true beauty, tall and confident, who could marry above her caste; but her younger sister had chubby cheeks that looked as if they were storing food. Her cheeks made her tiny mouth look even tinier, but she was still possessed of large shining eyes and her body was plump yet well proportioned. Pleckoo imagined she might be grateful to have his attention.

When he pushed through the door's flap, he stepped out into an intense sunshine that candied everything it touched. Whatever he had imbibed—probably cannabis—it made him unsure of his legs. The world seemed unsteady as he took a few steps, then realized he had to find his own feet. Once he did, he was walking—this amazing ability to move with legs instead of sit like a stone. What a fantastic thing! As he watched the walking men ahead of him, he thought it astounding that each of them did it so differently. Some of the men had a strange, comic stride and others had a grace and fluid strength. Some men, crippled in the war—*a war that I waged against them!*—walked with an evident pain that was heroic and beautiful. At that moment, Pleckoo was humbled.

These men of Bee-Jor, and even some of their women, had risked their lives and fought against Hulkrites to live in what they called the New Way.

The middenite men from other houses were joining them with their women following close behind. But something had changed in the separation of sexes; the women were not completely divided from the men, but followed them closely and called and joked with them as they walked ahead. As all of them moved forward, Pleckoo had to will himself not to turn and look at the females; this cannabis had revealed to him how magnificently beautiful they had always been. Regardless, he knew it was still not acceptable to look openly at a woman other than one's own wife or mother, and only in private. That much had not changed on the Slope—or Bee-Jor if they wanted to call it that.

Pleckoo was unsure of where they were headed but he did not care—he just wanted to keep going, to take in the unending beauty of Palzhad and of the very world itself. They arrived at a ring of houses three above their own—different castes were going to mingle! This ring of dwellings had finer houses and a larger outdoor shrine. Near it was a pyramid-shaped structure under construction, which had the beginnings of some strange markings carved into its top layer. Next to the shrine was its idols keeper, who pulled a cord attached to a tower with a carillon of wooden bells that sounded different pitches.

A priestly sled arrived and out of it came one of the old Palzhanite priests and his acolyte—a dark-skinned young man!—who nodded to the idols keeper, then struggled up the steps of the pyramid. When the two reached the top, the people quieted as the acolyte unrolled the scroll. The priest looked on the scroll's drawings and then began his recitation. "These are the eight essential laws of Bee-Jor from which all other laws will descend," the priest shouted. When he had finished reading, he returned to the ground and nodded to the idols keepers before reentering his sled.

These laws and their reciting are the work of Anand, Pleckoo realized. He had a memory of Anand as a boy of ten summers who had followed him everywhere and looked up at him with awe and admiration when he had performed feats of strength or killed attacking mosquitoes by ripping out their needles from their faces. And Anand had always thanked him, quietly, with tearful bows of the head when Pleckoo had protected him from the taunts, fists, and knives of the other boys who hated him for being the darker-skinned roach boy.

And now Anand wants to protect all the abused of the Slope with his laws. As Pleckoo pondered this he felt a chill down his spine and then stiffness in his chest as a wave of warm feelings overwhelmed him—it was love for his little cousin. Pleckoo feared he would start crying like a woman and forced himself back to the present, to the beautiful new world around him.

He watched as Glip went to greet the foreman of this upper ring, a man wearing a large mite-scraper around his neck that was painted locust-blue. Glip smiled, and presented the foreman with a barrel-jar that likely contained more of what had been drunk that morning.

Behind the shrine was a series of tall, vertical drums and scattered around these on the ground were smaller percussion instruments. The man with the kerchief who Pleckoo had dubbed Silent Cricket handed him a hollow, stoppered seed that sounded as if it had ground sand inside it. Following Silent's example, Pleckoo raised it over his head and approached the shrine and shook it as an offering to the gaudy idols. Some of the altar's idols were being bathed, scented, and freshly dressed before they were returned to the altar. Among them was a newer one, a carved likeness of his cousin as the demigod Quegdoth set before the chubby moon idol, Glowing Mushroom. They had depicted him with dark purple skin and astride a night wasp that no longer looked like a fierce demon, but carried a look of submission and defeat. *Is Anand really a divine being?* Pleckoo wondered. *Since we are related—does that make me divine too?*

Looking at the idol of Quegdoth, Pleckoo felt envy, a deep wound, and a tug back to the mass of suffering that had followed his failure to take the Slope. He shook his head hard to release those ugly thoughts and felt them fly out of his ears like a swarm of midges. His vision blurred and doubled, and when it cleared he saw the idols keepers facing each other to blow on their thorn horns. The horn's sharp blasts pulverized the last remnant of dark feelings inside Pleckoo. He was ready to celebrate.

A man began drumming and others followed his beats or pounded their own to blend with it. Though he was given no instruction, Pleckoo shook his seed as he wanted. The rhythms intertwined and grew like a pleasant, flowering vine to a place in the sky where all Bee-Jorites could dance in a spiral up the leaves, and join the gods in their tree palace. When he looked over at the women, he saw they were spinning, with their colorful skirts spreading and rippling, like whirling flowers. Pleckoo wept happily to realize he had somehow ended up in Paradise without dying—*I am here!*

As he looked up and into the sky, all the gods of his youth were standing as giants in a circle around him. Termite reached out the middle of His six arms to join His hands with Grasshopper and Ant Queen. And then, the black and lovely Goddess Cricket approached the other gods in a cloak that trailed the star-spattered night behind Her. When She arrived, the other gods bowed to Her.

It was late afternoon when Pleckoo awoke inside the vast twig and leaf tent that had been erected for the day. He tried to remember the moment of exhaustion

when he put down his seed and left the round of chanting and dancing. As he lay with the other men on rag
rugs, the women filtered through to hand out cones of
liquid. Pleckoo slurped it, and tasted a touch of honey
and some kwondle bark extract that he knew would
revive him.

When he stepped outside, he looked out to his
right to see boys and girls were riding on ants for no
reason other than pleasure. They were visiting with
other children who were of higher castes and better
dressed—some were even wearing royal yellow. On
his left, he saw Naloti and the other women preparing the evening's feast. The main course was hairy
yellow scorpions that had been baked in the sun-kilns.
Their stingers and venom glands were in a vat that
Little Grinner was hauling back to the midden. Glip
and Silent Cricket arrived to help the women with the
strenuous task of cutting into the scorpion shells. "Give
us a hand, Vleeg," Glip shouted to him, and Pleckoo
picked up a handsaw, which he used to break open
the hard claws and tail segments to release their firm,
sweet meat. His stomach grumbled when he remembered the delicious taste of scorpion flesh, something
which had a good chew. When the chest cavities were
opened, the women scooped out the gray tomalley,
which they thinned with barley beer for a sauce.

"Have you ever eaten scorpions?" asked Glip.

"Yes," said Pleckoo.

"Really? Where?"

"In Hulkren."

"In *Hulkren*? *You* have been in Hulkren?"

Pleckoo panicked, tried to contain his breathing. Above his face kerchief, he saw Silent Cricket furrow his brow and squint in suspicion.

"I ate them once . . . with the Britasytes . . . on the way from Gagumji. The *scorpions* were from Hulkren."

"They are a special treat," Glip said after a pregnant moment. "Even better tasting after imbibing the divine leaf."

"Divine leaf," Pleckoo repeated. "Cannabis."

"That's one name for it. It's a gift from Goddess Cricket, whose children are very fond of it themselves. It's what makes crickets so happy that they sing through the night. Tonight, offer your drop to Cricket before sucking it up, and She will bless you with the most intensely holy experience. Look, here they are now."

"Who?"

"The priestesses of Cricket."

Pleckoo watched as women with shaved heads and long, floating antennae passed through the crowd and to the shrine, where they brought scent-offerings of evening primrose in soaked wadding to set before the idol they resembled. The priestesses were wearing rough, grass tunics with a back end that resembled the three-pronged tail of a cricket, with its thorny egg-laying pipe in the middle. Attached to the back of their ankles were two large false legs that rose and fell with their movements and completed the illusion of a cricket walking upright. Some distance behind them was a taller, light-skinned eunuch with a noble bearing; he wore layers of diaphanous gowns and a tiny jar of something around his neck. He had a kind smile in a plump face, and nodded to all over his clasped hands. His embroidered sleeves draped to the ground, and his hair was powdered a garish pink and cut to look like a spiderling riding on his head. As he passed, the people were not reverent, but cheering and applauding.

"Who is . . . he? A priest?"

"You are in for the best treat yet, Vleeg. That is Brother Moonsinger from Mound Loobosh, the seat of learning. Moonsinger is blessed by Goddess Moth with the gift of storytelling. And tonight he will recount the glorious victory of Commander Quegdoth and the People's Army against the Hulkrites and their leader, Pleckoo of Hulkren, a middenite from Cajoria."

CHAPTER 22

LIES OF A EUNUCH

Pleckoo wanted to touch his face to make sure he was still wearing his kerchief, then felt it flapping from his heavy breathing. He worried he could not hide his reaction to Glip's mention of his real name. Silent Cricket was giving him the sideways glare. With no idea of what to say, Pleckoo continued to work.

"Are you all right, Vleeg?"

"Yes. I'll take care of these," Pleckoo said, motioning to the pile of baked scorpions. Silent and Vleeg cocked their heads.

"We'll help you," Glip asked. "That's a lot of work."

"No. Hard work will do me some good."

"Not too hard. It's the eighth." Glip and Silent shrugged and walked off.

Pleckoo poured his rage and fear into his sawing and snapping of the scorpions' corpses. His arms ached from the difficult work, and he found himself grunting and cursing under his breath, and hoping that the others would mistake his tears for sweat. When Naloti and the women returned to scrape out the meat from the opened shells, they seemed pleased and astonished. "You've worked hard, Vleeg," she said.

"What else needs doing?"

"Our sun-kiln needs cleaning," she said. "But it's hot, messy work and . . ."

"Gladly," he said. "Bring me what's needed."

The kiln was dragged on its runners to the shade and Pleckoo pulled out its opening panel and entered its dome of refractory crystals. It was still very warm inside as he broke open pods full of soap-weed liquid. He took a rough thorn brush to scrub the scabby remains of burnt creatures from the oven's floor, stinking with rancid oils. When he was sure no one could hear him, he shouted at the resistant dirt and whispered the round of Hulkro's names to calm himself. When he emerged from the oven, the others stared at him and he knew he must look grimy and mad as he stood over a pile of greasy scrapings. Woozy with exhaustion, he slumped and fell but was quickly picked up by others who righted him. Moozak, without a grin, handed him a water bag as the carillon summoned the people to the evening feast. "Come on, uncle, drink," he said. "Lean on me if you need."

Pleckoo shook his head, then stood his tallest and walked to the tent with his chin up. It was crowded and noisy inside what was called "an eighth day tabernacle." The people cheered when the idols from the shrine were brought in and set on a tiered altar where glow-fungus in kettles was positioned to illuminate them against a backdrop of the moon deity. The idol of Cricket was saved for last, brought in on a glittering litter, and set on the altar's tallest pedestal. The idols keepers were on both sides of the altar, waving perfumed leaf fans as the worshippers seated themselves.

As Pleckoo took a seat at the leaf for the middenites, he was joined by Mlor and Kelvap, who nodded to him on each side. Silent Cricket sat next to Mlor, acknowledging Pleckoo with a faint nod. He realized they must have made a vaguely strange sight, the four of them, hiding their faces with kerchiefs. Once all were seated around the leaf, Naloti and Glip circled it to dispense the evening's drop of cannabis liquor. Following the example of the others, Pleckoo took the flat knife with its drop and raised it up to the idol of Cricket before he tucked it under his tongue. *I hope it's strong,* he thought as he felt the drop burn, *and will deafen me to what I might hear this evening.* The taste of this drop was stronger, more bitter, and he quickly felt its effects. His worries did not go away but expanded and consumed him. Soon he felt he had lost control of both his body and his mind.

When he looked at the others around the table, as they happily discussed what they were about to eat, he thought them all odd and ugly. When Kelvap turned to him, Pleckoo found his eyes to be monstrous and bulging, like those of a yellow jacket wasp. "Got us a real feast tonight," Kelvap said. "We heard you was hard at work cracking open them scorpion shells."

"Yes . . . I . . . I was," said Pleckoo, unable to think of anything to say. He imagined that under his kerchief, Kelvap's mouth had serrated mandibles and he was going to use them to tear out everyone's throats. Pleckoo's limbs felt suddenly heavy and his mouth felt impossibly dry; how could he eat when he felt like this? His bottom felt the heaviest, as if it had turned into a rock he could not lift.

The crowd cheered when platters of the prepared scorpions were carried through the tabernacle, then presented to the idols before their distribution to the crowd. Pleckoo was handed a generous amount of the meat, which had been cut into chunks, mixed with a sauce, and then returned to a piece of the shell it had come from. The others were delighted by what was given them, but the more Pleckoo stared at it, the more the meat looked like a strange and ugly mess that stank from sour beer. The pieces seemed to be moving, and for a moment he was sure they were a mass of tiny maggots squirming over and through each other, about to crawl out of the shell and up his arm.

He forced himself to eat, but as he looked around the leaf, the middenites' conversation seemed too loud, and the words were a pelting to his ear. They had worn their best clothes—the castoffs of merchants—but the beauty of them only heightened the ugliness of the wearer. The quick movements of the women's hands and arms resembled black-widow spiders as they crawled around their messy webs, waiting for husbands they would devour after mating. The men's arms looked all too much like the legs of the hairy and hideous corpse-flies, which gathered around middens and rubbed their front claws as they prayed for a meal of rotting flesh. As Pleckoo looked at the circle of faces, he was convinced that they were nothing but low-caste creatures who were ridiculous if they aspired to be anything other than laborers in service to the highly born.

"Vleeg, how goes it?" Glip shouted at him. "Need another drop?"

Pleckoo shook his head. "No. This spirit is . . . too powerful."

"You have been fucked by thunder," Glip said, and everyone laughed. Never before had laughter sounded like a beating to the skull with mallets.

"Drink," Glip said, pushing a bowl towards him with a doming drop. "It's just water. Now breathe deeply, in and out, and it will cast out your dread."

Pleckoo took a good suck of water and breathed as deeply as he could, but it did not calm him. As he inhaled, the whole world seemed to expand and distort, and as he exhaled it shrank and shriveled. It seemed like several long nights before the feast was consumed, but finally, someone took away his uneaten portion. The crowd quieted as the priestesses of Cricket appeared at the tabernacle's entrance and made their way to the altar, sounding their chirp harps with the rise and fall of their false hind legs. The Palzhanite High Priestess of Cricket was last to appear. When she reached the altar, she bowed to her favorite idol, then turned to face the crowd. Her acolytes surrounded her, facing in the positions of the Four Directions.

"All kneel," she said, and the crowd went to their knees. Pleckoo felt humiliated to join them in this disturbing position.

"All hail Goddess Cricket," she shouted up to the tabernacle's ceiling. "Hail the Queen of Night, Defender of Bee-Jor, and Enemy of Ignorance. All hail!"

"Hail Cricket!" returned the crowd.

"To Cricket, we say thank You, for the bounty of this feast on the eighth day of rest."

"Thank You, Cricket," shouted the crowd.

"We thank You for the present peace, and for the

death of Tahn and the defeat of the Hulkrites, who suffered in unholy ignorance. May we never war again except to defend our righteous own and Cricket's beloved Commander Quegdoth. Hail Quegdoth."

"Hail Quegdoth," they shouted. Kelvap elbowed Pleckoo for his silence.

"Hail Quegdoth," Pleckoo whispered, but his old anger was rushing back and building. *The only thing crickets are good for is eating! Just as the singing of crickets invites hunters to slay them, so are these Palzhanites inviting their own destruction!*

"The Goddess needs your silence," shout-whispered the high priestess, and the tabernacle quieted. Faintly, from a distance, they heard the chirping of real crickets. "Ahh," said the priestess. "The Night Musician may give this feast Her greatest blessing."

The priestesses began playing their harps together in a quicker way, as the lure of males to attract females. Pleckoo heard a thump on the roof and saw a bend in its ceiling. More thumps followed and he realized crickets had landed on the tabernacle.

"She comes! Hail Cricket!" the priestess shouted as a tubby, dark, and shining cricket entered the tabernacle, with her long antennae twitching around her head. The people rose, pressed hands together, and bowed to the cricket as it crawled its way to the altar. Some made contact with it, touching its legs or tails, and then wiped its oil on their hair and faces. Soon other crickets entered and followed the first to the altar. The priestesses halted their chirping to lower their heads and arms, and knelt to assume the mating position.

Pleckoo knew from the crickets' thicker bodies and egg-laying tubes that they were females, and he watched in disgust as they mounted the priestesses. The crickets had been fooled into mating, which for them meant mounting the males. In this bizarre ritual, the priestesses had posed as *male* crickets and now they were using their hands to insert something in the crickets' orifices that looked like a drop of semen. It grew stranger yet when the crickets pushed each other away to mount with the different "males."

As the crickets lay atop the priestesses with their dwarfed wings spastically flapping, the crowd got up on its feet. They went to the tabernacle's edge to retrieve their drums, seed shakers, and rhythm scrapers, then entered a frenzied dance of bouncing and twirling in circles that pulled together, then blew apart. Once the crickets felt they had been thoroughly inseminated, they dismounted. Some climbed to the ceiling, where they hung upside down to observe the feast from above. Others crawled for the exit, and the people followed these to the outside and watched them leap away as they shouted thanks and good-byes and invites to return.

Pleckoo wobbled as he stood with the crowd outside, feeling weak as he watched the departing insects. He hoped his contempt for what he had witnessed was not visible in his crunched brow. The people got excited again when they saw the largest platter yet coming towards the tabernacle, one so wide that the leaves of the entry had to be rolled back to allow it to pass. The platter was on runners, dragged by young girls with muck-covered arms. Sitting atop a vast slab of rainbow quartz was a dark, glistening effigy of Goddess Cricket. The platter was hauled to an area below the altar, where it was spun eight times as the crowd leapt and chanted Cricket's names.

The high priestess took the sharp end of her staff, muttered a prayer, then cut off the effigy's mandible, which she picked up and gnawed on. She was joined by the other priestesses in cutting the effigy into morsels that were passed through the crowd. Silent handed Pleckoo a piece to eat that felt cool and sticky in his hands, and he realized it was a sweet of dried fruits, grain, and honey. He looked at Silent as his kerchief bobbed up and down with his chewing. Pleckoo was sure that the man hated him, was suspicious of him, and if he could speak, he would only be insulting.

The high priestess led the other priestesses to the side of the altar, where they crouched to enjoy their sweets. From outside the tabernacle, a new procession was making its way in. Three young and plump eunuchs—perhaps of fifteen summers—made their way to the altar dressed as different moths. One was a white-and-black many-spotted moth, another was a scarlet-painted lichen moth, and a third was a mottled crystal moth. Each carried a staff with a replica of Goddess Moth at its top, and as they walked, their replicas' wings shook out a fragrant powder. Brother Moonsinger followed behind them in a garish evening costume: a split cape of dark blue with indigo stripes over a red tunic. The costume rendered him as the bloody-shouldered demon moth, an insect that was easily mistaken as a night wasp and was almost as feared. His antennae were cables of scarlet fuzz that rose up high, then fluttered at the top.

Pleckoo's hatred for this sexless creature deepened into a chasm. Moonsinger wore powder on his face to heighten his lighter skin, and his chubby cheeks were accentuated with rouge. His lips were painted a bright orange, and his eyes were rimmed with the same cosmetic that thickened his lashes. When he reached the altar, he turned to the audience with his draped arms over his face and then slowly lowered them. With his shaved head and yellow complexion against the black of his enormous cowl, his face simulated the full moon floating in the night sky. The younger eunuchs stamped with their polls to quiet the worshippers.

"Who is Vof Quegdoth?" Moonsinger shouted through the gathering in a voice that was masculine yet melodious, and drew in every ear. "Turn your ears to me, and I will tell you who has made this Feast of the Eighth Day possible."

Pleckoo was nauseated as Moonsinger extended his draped arms and cocked his head as if offering a hug to all. The tabernacle quieted to reveal no other noise than distant crickets and cicadas.

"Locust so loved the world that he mated with a roach woman, the Virgin Corra, a pure and virtuous descendant of Madricanth."

The Virgin Corra? She's a Britasyte slut!

"Corra had been separated from her clan of noble roach people. It was the harshest of winters, when the morning dew was locked up in crystals that are painfully cold to the touch. It was a time of such coldness that when people spoke, they could see their words as little clouds. The creatures of Mother Sand were dead or in hiding. The leaf-cutter ants of the Slope were in the deepest chambers, covering their ant queens as living blankets to keep them warm. Everyone prayed to Pareesha, Goddess of the South Wind, that she would rise early from her Long Sleep at the Edge of the Sand, to blow her sweet and warming breath and bring an early spring.

"The roaches of the clan were dead or dying from the cold, and unable to lay the eggs that the people of Madricanth rely on for sustenance. In search of food for her family, the Virgin Corra wandered into the brittle weeds near the midden of Cajoria, where she collapsed from hunger and sank into a sleep she did not expect to wake from. It was night when she revived, in the arms of a middenite whose tongue and teeth had been destroyed. Yormu had come to the weeds to take his own life when he stumbled upon Corra, and felt the cold skin of her corpse. Something sparkling landed on her body. Yormu the Mute looked up to see a shower of stars falling from the sky to cover Corra with their gentle lights. She rose up—revived!—and gasped to find herself staring at a tongueless and toothless man. He was just as astonished.

"'Who are you?'" she asked Yormu, then realized he could not answer. A voice rumbled like thunder that spoke in both their tongues.

"'He is Yormu, a Slopeite from the mound of Cajoria,' said the Voice, 'and he is your husband.'

"'Who are you?' Corra asked of the sky.

"The weeds turned green, blossomed, and fruited with phantom berries, then parted to reveal a great, glowing being who crawled to them on six legs and filled the fields with the blue light of heaven. 'I am Locust, Lord of the Sky,' said the God of Creation. 'And I have chosen you, Corra of the Entreveans, to bear my son, who will be known one day as Vof Quegdoth. He will bring peace, end suffering, and raise up all men and women as the People of One Blood.'

"And then Locust turned to Yormu and stroked him with His bright antennae. 'I have chosen you, Yormu, to raise my son as a humble middenite, so that he will know poverty and injustice and the hopelessness of a life determined at birth. For too long, Mantis and Ant Queen have ruled my Creation and fomented war and cruelty and hatred. Raise my son as one of you, and when he is ready, he will know his real Father.'

"Immediately, Corra swelled with a pregnancy and only one moon later, when spring had arrived, a child was born. He was given the name Anand, which means 'worker' in the old tongue. And work he did—the most humiliating, gruesome, and soul-crushing work, as he ported filth and cleaned chamber pots and hauled corpses to the swamp. And he would know, all too well, the life of an outcaste—for among the outcastes, he was an outcaste, a boy who was abused and tortured for his status as a half-breed. Only two Cajorites would ever acknowledge him: the first was Terraclon, a boy blessed with two spirits; and another half-breed, Pleckoo, the spawn of a yellow-skinned rapist."

At the mention of his name, the crowd hissed their contempt. Pleckoo tried not to shake with rage, then disgust. He watched as some of the men rose up to spit and curse his name, while others feigned pissing. Some women stood and shook their fists, and made the motion of clawing out eyes.

Moonsinger hesitated for a moment and looked in Pleckoo's direction. *He looks like he's staring right at me,* Pleckoo thought. *Or is it the cannabis that makes me think so?*

"Yes, they were close once, Pleckoo and Anand— drawn together by blood, by gifts, by intelligence . . .

by a sense of a different destiny than the one to which they were born. Anand was forced into a Fission march to Dranveria, where he would learn, unexpectedly, of his divine heritage and partake of heavenly wisdom. It was there, in the Land of Miracles, that Anand learned the worship of Bee could restore arms to the limbless and eyesight to the blind. Her Healing Honey could be poured on the disfigured to grow new noses, tongues, and ears. In Dranveria the righteous and devoted could be made prosperous and beautiful."

The audience was rapt, murmuring in ecstasy as if their own transformation had begun. Pleckoo's heart was thumping. Was it this wicked drink that was distorting his hearing, or did he hear that a nose could be regrown in Dranveria?

"Pleckoo, who ran from the Fission, turned to the Termite demon, and welcomed His seduction," continued Brother Moonsinger. "On the night before the Fission departure, Pleckoo wandered into the weeds and prayed to Mad-on-Turpentine to guide him to His realm. Termite manifested Himself as Hulkro, in His human aspect, and stood before Pleckoo with His naked and powerful body and a demand for His obeisance. Pleckoo agreed and gave Hulkro his mouth and then . . . his bottom. Pleckoo was filled with the Termite Lord's corrupting seed, which poisoned him with an unending hatred and a hunger for rape and thievery and killing."

This is outrageous! Pleckoo thought, and almost screamed it aloud. *I have never been anyone's flower boy! How dare they defame Lord Termite as a boy lover! Sacrilege!*

"The Termite guided Pleckoo through the Slope and into the Dustlands," Moonsinger continued, "where he rose quickly in the Hulkrish army after submitting to the bodily desires of Commander Tahn. Together, they plotted to conquer the Slope and extend his murderous empire."

And now he defiles Tahn as a deviant!

The crowd was hissing again. Pleckoo's rage had overwhelmed the influence of the cannabis, and his mind grew clear. He was ready to rise up and use his bare hands to tear out the tongue and throat of Brother Moonsinger. Next he would rip off his limbs, and use them to beat to death every last person who listened to these lies. But all he could do now was sit and listen. Moonsinger, hesitating again, looked as if he had forgotten the chain of words, or was about to change them. He seemed to be looking again in Pleckoo's direction.

"Tonight, I must skip over the details," Moonsinger said, "for I have a different ending to this story—a new one you have never heard before. Vof Quegdoth's victory was incomplete over the Hulkrites. As the Laborers' Army battled the Termite worshippers, so did Locust battle Hulkro in the Heavenly Realm.

Termite enlisted Ant Queen and Mantis to come to His defense, while Locust allied with Madricanth and Cricket. Their battle was bloody, and flooded the Heavenly Plain with a watery lymph that rained on the Sand for seven days. Termite was weakened, but crawled off to recover and grant one last boon to his beloved Pleckoo, the mortal who had worshipped Him so deeply."

Moonsinger took a sharp breath.

"After his defeat on the Slope, Pleckoo retreated to Mound Jalal . . . in the Dustlands," sang Moonsinger with a rising tension in his voice. "At Mound Jalal, the last of his men sacrificed their lives to allow their commander to escape. Pleckoo wandered through the northern Dustlands, then returned to the Slope to a place where he might hide in plain sight."

Pleckoo's heart was beating so hard he was sure it was about to break his rib cage. Moonsinger pointed at him.

"Behold the most brazen of all men, the most offensive, the most outrageous! There, eating our food and imbibing our drink, may be the enemy of Bee-Jor himself . . . Pleckoo of Hulkren!"

Pleckoo stood to run, then felt the dig of a knife at his back, then the painful point of a sword in his chest. At the sword's end was Silent Cricket with his unblinking, smoldering eyes. He pulled down his kerchief to reveal a face like Pleckoo's own, with a missing nose.

"How would we find them? And how would we know they had this power? And would they eat roach eggs? Slopeites have been told for centuries that they are a poison that only Britasytes can ingest."

"Until we sort that out we can export urine from you or some other queen. This is not a rare substance."

"But it's more than that, Anand. A mound needs a queen and a king, to lend it stability and continuity— especially in a time of change."

"Perhaps," he said. "Palzhad is a poor, weakened queendom that has never recovered from the Hulkrish raid. At the moment, it faces the threat of refugees and some problematic Dneepers. What royal could we ever get to rule there?"

"I would," said a voice from behind them.

They turned to see Trellana standing near a tunnel portal. The maidservants with her were pulling out a second figure, King Sahdrin, who looked disturbingly fragile. Each of his movements was a feeble struggle, as he was lifted up to assume his crutches.

"You would live in Palzhad?" asked Polexima with a doubtful chuckle.

"I had planned to," said Trellana, "when we thought you were lost. It was to be the home of all the Fission pioneers returned from that vile little nation with its savages on red ants."

"Trellana, you are married to me," said Anand. "And I govern from here, with your mother."

"But there is no longer a need for me to be here. Not for the next eight months."

"You are ...." said Polexima.

"Pregnant, yes. Inside me are at least one, maybe more, little dark-skinned eyesores." A maidservant handed her and the king their drink-bags.

Anand stood as he watched them suck their liquor. "Do not speak that way of my children. Of *our* children. Why are you drinking spirits?"

"Why wouldn't I?"

"You won't. Until our children are born. And then you can turn them over to a milk nurse—one who will not indulge in spirits."

"That's ridiculous," said Trellana. "Fermentation will do them good. It will give them a happy womb, and make them the kind of babies that sleep well."

"Spirits will impair their vision and hearing and give them small heads—make them stupid. At the moment we have enough stupid royals."

"Do not speak to my daughter in that tone," rasped Sahdrin. "Polexima enjoyed spirits while Trellana was in the womb."

"Obviously," said Anand. "Excuse me, Polly."

Trellana looked at Anand as if she were about slap his face with her drink-bag.

"Your ignorance can be forgiven but you are now informed," Anand said. "I am determined about this. In Dranveria it is a crime for a woman to drink spirits during a pregnancy . . . and it will be a crime here as well."

"I will drink what I want," Trellana said.

"Not if I lock you in a cage."

Anand watched her fume and purse her lips as Sahdrin hobbled towards him, staring with his good eye.

"You would not dare!" shouted Sahdrin. "I may be nothing more than some ancient sack of flatulence, but I will use the last of my pathetic life to stop you from caging my daughter!"

"He *would* dare," said Poleixima. "And I'm sure he would be kind enough to lock you up with her. The people of Dranveria are wiser than we. If they have determined that drinking fermentation during pregnancy is bad for a child, then they are right. I have always sensed this was true. I did not drink when I was pregnant with Nuvao."

"So not drinking results in an effeminate son?" said Trellana.

"Not drinking results in kinder children—who are smart and want to learn things," said Anand.

Trellana was quiet for a moment. "I would give up spirits for the next eight months," she said, "if I could reign over Palzhad."

Anand was quiet, wondering what she really wanted.

"Say yes, Quegdoth, and I'll have one last night of indulgence," said Trellana before she took a deep draught from the drink-bag. "I think the distance would do us both some good."

Anand looked to Polexima, who cocked her head and shrugged. "I have an idea," said the queen. "I'll need to speak with her brother. If the two of them can agree on something this might just work." Anand signaled for a messenger to fetch Nuvao.

"I would agree to just about anything to get away from here," said Trellana.

"Then agree to stop drinking," said Polexima. "We will need your full presence to discuss this matter."

"If this is my last night of drinking, then I will enjoy all I want," said Trellana, signaling to her servant to bring her more.

CHAPTER 24

NOT A CAGE

I should just jump forward, impale myself on his blade, and end my life, Pleckoo thought. But he couldn't; his limbs were shaking, his mouth went watery, and then he vomited. The crowd backed away as he fell to his hands and knees to empty his stomach, and then he shook with dry heaving. They were screaming, poking him with their weapons, kicking his behind. As he looked up at them, he felt a slime dripping down his chin. "I am not Pleckoo!" he tried to shout, and heard himself as someone weak and womanly as he stood and wobbled.

"You are not Vleeg of Gagumji!" he heard from No Longer Silent, whose blade was piercing his tunic.

"Don't kill him!" Glip shouted. "Tie him up! We've been told he must be kept alive!"

Two men grabbed Pleckoo by the ankles and yanked him sharply; he fell forward and onto his face and felt his skull smack against the sand. His wrists were grabbed and pulled behind him and he screamed as his arms were nearly wrenched out of their sockets. Ropes gouged deep into the skin of his wrists as they were bound, and then he felt the agony of being pulled to his feet with the loop of his distended arms. The kerchief was ripped off his face as he was pushed through the maddened, screaming crowd, with all of them waving knives and swords. They grabbed the hair on his head and that of his beard and yanked it out by the handfuls. He was stripped of his garments, even his loincloth, and pushed naked to the exit as they stomped on his toes, kicked his legs, and spit on him until he was covered in gobs. When he was pushed out of the tabernacle, he saw a cage perched atop a sand-sled, waiting just for him.

They suspected all along, he thought, *and planned this! But why is this cage on a hauling-sled?*

Inside the cage were several men waiting with coils of rough ropes. They reached down for Pleckoo, jerked him up by his armpits, and then dumped him on the cage's floor. The cage was surrounded by the crowd who jeered and cursed as Pleckoo's limbs were spread, then tied to the back of the bars. The ropes were wound hard over his limbs and torso until he was covered in them, a second torturous skin. He could only move his head, which looked upwards as he prayed to any god that would listen. "I can't breathe!" he shouted when he felt the constriction of his chest as his breathing went rapid and shallow.

The cage was growing darker when he saw young men climbing up its bars, shouting their curses at him. When they reached its top, they pulled up their tunics and showered him with their piss. As soon as they descended, new boys took their places. The crowd shook their fists, shouted their curses, and hawked their phlegm and spat.

The sled lurched, and he saw it was being pulled further up the mound where the higher castes could start a new round of humiliations. Young men climbed up the cage again and Pleckoo felt the ropes dampening. The shrieking and screams grew louder and felt like pine needles, piercing his ears until they pricked his brain. His breathing grew more and more shallow until he felt flashing waves of a sharp pain over his skin, and then a spastic trembling of his bowels before he lost control of them. A darkly sour stink filled his nose before he entered a stupor that softened the world and turned it into a distant nightmare.

It was sometime near midnight when he roused to a ringing in his head. He attempted to clamp his hands to his ears, then remembered he was bound up like the wrapped prey of a spider. He looked down at the cage and saw the piss-wet floor glimmering in the moonlight, then he looked out and saw a quieter gathering of nobles around him. Over their heads he could see the grimy walls of one of Palzhad's palaces, and he realized he was at the dew station of the topmost circle of the mound. The people who surrounded him spoke softly and were well dressed, the remains of the mounds' royals and its war widows, priests, and their servants. The boys among them were not crawling up the cage to piss and spit on him, but he could hear the hatred in their voices as they loudly whispered insults like "the murderous filth worker" and "Termite's catamite."

Pleckoo strained against the ropes but it was useless. It was an agony to hang on the bars with the ropes' fibers violently scratching into his skin. Among other pains, his mouth was completely dry from thirst. Quietly, two men approached the cage's door after it was opened by the guards. Pleckoo recognized the men as the sheriffs from the market. One of them carried a drinking bladder with a long tube at its end.

"Hello, Pleckoo," said the one with the bag whose neck bulged with a butterfly-shaped goiter.

"That is not my name."

"Really? You are not Pleckoo, the noseless middenite from Cajoria who claimed himself as the Second Prophet of Lord Termite?"

Pleckoo was quiet. *I will not deny that.*

"I can't hear you," said the sheriff. "Are you not the

Commander Prophet Pleckoo, the Chosen Successor of Tahn the First Prophet?"

Pleckoo could not speak. *Please, Hulkro, inspire me*, he prayed.

"A simple 'no' will do," said the second sheriff, a man with one eye sewn shut. "If you want to save yourself."

"Only the One True God decides who speaks for Him," Pleckoo rasped.

"Drink this," said Butterfly Goiter, who held up the drinking tube of the bladder.

"What is it?"

"Water."

"Why give me water? Why not just kill me?"

"Because it's against the code. You are wanted alive until you are proven guilty."

"What will you do with me?"

"We're bringing you to Cajoria. To be identified," said Sewn Shut. "Would you happen to know anybody there?"

One more unbearable shame, Pleckoo thought. *My demise will be in Cajoria.*

"Why Cajoria?"

"It's where Commander Quegdoth governs, the capital mound. We've got a few places to stop along the way," said Butterfly Goiter. "I'm sure quite a few people would like to make your acquaintance."

Anand is in Cajoria, Pleckoo thought. *Where they're taking me.* He shut his eyes and there was a sudden silence and a delicious sense of plunging. Soft lights flickered within the blackness and a fallen log rolled up to him, covered with scales of blue glow-fungus. Hulkro crawled out of the log in His aspect of the Termite King and raised His lacy wings. "Stay strong, Pleckoo," He said with a voice that vanquished the pain. "And know that you are not in a cage. You are in a cocoon."

CHAPTER 25

GROWING GIANTS

Trellana was arriving in her sedan chair on the edge of Cajoria's ant-riding course, surrounded by servants and 123 trunks of essentials that were coming with her to Palzhad. She had been up all night, going through all her possessions and deciding which she could do without and which she could send for later. It had taken the palace servants all the morning to pack her trunks and then port them to the sled dock.

"That was just exhausting," she said to her parents as her chair was set down.

"We will miss you, Trelly," said Sahdrin, and she saw that his face drooped more than usual.

"You don't have to miss me, Daddy. Come with me. It's not like Mother will miss you."

"I cannot," said the king. "Perhaps when I feel better. If I ever feel better."

"I am sorry you will not get to share my little adventure," Trellana said with a smile she knew revealed her excitement.

"Trelly, I have told you," said Polexima. "You should lower your expectations. Palzhad is not like Cajoria. It is likely even more different since the war. They are far less reverent to royalty. And they are fond of some much older traditions of which, I am sure, you are mostly unaware."

"I will make it my own," said Trellana. "And set an example. I imagine the Palzhanites will welcome a young queen from the North, someone who can bring charm and splendor back to their mound. I imagine they would just adore, as anyone would, an elaborate and traditional anointing ceremony. Perhaps we can invite some royalty from the Old Slope."

"I imagine that what the Palzhanites would really welcome is a steady supply of queenly urine," said Polexima. "So that their ants can continue to defend them against these refugees from the South . . . as well as enemies in the East and West."

Trellana winced at her mother. She was wearing the most ridiculous cricket robe yet—this one was the bright green of the tree-leaf crickets who thrived in the late summer.

"Mother, did Terraclon sew something new for you? Out of some very stale cloth?"

"This actually came with me years ago when I first arrived at the mound—a gift from your grandmother, an heirloom. She wore it during the Nights of Awe that celebrated Cricket and Moon and the other nocturnal goddesses. That's a feast they still celebrate in Palzhad."

"And you wore *this* to say good-bye to me."

"To say good-bye to *her*," said Polexima. "My mother, *your* grandmother, who was a devotee of Night Singer. It would do you well to honor Cricket at Palzhad. When you are unsure of your way, you should look to Her, ask for Her guidance."

"I am sure I will be praying to Her on hot summer nights when Her offspring get too noisy."

"The sled is coming," Sahdrin said as the train of hauling ants came into view. The riders seated at the head of the ants slowed them with the new technique of scented gloves applied to different segments of the antennae. Trellana was mildly shocked and deeply annoyed. The ants were not hauling the Royal Sled of the Mound of Cajoria with its three-tiered cabin. Instead, it was a lesser vehicle, a priestly conveyance, which was not even the carriage of His Most Pious.

"They've brought the wrong sled," Trellana said.

"Unless this is the one for my trunks." She heard the sound of marching and turned to find a formation of foot guards making their way towards them like a living fortress. From out of its middle, Anand appeared with that vulgar, mincing Terraclon at his side.

"You have ordered the wrong coach," Trellana said to Anand.

"I have not," Anand said. "We are taking precautions."

"Precautions? Why?" asked Polexima.

"It may be nothing—but there are reports that some of the ants of our eastern mounds are growing giants in their nurseries."

"Seed Eaters preparing an attack? In the autumn?" said Sahdrin.

"I am sure they think we are weak and vulnerable after the war," said Anand. "In any event we will need to get Trellana to Palzhad as quickly as possible. While we still have locusts, what I really think is that she should fly there and let the trunks come later."

"I am not flying to Palzhad on the back of a *locust*," Trellana said, and glared at Anand, whose skin seemed darker in the sunlight. "You are just making up this noise about an eastern threat to deprive me of a procession suitable to my rank."

"Yes," said Anand. "I live only to deprive you." He looked at her with barely stifled hatred. "You cannot take all these trunks on your *journey* to Palzhad."

"Why not?"

"You can take as many as fit in the sled's trunk storage. And no, we will not be arranging a second train to port the rest of your dresses and jewelry and whatnot to Palzhad." He turned to his guard. "Defenders, take good care of Princess Trellana, soon to be Queen Trellana of Palzhad of Bee-Jor. Be ever alert."

Half the guards stepped forward to join Trellana's procession, leaving the other half to guard Anand and Terraclon.

"These guards are all going with me?" she asked. "All these men?"

"Two are women. And yes, they are all going, in addition to your royal guard as a part of your protection."

"You mean to keep an eye on me."

"No. To keep *eyes* on you. Thirty pairs exactly."

They heard a faint buzzing and looked up to see a loose formation of locusts coming from the East. They landed in their usual, haphazard way. The pilot of the one falling closest to Anand was jarred by the landing and nearly fell off of his saddle. He straightened his helmet gone askew before slapping his chest, and then patted his locust's head as he addressed Anand.

"Commander Quegdoth," he said. "We have sighted Seed Eater armies gathering forces in their west."

"Near which mounds?"

"At least two including Callabeeth and Eglosso."

"And likely Zerabel, Xixict, and Shishto," said Polexima. "They have already taken Dinth and

Habach, whose people we are still relocating. Those are the seven annexed by the Slope in the last two centuries."

"You mean stolen," said Anand. "The Seed Eaters are *taking back* what used to be their mounds."

"I suppose *stolen* is the right word. But they are Slopeish—or rather, Bee-Jorite—mounds now, occupied by hundreds of thousands of our people."

Anand turned to Terraclon. "Ter, I've got to get up there, see for myself. The Seed Eaters feint an attack at one place, then pounce on another. I've got to determine where they're really attacking."

"I'd go with you if I knew how to fly."

"Start learning," said Anand.

"Really?" asked Terraclon in a happy shock, his mouth agape.

"Start today. We need a pilot for every locust we have." Anand turned to the pilot before him. "Is this locust fresh enough to fly back to the Southeast border?"

"Yes, Commander. I believe so."

"Then make room."

Anand was climbing up the locust's leg when he noticed a messenger racing with all his speed towards him, wildly waving his hands. "Commander! Wait!" the boy shouted. "You must wait!" The boy was out of breath, barely able to speak.

"What's the matter, young defender, that you're giving me orders?"

"A message from Palzhad. They think they've got him!"

"Who?"

"Pleckoo!"

"Say that name again."

"Pleckoo! They've captured a man who fits every description. They're porting his cage here now."

Polexima staggered, dropped her staff, then fell on the ground to sob. Trellana did not know if her mother was crying out of fear or relief or both. Anand and Terraclon looked at each other, stunned by the news, and panting.

"Send a message back," said Anand with a tremble in his voice. "Twenty guards are to accompany this man—who might be Pleckoo—in his cage back to Cajoria. And they must never leave him out of their sight. Tell them *he must be kept alive.*"

"Why do you want him alive?" asked Trellana. "Cut his throat and be done with it. You can identify the corpse later."

"If it isn't Pleckoo I'd be killing an innocent man."

"I know why you won't gut him," whispered Terraclon.

Anand was silent, then gave Terraclon a look that was a grudging acknowledgment . . . and a warning to keep quiet.

"I'll be back as quickly as possible. Ter, I need you to look after Polexima."

"Of course."

"And learn how to fly."

Anand and the pilot flew off without even looking at Trellana. She turned to look at Terraclon, the strange, dark-skinned outcaste, as he comforted her mother, who rocked and cried as she relived some memory. Sahdrin watched his wife in silence, sighing as he rubbed his false eye before signaling to his servant to lift his drink-bag for a swallow.

"Well, I suppose this Pleckoo person must be something awful," said Trellana to dispel her own discomfort. "I am glad he will be gone from Palzhad by the time of my arrival. Let us get on with this procession, shall we?"

As Anand flew towards the southern end of Bee-Jor, he could see little below him. The only thing in his head were visions of his cousin: Pleckoo, the proud and ambitious middenite he had toiled with and shared his dreams. Pleckoo, the humiliated reject returning from Venaris with a bloody defacement. Pleckoo, the warrior wearing the White Paint of Submission as Tahn's rising favorite. *I will clear my head,* Anand determined. They reached the Tar Marsh where Anand looked down at workers engaged in the dangerous, messy work of gathering tar, so much in demand for the building of better shelters by newly prospering Bee-Jorites. "Turn north and keep east of the border wall," he said to the pilot, who veered the locust into a turnaround against the south-blowing wind. But as Anand forced himself to search for signs of Seed Eaters massing to attack, he was still imagining his cousin behind him, stalking him in the air with an obsidian arrow aimed at his neck. *And as for obsidian . . . was it Pleckoo who cut my leg from the bottom of our sand-sled?*

As they flew above the border wall, Anand looked down at the Seed Eaters' innumerable villages that were far from their ant mounds. Clusters of hollowed pebble dwellings were squeezed between nearly every clump of the barley grass that grew in broad patches between their oak trees. Anand could just make out a band of hunters in one village, standing atop a flat rock as they shot their arrows up at his locust, unaware of its human riders. One arrow climbed up next to Anand and seemed suspended for a moment before he plucked it out of the air to regard its making. It was imported—made by the Beetle people from their pine wood. *And it had to have been sold to them by Britasyte traders*—a thought which made him frown.

To the west, he could see Mound Culzhwitta, and over the border wall on the east he saw what looked like the first of a military encampment on the Seed Eaters' side. Here and there were a few cages full of ants, and he sighted scattered soldiers in their brown chitin armor as they supervised the digging of their sacrificial pits. *But that's a feint,* he decided.

Barely anybody there! Just enough harvester ants at the border to deceive the leaf-cutters into growing giants. The south wind was blowing harder when they reached Mound Eglosso where to the right, over its border, was another modest Seed Eater camp. *One more ruse.*

Anand counted four more feints, one next to each of the next four border mounds, until they neared Mound Shishto. *It's got to be Shishto they've set their sights on,* he thought. He sniffed the air for the scents of Seed Eater soldiers and harvester ants, expecting that the real encampment would make itself obvious soon. The pilot steered them over an expanse of scrubby oak trees, and then arced up when they reached a cluster of mature ones. Several of these were hundreds of years old, wrapped in chunky armor-like bark and barely compromised by the leaf-cutters.

The largest and most magnificent of the oaks had a thousand undulating branches that spread from a broad and ancient trunk. The branches on the tree's eastern side extended over the border wall to the Barley Lands. Under these branches, Anand could make out tawny-skinned women working in teams of three to roll away the acorns. On the Bee-Jorite side, the acorns were far more abundant, covering the ground by the tens of thousands. All of these acorns were neglected and rotting or infested with the grubs of the long-snouted weevil. *Why do Slopeites let acorns go to waste?* Anand asked himself. *That's food for a hundred thousand down there.*

Mound Shishto came into view. It was wider and lower than most leaf-cutter mounds, a reminder that it had been built and occupied by Seed Eaters and their harvester ants before it was "annexed" and rebuilt by Slopeites. It had only two crystal palaces at its top, with a third at the beginning of its construction. The uppermost rings were typical of Slopeish building, with pink rectories and black-sand barracks, but the dwellings on the lower rings were in the Seed Eaters' style, and included houses with walls of chipped quartz on the lower levels and hovels with roofs of acorn caps. Anand looked east into the further distance and felt a growing discomfort in his stomach. He smelled or saw or heard *something* that tightened his gut, even if he could not yet identify it. As he looked down at the border, he saw nothing but scattered villages. *No feint here! The real encampment is nearby, but deeper in.*

"Further east and lower," he commanded the pilot.

"Over the *border*, Commander?"

"Yes, but be ready to turn around."

The pilot turned to look at Anand briefly, his face betraying his apprehension at the moment the locust made a brief halt of her wings and plummeted before resuming flight. Reaching for the upper and outside segments of the locust's antennae, the pilot changed her pattern, and Anand sighted a clearing near a patch of bright green. *That's got to be it!* As they got closer, he looked down and saw just a few ant cages and a mere squadron of Seed Eater soldiers whipping the slaves of a pit excavation. *It's just one more feint*, he realized, *but a little further inland. From where are they planning to attack?*

"Back to Cajoria," he commanded when the locust continued towards a patch of clover with pink and white blossoms.

"She's not obeying!" said the pilot.

The locust made an abrupt landing in the clover, landing on a sprig, which collapsed under her. Anand and the pilot were jarred and thrown forward. The locust righted herself and was already eating as they reseated. Anand looked to the sky and saw the sun was rolling lower.

"We have to let her eat, Commander," the pilot said. "She needs the water."

"She does," Anand said. "But we're not safe here."

They waited, listening to the locust chew, when they heard the *twang* of strings and then the *whoosh* of arrows, followed by the sound of boots on sand.

"Shit!" Anand said. "Up! Up!" The pilot clamped his hands at the antennae's roots, which sent the locust bucking and into short jumps before it took an erratic flight. Anand looked over his shoulder at the encampment's soldiers taking aim. Some soldiers were opening the cages, releasing their ants and mounting them. The pilot leaned in when, at last, the locust straightened its flight, veering upwards as Shishto's border wall came into sight. The locust flew hard, and Anand was almost relieved as she neared the top of the wall, then crashed into its peak. Stunned or dead, she slid down the wall's slope of sand and ant droppings. Anand and the pilot were dragged after her in the tangled ropes of the saddle rig. The hot pain of his leg wounds was reignited as they bumped down the wall.

"Are you all right, pilot?" Anand asked when they came to a stop.

"I think so," said the pilot as he strained to pull himself from the stirrups and reins. Anand crawled over the dying insect to see Seed Eater villagers filtering out of the barley grass with crude pikes at the ready. They feigned a threat with their weapons and weakly shouted at the invaders. Their tongue sounded like a violent snorting and throat-clearing. All of them, including the women, wore little more than a rag or some woven straw to hide their genitals. Their cheeks were sunken, their rib cages were visible, and their arms and legs were no more than bones wrapped in shriveled skin.

"You can have this," Anand said to them in Britasyte, Dranverish, and Slopeish and then pointed to the locust with an opened palm. They understood his gesture if not his words, and converged on the locust, using their pikes to stab into its abdomen. After making punctures, they yanked out circles of chitin, then dropped to their knees to hungrily lick at the dripping lymph. When it stopped dripping, they thrust their heads inside the cuts to continue slurping. Anand and the pilot looked at each other, ashamed to witness such an extreme display of starvation. An old woman emerged from an acorn-capped shelter, and walked weakly towards the locust with a sling over one shoulder. As she got closer, Anand realized she was not so old. Inside her sling he could see the thin arms of a withered and skeletal baby that was sucking at her withered breast.

No one made room for the woman to partake of this sudden feast. She stood nearby, pacing with despair, pleading for her share.

"Why are they excluding her?" asked the pilot.

"She has no husband. Maybe she slept with someone else's and her child is a bastard. I'm going over to her. Look out for me."

The pilot nodded, and raised up his blowgun to protect Anand as he unsheathed his sword and strode to the locust's end. Anand heard the weak crying of the woman's infant as the villagers turned and stared at him. Some of the men shouted at Anand and threatened him with their pikes. When they came too near, Anand used his sword to knock their weapons from their hands, then motioned them with a sweep of his sword to step back. They quieted to watch him raise his blade over the locust's abdomen, then chop at its end until it fell away.

Picking up the end by the ovipositor, Anand walked towards the starving mother and held it out to her like a great cup. She reached for it, struggled with its weight, then sucked deeply of the lymph. Inside the cup were two partially formed eggs, which she squeezed up and out of the tube to chew on. She looked Anand in the eye and nodded her head in thanks. The others in the village were warming to him and nodded their thanks as well. Someone with a second piece of cloth wrapped around his head, perhaps their chieftain, was saying, "*Shpeebo, shpeebo,*" and pressed together his hands in the motion of gratitude. Suddenly, Anand heard the clacking of a wooden bell and looked to the pebble tower to see a sentry with an orange helmet rise up from what must have been a nap to sound a warning that spread through the grass.

The barley stalks behind them were twitching and bending with new arrivals—harvester ants were crawling out in their speedy, jerking way with armed riders on their backs. *Those are the soldiers from the feint,* Anand realized. He looked at the ants with their massive heads and bearded mouths, and panicked when he saw them turn and raise their legs to shake their abdomens.

"Run!" he said to the pilot, and they scrambled up the collapsing border wall in hopes of reaching the other side.

attackers. His darts landed in the opened mouth of one bowman and the cheeks and chins of others. They went into spasms, violently shaking and losing control of their ants. Anand knew more soldiers on brown ants would be racing up to replace them.

"Can you climb?" Anand shouted to the pilot.

"We have to," he said. The two resumed painful ascents up the crumbling wall, when the pilot reached for a sand grain that dislodged and he slid again. A new barrage of arrows sailed towards them. One whizzed past Anand's ear and broke in the wall. The pilot screamed when an arrow pierced his hand. Anand grabbed the pilot by his wrist and pulled them up, using his pain-wracked legs when an arrow grazed Anand's neck and lodged between his helmet strap. He raised his heel on a shelf of quartz, which snapped. The two men slid again.

A shadow was over Anand when he realized a mass of yellow ants was crawling down the wall. Ten, twenty, and then thirty leaf-cutters were pouring over his body, some stepping on his face with their scratchy claws. The leaf-cutters had raced into battle, stirred by the odors of harvester ants. Immune to the harvesters' toxins, the leaf-cutters reached their enemy and sheared away their antennae and clipped off their legs to leave them immobile. The harvester ants attacked the leaf-cutters by clamping on to their stout abdomens to insert their stingers, but the leaf-cutters were overwhelming.

Arriving Seed Eater bowmen jumped from their embattled ants. Some men were caught by the quicker leaf-cutters and screamed when they were made limbless. They were silenced when they became headless.

More leaf-cutters crawled over the wall as a stream of harvester ants wove out of the barley grass to confront them. Anand struggled to flatten himself and cover his face when he heard voices and realized Bee-Jorite sentries had arrived on antback. "Down here! We are Bee-Jorites!" Anand shouted. Men wearing breathing filters and quartz goggles dropped from their saddles and threw down rope loops to pull him and the pilot up to safety. As they were lifted up, more of the wall crumbled beneath them and left an even larger rupture. Once on the Bee-Jorite side, Anand and the pilot were carried to the underside of a watchtower, where they were set on mattresses of bound grass.

"Thank you, Bee-Jorites. Tend to this pilot's wounds and then patch that section of the wall as quickly as possible," said Anand to his rescuers.

The men surrounding him were slow to react.

"Come on, men. Quickly. We can't have the Seed Eaters accuse us of invading their country! We're not ready for war."

"Sorry, Commander," said one of the astonished men. "Just realized you is Vof Quegdoth!" The men bowed to Anand, then ran to the break in the wall.

They hastily piled up sand grains and pebbles and resprinkled the ant pellets on its eastern side.

Anand looked over at the pilot, who lay on his mattress, shaking and taking shallow breaths as his wounds were bandaged with egg-cloth. When Anand's lungs cleared and his eyes stopped stinging, he rose to join the others in the wall's repair by passing sand grains up a chain of workers. The defenders tried and failed not to stare at their leader as he engaged in common labor.

After the wall was patched, Anand stood atop it and peered down at the village and its wretched people as they reemerged from their shelters. They wandered in hesitation through a wealth of ant corpses that would feed them for moons. Anand sighted the starving woman and her baby as she used a hand axe to sever a head from a dead leaf-cutter, then rolled it back to her shelter. Helping her were some sickly, stick-like children who had barely the strength to move their limbs. *Too, too many children everywhere on this Sand*, Anand thought. *And not all of them wanted.*

He looked to the sky and saw the sun was low in the West. "I'll need a locust, first thing in the morning," he said to the border sentry in charge, a man with the dark skin and hair of a laborer and the splotchy skin of a tar worker.

"Yes, Commander," said the sentry, meeting his eyes. "Will you join us for supper?"

"What?"

"The evening meal, Commander. Will you join us, if you're spending the night here?"

"Oh. Thank you. Yes."

"I am Defender Utchmay. An honor to serve you."

Food was the last thing on Anand's mind, even though he realized his stomach was noisy with hunger. He was relieved when sometime later an ant-drawn coach arrived near the watchtower to bring them to the mound's main artery.

"Can you ride?" Anand asked the pilot. "Are you hungry?"

"Yes to both, Commander."

"I should ask your name."

"I am Omal."

"Defender Omal. Thank you for your brave service today. You have suffered much for our country."

"I would do it all again, Commander. For Bee-Jor. And the Son of Locust."

The coach brought them to a station where they boarded an ant train carrying working people home. As they were riding up the merchants' rings, Anand saw Shishtite war widows in tattered yellow dresses. Some were returning from the market to modest homes. A few were idly sitting outside on pebble benches and minding their children or fingering prayer beads. When they noticed Anand, they began shouting to each other and he heard them call him "the Alien" and "the Dranverite" and "Polexima's

Seducer." Some came forward to stare at him when the train halted to drop off passengers. The widows pelted him with rotting mushrooms and human filth from chamber pots.

The widows were targeted with darts and one's chamber pot came spilling over her own head. Anand turned to see the passengers of the ant train shooting their blowguns, then laughing to watch the women fall into fits and flail within their grubby gowns. The widows' sons—some on the verge of manhood—stared at Anand with open hatred as he removed his stained tunic to reveal his Dranverish armor. When they reached the next ring, Anand saw a Shishtite priest complying with his edict to read the Code of Moral Conduct at day's end atop a monument under construction. The priest read it with a passionless singsong, but it still made Anand smile.

It was dark when the train approached the plaza of the black-sand barracks. Anand saw a spread of bobbing fungus torches, and then a vast crowd who quieted at his approach. He was apprehensive and searched through their darkened faces for weapons and other dangers. Defender Utchmay stood atop his saddle to speak.

"Shishtites of Bee-Jor! We are honored by the presence tonight of the Tamer of Night Wasps, the Son of Locust, the Commander General of the Free State of Bee-Jor. All hail Vof Quegdoth!"

A great cheer went up as Anand and Omal descended from the ant train and were escorted up the steps of the clearing's dew station. The people went into a state of devotional frenzy and chanted the round of Anand's names. Some had attached blue prayer banners of Locust to the tops of their torches and waved them. Shivers ran down Anand's spine as he was bathed in the sweet warmth of adoration. A moment later, he chided himself. *Roach Boy, they don't love you, they love some idea of you. They think of you as one of them and at the same time as something better. You must never believe yourself to be anything other than human because someday they'll forget you and throw their love at someone else.* He motioned with his hands for the crowd to settle. "You are kind," he shouted. "Too kind!"

His simple words sent them back into a frenzy and he worried their cheering might never end. "I need your silence," he said several times with a mild sternness. Finally they quieted.

"You have all fought bravely or supported our effort to win this new land of Bee-Jor. But our work has just begun and an eastern threat arises. The ugly truth is that several of these border mounds were built by Seed Eaters and their harvester ants when this land was in their possession. These mounds were stolen by the Slopeites, including this mound of Shishto."

The crowd was *too* silent before low murmurs trickled through them in a cold current.

"The offenses against the Seed Eaters were never of *your* doing, nor of your fathers' fathers. The offense of stealing foreign land belongs to the bloodthirsty generals and the greedy royals of the Once Great and Unholy Slope. It was they who stole these mounds and forced our people to inhabit them after a Fission lottery. It was the Slopeites who left you—who are guiltless—to defend this mound, the only home you have ever known, against a people whose claim to it is true."

The crowd got even quieter.

"We must be prepared for war," Anand shouted. "But there is something else we must be prepared for."

Anand puffed his chest, looked left and then right.

"Change!" he said. "To make a truer Bee-Jor, we must be willing to make ever more changes." In the nearby faces, Anand could see the people were in a confused silence.

And why wouldn't they be, when I am just as confused myself.

"In their own language, the Seed Eaters call themselves the People of the Barley. Yes, they are *people*, in every way—people who are filled with warm, red blood. They are our cousins, and before warring on them, we must see if we can live in peace *with* them. The Slopeish royals want you to hate the Barley people, to see them as less than you. The Seed Eaters have an emperor who tells them to hate us right back. This . . . must . . . *change*."

Anand knew he had lost them. The crowd was shifting uneasily, looking at each other in uncertainty.

"Bee-Jor is an ideal we must strive for," he said after a silence, "an impossibility to achieve on the Sand. But a part of that ideal is to accept that all people—brown- and yellow- and *tawny-skinned*—are one human family. And ideally, we are a family where each of us wants and works for the well-being of all."

The crowd did not cheer his last statement, but a smattering of clapping turned to sustained applause followed by whispered discussions. To Anand's relief, dinner arrived and everyone took seats as leaf platters were unrolled. Anand sat and tried not to look as tired and achy as he felt. He looked over at the nearby leaf, where he was being admired by richly dressed men and women of the merchants' caste, who raised their drops of liquor to him. They were seated on cushioned stools and had a servant scampering among them who brought Anand their barrel to share their drink. *No spirits,* he thought. *I need a clear head.* He returned their broad smiles, happy to see their presence among the new class of soldiers, and dipped into the air above the barrel with its scoop and feigned taking a slurp from it.

Some serving women arrived in groups of six with

platters on their shoulders. Anand was alarmed to see that the main course was harvester ants, which they had probably caught with baited rope traps that were hurled across the border. As the guest of honor, they set the first of the ants before him. It had been baked in a sauce of barley vinegar and mashed squash and then decorated with sprinkles of honeyed squash bugs. When the ant was broken into, the cooked lymph oozed out in a thick gel.

Anand was surprised by the platters and bowls on the eating leaves, which were finely decorated and glazed. Utchmay cut a fragrant drop of liquid from a nearby barrel and passed it to him in a slurping-cup embedded with fine crystals. Anand took a shallow lick of the drink and left the rest, even though the spices of the food left him thirsty. *I can smell the cannabis in it,* he thought, *and this is not a night for cannabis either.*

"Commander Quegdoth," said Utchmay. "How soon is the war with the Seed Eaters?"

"That is up to them," said Anand. "But I'd say it is soon. What position did you hold before the war?"

"I was foreman of the salvagers' caste, as was my father before me. But look at us now—eating ant meat in the black-sand barracks." He raised his cup to Anand and slurped from it.

"Defender, are all the war widows of this mound living in the center rings now?"

"They are."

"Were they relocated there? Forced to leave the barracks?"

"They made that decision all by themselves. They was instructed to combine households and welcome veterans and their families to the barracks and officers' rings. But they never accepted us—refused to look at us, much less live next to us. They wants to be among themselves, which be fine with us. 'Polluted darklings' is what they calls us."

Anand heard a sudden quiet and a rustle of low voices on his left side. He turned to see three men in priestly garb approaching him with the awkward gait of men in ball-shaped shoes. When they reached the platform, he saw their prominent miters shaped in the images of Grasshopper, Mantis, and Ant Queen. The priests did not bow but nodded to Anand from under their small torch of shriveling glow-fungus.

"Commander Quegdoth," said the oldest of them; he sounded as if he had a little ball balanced on the front of the tongue. "I am Lamonjeeno, High Priest at Mount Shishto. We welcome you to our mound. We would have made arrangements for a more gracious reception if we had known you were coming. As it is, we request your presence in the royal palace of Their Majesties, King Wahdrin and Queen Omathaza."

Anand looked at the priests, whose faces held a poorly masked contempt for him.

"What a gracious invitation," Anand said. "And may I ask about the nature of this . . . reception?"

Utchmay and Omal were looking at Anand and the priests, fascinated by their commander's sudden air of royalty as he imitated their speech through his Dranverish accent.

"You may, sir," said Lamonjeeno as he adjusted his miter shaped like Ant Queen. "Their Highnesses have some matters of importance they wish to discuss with you—matters they believe you would also find . . . pressing."

Anand hesitated, searched the eyes of the priests, and wondered what ambush lay in store.

"Tell Their Majesties I would be honored to join them," he said. "I and a number of my . . . company."

The priest failed to hide his frown. "Certainly, Commander. You and your guards will be welcomed."

"After we've finished eating . . . if you wouldn't mind," said Anand. "Would you care to join us? We have more than plenty."

The priests looked at each other and raised their eyebrows.

"We will. Thank you," said Lamonjeeno, to Anand's astonishment. The priests gingerly climbed the steps, then sat at the edges of the leaf, their legs splayed behind them instead of crossed before them. As they filled their platters, their miters bobbed and bent and caressed each other, as if they were puppets whispering secrets in a show.

As they ate, the priests spoke to no one, not even

each other, and they were oblivious to the stares of the crowd, who curiously watched them eat and drink.

"**W**e must congratulate you," said Queen Omathaza on her throne in the empty gloom of her barely lit palace. The throne was not at the top of the stairs, but arranged with the others near the bottom of the steps. Anand saw this as progress.

"On what, Queen?" said Anand. He looked from her to her aged husband, Wahdrin, who twiddled his braided, white beard. The priests who had summoned Anand were resuming their places to their monarchs' right where their torch's weak light was added to the dim tableau.

"On so many things," said the queen, whose gown was squeezed between the arms of her throne. "Your victory over the Hulkrites. The creation of your new nation. For the upending of . . . everything."

Her words are bitter, Anand thought, *coated with honey, but bitter as tar*. On the queen's left was a cluster of women in grand dress who he thought might be her daughters or sisters, until he discerned that their foreheads were painted with the blood slashes of war widows.

"Things needed to be upended," said Anand. "For most of us."

"I don't know that we would agree with that," said Wahdrin in his thin, breathy voice. "You would agree that there are dangers in instability."

"I would," said Anand. "But instability can lead to an improved stability. For *more* of us."

"How is my cousin, Queen Polexima?" the queen asked.

"She is well," said Anand.

"And her daughter? Your wife . . . of sorts?"

"As well as she can be."

"We have heard Trellana is on her way south. To be queen of the Palzhanites."

"Yes. She is assuming that . . . honor."

"That will do her well," said Omathaza. "A queen needs her dignity."

"We all need dignity," said Anand. "Or rather, we all need the respect that is due to each and every human." Anand shifted in the rough chair they had set across from them as his guards stood behind him, facing the chambers' entries. Servants entered and set a simple offering of withered mushrooms and cloudy water in a bowl before him. "What may I do for you, Highnesses?"

"We are not well treated," said one of the war widows from out of the darkness. Omathaza and Wahdrin looked over at the woman, offended that she had spoken out of turn.

"And who would be speaking?" Anand asked.

"Apologies, Commander Quegdoth," said Omathaza.

"I'm afraid that protocol, like so many things, has fallen to the wayside these days. May I present the wife of Commander General Walifex of Shishto, the Widow Walifex."

"My deep condolences for your loss, honored widow," said Anand.

"But it is not just our men we have lost," the widow wailed. "We have lost our homes, our servants, our way of life—all we have been accustomed to."

"If I may inquire," said Anand, carefully choosing his words. "What did you work so hard at that earned you the privileges to which you have grown accustomed?"

Walifex's mouth fell in disbelief and began to quiver.

"Your question is appalling! I believe it is obvious!"

"Forgive me if it is not obvious to me," said Anand.

"Our sacrifice!"

All the widows began crying in an exaggerated way and looked to the ceiling as if requesting mercy from the gods. "All of us—as girls of the martial caste— married as soon as we experienced our first bleeding. And all of us were pregnant soon after. We gave our lives, our wombs, our breasts, to the breeding of as many males as possible. We filled our army with the most capable soldiers—soldiers to defend this mound of Shishto and our Great and Holy Slope. Without our *children*, this nation would have been trampled by our enemies and overgrown with barley and pine trees."

Where to begin, Anand thought as the widow continued.

"And now we have made the greatest sacrifice of all—the loss of our husbands, fathers, brothers, and sons to the menace from Hulkren. And how have we been rewarded? To be forced from our houses to live in hovels in the center rings!"

"Who forced you? And how did they do that?"

"The untouchables! They threatened to touch us! Some of us *were* touched! We were polluted! And now our very houses are polluted!"

"Madame, with all due respect, touching someone . . ."

"We exist on little more than mushrooms and water and are clothed in old rags," she shouted, interrupting. "And we are treated as if we are nothing more than bloodsucking mites!"

Anand was quiet. "Madame, you will listen to me now, please. You would not be alive, you nor anyone else here, if it were not for the sacrifices of the Laborers' Army." Anand gestured to his guard and caught the eye of a woman among them. "It was men and *women* like these who destroyed the Hulkrites. Most of the defenders are laborers who continue their *usual* work. What, may I ask, are you and the war widows contributing now that the Hulkrish aggression has passed?"

"The question is outrageous!" shouted the widow.

"What would you expect us to contribute—in our grief?"

"That would be up to you. What manufactures can you offer? What services?"

"Those are not the duties assigned to our caste!"

"There are no more castes!" shouted Anand, unable to contain his ire. "If the soldiers of your caste were so good at fighting, then where are they now? Why is *my* army, made up of laborers, still alive to defend Bee-Jor?"

The Widow Walifex did not answer, but joined the others in a sobbing mixed with shrieks as they looked away from Anand.

"Commander Quegdoth," said Omathaza, who signaled to a priest to hand her his torch. She rose from her throne, raising the torch as if it were a club she might use to beat Anand. "These women—these *kinswomen* of mine—are not inspired to loyalty at the moment. They no longer inhabit the homes of their ancestors."

"I would agree with that," said Anand. "Since their ancestors *did not live* in Shishto. I am told the war widows left the black-sand barracks of their own volition—that they would not abide laborers as their neighbors."

The queen came closer to Anand. "What they could not abide, Commander, were the people who assumed these noble dwellings, then desecrated them with their trash, their stink, their harsh voices, and their ignorance and arrogance. These noble women had no choice but to flee from an invasion of darklings who simply don't belong here."

Anand's chest was heaving. He fingers were tightening into fists as anger—so familiar to him—took over his being. *Breathe deeply,* he reminded himself. *Think before speaking.*

"Madame, I believe you asked me here to request something. Is there something I can do to improve some situation?"

"Commander Quegdoth. You may not see the value in supporting our war widows or our priesthood. But you do see the value of maintaining a royal presence at this mound . . . a sorceress queen."

Anand hesitated, took a breath. "I do," he said.

"We must all feel comfortable where we live," Omathaza said. "Respected and safe. I do not feel much like a queen when my clothing and furnishings are bartered for a morsel of worm meat. And my wellbeing is hampered when my kin are humiliated—my good cousins who lost all their men in this war."

The queen was silent, stepping towards Anand as she met his eyes and looked over the brown skin of his face. The torch revealed her own face, which he could see had once been beautiful and plump and had now become slack and wrinkled.

"Anand of Cajoria. What will you do for us royal and military females in *all* of your new nation?" she hissed through the vaguest smile. "So that we will do what *we* must, so that your Bee-Jor and its ants and structures survive?" She cocked her head and looked at him as if he were some juicy flesh-fly she had trapped and was eager to slaughter and eat.

Anand grinned even as his anger turned to rage and he nodded in grudging respect of her cunning. "Your point is well taken, Omathaza, and warrants further discussion," he said through gritted teeth. "If you will excuse me now, there are other *greater* threats to you and yours that I must consider at the moment."

CHAPTER 27

A CLAN DIVIDED

The Entreveans' caravan was approaching Mound Venaris when a faint buzz overhead made Daveena look to the blinding light of the noon sun. Distant black objects were falling, getting larger, and then revealing themselves as blue locusts. Most of them landed at the head of the procession, but one fell near her sled, and its young and inexperienced pilot struggled to guide it back to the others in the crawling mode. Chieftain Thagdag sounded his thorn horn, and the chain of sleds halted as a message was passed up through the sleds. "Madame Anand, did you hear that?" said Punshu over his shoulder. "You are needed at the chieftain's sled."

Daveena's heartbeat quickened as she imagined who had summoned her. She walked quickly to the head of the caravan and saw the locusts being watered in a loose circle as their pilots remained seated and accepted offers of food and drink from roach women. As Daveena climbed the ladder to the riding ledge of Thagdag's sled, a hand reached down to pull her up and then into a warm embrace, which was followed by a tender kiss.

"Something must be wrong," she said.

"For the moment, all is right," said Anand with smiling eyes. They looked over at Thagdag, who seemed charmed and envious of their youthful passion.

"Do you need my cabin?" Thagdag asked.

"I shouldn't waste time," Anand said. "It's war. The Seed Eaters are preparing for an attack on Bee-Jor."

"They don't know it's Bee-Jor," said Daveena.

"Which is exactly what we must tell them as quickly as we can. The Entreveans must enter the Barley Lands and ask for an audience with Emperor Volokop."

"It would be dangerous to travel as far as Worxict," said Thagdag. "I've never been there. Others have been lost there. It's been decades since we went that far east. Once we got there, we have no idea if the emperor would receive us."

"We will arrive with a gift."

"What?"

"Something that belongs to them. But I need you to leave now."

"What about trade with the Old Slope?" asked Thagdag. "The priests are anxious for roach eggs … at all their mounds."

Anand considered the consequences of a weakened Slope poisoned by the Yellow Mold—that was an invitation to easy conquest by the Carpenter nation. *And they would march straight into Bee-Jor after that.*

"Then I need you to split off half your roaches and half of your clan to send to the Barley Lands. You will lead the other half to the Slope."

"Split up our caravan?" Thagdag asked with mild alarm. "And start another clan?"

"No! It's temporary. But we must meet with the Seed Eaters' sovereign as soon as we can."

"They won't let us very far if we don't have trade items," said Daveena.

"What do they want?"

"Cloth and thread—orange and blue are much desired, no black. They make their own embroideries and like fine needles. Their women and priests like jewelry made from rare beetle chitins as well as pendants and ear-bobs of pyrite. You can always sell them beads."

"And, of course, they like mushrooms," said Thagdag.

"Mushrooms? What kind of mushrooms?"

Thagdag shrugged and picked up a long, dried mushroom from his lunch.

"This kind—like the leaf-cutters grow. Should be

plenty available at Venaris. And we can trade them some of this honey and wax we've brought from Hulkren."

Daveena looked at Anand as he rapidly blinked, stopped breathing—he was shocked.

"Slopeites export their mushrooms to Seed Eaters?" he almost shouted, unable to contain his anger.

"They sell them to us, and we sell them to the Seed Eaters."

"Even as the people of these mounds were starving!"

"We have always traded them," Thagdag said, his brow furrowing under Anand's scolding. "The Seed Eaters' soldiers give them to their wives and daughters."

"Of course they do," said Anand as he grimaced. "Because they make women more fertile."

"There's a surplus of them now—dried, sugared, pickled, at all the mounds' marketplaces," said Daveena. "Now that the laborers are able to hunt and forage for decent food, the mushrooms are piling up."

"Then bring the Seed Eaters' mushrooms. For now," Anand said. "How long will it take to reach the eastern border?"

"With just a few roaches and a light load, they could be there in three days if they travel day and night," answered Thagdag. "Who will lead this little caravan if I'm to continue to the Slope?"

"She will," Anand said, jerking his thumb at Daveena who straightened with shock as her jaw dropped. Thagdag frowned and looked away.

"You're wary?" Anand said to him.

"I worry, yes."

"Chieftain, with all respect for your years and wisdom, Daveena will lead. She speaks the Seed Eaters' tongue as well as they do. And the Britasytes who go with her will obey her because she is, of course, my wife."

"Of course, Anand," said Thagdag, meeting his eyes. "But I worry because she grows heavy with your offspring. And she is . . . young to lead a caravan."

And she is a woman, I suspect he wants to say, thought Daveena.

"I am touched by your concern," Anand said. "But Daveena is no younger than you when you became chieftain."

Daveena turned towards Thagdag and made the slightest bow. "Chieftain, if I am in doubt about a situation we might face, I will ask myself what you would do."

Thagdag looked briefly at her and nodded his head.

"I will see you near the riding grounds of Shishto in three days, by midmorning," Anand said to Daveena. He patted her round and growing stomach. "Take good care . . . of everybody."

"My sadness is small, my heart is brave . . ." she managed to say after stiffening her lip.

". . . for I know I return with new tales of roaming," he completed for her.

"You're going back to Cajoria?"

"Soon," he said, descending the ladder. "I've got to make a stop first, make some arrangements—the gift for the Seed Eater's Emperor."

Within a few breaths, he was gone, flying north with his men. As she watched the locusts disappear into the sky's blue, she resented him for his brusque departure, then ached for his immediate return. She also wondered what it would be like to pilot a locust. *He's going to teach me to fly after these babies are born.*

"Punshu," she shouted, running back to their sled. "We're going to Seed Eater country. We'll need fresh roaches and everyone willing to risk their lives to see Worxict."

CHAPTER 28

SURPRISING NEWS

The sand-sled was not to Trellana's liking. It was too low to the ground, too small, and needed a fresh coating of lacquer. Its banners were faded and tattered and would not be replaced as they were considered "Slopeish." As they rode over rough patches, she felt as tossed as the beads of a baby rattle. The cushions were thin and flat and needed reupholstering, and there was barely room for the four maidservants she was allowed.

The worst thing about the sled was the unexpected passenger inside it: her brother Pious Nuvao. He was practically a stranger to her, and so unlike the rest of her brothers since he was the only one that had chosen the godly life and had lived most of it in Venaris. As he kept a soft yet watchful eye on her every activity, she knew he was not there for her religious guidance but to monitor what she ate and drank. Like their mother, he had adopted a simple woven garment of grass and long crickets' antennae that he let fly out the window as there was no room for them in the cabin. Around his neck was an amulet of Goddess Cricket, which he stroked when he mumbled his endless prayers to Her. Trellana thought he was all too pretty; why had the gods blessed him instead of her with such smooth, bright skin and large, entrancing blue eyes? And then he had those high-arching eyebrows, which gave him the appearance of being happily surprised by everything.

In the tight confines of the cabin, Trellana did not like smelling the breath of the others nor their bodily odors, as they all had to go without bathing. Their voices, even when whispering, seemed loud and harsh. The sunshine coming in through the windows was horribly bright, and worsened a headache that felt as if a lair spider had made its home under her skull. Her mother had warned her that she was about to go through the painful after-effects of giving up spirits, but she had not told her it would be so extremely excruciating.

The withdrawal symptoms were worse in the morning. The world looked blurry and unstable, and anything she fixed on seemed predatory and hungry. Large things looked ready to fall and crush her, and small things wanted to fly up and invade her through her nostrils. Even worse, when she closed her eyes she saw the oddest, most disturbing visions: living skeletons that traded bones with each other, ball gowns floating to the trees and shattering, the Sun eating Moon and then regurgitating him as bits and pieces that crawled away as whistling maggots. And always, at the back of her mind and in the quietest moments, she heard the agonized crying of her and Maleps's babies—the boys she had left behind in Cajoria. Sometimes when the crying got its loudest, she would look out the sled's window and see her sons—they had sprouted wasp wings and were shedding tears of blood as they hovered and pleaded for her return.

Trellana knew that all of these ugly daymares would vanish in an instant if she were allowed a good, long draught of some decent fermentation. Nuvao had denied her requests again and again, and even slapped her face once after she had attacked him with her fingernails while threatening to kill herself. "You won't have to take your own life," he said. "I'll do it for you. Or, if you like, we can drag you behind the sled, facedown, until your nose and lips are scraped off."

One thing that gave her the slightest relief was knowing that Cajoria, now the most dreadful of places, was getting farther away with each day of travel. But oddly, every time she looked out the window, she could still *see* the mound, even days after their departure. She even saw it at night when it was lit up like a million lightning flies that had crashed into a heap. One afternoon, staring at the persistent illusion, she determined to wish it away when she saw two great giants, as tall as trees, growing out of the sand with the smuggest and ugliest faces. The first giant was her strange and traitorous mother, who, as ever, looked at her with poorly concealed disappointment. The other giant was the Dranverite who smoldered with open contempt for her, his hand raising an enormous mallet to crush her sled into a splintery pulp. She pounded her skull to make these visions go away, but they were soon replaced by a swirling cloud of blood-red midges that spat and cursed at her as they swarmed around her head. When she attempted to swat them away, the midges invaded her coiffure by the thousands where they were soon engaged in noisy intercourse while expelling a stenchy gas.

Sometimes, when the headaches, the bone aches, and the skin-crawling were unbearable, she had to scream—she had to wail and quiver uncontrollably until she was exhausted enough to earn a little bit of sleep. One afternoon she awoke to find the visions were gone, if not the headaches. Her brother offered her wafers with bits of roach eggs and then a drinking bladder of fresh grass extraction. "Drink it and grow strong," he said. "It will help." The liquid tasted most foul, and she shivered involuntarily after swallowing it. She had no choice but to eat the wafers, which resulted in a catastrophe of flavors that ravaged her tongue. "I'm never eating these again," she said.

"You will," he said. "It's your duty as a queen and you know it."

"Why do they taste even worse now?"

"They were baked without sweeteners. Honey, syrup, and barley sugar are very much in demand now."

The procession had taken the traditional route south that connected the eastern mounds, but they had yet to stop for a courtly visit or to spend the night at a palace. "I'm afraid you are not quite presentable," said Nuvao when she asked him about it. Instead of bringing her to a royal dwelling for sleep on a proper mattress, they left her in the sled's cabin and bound its doors with rope locks to prevent her from bolting into the dark. Nuvao and the chambermaids escaped her nocturnal screaming and smelly night sweats by climbing up ladders to sleep in the abandoned hovels of common laborers, and then leaving them as soon as Sun arose.

One afternoon, with the symptoms of Trellana's withdrawal subsiding, Pious Nuvao accepted the first of some invitations from fellow royals to sup and sleep in comfort at the top of their mounds. Trellana and her entourage gathered with their hosts in the dark, empty palaces of Abavoon, Gorotika, and Shlipee where they dined, poorly, on mushrooms and dew water and whatever else might be scraped together. At Shlipee, Trellana's distant cousin, Queen Zherquees, presented the guests with the first meat of the journey. It was something that was undercooked and runny after it left the sun-kiln on what had been a gray day.

"What fine thing are we enjoying?" Trellana asked, pretending the dish was not bitter and gritty or tasting of excrement as she dipped into the mess with her mushroom wafer. "So kind of you to offer meat."

"It is a tarantula and not a fresh one," said Zherquees. "Dead already when they pulled it out of its burrow. I'm afraid what we are eating is from the abdomen. We ate the head and leg marrow last night."

"Well, it is meat all the same, thank you."

The dinner, like the ones on the previous nights, was another morose, quiet affair made up mostly of mourning women, some depressed priests, and the odd king or prince who was too debilitated or dim-witted to make conversation. *This will pass,* Trellana thought as she was handed a cone of dark, cloudy mead from what looked and smelled like a rotten barrel. Her brother snatched the cone from her hand.

"You have come too far, dear sister, to endanger your fetus with this," said Nuvao.

"Endanger your fetus?" said Zherquees. "Are you with child, Trellana?"

"I . . . I am," she said. "With children, I believe."

"Then we need to bring out our best spirits. To

celebrate. I believe we have one last jar of a rather young phantom-berry-wine I was hoping to let age but . . . yes, this is a special occasion."

"That won't be necessary, thank you, Zherquees," said Nuvao. "Trellana has made a pledge to go without spirits until her babies are born."

"A pledge to whom?" the queen asked.

"No one of importance," said Trellana.

"To the father of these children-to-be," said Nuvao.

"Oh," said Zherquees. "Him."

"Trellana's second set of children are the first to be born from the union of a Slopeite and a Dranverite," said Nuvao. "The first issue of the Great Defender and a Slopeish royal."

"No wonder she wants a drink," said Zherquees. "And I will make sure she has one." The queen raised her hand as a signal to her servant when Nuvao grabbed it and pulled it down sharply first, then gently when he realized his error.

"That will not be . . . necessary," he said as he watched her face go wide with shock.

"Pious Nuvao, you are in my home," said the queen. "As my guest."

"Forgive me . . . Majesty," he said. "I meant no offense. But the future of our nation is invested in the sound mind and bodies of Commander Quegdoth's children. He is of the firm belief that spirits imbibed during pregnancy make for weak, sickly, and stupid offspring. This is wisdom from Dranveria—a nation we know to be superior to our own."

"I believe the Britasytes also hold this ridiculous belief about pregnancy and what should not be drunk," said Zherquees. "Are they our superiors as well?"

"Yes," said Nuvao. "They are masters of different tongues, as well as trading, crafting, and other skills. A brilliant people."

"How I long for the old days," said Trellana. "Those days when Dranverites were nothing more than some story told on long winter nights . . . and when Britasytes were nothing but some wandering roach trash."

"The old days are not completely gone," said Zherquees.

"No?" said Trellana.

"The Old and Noble Slope does not just survive in the West. It thrives."

"Does it?" asked Nuvao, one eyebrow lifted. "Perhaps you have received different accounts here at Shlipee than we have in Cajoria."

"Our military is about to take back Mound Teffelan. They are driving those Beetle Riders back into their pine trees."

"That is surprising," said Nuvao. "That is not what we have heard."

Trellana felt a flush in her cheeks and her heartbeat

quicken. "They have taken back Teffelan? That is not so far from Palzhad. Perhaps when there is peace they will invite us to a victory ball."

"If this is at all true, I shall be glad to accompany you . . . to a victory ball," said Nuvao.

"The men of Teffelan are supposed to be quite handsome. And very good hunters," said Trellana.

"Sister, may I remind you that you are married. And pregnant," said Nuvao. "And most of the men at Teffelan and in the Old Slope are mostly very old or are not quite men yet." Trellana looked at her brother with pinched lips. She was dunking a fresh wafer in the tarantula dip when she dropped it and decided she had lost her appetite. A silence followed in which she heard someone's snoring . . . old King Titzock had fallen asleep and no one was bothering to wake him. His wife, the queen, just looked at him, mildly annoyed, before she slurped up her mead.

"I . . . I hesitate to bring this up," said Zherquees in the silence as she turned to Trellana. "As communication is so unreliable between our nations. But we have heard that . . . heard . . ."

"What?" said Trellana.

"We have heard your husband, Prince Maleps, may be alive—may even be leading the battle against the Carpenter People."

"*What?*" Trellana felt a wave of joyous warmth roll through her, something that had finally vanquished her headache. "What have you heard? It might be his brother, Kep, that's alive. They were twins."

"You mean they *are* twins," said Zherquees. "Kep has been sighted as well, with Maleps."

Trellana emitted something that was like a laugh, a gasp, and a cry of relief.

"What a lovely dinner!" she said. "What lovely days ahead!"

The following morning, for the first time in her life, Trellana rose from bed without anyone prodding her. She was eager to get back in the sand-sled and proceed towards Palzhad, offering excuses to her hosts' servants for not joining them at the sunrise prayer and the morning meal. "I simply must get to Palzhad," she said to Zherquees's chamber mistress. "They are relying on me. We have heard the vaguest wisps of the Yellow Mold are making an appearance, and so we kindly ask Her Majesty's forgiveness, and thank her for kindness. Please let her know we must be on our way and will extend an invitation to her soon."

Nuvao was looking at Trellana with something like bemused contempt as they entered the sled's cabin. She could see in his face not just her mother's fine features, but her weakness for worry. *The two of them think too much*, she thought. *But I will not let him ruin this very beautiful morning.*

"Ladies," she said, addressing her maidservants

with her first smile in a fortnight. "We will need to think about a post-anointment gown."

The servants burst into smiles and happy gasps, and a lively discussion of options ensued. Occasionally Trellana looked at her brother, who was annoyed by the discussion of pleats, hemlines, and lace patterns that consumed the morning. The conversation finally ended when the procession was forced to halt and then pulled to the side. They heard the jeers of a rough-looking crowd from Mound Destroppo, which had gathered at the route's edges. At first Trellana feared they were under attack, that rogue laborers had left their work to raid her procession. Nuvao pulled up the window flap and they saw guards mounted on hauling ants that dragged a prison cage on a sled. The laborers were hurling trash and sand grains at the cage, whose inhabitant was tightly bound to its bars with a thickness of ropes.

"Good gods in Ganilta! It's Pleckoo!" said Nuvao.

"Pleckoo. Really," said Trellana as she looked at his ropes. "I don't imagine he's terribly comfortable."

"He is not," said Nuvao. "We are witnessing an extraordinary moment!"

"At the moment he's in our way," said Trellana. "I'm perfectly willing to cut his feet off myself and have him bleed to death if that speeds things up. We would never have tolerated this on the Old Slope. A day or so is long enough to torture someone—inflict some pain, drain some blood, then make an example of his corpse."

Pleckoo was suffering from thirst as the ant train slowed at yet another mound, where a fresh rabble gathered to torment him. *Anand wants everyone to get their chance, so they can all tell their grandchildren about the day they got their licks in,* he thought. He looked through the bars, then noticed a large Cajorite sled across from him with its faded banners flapping in the breeze. Its passengers were looking out their window at him, covering their noses to cut off the stink of the filth that had gathered on the sled. From behind him, he heard the growing crowd of haters as they poured out of the weeds to rattle his cage, climb on top of it, and rain down their piss. The guards ordered them back, and when they had order, they opened the cage's door. Short ladders were set on both sides of him and he knew they would be climbing up to force liquids down his throat again.

No, not this time. I will not open my mouth, he determined. *I will die of thirst before I reach Cajoria.*

"Breakfast!" Goiter shouted at him. "Be a good boy and suck the titty." Pleckoo gritted his teeth as Sewn Shut readied to jam the tube of a squeeze bag down his throat. Pleckoo shook his head as best as he could.

"He's not happy today," said Sewn Shut. "Come on, Pleckoo, open up. Or we'll have to get this tube past your lips by knocking your teeth out."

"And you don't want to eat your own teeth," Goiter said to him, "They'll really hurt coming out your other end. So suck down your breakfast."

Pleckoo only gripped his molars harder, grinding them.

"I've got an idea," said Sewn Shut, who suddenly plunged the bag's tube into Pleckoo's nose cavity, then squeezed the contents. He choked, then drowned on the liquid as a panic exploded through him. He blacked out, and when he came to, he felt the tube deep and scraping into his throat and then his stomach quickly filled to bloating. He retched and spat up something deeply rancid before they yanked the tube from out of his mouth.

"That's a good little Hulkrite," said Sewn Shut. "Now go out and play."

The guards left the cage and retied its door. "Have at him!" they shouted to the crowd, and Pleckoo felt the cage rattle as boys and young men climbed its bars.

This trial will end, thought Pleckoo as his ropes were soaked anew. *And Hulkro will help me kill every last infidel of Bee-Jor.*

gentle contact with the sand. Anand had not experienced such a perfect end to a flight since flying with Jidla in Dranveria.

"Well done, Ter. I'm surprised," Anand said as he jumped down.

"Were you expecting less?" said Terraclon, wrinkling his brow.

"Of course not."

"Then why are you surprised? Because I'm a two spirit who can pilot a locust?"

"No! I'm surprised that you learned so quickly."

"So quickly? Because I'm usually so slow?"

"Why are you giving me such a hard time? I was complimenting you."

"When do I usually give you a hard time?" Terraclon said, then looked away to hide his glistening eyes.

"You know, you could just say something like, 'Be careful, my friend. I'll miss you.'"

"There you go, charming yourself again. Oh, I forgot . . . you're a god. Or at least a demigod, I'm not sure."

Anand rolled his eyes, gave with a quiet laugh. "Fly high when you're scouting inland. Don't let them sight you."

"I will. Why are you sure they're coming at all?"

"I am told that before they go to war, they dig pits before an idol of their moon god, Lumm Korol, whose mount is the Night Mantis. The pits are filled with the old or sickly or crippled who are shot or stabbed when they try and escape. When they're all dead, barley seeds are rolled on top of the corpses. And when the pits are refilled . . . they go to war. They've prepared those at the feints and likely somewhere inland, where they're really gathering."

"And I thought it was shameful to be a Slopeite."

"Don't fly alone. Take a squadron. Locusts are less dependable as the days get shorter and cooler."

"I'll be careful."

"And, Ter, I know I don't need to ask, but—look after my dad when you can. And Polexima. I think . . . I know she gets lonely too."

Terraclon was startled. "I suppose she does," he said. "So do a lot of people."

"We all get lonely."

"Then why do we feel such shame to admit it?"

"I don't. Be careful, my friend. I'll miss you."

"Right, Commander. All that."

Anand walked away to a cluster of yellowing mallow plants.

"Anand!"

He turned and looked at Terraclon, who wore his most serious face. "What, Ter?"

"Don't come back empty-handed."

Terraclon smiled to reveal his oversized teeth before he coaxed his locust back into the sky. Anand took a sniff of the tart air and walked to the mallow cluster, where the Britasytes and their roaches were waiting for him. Punshu emerged from out of the mallow's shadows with a scented roach cape to disguise Anand's ant-scent. As he tied it under his chin, Anand took a deep whiff of its rich and complex aromas, then was plunged into early memories of his first visits to roach camps—those places where he felt happily at home among a homeless people. His happiness expanded as he entered the depth of the mallows' shade and sighted Daveena on the riding ledge of their sled, where she was intensely at work on a garment. He ran to her, and as they plunged into each other's warmth, he rubbed his palm over her belly and felt her swollen naval.

"I'm going to have days with you," he said between warm, wet kisses.

"Not easy days. I've got something for you, in an orange that will please the Seed Eaters," she said after leaving his hungry arms. She held up a man's traditional Britasyte tunic to wear under his roach-wing cape. The garment was as bright as a spring poppy, with a subtle pattern of roaches racing after each other in a darker shade of orange. Anand smiled as he admired its subtle qualities and the way the spiraling pattern continued without breaking over the seams. "It should be able to hide your under-armor," Daveena said, showing him the tunic's quilted padding on its insides.

"It's very beautiful," he said. "Like its maker." He pulled it on over his armor and it felt slightly snug, something that would improve after a few days of wearing. Daveena's eyes were running up and down her husband's naked legs, which retained patches of scabs.

"My legs are good, don't worry," he said.

"You know I married you for your legs," she said. "And I can't bear seeing this kind of damage to my investment." She went inside the cabin to retrieve some roach salve, and a moment later his legs were glistening, smoother, and soothed.

Once the caravan was assembled, Punshu and other Britasyte men unfolded the pole of an enormous banner with the embroidered image of an orange roach. When they reached the border wall, they raised the banner to full height. A Seed Eater sentry in their distant tower signaled recognition of the entering roach tribe by raising a banner of their own, one with a dark orange background and the bright green figure of Katydid the Barley Goddess.

"Break it down!" Anand shouted to the Shishtite guards, and a section of the wall was disassembled in a swathe large enough to allow for the caravan's passing. Anand and Daveena rode at the head of the sandsleds, behind grass shields on the riding ledge, with Punshu as their driver. The boy leaned in, fiercely, as if his chin were a dagger cutting its way through the wilderness. He had split his long curls into three separate tails on the back of his head, and thrown back his cape to reveal a new tunic of orange silk with flame patterns, something drawn from the memory of the war against the Hulkrites.

Anand looked behind him as the caravan completed its passage to see the wall being quickly rebuilt by the Shishtite guards. Ahead of them was the Seed Eaters' low, rough wall before the grim little border village where he had crashed with Omal. Its inhabitants were shyly emerging from their shelters and perched atop their pebble mound to marvel at the sparkling sleds and their extravagant carvings. The woman with her baby in a sling appeared, followed by the rest of her children or siblings—Anand wasn't sure. Anand thought all of them looked better, less haggard; but their eyes still seemed too big in their withered faces. The chieftain, wearing his rags of grass cloth, appeared from his dwelling at the top of the mound with two wives and at least ten ill-fed and poorly clothed children. Their low wall was disassembled by men who strained to remove its sand grains, then fell in exhaustion.

Daveena bowed to them all once they entered. "Thank you, glorious Barley people, beloved of Katydid, for kindly allowing us passage through your beautiful and gracious land."

Anand knew what she had said from a few words—the customary greeting—but he was still stumped by Yatchmin, a language that bore no resemblance to any he knew. He was thrown by the word placements and what sounded like a complete lack of vowels. He cleared his throat.

"Daveena, tell them that Commander Quegdoth, the ruler of Bee-Jor, formerly known as the Slope, sends his warm greetings and a gift of food," Anand said, and Daveena nodded towards him, then shouted out the translation.

Anand and Punshu unfolded the roach banner's pole again to bring it to full height, then waved it atop their sand-sled. The Barley people and Britasytes heard a gentle rumbling and turned to see Bee-Jorite guards all along the border walls pushing acorns over it that rolled to the villagers. One of the acorns, older and darker, came closest to the village and the youths ran out to it and squealed with delight to find holes in its shell. They set to work with their ant-pincer daggers and yanked out the white weevil maggots inside the acorn, then ran back to the mound while licking and nibbling on them as they squirmed in their arms. The woman with the baby gasped when she recognized Anand. She smiled and waved at him with her free hand, shouting, *"Shpeebo crasshpy shirca!"*

"What's she saying?" he asked.

"You have an admirer," said Daveena. "She says, 'Thank you, handsome sir.'"

"Tell the village chieftain that Bee-Jorite acorns have been rolled to the border villages all along

Shishto as an offering in peace. Ask him to pass this news through their . . . um, beautiful empire. Tell him the new nation of Bee-Jor respects the nation of the Barley people and wants to be their peaceful neighbor."

Daveena shouted Anand's message to the villagers as a scattering of harvester ants came through the weeds, raised their antennae, then quickly turned and sped away after detecting roach-scent. Anand ordered the procession to resume. He felt strangely unsure of himself as he looked out at this foreign nation from the lower perspective of a sand-sled. At this intimate level, the Barley Lands looked harsh and primitive and evoked an eerie sadness. When they reached a mass of scrub trees where the sand route split, Punshu veered them right.

"This is the way?" Anand asked as they traveled through almost identical villages, all of them densely spaced. "This is the usual route?"

"Yes," she said. "It's the route we've traveled for centuries if we're going to Durxict first." He looked up at the pebble tower of the passing village, which was like a thin pyramid with a rope wrapped around its top that connected it to the tower of the next village. He noticed men at the top of these structures looking down from platforms with bows at the ready and quivers full of arrows.

"Are those religious structures or watchtowers?" he asked.

"They are both," she answered.

"And are those soldiers or sheriffs on top?"

"Both," she said. "They don't distinguish between the two. The closest word we have is *sentry*."

As the caravan continued east, Anand was uncomfortable to see masses of villagers leaving their dwellings to gather at the edges of the sand route. They looked at the Britasytes from behind pebbles or tufts of weeds or with a shy, sideways stare. It was all the more eerie that they did so in complete quiet, shushing their children if they tried to speak.

"Do they always gather like this?" he asked Daveena.

"Always."

"I don't like it. A predator is silent before it strikes."

"We are all quite safe."

As Anand looked at this long wall of gaunt, raggedy villagers, he tried to ponder their existence. If this was their future, it was no wonder Tahn was able to lure so many Seed Eaters into Hulkren.

"When do we stop and trade?" he asked.

"Not for two, maybe three days. Until we reach Durxict."

"Why not before?"

"Do these people look like they have anything to trade?"

"That's what worries me. We have plenty they might like to take."

"They wouldn't dare. They are more obedient

than you know." Daveena tilted her head up to the men in the watchtowers. "They know very well not to molest roach trains bearing goods to the mounds."

Anand looked over the people's heads to see a few scattering harvester ants as they sniffed, then retreated up to barley stalks to wave their antennae. Some were shaking their abdomens, and a whiff of their poison reached the caravans. "Breathing masks," said Daveena when the smell thickened and began to irritate their lungs. "They've sensed some leaf-cutter-scent." She went to a seed chest and retrieved masks with filters and their connected quartz goggles, and passed them to Punshu and Anand as others in the sleds behind them did the same. When they reached the top of a grade by late afternoon, Anand saw the first human-inhabited ant mound and what looked like a larger, secondary city next to it.

"Durxict?" Anand asked.

"Yes," said Daveena.

Sometime after the sun grew larger and softer, Daveena gave an order. "Pull over, Punshu. We'll spend the night here."

"Why spend the night?" Anand asked "Let's keep going."

"Night travel is not permitted."

"Why not?"

"Because they say so. We'll camp here."

"Here? On the sand route?"

"There are no clearings large enough to accommodate us until we reach the city," Daveena said. "We will camp here, leaving enough room for any Seed Eaters to pass on foot if they need."

"And we'll be safe? Surrounded by all these starving Seed Eaters?"

"Anand, you are new to the Barley Lands. But it has always been this way. You did put me in charge, didn't you?"

"I suppose I did," said Anand as he looked out at masses of people coming out of the barley stalks to stand or sit and stare at them in the falling darkness. "So are all these people going to just watch us and our sleds while we're sleeping? Just what are they expecting?"

"A little entertainment," she said. "That is what we do."

"But we haven't brought anything—no stage or costumes or fungus lights."

"They are very entertained at the moment. All we have to do is stand here and be ourselves and they will find it fascinating. They can't wait to see us eat. And later, if we bring out our drums and sing a little in the dark, it will be their best night in moons."

"You're being sarcastic."

"I'm not."

"Should we invite some of them to join us at the meal?"

"Not permitted."

True to her word, the silent Seed Eaters watched the Britasytes as they docked their roaches and fed and watered them. Later they watched as the roach people ate a simple dinner and then visited among each other's sleds. The Britasytes were oblivious to the hundreds of quiet watchers—all of them but Anand, who looked back at them and wondered if he should pity them for their deprivation or envy them that they were so easily amused. When it grew dark, it got very dark, and not one of the Seed Eaters had a torch of any kind. Anand could see them only as solid black shadows, and he was sure that was how he appeared to them.

"We should sing now and drum a bit," Daveena said. Anand stumbled in the darkness of their cabin for a drum for himself and a grater and rubbing stick for Daveena. They began with a slow and simple rhythm and were soon joined by drummers on other sleds, who weaved their variations into the beat. Daveena sang the first song of the night in Yatchmin, and Anand was taken with the honeyed sadness of the tune. He was just wondering what the words meant when she sang the Britasyte translation.

> *I will get through this life,*
> *Will suffer for my pleasure.*
> *I'll ask what my emperor needs,*
> *Not waste my time in leisure.*

"But it's instructions on how to be a good slave. Suffer for the rulers now, paradise later."

"Singing this song allows us to travel these lands. They might have a problem with a tune called 'Let's Kill the Emperor and Raise Ourselves Up.'"

They continued on the route for two more days and two more nights, until Punshu veered right before a shallow pond and a cluster of beautifully crooked sycamore trees that had fallen and sprouted new branches along the lengths of their reclining trunks. They continued to Durxict through stands of barley and other seed plants, including chia, red wheat, buckwheat, maize, and autumn amaranth, the latter of which Anand had eaten in Dranverish dinners. Its densely packed flowers bloomed in pendulous ropes, and their bright maroon provided the first real color they had seen in days. They continued past piles of accumulated pebbles on Durxict's edge and saw workers in the process of sorting them, breaking them down into smaller sizes, or chipping at them to shape into building blocks.

As they got closer to the mound, they entered into an irregularly shaped wall that surrounded a slaughtering ground. Countless cages of living insects were stacked one atop the other. On the ground below, they witnessed ritual slaughters with priests dressed as the insects they were killing—Katydid, Cricket,

Grasshopper, and Locust. Other cages held insects being killed by different priests who honored Aphid, Black Weevil, and Red Mite.

The dissected insects were dragged by travoises into the next walled encirclement, another strangely shaped structure with an area in its west that had been cleared. On the eastern side was a busy market crowded with chaotic rows of tables and stalls under woven grass tarps. The orange-haired Durxites watched as the roach caravan took its place in the clearing. Anand heard the market quieting as sellers and purchasers turned to look at them in a way he did not like.

"Now what?" he said to Daveena.

"We wait for permission to market," she said.

"Why does no one ever smile here?"

"It's disrespectful. If you show your happiness, it incites people's envy. Keep your joy to yourself."

"Or infect others with it."

"Simply not done."

As they waited for permission, the caravan made its usual if smaller camping arrangement by arranging the sleds in a circular position, as the wranglers assembled the roach pen and then herded and tethered the insects inside it. Anand was astonished by how different the people of this mound looked when compared with the scantily clad villagers of the borderland. The ones standing and staring at them were wearing long, embroidered robes of rich, deep colors, and all of them incorporated the bright orange fuzz cloth of velvet ants in their collars. On their heads were one-, two-, or three-pointed nimbus hats that were decorated with strung bits of Britasyte beads. In back of them stood mysterious figures in tent-like robes wearing orange bonnets with long antennae for negotiating with the harvester ants. As for the ants, they had fled the Britasyte's roach-scent and were scurrying along the top of the wall, their antennae waving, as they retreated into the mound and left a faintly poisonous toxin that made Anand's eyes water.

"Are those merchants?" Anand asked Daveena as some of the nimbus-hatted came closer with the most severe look on their faces.

"They are. They are disappointed there are so few of us."

"How do you know?"

"I can see it on their faces."

"You can? They look as glum as everyone else."

"They are glummer than usual. Come, we have to assemble before our sleds and wait."

Daveena stood in front of the sleds and was joined by Anand and the rest of the Roach Clan, all of them facing front, standing stiffly, as if for a military inspection. "Give me your arm," she said to Anand, and she held it with her right hand as her left held a brown lacquer box. Anand looked up at the crooked yet towering wall of glued and reinforced pebbles and saw a few harvester ants poking their heads over its top, their beards brushing over its rough surface before they retreated. From their pen, Anand heard the roaches as they clicked and pivoted, sensing so many nearby ants.

"The roaches need feeding and watering," he said to Daveena.

"We will do nothing until we receive official permission."

"Whom do we get that from?"

"We are never quite sure. But someone will approach. They want very much to trade."

The people of the market quieted as all waited for something to happen. At last Anand heard a strange and rhythmic sound growing stronger. A procession of drummers appeared with nutshell kettledrums, which they brushed/tapped with sticks that ended in stiff bristles. Four large and muscular men wearing pied orange and green garments marched in a slow unison, as one of them instructed, "Shmug," before they took each step. Atop their broad shoulders was a sedan chair and a weirdly oblong cabin with a screen that hid its occupant. When the sedan was set down before the Britasytes, its carriers lifted up the cabin to reveal its occupant. He remained seated on a magnificent chair, or perhaps a throne, the back of which was carved and gilded into a radiant sun-disc. The young man had strange features that Anand had seen somewhere before . . . a heavy lower face, large thick lips, and eyes with a pleasant fold over them. He was

wearing a thirteen-pointed nimbus hat, and his thick
hair and beard were an abundance of long, thin plaits
that had been combined into larger, cable-like braids
that were cinched with orange bead clasps.

He looks like a Bulkokan! Anand realized as the
man made a faint wave of his fingers as a demand
for Daveena to come forward. She pressed her hands
together and bowed and waited for him to speak.
Once he did, she opened up the box before him and
its upper lid glinted with a pleasant yellow sparkle.
Anand knew that inside it were one hundred wafers
of the Holy Mildew. The man, whoever he was, accepted the box, set it on his lap, and clasped his hands
over it. As he conversed with Daveena, she answered
each of his questions with a bow of her head, and at
one of them, she pointed to Anand.

The young man was shaking his head no. Anand
heard Daveena's voice as it got more excited, louder,
but again he shook his head no. Anand started to
speak to her when she threw out her hand to quiet
him, followed by a glare over her shoulder. She curtsied lower, then made her request. After a moment
the man nodded, permitting her to return to Anand.

"He is the princeling, a Dur Knazhek. His father is
the Dur Gorodz, the Grand Prince of the mound and
brother of the emperor in Worxict."

"Will they meet with me?"

"No. The Knazhek said he will pass our messages
to his father, who will pass them to the emperor. He

says the emperor has never met with an outsider. He will only consider their messages."

"And you have told him it is urgent, that we want to avoid a war and have come with an offer of a peace treaty."

"I have told him, but he says they are very eager to wage war on the Mushroom Eaters. He says the Slope can rename itself, but that does not make it a new or different nation. Emperor Volokop wants his mounds back."

"Ask him if I may approach."

Anand opened his roach-wing cape to reveal the orange tunic inside and then bowed. He saw the princeling was intrigued by the brightness of the cloth. Daveena made her request, and he shrugged before he motioned Anand to come forward.

Anand lowered his head, then stood at full height and kept his cape open with his elbows set back. "Our deepest gratitude for meeting with us today," he said, and Daveena followed with a translation. "And our gratitude for allowing our caravans to travel in your lands and conduct commerce. Soon, we should like to bring you the fabled goods of our newest contact, the greatest, richest, and most powerful nation on the Sand."

Daveena hesitated and looked at Anand with widened eyes. He urged her to relay his words with a sharp pointing of his chin. As she spoke, the princeling leaned forward in his throne and looked at Anand with eyes that popped open and dilated. He asked Daveena a question.

"He is asking if you speak of the Red Ant people of the Northern Unknown Beyond the Sweet Blue Lake—what we call Dranveria."

"Tell him yes."

"Are you sure? They may be enemies."

"Tell him yes, I speak of the Dranverites, a people who seek peace with their neighbors."

She curtsied, answered the question. From the volume of his voice and the look on his face, Anand could see the princeling was scolding her. She turned to Anand, short of breath.

"What's wrong?"

"He's angry with me because I hesitated in my translation. He is asking if you have had direct contact with Dranverites."

"Tell him the truth. Tell him I *am* a Dranverite."

The princeling stood up and stared at Anand.

"I don't think I need to translate that," Daveena said. The princeling spoke sharply with one of his sedan porters, who ran off. He spoke to a second porter, who ran off as well.

The princeling stared at Anand and Daveena in silence.

"So much staring," Anand said. "Don't they know it's impolite?"

"I'm going to ask him if we can trade our goods

now," she said, "but only to fill the silence." The princeling nodded his head.

A second sedan with two chairs appeared, and the princeling pointed sternly to it as an order that Daveena and Anand should get on top of it.

"I sense we are in trouble," Anand said.

"Not too much trouble. Or we'd be walking behind him."

"Britasytes, sell some goods," Anand shouted. "Keep half to trade for the journey home—you may need them."

The Britasytes pulled down the tables attached to their sled's sides and arranged their goods.

"Punshu!" Anand called to his driver. "If we are not back by sunset, you are all to return to Cajoria—immediately—and contact Pious Terraclon and Queen Polexima. Tell them we are captives."

"We won't leave without you!" Punshu shouted.

"You may have to. You must . . . for everyone's safety."

Anand saw the worried look on Punshu's face as he struggled to look fierce. Anand and Daveena sat on the sedan's comfortable, cushioned chairs and were hoisted up and onto the shoulders of the carriers who followed the princeling's sedan. They entered a wide tunnel that opened into another walled, oddly shaped ring of more than twenty stories. The walls had hundreds of large, open, and arching windows throughout its bulging pebble construction. Seated under each arch was one man or one woman in colorful, flowing robes and jackets with broad shoulder pads and each of them wearing a nimbus hat. Most of them had their eyes closed in prayer but some opened them to watch as the sedan chairs passed.

"Who are they?" Anand asked.

"Priests and priestesses," Daveena answered.

"What are they doing?"

"They are communing with their gods," she said.

"They appear to be doing nothing," Anand said. "Which makes them typical of clergy everywhere."

"Shh," she said. "This is their prayer wall. They believe if prayers are not constantly made to each of their deities that the slighted ones will get jealous and angry and curse or neglect the mortals."

"As I said. Doing nothing," he whispered. "Where do you think we're going?"

"To meet the Dur Gorodz, I hope," she said. "I've never been in one of their palaces. Why did you tell him you're a Dranverite?"

"Because I sensed they would want to meet one."

"How do you know they won't imprison you?"

"I suspect we are already their prisoners. It's a risk I'll take to avoid war with them—one we might not win."

The sedan chairs entered into another walled circle, which Anand realized was a stable that housed drawing insects and sand-sleds. The Seed Eaters' sleds were longer and lower and resembled something like centipedes in their design. The scales under the runners were densely packed, and looked to be crafted more for a comfortable ride rather than a speedy one. Anand and Daveena's sedan chair was set in a slot at the top of a sled. Wranglers appeared wearing rough, oily clothes, and led eye-spotted bean beetles to the reins with lure sticks whose ends were a stinking speckle bean, fermented in tree sap.

The princeling stared at the two of them from his chair.

"Ask him where we're going. Maybe the Gorodz is out hunting or something."

Daveena spoke with the princeling, whose words were clipped and whose tone was stern. He made angry gestures and pointed east.

"Are we meeting the Gorodz or not?"

"No," she said. "He's sending us to meet the emperor."

CHAPTER 30

A NEW QUEEN FOR MOUND PALZHAD

"**G**ood gods on Ganilta," Trellana said when the sand-sled slowed again. "What's in our way now?"

Bevakoof, the eldest and plumpest of her maid-servants, peered out the window and blinked in astonishment. "Your Highness, it is acorns!"

"Acorns? Very well. Let's have the guards roll them away."

"They *are* being rolled. But it looks like hundreds of them—maybe thousands—in the route."

"What?"

She looked at Nuvao, who shrugged, unconcerned, as he unrolled his cylinder of scratching paper and went to work with his stylus. Trellana left the cabin, and after pinching her eight skirts together she made the difficult climb up the spiral staircase to its observation perch. She looked out and saw masses of people rolling acorns up the sand route. Behind most of these men were their families—wives and sisters and children—hauling their possessions behind them. Trellana was confounded, and returned to the cabin.

"It's the oddest thing," she said as she watched her brother scratch into his roll. "Why are thousands of these people rolling acorns to Palzhad?"

"Perhaps they were asked to roll them," Nuvao said.

"Why?"

"So that they could be split open and eaten."

"Eaten? By whom? Acorns are very bitter."

"The refugees in the border weeds need food. I am sure they can abide a little bitterness at this moment."

"Why would we feed the refugees?"

"Because they are starving."

"What do we care if they starve? They aren't Slopeites."

"Some of them were, or may be, Slopeites. Or Bee-Jorites, if they choose to live on this side of the border. All the rest of them are human beings . . . like we are."

"Oh, I see. This is one of the Dranverite's notions."

"And Mother's. If you had ever known starvation, you might understand why they would want to end it."

"We have all been hungry, Nuvao. There are worse pains."

"Hungry and starving are two different things. You have never known starving—when a person is powerless to get food, when hunger turns into a debilitating weakness that can lead to death."

Trellana returned to the top of the sand-sled's perch and shouted through its amplifying-cone to the people in the sled's way. "Your attention, subjects! Attention! Roll your acorns to the side. We are passing."

She saw the people turn and look at her, then return to pushing their acorns.

"Subjects! I command you to push your acorns to the side!"

Nuvao was climbing up the spiral towards her. "Allow me," he said, displacing her before the cone. "Good day, citizens of Bee-Jor. Our kindest thanks from Commander Quegdoth for your help in feeding the starving," he shouted. "In the meantime, would you be so kind as to roll your acorns to the side of the sand route? We have need of getting Princess Trellana to Palzhad, so that she may offer it her protective essence. Your cooperation would be most appreciated."

The acorn rollers looked at Nuvao, who bowed to them, and then at each other before they pushed their large and pointy seeds to the route's sides.

"Thank you! Thank you, thank you," said Nuvao, and the procession lurched forward. "The New Way, Princess," he said to Trellana as he stepped down the spiral. "You would be wise to learn it, embrace it, practice it."

"I am *Queen* Trellana," she said.

"Not yet."

When Mound Palzhad came in sight, Trellana stepped back up to the perch to take it in. Sun was ending his daily journey and glowing warm and golden over the mound. Trellana was taken with the crystal palaces, which were tinted with amber and rose through their intricately interlocking sand grains. The palace's old and ancient walls had an enriching patina of age, and its darkly stained grout was a spread of lacy patterns. A thin parade of leaf-cutter ants was returning to the mound's opening with sunny yellow leaf clippings. Below, near the laborers' rings, she saw the massive tangles of infamous weeds that radiated in a wilderness.

"Those weeds are unacceptable," she said. "I am sure the lower castes get up to all kinds of mischief in them."

"Mother has told me the weeds of Palzhad provide a rich variety of products that all Palzhanites enjoy," said Nuvao. "They have been less reliant on the mushroom for years."

"Less reliant, really. That will change."

As they passed through the weeds, Trellana saw

very few Palzhanites. A few children were playing in them and occasional foragers and hunters emerged to look at the sand-sled with a mild curiosity. They noted its long and yellow mantis-wing banners, but few of them had the good sense or decency to stop and bow or even nod their heads. As the sand-sled climbed higher and darkness fell, it passed through the empty rings with their neglected dwellings before reaching those with clusters of Palzhanites returning from work, or from drawing the night's water. Most of Trellana's new subjects gave her sled the most cursory glance before returning to their tasks or conversation or their walk home.

"They did know I was coming?" she asked.

"Who?" said Nuvao.

"The Palzhanites."

"Of course. I am sure they are relieved to have a queen again."

It was near evening when they reached the black-sand barracks. Trellana was frightened to see so many dark-skinned people gathered around its dew station, dining outdoors under the moonlight and conversing in the loud, coarse way of the lowborn. She was relieved to pass through the priests' rose-quartz rectories, but disliked seeing that the statues and carvings were dingy; some of them even looked blackened, as if the gods had become as darkly pigmented as the laborers. As the sun sank below the horizon, so did her heart, but it rose again when they reached the crystal palaces and she saw a wealth of lights and a few priests dressed in their very finest. *A little too fine*, she thought. *Those look like the anointment robes!*

When the sled stopped, an abundance of leaf-cutter ants erupted from the mound's main opening to run their antennae over the new arrivals. A variety of scents were agitating the ants, but after some time they found leaf-cutter kin-scent on all its human and ant arrivals. After Trellana stepped out of the cabin, her servants straightened her skirts, righted her crooked antennae, and primped her simple travel coiffure to make her more presentable.

"Welcome, Princess Trellana," said His Most Pious Ejolta. "We have just time," he said.

"Just time for what?"

"The anointment. Your coronation as queen."

"The coronation is *tonight?*"

"Yes, of course. Your essence is needed. Right away. It's been very damp this last moon, and I believe you are aware that we are smelling and seeing the first touches of the Yellow Mold."

"Well, I'm quite willing to fulfill those duties but . . . I had hoped to plan something for my anointment . . . to invite some of the other royals from the nearby mounds for a proper celebration."

"Well, of course, Princess, but it is not our custom to let a princess fulfill the duty of a Sacred Wetting. It never has been."

"I was crowned queen in Dranveria. And, later, of Cajoria."

"Yes, but not of Palzhad, which must have its own rightful queen. These are difficult times and I'm afraid that celebrations cannot be part of them. We planned to anoint you in a simplified ceremony just as soon as you arrived. It's been arranged for some time, including the approval from the gods. You were informed, yes?"

"Yes, she was," said Nuvao, turning to her. "I believe I did tell you, Trellana."

"I might have remembered if you had," said the princess, spitting each word.

"You weren't quite yourself when I did, having enjoyed your last indulgence in some spirits," he said. "Your maids might remember."

The servants looked among each other and made the faintest of nods. "It was discussed, Your Highness," said Bevakoof, making a slight bow and looking away.

"Show the princess to her chambers," said Ejolta to an old but sturdy-looking palace servant who stood nearby with a torch.

"This way, Your Highness," the servant said after a shallow curtsy that revealed her aching joints. "I am Barhosa. I served your mother and your grandmother. I am honored to serve you."

"Proceed," said Trellana as Bevakoof parted the slitted opening and helped the princess through to the palace's insides. They made their way through bleak halls to what had been Queen Clugna's chambers. Trellana took in the stark spaces and was disturbed by the lack of carpets, furniture, and tapestries.

"These are terribly empty rooms," she said.

"It's a terribly empty palace," said Barhosa. "All four of them. They weren't always so dreary."

"When was it less dreary?"

"Before your mother left for Cajoria, when she was Princess Polexima. Such a sweet and intelligent beauty, your mother. She brought what we had to her new home in Cajoria—her dowry."

They entered the queen's bedchamber, which was as lacking as the rest. A bed was prominent and a chair and a chest were against the wall. The mirror— such a small thing—had lost its glimmer. Trellana's face fell, then so did her head.

"Are you all right, Highness?" Barhosa asked.

"No," said Trellana. "It's been a tiresome journey. Very, very tiresome."

"All right, then. It is time to get ready. They are gathering in the throne room now."

"Not in the cathedral?"

"No, Highness. We haven't got enough torches to illuminate it, or the time to travel down. We have one of your grandmother's wetting gowns if you have not brought your own."

"I have," she said. The chambermaids arrived with the first of her trunks, set them down, and looked around the room's undecorated walls, at its dark ceiling and out its hazy windows with a view to a blackened sky. Trellana saw her own disappointment in the servants' faces. *This was all a mistake to come here,* she thought. *Mother tried to warn me.*

With Barhosa's prodding to be timely, Trellana made her entrance to the throne room in the simple slitted gown expected of her. All the mound's priests were present—not very many—and scattered through the vast chamber were what remained of the upper castes. Among them were just a few war widows, and next to them were some younger, yellow-skinned women in dresses that were almost fashionable. All these women turned slowly towards Trellana, as if hobbled, and made short and truncated bows.

"What's happened to them?" Trellana whispered to Barhosa.

"They were captives of the Hulkrites. Almost killed in their return here. We think there may be more of them beyond the border wall, living among the refugees."

"I see. And why are there but a few war widows?"

"More than half this mound was killed before the war, in the Hulkrites' raid that captured your mother and stole our egg-layer." Barhosa dropped her head and shuddered as she was overwhelmed with the darkest memories. Trellana turned from her to a few merchants and their wives at the back of the chamber, some bearing gifts, and bowing to Trellana when they caught her eye. She thought they looked impatient as they paced and tapped their feet, and all looked as if their minds were elsewhere. A maidservant approached the thrones and fluffed each of the seat cushions when Trellana had a strange realization.

"Why are there two thrones?" she asked Barhosa, who stiffened with surprise.

"Well, of course there are two thrones."

"But why?"

"Trellana!" called Pious Ejolta, giving a brave smile as he signaled to her to come forward. "Take your throne, please, and we'll get started shortly."

From the eastern chambers, the Cricket priestesses entered in their noisy regalia. At the tail of them was a male figure in a sumptuous, golden tunic and brocaded pantaloons. Her heart jumped; had they found Maleps and brought him to Bee-Jor to be her consort?

As he got closer, she realized she was looking at Nuvao, who nodded at her with a faint grin.

"Shall we take our seats, Trellana?" he asked.

"*Our* seats?"

"Yes. This is my coronation too."

"Your *what?*"

"You are queen and I am king. We discussed this."

"We did?"

"Darling sister, I know you have not been quite right since your last bout of drink but this was what we agreed to. You pressed your inked thumb to several copies of a document—one of which I can produce if you like."

Her mouth opened but she could not form words. "W-w-when was this arranged?"

He walked towards her and whispered, aware that others were listening. "Ask Bevakoof and your maid-servants, who were the sworn witnesses. They inked their thumbs as well."

"*You* are going to be king? You are my *brother*."

"It would not be the first time a brother and sister have reigned. You didn't actually expect to be in charge, did you?"

Last bout of drink, thought Trellana. More than anything she wanted, she needed, a drink of the strongest spirit. Nuvao offered her his arm and she pushed it away to tumble onto her throne and slump. She fell into a pit of sadness so extreme that she was oblivious to the ceremony taking place around her, until she felt hands working the scented oil of Pal-zhad's ant queen into her hair. A royal crown with its bejeweled antennae was clamped onto her damp head. They turned from her to her brother, who sat up straight and grinned with his chin up as priests and priestesses marched around his chair in a chant. Ejolta set the gold and amethyst antennae on his head and named him King Nuvao the 17th.

"Rise, King and Queen of Palzhad," said Ejolta. "And greet your subjects."

No sooner had everyone risen from their bow than Ejolta continued. "Your Majesty, your holy essence is required. Come this way, please, after offering your obeisance to your ancestor, Goddess Ant Queen."

Trellana's every effort was exerted to walk over and raise her scepter to the statue of Ant Queen on the altar at her side. A moment later she was escorted by her brother to the tunnel entry. The slitted diaphragm in the wall was opened and she was greeted by an ant-tamer. He bowed to her, next to a triple-saddled and bangled riding ant that awaited her and Nuvao at the top of the downward spiral. Her brother helped her up to the saddle, then joined her. As they made their way down for the first of her Sacred Wettings, she fantasized that the ant queen would reject her after finding an enemy scent. As an act of mercy, the egg-layer would use her mandibles to lop her head off as she urinated.

"You look terribly sad," said Nuvao.

"I'm just a bit disappointed," she said.

"You have no right to be," he said. "Not a woman of your privilege."

"Will you always be lecturing me, Nuvao?"

"I suppose so. If you will always be so self-involved."

"What if he comes back?"

"Who?"

and a place for children to climb and hide in as they chewed on its remaining flavorless leaves.

Around the princess and the other Ledackis, the camps had been shifting and growing more crowded. Frequent skirmishes broke out as people were consolidated by a common language or a skin color or a place of origin. Other Ledackis, on learning their princess was among them, had been drawn to Jakhuma, and remained with her to share what meager food they had. At night, the Ledackis weakly sang their prayer-songs for delivery from the Waiting. When their numbers continued to expand, the camps surrounding them made flimsy barriers of broken twigs, sand grains, and whatever trash they could pile up.

One midmorning the baby unlatched from Kula's shrinking breast after its milk was depleted. She gave him her other breast, which held but a few drops, and then she grimaced from a sudden pain. "Sweet baby!" she said. "Sucking harder does not make for more milk!" When she pulled the boy away, he gave with a piercing cry that was an echo of everyone's hunger for food, for comfort, for certainty. Across from the Ledackis was a swelling camp of light-skinned people who looked up from their own miseries to stare with hatred at the Meat Ant people and their noisy brat. "How about shoving some cloth in its mouth?" shouted a woman in native Hulkrish as she clutched the chunky jewels around her neck. "Or maybe he might like to suck on my fist."

"How about if I rip your lips off your piss-colored face," shouted Kula, making a claw with the long nails of her hand. "And then stuff them in your ears so you can get some quiet."

The light-skinned woman stood, looked to the sky, then began cursing in Hulkrish. "Wife of Termite, Gracious Layer of Eggs, blind this woman's eyes, and make her entrails ever runny! Dry and harden her vulva!" sang the woman as she made the sign of short, curly antennae above her head. A moment later, Kula recognized the woman from her showy jewelry, likely stolen for her by some thieving Hulkrite.

"You!" Kula shouted, stepping towards the boundary of trash. "You're the Hulkrish witch who tried to steal our sled!"

"You! The black Ledacki she-wasp who stole that sled from the Hulkrites! Where are our swords?"

The two reached down and lugged up sand grains and held them over their heads, threatening to toss them. Surrounding tribesmen on both sides heaved up their own grains, ready to fight, and crowded the barrier. Sebetay, the bare-chested young man with his black and shining skin, made his way from the Ledacki camp's northeast edge. As the two camps howled and hissed their threats, he took to his knees before his princess.

"Sebetay, what is it?" Jakhuma said through nervous breathing, her eyes on the impending battle.

"Princess Jakhuma, they are shouting something about *food* in the northern camps," he shouted. "Something is coming—from over the wall."

"From Bee-Jor?"

"Yes, from Bee-Jor."

"Climb and tell us what you see," she said. As he went towards the tumbleweed, she shouted so that all could hear her.

"Food!" she shouted from deep inside her, then repeated it in Hulkrish.

The Ledackis and the Hulkrites lowered their sand grains as the word *food* spread like a sweet breeze through their camps and those north and south of them. When he reached the top of the tumbleweed, Sebetay shouted down to Jakhuma.

"Princess, I see a stream of something. They are round and long and tumbling over the border wall— something pointed on one end."

"What if it's not food?" shouted Kula. "What if they're sending barrels of poison?"

"They are rolling them up the Petiole!" Sebetay shouted. "Hundreds, maybe thousands of them!"

Everyone quietly waited, pacing and praying, their hopes growing as the sun made its slow progression in a sky thickening with clouds. At last, they heard a rising noise from the camps deep in the South, a mixture of screams and cheers. Bee-Jorite soldiers were marching up the Petiole, like a human plough, waving swords and threatening arrows and destroying the flimsy borders between the camps. "Move aside by order of Commander Quegdoth!" shouted a yellow-skinned leader at the head of the procession. Given his loaded bow, Jakhuma might have mistaken this leader for a native Hulkrite were it not for his strange tongue. The soldiers behind him were mostly dark complexioned, some nearly as dark as herself. These soldiers were followed by a long and wobbly parade of acorns that were rolled by a more common people. More of these continued, with more acorns for the last of the settlements on the edge of the Dustlands.

Once the acorns were positioned in a loose chain, the soldiers and common people filtered back and around them, keeping swords, arrows, and blowguns at the ready. The refugees stared at these Bee-Jorites in fear and awe. After they left, the hungry went to examine what had been left behind.

The gift was a very mixed lot. Some of the acorns were green and too firm; some were desiccated and shriveled, and many were old, rotten, or moldy. A few were aged, dried, and perfectly golden and would yield a fine and nourishing flour once their hard shells were broken. Others were beautifully infested with weevil grubs while some were hollow and rattled with the dust of grub corpses.

"Who has sent us these acorns?" Jakhuma asked in Hulkrish to one of the last of the returning solders, with a face as dark as her own. He did not understand her until she repeated it as "Who gives food?"

"Commander Quegdoth of Bee-Jor," said the man in Slopeish, a tongue that was not unlike Hulkrish. "And Queen Trellana and King Nuvao of Mound Palzhad," he added.

"Quegdoth," she said to herself. *I know that name. Wasn't he a Hulkrite?*

The refugees on both sides of the acorn chain peered at each other through the gaps between them. Jakhuma looked at the seeds and knew they could not pull them in—they would have to step into the Hulkrish camp and push them from the other side.

"Ledackis!" she shouted. "Push half these acorns into our center. Leave half for those jaundiced termite-eaters over there. Watch your backs!"

Sebetay summoned several men in his vicinity. "Come on!" he said, taking out the curved dagger made from the ghost-ant mandible he had smuggled out of Hulkren. "Keep weapons at the ready!" he shouted. The Ledacki men approached a ripe yellow acorn and turned its sharp point away from them. They made threatening war hisses as they followed Sebetay to the seed's other side, forced to step over and through the scattered detritus that had marked their camp's lines. As they pushed the acorn into their camp, they were rushed by yellow-skinned assailants making the Hulkrish war whoop. "That's ours!" they heard in Hulkrish voices.

Sebetay felt a spear's tip under his shoulder blade. He spun and howled, and bared his teeth, then whipped up his blade to slash at the face of his attacker and cut off his ear. The man fell to his knees and screamed as Sebetay kicked him under his chin and sent him flying into his fellows. Other yellow skins rushed the Ledackis with a mix of axes, pikes, and daggers.

"Get these seeds into our camp!" Sebetay shouted to the boys and women, who obeyed and took over the rolling as the men turned to defend themselves. As the bobbing, erratic acorns were pushed into the camp, Jakhuma was jostled in the panicked throng. The acorns upended, then fell as they were rolled, threatening all with their sword-sharp ends.

"Look out!" Jakhuma screamed to a cluster of Ledacki boys when their backs were rushed by a gang of Hulkrish youths raising clear swords of ghost mandibles. They thrust at the little Ledackis, surrounded them, and pushed the smallest of them hard into an acorn's spike. The boy screamed when his back was pierced. When he fell forward, a pike was thrust in his chest. Sebetay ran towards the Hulkrish youths, raising his dagger to distract them, then threw himself up, rolling in the air to kick through the head of the tallest youth with the toe spikes of his boot. The youth fell, the toe spike stuck in his bleeding skull. His eyelids fluttered before his face went still. His fellows grabbed him by his arms to pull him away, when Sebetay used his curved dagger to chop through their wrists, their hands falling and twitching on the sand. The Hulkrish invaders pressed through a gauntlet of attackers, wildly waving their swords as they were threatened with a wall of jabbing pikes. Those that were pierced were held in place, so that Ledacki swordsmen coming from behind could saw off their heads with the serrated mandibles of meat-ant swords.

When the brawl subsided, Jakhuma saw that a good number of acorns had been rolled into their center, but at what cost? She pushed through the shocked and wailing crowd to the camp's barrier to take in the number of dead and wounded. Her gasps turned to weeping when she saw that the corpses included that of a young mother, still clutching her baby in swaddling. Jakhuma lifted the infant and it felt all too light. From her bright underclothes, she saw it was a girl, a girl whose eyes were all too big. When the princess pressed the infant to her chest, she knew in an instant she was forever bound to the little creature.

Not far from her, a few wounded Hulkrites, boys on the verge of manhood, crawled or limped back to their own side. One young man carried a corpse over his shoulder, using him as a shield. "You cannibals won't be eating my brother!" he shouted. Jakhuma looked at him with pity, then realized she did not know where Kula was. "My servant! Where is my servant?" she shouted. "Kula!"

"Over here, Princess," Kula said, descending from the tumbleweed in a brief rain of its flaking bits, and flicking them off the face of the baby, which she held in one arm.

"How is No Name?"

"He lives."

Kula opened the dirty blanket that held the baby. His eyes were closed and his arms and legs seemed too still. Kula opened one of the little fists he was making and Jakhuma watched as his tiny fingers curled back together and his eyes blinked open.

"I must eat and drink—to get him some milk," Kula said.

"And some milk for this little one too," said Jakhuma, showing Kula the stick-like baby. "Maybe I can make milk. I will pray to the Cloud Goddess."

"Pray, yes, Princess. But if you want to make milk, you need someone to suck hard on your nipples. Five or six times a day."

"A baby?"

"Not strong enough. An adult. I would rather not do this . . . if you don't mind."

"I'll do it," said a man behind them. Jakhuma looked to see Sebetay behind them. The sweat on his face made his scars more pronounced and shine with a strange beauty. He looked depleted after the conflict and was still catching his breath. "Not in a disrespectful way, Princess. As my duty. To save this young baby who is a beloved member of our scattered tribe. I will do whatever you ask."

Jakhuma nodded. The five walked to the center of the camp where the acorns were already in the process of being sawed and cracked open. The infested ones were harvested of their weevil maggots. Many of the maggots were dead and moldy, many of them were dried and flaky corpses. One acorn held some smaller wasp-gall maggots, which were alive and plump and had turned the inside of the seed into a crumbly and tasty pulp.

"Ledackis!" Jakhuma shouted. "Pregnant and nursing women will feed first. Give them these fine, squirming maggots." Her voice shocked the baby in her arms, whose arms trembled as she burst into a delicate sobbing. "I am sorry, little one," she said while looking into eyes as dark and sad as a lonely night. "I have no milk to give you yet. But I will make . . . or get you some. And I promise your dead mother, whoever she was, that I will bring you to some better place."

The dried and golden acorns were opened last. The men used hand-axes to hew chunks from their soft, powdery centers. Jakhuma joined the other women in shaving the chunks into chips and bits with the edges of knives and swords. She tasted one of these chips and found it pleasantly starchy at first, followed by a bitter aftertaste that dried the insides of her cheeks. When all the acorns had been emptied of their nourishment, the princess ordered the shells to be moved. "Bring them to the edges of our camp to make a wall," she commanded. The Hulkrites turned from processing their own acorns to sneer at the Ledackis as they raised their fence of shells. When it was completed, Sebetay and other men gathered up the severed heads and limbs of the Hulkrites and threw them over the fence. The Hulkrites screamed in horror or keened with grief as they examined the faces of their dead. Their surviving men reached for their weapons, threatening a new feud. Instead they chopped up the bodies of the dead Ledackis on their side and returned the gruesome favor.

The sun was setting when Jakhuma handed the infant girl to Kula to nurse, as Sebetay held Khali Talavar's baby. *I must stop thinking of him as that Hulkrite's baby,* she thought. *I must give him a name.* She loosened her clothing and climbed up and into the tumbleweed to survey the camps before darkness took over. All across the camps, she saw that acorn shells had been used to create a patchwork of border fences. As she looked deeper south and then north, she realized the dark-skinned refugees had somehow gathered and consolidated in camps on the east side. The light-skinned people had all migrated into camps on the western side including people of Hulkrish, Slopeish, and Seed Eater stock.

Of all the distressing things she had seen that day, this new development disturbed her most . . . and she wasn't sure why.

She looked up to Mound Palzhad as the dying sun spread its light on its delicate palaces. A meager parade of ants was returning with the yellowed leaf cuttings of autumn. As Jakhuma looked west and over the wall of acorn shells, she saw the yellow-skinned worshippers of Termite as they nursed their wounded and prayed over their dead in their native tongue. The Hulkrish words ignited memories that sickened and frightened her. She could smell the breath of the cruel rapist who had taken a liking to her, and forced her to share his mattress when he was home from wars. He had never called her by her name, had never told her his own, and each time he released into her, he squeezed her breasts until she shrieked from the pain. Jakhuma shook the memory out of her head and looked back to the palaces of Palzhad, as their crystals glowed with a bloody red from the last of the crimson light.

How can that be Bee-Jor? she wondered as she listened to the Hulkrites' droning prayer-songs on their knees before a chip of wood. *How can that place over there be a paradise on the Sand if we are supposed to share it with those people?*

She stared at the palaces until their silhouettes disappeared in the blackness of night.

sight of the sunlit stadium on the mound's south side filled Pleckoo's empty stomach with little demons that vomited fire inside him.

"What's that?" said the voice of Butterfly Goiter below him as they tethered fresh ants to the reins of the sled. "You want us to kill you? Before you've had breakfast?"

"Why would you want to be killed now, little Pleckoo?" said Sewn Shut, looking up. "They've got so much planned for your homecoming."

"Right. From what we heard you're getting an assembly—and it's all in your honor, Pleckoo! Everyone from mounds all over Bee-Jor is coming—just to see *you*."

"Maybe after that you can die. Haven't heard how yet. Won't be bathing you though—too quick and a bit too usual."

"I've heard that if it's a sunny day, they'll be putting him in a sun-kiln."

"No, not the sun-kiln, because then we can't hear him scream. I like this idea of nailing him to a pole until he dies of thirst. And then we lacquer him and attach his mummy to a plaque to hang in the markets as a warning against termite worship."

"Whatever they do," said Goiter as he entered the cage and climbed up the ladder to feed Pleckoo, "we've got our own plans. I'm thinking of ripping off his ears and fingers and selling them as trophies."

"Not a bad idea. Wonder what we could get for his balls?"

"Not sure. Probably get a better price if we keep them together as a matching pair."

The guards sniggered as Pleckoo was forced to suck down the bladder. He felt the tightness of the ropes as he squirmed with panic while imagining the knives of the guards coming towards his body. It reignited his worst memory, of losing his nose with its endless bleeding and the radiating pain that burned through his face for days. As the sled was tugged into the weeds of Cajoria's outer rings, he panted and mouthed all of Hulkro's names in ever quicker rounds. The laborers working in the weeds were shouting to each other, running out to the route to jeer him.

"Look! It's Pleckoo, the Termite's catamite!" shouted one old man as he hobbled up on crutches and revealed the single tooth in his mouth as he grinned. "Catamite, catamite, catamite!" he repeated, and others took up the chant along the route. Foragers, hunters, and dew gatherers left their work to stare at the passing cage and to shout and spit and laugh. "Welcome home!" shouted a hunter, who held up a moon roachling that scissored its mandibles. "We've prepared a right nice feast for you, Pleckoo! Or rather, we've prepared for some things to feast on *you*." The jeering increased to an ear-jabbing din until it all turned quieter. The insides of Pleckoo's ears were as battered as every other part of him, and finally, it seemed, they were failing. He hoped the silence meant that he was deaf now and that blindness would be next, followed by the loss of touch and then . . . death. Soon he would feel nothing and be free of the ropes, free of humans, free of the Sand. *Have you killed me, Hulkro, taken me home? I beg you . . .*

But it wasn't death. It was sleep . . . or something like it. He woke with a start when the cage was shoved off the sand-sled to tumble, over and over. He felt his head nearly snap off his neck and heard the crack of its bones, then heard a harsh ringing in his ears. He was upside down when his stomach tightened, then released its contents all over his face, filling his nose and stinging his eyes before he was righted at a dew station on Cajoria's lowest ring, just above the flats. The cage was near to one of Anand's new stone structures, with its scrawls and pictures that related his laws. A mob was gathering to curse and shout and spit at the cage with so much sputum that Pleckoo could barely see through the bars.

Something shifted within the crowd when they quieted and parted to allow the passage of a smaller mob that looked both strange and familiar. They were clean and decently dressed but he slowly realized he was looking at his cousins, uncles, and aunts from the midden. After staring at him in a hateful silence, they pulled away for another arrival: a man and woman he was slower to recognize as his mother and her husband. Their hair was cut and combed and their bodies were thicker with nourishment. Here was the man he had called "Father" with a trimmed beard and a dyed tunic, the man who had groped him in the middle of the night, who had grabbed him in the weeds and pushed his head to his crotch and then beaten him for resisting. And now that man was grimacing in rage, brandishing a bright, new dagger and ready to make the first cut. His mother was shaking when she looked in her son's eyes, then began convulsing as she bawled.

"Pleckoo!" she shouted. "You have shamed us for eternity! Your sins poison us in this life and the World to Come! You have made me the mother of a Hulkrite! Of the worst Hulkrite! A demon worshipper who would have slaughtered his own mother! I cannot live with this shame! I am taking my own life . . . but not until I see you suffer for your crimes and die."

"We always knew you was worthless," shouted his father, "that you would bring us shame. But this is the greatest shame of the ages, the shame that knows no end."

His mother came towards the cage when the guards blocked her. She straightened herself and turned to face the growing mob. "I renounce this man! I disown him!" she screamed. She turned back to Pleckoo, grinding her teeth and jutting her chin. "I don't know you, Pleckoo of Hulkren, you man-whore to Hulkro!" she screamed, and then spat a great, sliding gob at the cage, then collapsed into her sobbing as her husband went to pull her up.

My mother is a victim of ignorance. Her stupid words mean nothing to me. My mother hates me—so what, he told himself. But then his eyes ached and were making tears. He felt a trembling as his lungs tightened and his body spasmed. *I will not sob like a weak woman before them, not these middenites. Please, Hulkro, if You are going to rescue me, please do it now.*

"Go ahead and cry like some little girl seeking pity. You'll get none of it from us, you man-slut," shouted his father. And with that, he turned his back on Pleckoo.

The crowd began shouting, "Man-slut," in unison when Pleckoo smelled a sweet, woody odor. "Thank Hulkro," he rasped to himself, relieved that his prayer was being answered: the smell of fresh pine was Hulkro manifesting as the Great Wood Eater! At last, He was arriving with a sweet drink of soothing turpentine and would free Pleckoo and carry him up to the World Beyond Stars. The crowd stopped their chanting and was parting, but instead of his god flying towards him on lacy wings, Pleckoo saw a train of carrier ants lugging a cargo-sled. Guards in red-stained armor were sounding thorn horns. "Make way for Her Highness!" the guards shouted, and the crowd turned silent and bowed their heads as

Queen Polexima rode up on a bangled ant. Pleckoo did not recognize the hairless woman he saw through the bars, someone who was dressed in the preposterous garb of a Cricket priestess. She came closer to the cage with her chin up, her lips stiff, and her eyes unblinking as she stared through the bars. Her chest was heaving and her teeth were clenched in rage.

"Make way for Their Piouses Dolgeeno and Terraclon," shouted another guard. Pleckoo looked in disbelief to see a draped and powdered riding ant with prayer sashes tied up its legs that supported both Dolgeeno and Terraclon, the latter with stripes painted on his brown face. Both men were dressed in the purple garb and jewels of the Ultimate Holy! In the center of all his pain, Pleckoo felt a chilling envy to see that Anand's only friend, that ridiculous, flitting butterfly, had been raised to the level of highest priest. Polexima turned from the cage. "It is him," she said to the priests. "It is Pleckoo of Hulkren."

"It is Pleckoo of Cajoria's *midden*," said Terraclon as he urged the ant forward for a closer look. The old, fat priest looked at Pleckoo with drunken indifference, then turned away from him, casting his gaze down. Dolgeeno slouched and had a roundness to his shoulders that suggested his own defeat. Terraclon cocked an eyebrow and spoke in the haughty way of priests. "Welcome home, Pleckoo. We have heard the most sensational things about you," he shouted before his face turned into a snarl.

"Anand's planning something very special for your homecoming, he is," he added, returning to the guttural accent of their caste. "Bring it forward," he shouted to the guards behind him who went to the sand-sled and raised up a block of wood on their shoulders. They set the block before Pleckoo, who saw the source of the sweet smell—it was pine wood, with a fresh termite track on its surface.

"This is a home of your invincible termite god," said Terraclon. He signaled with his hands for the men to turn the block around. Glued to its back was a crushed termite king with ragged wings. "This will keep you company at the assembly during your denunciation," said Terraclon. "You can pray to it! Beg it for mercy! Demand it release you from the days of torture ahead. And all the world will see your god is nothing, a blind and powerless drunkard who will let you suffer before you die."

Terraclon came closer. "When your beloved cousin returns, we'll hold an assembly, a trial and then a days-long execution. We're thinking about a death by a hundred thousand cuts, one for each of your victims. Also in consideration is the careful removal of the bones from your body, one at a time, to set before your Hulkro as a sacrifice. You'll be alive but like some helpless, quivering jelly."

"I can't bear to be in his presence another moment," said Polexima to Terraclon. Pleckoo saw her familiarity with the little flower boy, and it disgusted him. The queen turned to the cage and stared in Pleckoo's blinking eyes. "Anand's asked us to wait to exact his justice," she said. "But before he arrives . . . I can think of a number of things I'd like done to a rapist. He should know exactly how it feels, and in the presence of spectators." The mob lowered their heads as the royal party turned and exited.

Anand! Polexima had said his ugliest of names, and a new anger was rising up in Pleckoo, that sweet and empowering rage that had always served him. *I can break these ropes with Hulkro's blessing,* he thought, *then smash through this cage to kill these unfaithful.* Pleckoo felt strength building in his muscles and then willed his limbs to move, to stretch and then break the ropes. Hearing himself grunting, he strained and heaved before he felt himself snap and fall into a black void. When he returned to consciousness, he was in the same cage, bound by the same ropes, but bleeding from new chafing. As uncontrollable waves of grief ran through him, he gritted his teeth to stop his sobbing when he noticed a third mob had arrived to feast on his suffering. Their laughter was all too loud and pierced him like a thousand daggers when he realized it was Keel, the midden's cruel foreman, with Tal and his other sons. All of them had been gorging on food that had stretched the stitches of their fancy clothes.

Anand and Daveena were grateful for the moments they could stand.

One of the few sights to break up the landscape were growths of the paddle cactus, a clustering plant with thick, juicy leaves that were spotted with prickly dots of sharp hairs and had edges lined by sharper spikes. At the top of the paddles was their round and intimidating red fruit. These were covered in patches of hairs that could break off and sink into human skin, resulting in a painful irritation or even death. Anand remembered eating pickles and preserves of cactus fruit in Dranveria, but only on special occasions, as they were expensive and dangerous to harvest. As they passed one of the clusters, Daveena pointed out a crew of thickly padded men at the tops of ladders who sawed at the crimson spheres. One of the men had slipped and fallen, and he dangled from a paddle spike that had caught the back of his clothing. Anand was worrying for this man when the beetle driver tossed Daveena another squeeze bag of water and some ground seed cakes without halting the sled.

During the day, the sled kept to the left of the route to allow for the passing of foot soldiers marching west by the tens of thousands. That sight filled Anand with dread. How many of them had massed at the border? And near what mound on the border? Would the war be over by the time they returned—if they were allowed to return? Who would ever come to rescue him and Daveena in this place?

"I'm sorry I'm so quiet," he said to Daveena during another stretch of tedium.

"I'm as worried as you are," she said, and took his hand.

His worries deepened as they went deeper into barley country and they saw another frightful parade of foot soldiers, followed by a longer chain of supply-sleds. These were followed by a train of sled-cages packed with harvester hatchlings, ants whose poisonous spews would be potent by the time they reached the border. It was the fifth day of traveling when they fell in the shadow of an ancient, massive oak tree with a monstrous tangle of above-ground roots. The driver stopped to offer a prayer to the tree and tapped his head, his heart, and his navel and Anand sensed they might take a turn.

The right half of the tree was dead and scorched by the suns of a thousand summers. Its gray and withering arms pointed weakly to the South, and the sled's driver seemed to obey the tree when he looked up, then steered the beetles right, and onto a route that traveled through a grotesque complex of bulging pebble structures. Not all of the structures looked inhabited, and only a few of them looked purposeful. Those that housed humans had crooked quartz windows, which did not seem placed so much as clutched by their pebbles. The black, dust-covered tar that glued these pebbles together looked as if it were oozing from them. Much of the tar had dripped down in thick splotches that held the corpses of long-dead midges, gnats, and hoverflies. As Anand and Daveena went deeper into the strange cityscape, it seemed to be popping up before them, assembling itself by some powerful magic and growing ever taller and stranger.

"I feel like I've drunk the Mildew," Daveena said.

"Exactly," Anand said as they passed through dwellings that seemed randomly strewn through the barley grass. "It's so weirdly ugly, it's kind of . . . beautiful." They were stunned by the buildings' magnificent irregularities and random shapes. Some buildings resembled clusters of warted wasp galls and others were like the low, radiating bark fungi that grew near tree roots in summer. Other dwellings had round or boxy understructures that were almost conventional, but they had free-form roofs that resembled wrestling fat men or piles of wrinkled and rotting fruit. Some roofs incorporated acorn caps that tilted or appeared to be sliding off, or were sometimes stacked for a wobbling effect. The facades of these dwellings—if they *were* dwellings—were decorated with grooves that resembled the contorted mating channels of cicadas on tree branches. Their walls had multiple hollows, the insides of which were painted with random, lacy designs of curlicues in green and orange paint.

The structures were increasing in height, and obscured the ant mound that Anand knew had to be behind the city, as he saw as many harvester ants as he saw humans. The bearded ants with their large, grain-chewing skulls came close to the Britasyte visitors, but would just as soon flee from their roach-scent and speed away in a curved and indirect way in keeping with the place itself. The few ants that wriggled their abdomens and sprayed their noxious scent in defense were attacked by a patrol of men with long quartz swords who cut off the ants' stingers. Most harvester ants stayed well above the city, crawling on its roofs, or at the top of the ovular walls that led to the palace.

The well-to-do men and women of Worxict walked slowly in their voluminous but stiff-looking gowns, and their heavily ornamented nimbus hats were like a weight to be balanced. Walking ahead and in back of the well-to-do were their servants, whose bodies looked freer in loose garments of uncolored cloth. On top of the servants' heads were the large, oblong bonnets with long tying sashes. On the sides of the bonnets were something like wings, which made a light snapping noise as they flapped. At the front of the bonnets were stamen-like antennae that the servants used to negotiate with the occasional probing harvester ant.

As before in Durxict, the sled entered into a series of wall rings that led to the palace. And just as before, the first ring housed a market, but this one was stupendous, as large as a pond and with an unnavigable maze of stalls and tables. Through this maze moved thick, alternating currents of marketers bearing baskets and sacks on their heads or dragging a decorated sand cart. As the sled rode up the market's central route, the marketers pulled to the side to stare at Anand and Daveena with the same eerie quiet as the villagers who had gawked at them in the barley grass. Most of the marketers were servants wearing the enormous bonnets, many doing the bidding of a nearby master or mistress.

The market ring was followed, as Anand expected, by another prayer wall; but this one had not hundreds but thousands of seated clergy chanting to the Seed Eaters' innumerable deities on the floors of the arched windows. Most of the clergy chanted upwards to the sky, but some were chanting downwards, perhaps to gods living underground. Anand could see carvings of the deities in the wall's hollows, which depicted most of them as having insects' heads, but human bodies. On the left side of the wall ring was a section where perhaps a hundred priestesses in bright green cloth communed with the Katydid Goddess and chanted in unison. Next to them, on the right side, was a section where a hundred priests in dark-blue and white robes honored Lumm Korol, the moon god. He was depicted with bright white skin and a very round head, and was mounted on a dark blue mantis, with its claws up and its ruffled wings fanning from under its elytra.

The sled continued to the prayer wall's back end, through an opening shaped like ovals colliding with triangles. Dangling from the opening's top were windblown strips of bee velvet spattered with stripes and speckles of brilliant colors. When the sled passed through these strips, Anand and Daveena gasped to enter one more towering yet lopsided ring structure of forty or fifty stories. These walls were thickly embedded with cunning carvings of humans, and all of them were wrapped in a true gold. Custodians in orange bonnets were at work on cleaning dust from the carvings while gardeners in green bonnets worked on the ground at uprooting weed seedlings and fungus from the spaces between the tiles.

"Who do you think they were?" Anand asked as he looked at the carvings.

"Ancestors, most likely. Their lines of royals."

"This nation is older than I thought, if they've had hundreds of emperors. Look at those," he said, pointing up to the third row. "Those carvings are less skillful. And the faces change after that. The eyelids have folds and their chins have grown."

"You're right," she said. "That must have been the point of some conquest."

Ahead of them was a narrower opening to one more tunnel, the roof of which was a rippling structure of interlocking orange crystals. After they entered this tunnel, the sled wove through its winding sides, and Anand and Daveena gawked at its walls, which were encrusted with a wealth of golden and silver pyrite. The tunnel ended, at last, at a vast and tiled plaza before the emperor's palace, set at the foot of the capital's massive ant mound. The plaza was covered with bonneted custodians who brushed and polished asymmetrical tiles sliced from stones of the purest white. Anand and Daveena held their breaths as they took in the most overwhelming structure yet, unsure if this *was* a palace or just some strange and unfathomable vision.

"This palace, if that's what this is, is not atop the mound but before it," Anand finally said, feeling dizzy.

"The mound couldn't support something like this at its top," said Daveena. "It's too much!"

Sculpted pebbles bulged across the palace's meandering walls in thick veins that clustered, then tapered, like upended tree roots in a pattern that was dizzying to the point of maddening. The ends of the palace had no corners, but were thick ropy structures that undulated downwards and slithered through each other, like a pile of worms that had made love in an orgy, then collapsed from fatigue. On the palace's roof were thick clusters of innumerable towers, with tops that ended in bizarre sculptures of imaginary insects and flowers of impossible intricacies. Great, sliced-quartz windows with almost perfect clearness made up much of the facade, and from behind them, courtiers were gathering to look at the expected strangers.

"Are we sure we've not imbibed something that produces visions?" Daveena asked.

"We haven't," Anand said. "Because we're seeing the same thing. I am sure the architects of this palace wanted us to feel this way . . . sick and intimidated."

"You mean frightened . . . if I am being truthful," said Daveena.

"Yes, I am a little frightened myself."

"Which assures me that you are the sensible man I married," she said, reaching to link his arm. "I might also add that I feel a touch underdressed," she said, and then nodded discreetly at one of the windows, where a number of court ladies had clustered. They wore long jackets with thick embroidery that looked embroidered again. The high, broad lapels of the jackets made the women's long necks and faces look like the stamens of the swamp lily. The gowns underneath the coats were a thick orange silk covered with layers and layers of a diaphanous lace. The women stared at the strange visitors over fans of jewel-beetle chitin that changed colors as they were flapped. None of these women wore antennae, which signaled a lack of contact with ants or exposure to the outdoors. Faceless attendants under pink bonnets stood near to these women, awaiting orders.

The main entry on the palace's left side—nothing looked centered here—was like the shape of a butterfly partially emerged from its cocoon. The entry's door slowly lowered with a rope mechanism, to become a bridge that the sled rode over to enter the interior. When they were finally inside the palace's chamber, it was so vast they could not see the walls of its south end. The sled stopped and its driver, a man who had said nothing to Anand and Daveena, bid them to step down, something awkward to do since they had not been offered a flight of steps. Anand, wobbly from poor sleep and weak from endless sitting, felt like a child climbing down from a weed, and not at all like a dignified envoy when his feet finally touched the floor. He helped Daveena down by grabbing her legs and setting her on a dizzying array of striped tiles. From a distance, the courtiers watched them while sticking close to their walls as they whispered behind their fans. Anand wondered how the chamber was so well lit, when he looked up to the ceiling and saw it was a spiraling dome tower of crystals, cemented with an orange resin. The chamber was richly furnished with chairs, divans, and tables all carved in a similar, unbalanced style and placed near the walls to leave a vast and empty center.

"I don't think this is the throne room," Anand said.

"I'm not sure what room we're in," said Daveena. "But I still think I'm dreaming."

Anand shook his head. From out of the distance, a guard of at least forty men appeared, wearing a lacquered armor made of hardwood covered in ant chitin, with its perforated panels tied together by twine. The guards carried weapons—bows and arrows and naked swords—that were highly ornamented but looked dangerously sharp. Their leader stepped out from the formation. He walked in a curving way towards the strangers before pointing to Anand's sword and dagger as he spoke in *Yamich*.

"He says, 'No stranger stands before the Divine Emperor of the Center of the Sand with weapons on his person,'" said Daveena.

"He wants me to give him my blades? A sword is one thing, but a Britasyte does not surrender his dagger."

"He's suggesting—in a polite way—that you surrender your sharp things if you want to meet his emperor."

"All right. They don't appear to know what a blowgun is. Don't tell them."

Anand unsheathed his sword and handed it over by its handle. More reluctantly, he gave them his dagger, the one that Terraclon had made for him before the Fission Trek. The guard's leader looked at both briefly and then at Anand in curiosity before he walked backwards in a curve to his formation, arranged like a crescent moon. Anand heard a clattering of rattles in the distance. The guards split into two formations to allow for the entry of something or someone. As Anand waited, he and Daveena took in more of the palace's interior. The walls in the near distance were hung with skillful tapestries, most of which had taken several lifetimes to complete. All of them seemed to be religious in content, and featured insect-headed gods riding atop clouds, or growing out of rich, dark soil, or emerging from the insides of flowers to bestow boons or seeds or jewels on adoring humans with orange hair. Around the chamber, the two heard clicking and tapping sounds from the insides of ovoid cages perched at the ends of spiraling pedestals. Inside these cages, Anand could see rainbow-colored shield-beetles eating basil and mint leaves to release their aromas.

The distant clattering got louder as Anand and Daveena sighted what had to be an indoor sled coming towards them. Fifty boys dressed in an armor of golden beetle chitin were hauling in the sled. At the back of the sled was a large, upright disc of a blood moon with spatters of grey blemishes painted across its face. Atop the sled was what looked like a cloth replica of the palace itself, complete with a random spray of carvings of harvester ants wrapped in true gold.

As Anand looked at this astonishing replica of the palace, he slowly realized that it was a garment. Protruding from the very top of the garment, through a collar, was a bearded head wearing a crown made from green and orange poppy jasper in the shape of a broken arrowhead. On the other side of the sled was an old man wearing a tall, thin hat that seemed to grow like a sprout out of the pile of his wormy braids. This man wore a simple, baggy blouse of white and blue over tight green pants with a design of tendrils that curled up the thighs. His white and orange beard was braided into seven ropes of various lengths, and when he opened his mouth to speak, he revealed teeth that were stained with the same green as his pants. Daveena nodded her head to him when he finished speaking.

"He says, 'I am the Holy Father of the One True Faith of the Barley Lands,'" said Daveena, translating. "'You stand before His Imperial Majesty, the Emperor Volokop, the ruler of the Center of the Sand, the direct descendant of the Barley Mother Katydid and Her consort, Lumm Korol, God of the Night Sky and Tamer of Blue Mantis.'"

"Your Majesty," said Anand, bowing. "We are humbled to stand before you and honored by your welcome. I am Anand, a Britasyte trader, and this is Daveena, my wife."

The emperor shouted a brief command.

"He says, 'Come closer, I want to look at you,'" said Daveena, then she and Anand stepped forward until the Holy Father bade them come no further with a pointing of his gold-wrapped barley stalk. Once they were closer, Anand could see that the emperor's face was as off kilter as everything else in Worxict. One eyebrow was larger and thicker than the other, and arched higher over his right eye. His left nostril was wide and round while the right one was small and narrow. His lips were thick and bulging on the left side but tapered to thin lines on the right and when they opened they revealed long and crooked teeth that seemed to be fighting each other.

"'You are Britasytes,'" Daveena said to Anand, interpreting for the emperor. "'But one of you have also made this claim of being a *Dranverite*, a rider of the red ants from the northern unknown.'"

"I am a Dranverite," Anand said, "a member of their Collective Nations. This is a choice I made, which they welcomed. I am also a Britasyte roach person as well as a member of the free State of Bee-Jor. I bring you a message and an offering from the Bee-Jorites, the new nation that has risen on your western border."

Anand looked at the emperor's face and at that of his old priest, and saw their resemblance to the bee people of Bulkoko: all of them had that same fold that covered their eyelids.

"'An offering from the Bee-Jorites—really. How can a man have three loyalties?'" Daveena interpreted for the emperor as he cocked his head left, then right.

"I can," Anand said. "One can be a Britasyte and a Bee-Jorite and a Dranverite within our new nation. We are fifty-one united mounds in what was once the eastern region of the Slopeites' United Queendoms. We have separated from our mother nation to create a better one, a country where the welfare of the people is primary—a place where all may aspire to a happy life."

"'Welfare of the people! Happy lives for all! Astonishing!'" Daveena relayed the emperor's condescending tone. "'Are you saying the Mushroom Eaters no longer aspire to steal my lands for their people to occupy, and for their ants to strip of its leaves and grass?'"

"Yes," said Anand. "We abjure any territorial expansion. As a demonstration of our respect for your nation, and as acknowledgment of the crimes of the Slopeites, we are returning the mound of Xixict to you and we will not attempt to retake the mounds of Dinth and Habach. We have already relocated our people from Xixict to our northern mound of Palzhad. You will find no resistance from our Bee-Jorite defenders when you resume occupation of what was always your mound and its surrounding territory."

The emperor and his priest looked at each other and then back at Anand after the translation was completed. When the emperor spoke again, he was shouting.

"'Only one of my mounds being returned? Seven mounds were stolen in the last two hundred summers. What else do you Bee-Jorites have to offer us when my people ache for space?'"

"We are willing to negotiate further concessions."

"'I'm not interested in concessions. I want *all* my mounds back.'"

Anand had figured out what the emperor had shouted before Daveena had begun her translation.

"Majesty, we are a new nation, facing many struggles," said Anand. "In time we could work out a plan that would allow for ...."

The emperor interrupted Anand before he could finish.

"'Whom is it you really speak for?'" Daveena

translated, and then added with a whisper, "Speak carefully, my love. He'd be eager to imprison the commander of the Bee-Jorites' army."

Anand hesitated. "I represent the people of Bee-Jor as well as the wandering tribes of the Britasytes. We are one nation now."

"'But you are different races.'"

"Yes. But we are all humans."

"'You do not speak for the Dranverites?'"

"I do not. Not at this moment."

"'So Dranverites are not coming to your defense in our coming war on your . . . Bee-Jor?'"

"We do not need to war on each other," Anand said.

"'Why would we not war on the Mushroom Eaters, when they are weak and recovering from the attack by Hulkrites? You call yourselves by a different name now, but it doesn't mean your ancestors didn't slaughter our people and steal our land.'"

"Slaughter—of both our peoples—is what we both can avoid. I ask that you not visit the crimes of the Slopeite royals on the common people of Bee-Jor. The commoners are not the descendants of Slopeish soldiers, but of the original inhabitants of the land, a brown-skinned cricket people."

"'I'll ask you again. Whom do you speak for? Who rules in this Bee-Jor?'" Daveena paused in her translation, looked at Anand with fearful, darting eyes. "'Tell me who sent you here!'" she completed.

Anand knew he had to speak quickly, could not hesitate. *Tell as much of the truth as possible.*

"The new ruler of Bee-Jor is also a Dranverite and a Bee-Jorite and was once a low-caste Slopeite," Anand said. "He is Commander Vof Quegdoth, a soldier who trained in Dranveria, spied among the Hulkrites, then raised an army of Slopeish laborers to destroy the Termite worshippers in the War of One Night."

Anand watched as the Emperor shook his head and jutted his lopsided chin in rage.

"'This Quegdoth is the one who pushed the Hulkrites into our land, a trickster who forced us into his battle. This Quegdoth used my armies to defeat his enemies when the Slopeites proved too weak.'"

"Quegdoth knew that after the Slopeites were conquered that the Hulkrites would turn on your nation next. They would have destroyed you. If it had not been for Quegdoth and his army, the Hulkrites would be occupying this palace and replacing your harvester ants with their ghost ants after they raped your women, enslaved your children, and extermi- nated all your men . . . and you."

Anand watched as the emperor seethed before he summoned his high priest with a wag of his finger to come near. The priest took out a ladder from under his emperor's garment and set it against the carving of the moon. Once he had climbed atop it, the two whispered in each other's ears. As Anand watched them whisper, he thought what he saw would be wildly funny if the threat of a war wasn't all too urgent. After the exchange, the priest climbed back down, reinserted the ladder, then resumed his stance and harsh stare as the emperor spoke.

"'I want to know more about Dranveria,'" translated Daveena.

"Yes," said Anand. "I would be glad to tell you more. In the meantime, I request that you pull back your soldiers from Bee-Jor's borders."

"'Certainly not. In the meantime, you and your wife will be my guests.'"

"For how long?"

Daveena gulped before she made her translation.

"'For however long I decide. We will always protect you and the other roach people who travel in our lands. And you will be allowed to return to the Slope—or Bee-Jor or whatever you're calling it—just as soon as we have destroyed it to rebuild it as our own. And perhaps you can tell me how I might capture this Vof Quegdoth. I think he would make the most interesting pet.'"

CHAPTER 34

THE BEE PALACE

They aren't lazy, Zedral thought as he watched the Bulkokans hard at work on the building of their new home. They had decided on an oak tree they had determined was a little more than seventy years old and fully grown. It had a trunk that would not expand anymore, and sturdy branches that would serve as a foundation for their branch dwellings. The tree, dubbed New Bulkoko in their own tongue, was on the furthest ends of Bee-Jorite territory, in a place where both Cajorites and Britasytes seldom ventured. Anand called the forested lands further north the Buffer Zone, and he had explained them as a place where his Dranverite nation had no claims or alliances, but some loose agreements with innumerable tree peoples who dwelt in the forest's canopies.

"I'm still wary. This tree is very far north," Zedral said to Grillaga, his eldest wife, who had been translating for the Bulkokans when it was learned a few of them spoke the Carpenter tongue.

"Too far north?" she asked.

"We only come this far when we're starving, when the other weeds are emptied of game. I remember being here one night as a boy, when we heard what we thought were tree goblins torturing the cicadas. It might have been someone screaming at us to stay away."

"This is the tree they chose," Grillaga said as she looked in a mirror to pluck the hairs above her upper lip that had sprouted since her bleeding ended. "Things are well under way. Their spiral-ladder should reach the tree crotch by late afternoon."

"What are you doing to your face?"

"I'm making it as presentable as possible," she said, just as her twig tweezers broke. She reached for another pair in her vanity box.

"It looks painful."

"It is. But mustaches are only admired when they are worn by men."

"I suppose so," he said, when he was diverted by an approaching party. "We're getting another royal visit."

The men who had identified as three of the six king-husbands of the Bulkokan queen were strutting to Zedral's sled with their staffs stabbing the air as they bobbed. They stood before him, stiff and arrogant, without so much as a nod of the head.

"We'll need more saws and axes," said the first of them.

"And thicker ropes and more twine," said the second.

"And food," said the third. "And we'll have nothing to do with ant-grown mushrooms."

Zedral understood what they had said, and cut off his wife before she finished the translation.

"Tell them we will supply it all gladly," he said to Grillaga. "After each of them licks my asshole."

Her mouth dropped and hung open.

"You're speaking to kings," she whispered in Britasyte.

"Then these *kings* can lick my asshole. With their royal tongues. And their queen can lick yours."

"I'll tell them you'll send a messenger to Cajoria. Right away."

"Do that. Then ask these arrogant red-haired pricks why they need so much rope. Hopefully it's so they can hang themselves."

As the question was translated, Zedral studied the kings' faces and watched them shrug and wrinkle their noses at him.

"He says they must have more and stronger ropes." said Grillaga. "If they are going to hoist what will be their new bee palace into the tree's branches."

"A bee *palace*?"

"What we call a hive, I think."

"The sooner we get them up that tree, the better. I didn't imagine there was a people I could hate worse than Slopeites."

The king in the center had long front teeth that protruded over his lip, even when his mouth was closed. He raised his voice while slapping his staff in his palm.

"He says they must work quickly, before it gets any cooler," said Grillaga. "The queen bee has just enough time to lay eggs to populate the hive with workers that will feed her through the autumn and warm her during winter."

The three kings walked away with not so much as a good-bye.

The following morning, the requested supplies arrived and the Bulkokans were back at work. Zedral watched as they completed the spiral-ladder. Soon after, most of them were climbing up it to spread over the lower branches, then disappear in the leafy shade. Zedral worked through the morning, and was enjoying himself as he repaired a hunting bow, when he heard a loud creaking sound, then faint shouts of warning from inside the tree. The lowest branch was dipping and then it cracked and fell.

The Bulkokans spiraled back down the ladder and went to work on the fallen branch they had severed. With a fierce determination, they sheared its leaves and chopped its twigs, then chipped off its bark before slicing and sawing its hard wood into planes, planks, and beams. By late afternoon, they had assembled an open cube with multiple slats inside it, which they glued together with the last of their propolis. Soon after, the beams of the structure were covered with sheets of wood to make an impressively clean and bright-looking hive. When it was completed, the kings returned to Zedral's sand-sled with new demands.

"Grillaga, come here now!" said Zedral, calling to her at the back of the cabin, where she was at work with the other wives on a block of tourmaline that they chiseled into bits for beads and insets. "We're getting all six kings," said Zedral. "I need your second tongue."

All three of Zedral's wives stepped out to the riding ledge to see the royal males walking as a living hexagon. Grillaga gave them a brief nod of her head. The king with long front teeth spoke to her in a tone that sounded of pure insolence. He made aggressive gestures with one hand while shaking his stinger-ended staff with the other. She cocked her head at him as he spoke while glancing at Zedral with slit-ting eyes that betrayed her disgust. When the king finished speaking, he made an offensive sweep of his hand.

"I don't like it when my ears bleed," said Zedral. "Just what did he say?"

"He said they will need their roaches back, that they will build a cage for them at the base of the tree as a repellant to leaf-cutter ants and other insects. They want us to gather some green grass and grains for their roaches to eat, and some water for them to drink."

"What else did he say? Something's put a scowl on your face."

"He's said that tomorrow morning they are going to engage in their most sacred ceremony, the introduction of a queen bee to her palace. It will coincide with the ceremony of the ascension of Queen Ladeekuz and her Bulkokan subjects to their new tree home, the first of many in New Bulkoko."

"So?"

"So he's told us to stay away, to remove ourselves from their sight. It's a ritual that only Bulkokans can witness."

"And why is that?"

"Only bee people are allowed this privilege. He has told us we are not *quite* worthy—we were molded from Roach's droppings. Their ancestors, on the other hand, sprang up from the fallen honey drops of Goddess Bee. The ceremony is a holy moment meant only for Bee's chosen tribe."

Zedral was unsure of how to react. His bow was freshly strung, and he thought if he had an arrow, he might load it to shoot through the king's throat in order to sever his neck bones.

"Tell the kings that they can lick my asshole."

"Oh, Zedral . . ."

"This time I mean it. Tell them they can lick my asshole. Or I'm going to stand up and lift my tunic and spread my buttocks to show it to them."

Grillaga was silent.

"Tell him!"

Grillaga breathed loudly through her nose, then shouted her translation. Zedral watched as the kings bristled and bent backwards, as if blown by a powerful gust. They asked Grillaga to repeat herself, which she did in loud, clipped words. The speaking king stared at Zedral and spoke.

"He's asking me if you are well," translated Grillaga. "He wonders if you are not infected with an evil spirit and if you would like some of their medicinal honey."

"Finally! An offer of some kind," he shouted in a fury. "Tell Their Highnesses that I was ill, but I am much better now. I will accept some of their honey and I will accept that they do not want us to watch their ritual. Tell them that they might have *requested* this instead of *commanded* it."

Grillaga completed the translation as the humbled king bent his head and spoke in a softer voice. "The king asks if there is anything else you'd like to tell him."

"Yes. Tell him I still expect all Their Royal Highnesses to lick my dirty, hairy, shit-matted asshole."

"I'll tell them you wish them well in their new home and offer the blessings and protection of our mutual god, Madricanth, and that you look forward to a future of trade to benefit us all."

"If you have to."

The next morning, Zedral supervised the move of the caravan further south until it was out of view of New Bulkoko. When the clan was settled within a stand of catchweed bedstraw, Zedral went to his smaller dressing chest and pulled out his oiled leaf poncho and stemmed cap.

"Just where are you going?" Grillaga asked.

"To see this ceremony."

"You told them you wouldn't watch."

"I told them I accepted that they did not want us to see it. I did not tell them I would *not* see it. I hope that's what you translated, because I don't want to lie."

She was quiet. "Can I come with you?"

"Get dressed."

After donning camouflage, Zedral and Grillaga wound their way north through a mix of dry weeds and younger green ones, then crawled under a cluster of rippleseed plantain where they hid in its shade. They peered over a pebble-slab to find the Bulkokans in the midst of their ceremony. The cage that contained the bee queen had been joined to an opening in the hive. As the cage's front slat was raised, the mass of Bulkokans were on their stomachs, prostrate, in a circle. The kings made buzzing sounds as they pushed in the cage's back panel, forcing the queen bee and her attendants to crawl into their new home.

"Where is Queen Ladeekuz?" Zedral asked.

"That's got to be her on top of the cube. Look up."

Zedral noticed Ladeekuz sitting on top of the hive on an improvised throne of woven twigs with leaf remnants. Her head was tilted up at the sun and her palms were out as if receiving a blessing. When the queen bee was inside her new home, the six kings climbed up ladders on the hive's walls to join Ladeekuz and surround her throne. They held hands and swayed back and forth, making buzzing sounds in a strange pattern of long and short bursts.

"They're singing," Zedral said.

"Or praying," said Grillaga.

The rest of the Bulkokans rose and went to the side of the hive where they picked up ropes that had been bundled into cables. They walked outwards with the cables, stretching them tighter, until the hive began to rise. Zedral could hear the people straining as the hive was hoisted higher and higher until it reached a slot that had been gouged into the flat of a branch. When the hive was locked and glued into the slot's corners, the kings shouted to the people below, who responded with an ecstatic cheer. After the cables were released, all the Bulkokans raced up the ladder to join their royals in the tree.

"What are they carrying?" Zedral asked, noticing that the men and women had full hands.

"I'm not sure. It looks like a shield on the left arm."

"And pikes in the right hand," Zedral said. "Probably with bee stingers on their ends."

As the Bulkokans raced up the spiral, the shouting of the people seemed less like a celebration and more like the shrieks of phantoms. Once they had made it into the tree, the shrieking continued, mildly muffled by the evergreen leaves. A few moments later, Zedral heard what sounded like a chain of screams from the tree's upper branches.

"I'm frightened," Grillaga said. "They've gone mad up there!"

Zedral did not want to admit that he also felt scared. They looked into the east of the tree and saw falling, fluttering leaves as well as broken sticks and bits of bark. Then something else started falling from the eastern branches, something that screamed as it plummeted.

"They're falling!" Grillaga shouted. "From high enough that they could die! They're sacrificing themselves!"

"Or sacrificing others!" said Zedral. "This is what they didn't want us to see. Those look like children out there." He stepped out from under the plantain. "Run back to the camp and tell everyone to pull the sleds here now. Ride with the Two Spirit and tell him what you've seen."

Grillaga ran back to the camp as Zedral ran towards the tree, watching as more and more people fell to their deaths or an extreme injury. As he got closer, he gasped to see that the fallen were not Bulkokans, but a pale-skinned people with fuzzy yellow hair that was almost white at its ends. Many of them had been stabbed or shot with arrows, while some had simply been pushed. He heard the crying of one of them who had the good luck to land in a clump of green fescue. The wind had been knocked from her and she struggled to inhale. Her large, lavender eyes shifted in panic as Zedral came forward.

"I won't hurt you," he said, using all his strength to lift her into his arms, where she went limp, too shocked and weak to struggle.

CHAPTER 35

SURPRISING VISITORS

Trellana yawned and didn't bother to cover her mouth. She was bored and tired of standing before another rough, ugly dwelling and another rough, ugly family. "Welcome to Palzhad," said King Nuvao as he handed a bumpy sheet of paper and an ink bladder to a dark-skinned man whose family included two filth-covered brothers, six stinking sisters, his waddling, pregnant wife, and eleven children with crusty nostrils. "You and your wife and children have been granted the right to occupy the lot of this dwelling and its current construction by me, King Nuvao of Palzhad, and by my sister, Her Majesty, Queen Trellana, for as long and you and your descendants obey our laws. Do you swear your loyalty to Bee-Jor and to Palzhad and the Eight Laws, and all laws that will descend from them?"

"I do," said the man as he looked over the sheet of paper, which had a smeared impression of Quegdoth's ubiquitous code stone printed from a wood block. At the top of the sheet was some other writing that Nuvao read aloud as his finger ran under it. "Miptak the Split Toothed, Defender in the Laborers' Army, and mineral sifter, formerly of Mound Xixict, is granted lot 1737 and its existing building on the fifty-third ring of Palzhad."

Miptak coated his thumb in ink, then pressed it into the paper's corner as acknowledgment of his agreement. The king gave him a sheet in return which had other writing and numbers. "This is your deed, loyal defender. Keep it hidden and safe at all times. And never let it get wet. No one has the right to remove you or your descendants from this parcel that you have earned as long as you are law-abiding."

"Thank you, Majesty," said the man, and bowed. His family had been looking in awe at the wreck of a house they had received, a windowless, sand-and-tar dwelling that was dark with an ancient grime and broken in many places. The family stepped through the torn and flaking diaphragm of its one and only entry, and Trellana heard the usual gasps of delight as they compared it to the stilted hovel they had left on the flats of Xixict. She was irritated by this family in particular because the men, mineral sifters, were wearing a wealth of semiprecious jewels as necklaces, a treasure they were entitled to keep under the Dranverite's new edict. They had seen her staring at their jewels with an envy she knew she had not concealed. *Those are not real gems,* she thought, *just some rare bits of colored quartz. But I want them all the same.* It surprised her when the family's head, this Miptak with an awful gap between his broken teeth, jilted all protocol by speaking directly to her.

"Do you like my necklace, Majesty?" Miptak asked, fingering chunks of fool's tourmalines that were crudely strung with a coarse twine. She puckered her mouth as if having eaten something bitter, then gave him the slightest nod of her head.

"Would you like it?" he asked as he stepped forward and fingered the gaudiest of its tricolored gems.

I do want it—but that would be accepting a gift from a low-caste laborer. She made another awkward nod, still not making eye contact. He lifted up a gem to his eye and looked at her through its violet side. "I like it too. I think I'll wear it all my days," he said before grinning, then disappearing into his new home. Trellana fumed through her tiny nostrils as Nuvao smirked and shook his head. "Oh, Trellana. Would it be so awful to laugh at yourself once in a while? Just try smiling, and at least acknowledging the people at this mound are humans like yourself."

"I am not just any human," she said. "And how

many more times must you drag me out here for one of these housing assignments?"

"This is your duty, your privilege. Show them some respect, sister, and the people will return it to you as their queen. These are families that fought in the war, the war that saved your royal bottom. Why, these recent arrivals were forced to leave their old mound. They rolled acorns here over rough sands for more than a moon so that all of us, you included, might have something to eat besides mushrooms."

"My unending thanks," Trellana said. "But the only thing acorns are good for is to remedy runny bowels. Now can we go back to the palace?"

"We've a few more families waiting for their deeds. Then we can go home."

"We can never go home."

"I am at home," he said. "Why, it feels quite homey here in Palzhad."

After finishing the deeding of several more houses, Trellana heard a thorn horn announcing the arrival of an ant train at the ring's dew station.

"Run, Trelly," Nuvao said. "If we hurry we can catch that train. Wave your scepter and they might wait for us."

"I would sooner use my scepter to crush in my own skull than run after some ant train."

"As you like. But if you do crush your skull in, you'll miss tonight's surprise."

"What surprise?"

"That would be telling. See you at dinner."

Walking to the main artery, Trellana would not allow her guards to hail any of the returning foraging ants for her to climb and ride to the top as they were unsaddled, an indignity she would not suffer. She stuck her nose in the air and trudged up to her palace as the guards laughed at jokes they whispered behind her back. After they delivered her to the tunnel opening, they failed to bow and ask for permission to leave before departing.

It was dark and sadly silent in her chamber by the time she entered it. A single torch in its wall holster was all that lit the emptiness. Her servants from Cajoria stood nearby, slumped and quiet, having endured a day far duller than hers. She raised her arms over her head as a signal that they should undress her, and they seemed grateful for something to do. Barhosa entered the chamber after calling, *"Creet-creet."*

"Majesty, King Nuvao has suggested you dress for dinner tonight."

"Oh. This surprise he mentioned. Has someone arrived?"

"I believe so. I believe it is a man he has been entertaining for a while."

"You are not sure if it is a man?"

"I am not."

"It would be surprising if my brother were entertaining a woman."

Trellana turned to her servants, who were luxuriating in this little bit of news. "Ladies, bring me my crushed silk gowns, the yellow, pink, and scarlet ones with the low necklines. This pregnancy has thickened me and I may as well show off my . . . increased assets."

After Trellana powered her face with some old and clumpy bee pollen that had to be re-crushed in a mortar, she made her way quickly to Nuvao's chambers with two servants following behind to carry the tails of her trains. As usual, her brother was sitting on a floor cushion at a leaf platter as opposed to a formal chair and table. For some reason, he was shaking with laughter. The leaf was covered with worn, chipped-quartz platters that held generous pilings of pickled and dried foods, as well as a shiny lump of hoverfly loaf, whose top bore a cube of green mint jelly. It was not exactly a holiday feast, but it was more than mushrooms and morning dew.

A man's back was to her, a man she hated at first sight for his overly round shape. The folds of his back were apparent through his thin robe and they jiggled in synchrony with his laughter, which was a harsh howl mixed with effeminate titters and chopped up with irritating snorts. Trellana knew in a moment it was pointless to have oiled her breasts and worn her revealing gowns. The man stood, turned, and bowed to her, and worked at stifling his laughter.

"Trelly," her brother said through muffled snickers, "we are honored to have the celebrated Brother Moonsinger as our guest tonight."

"Your Majesty," Moonsinger said. "Such an honor to meet the woman who has agreed to rule Palzhad."

"You must forgive me that I am not familiar with you," said Trellana as she examined the moth-shaped cut of his deeply pink hair with its waxed wings. His face paint was unsettling; the dark lines around her eyes and his thickened, clumpy lashes made her think of colliding millipedes when he blinked.

"Brother Moonsinger is from Mound Loobosh," said Nuvao. "Now he circulates through all of Bee-Jor and has become quite famous."

"A famous tutor?" *How I loathe tutors, these horrendous eunuchs who stuffed my ears with poetry and history,* she thought as she looked for the testicle jar that should have been hanging from his neck.

"I *was* a tutor. And I am still teaching," he said, "but my lessons are no longer confined to royal ears. As Commander Quegdoth has urged us, we must share all knowledge with all people."

"Brother Moonsinger is our greatest storyteller," said Nuvao. "His performances are very much in demand."

"I see," said Trellana as she signaled to a servant to bring her a low chair so that she would not have to sit on a floor cushion. "Our tutors are now working as common entertainers in order to make their way."

Nuvao's face went dark for an instant before it brightened again. "There is nothing common about the Brother's stories, Trellana. They are skillful, thrilling histories, and as entertaining as they are educational. Perhaps the Good Brother will grace us with a story after dinner. In the meantime, you and I have something serious to discuss with him."

"Oh, do we?" Trellana said as she signaled to one of her servants to fill her quartz platter with some unusually decent food. "A bit of everything and a lot of that," she whispered after pointing to the loaf.

"As you know, Trelly, in the Great Division we gained Mound Venaris but we lost Loobosh, our seat of learning."

"I did *not* know that," said Trellana.

Brother Moonsinger's eyes popped in surprise. "Really, Majesty. I'm sure you might remember: it was negotiated that Loobosh would remain with the Slope since it is very much in the West," he said. "However, many of the Learned did not want to remain in the Old Slope. Like me, they wanted to be a part of a promising new nation where we were invited to impart our wisdom in this new profession of 'teacher' . . . not tutor."

"Well, how very generous of you," Trellana said. "Though I am sure it will be an exasperating challenge to educate so many deficient Bee-Jorites."

"It is quite generous," said Nuvao, his eyes rapidly blinking. "Brother Moonsinger is a very generous man who has provided us with this lavish dinner tonight, generously given to him by those *deficient* Bee-Jorites as a thanks for sharing his gift. And what, dear sister, may I ask, have you brought to the dinner-leaf tonight?"

Trellana sighed. *He's worse than Mother.*

"I have brought myself," she said, "to this godsforsaken mound where every moment is a misery, but all of them made possible because my essence allows these ants to thrive. The sacred mushroom may have lost its prestige, but may I remind you, our leaf-cutter ants are lethal defenders that keep us all safe."

"Indeed," said Moonsinger. "But your brother and I have been discussing a new prospect, one that may strengthen this mound even more, and one that will revive Palzhad as one of Bee-Jor's greatest mounds."

"I wouldn't dare try and stop you from telling me," said Trellana.

"The Learned Ones who left Loobosh for Bee-Jor seek a new home, a new center of learning. King Nuvao tells me you have plenty of room here in Palzhad, many empty rings with empty dwellings that need rebuilding. This is a neglected but beautiful queendom with an impressive history that appeals to men with curious natures."

They want to bring more prattling eunuchs here, Trellana thought. *Thousands of them to annoy me.* "Curious natures, yes. Are you telling me all the eunuchs want to live on Palzhad?"

"Yes," said Nuvao. "They do, and we should welcome them. They would run what Quegdoth calls *schools*, learning places for children, and later, they would have a higher place of learning—something called a *university*, which we could establish in one of the unoccupied palaces."

"We'll invite *all* the curious and the quick learning to be teachers. But first," said Moonsinger, suddenly serious, "we must end the practice of castration for those who enter the learning life. The Learned will never again be eunuchs."

"End castration? I thought it improved memory and intelligence. Along with weight gain. The fatter, the smarter."

"It does not," said Moonsinger. "Nuvao is no less bright than I am for having all his parts and for keeping a fine figure."

"Under the Eight Laws, it would be a violation to take away a boy's testicles," said Nuvao. "The mutilation of another's person."

"We've come to realize that the priesthood enforced this cruel practice to maintain control over the common people, to keep them stupid," said Moonsinger as sadness fractured his voice. "Remove the intelligent boys from the tradesman and working castes and one takes away the chance to pass on their seeds. The end results are dull masses willing to accept dull lives. That is exactly what happened to me, when I proved myself a bit too clever."

"Well," said Trellana. "If you tutors are only coming to realize this now, perhaps you are not as clever as you think."

To Trellana's complete surprise, Nuvao and Moon-singer laughed as loud as a tumble of rocks, and then they laughed some more. Servants standing near the wall stiffened and looked uncomfortable. Trellana felt a crushing envy.

"Whatever it is you are drinking, I would like some," said Trellana.

"It's not what we are *drinking*," said Nuvao. "And as ecstatic as I am at the moment, I will not allow you to break your promise to Quegdoth: no fermentation until your babies are born."

"Then what is it that you have eaten?"

The two started laughing again.

"Really, the two of you," she said as she pushed away her platter and wiped at sudden tears. "You have made this dinner in Palzhad as unpleasant as any other." When the two started laughing again, she felt as if a stopper in her heart had been plucked to release streams of sadness, regret, and despair, a gushing that filled her with an unbearable heaviness. Before she could stop herself, she yelped in the deepest pain and dropped off her seat to the floor. She lay on the tiles, feeling as if she had been paralyzed, once again, by a Dranverite's dart, and felt sure that she could never rise again.

"Trellana, this is very unbecoming of a queen," said Nuvao, suddenly sober and standing over her, looking down. "It is unbecoming of anyone. Get up, please. The servants are watching."

"You don't understand, Nuvao," she said. "I've no one here. Not my father or a husband or my babies or friends . . . no one who loves or understands me. And now the Dranverite has taken away my one great pleasure, my only relief."

"There are other pleasures besides drink," Nuvao said.

"Have one of these," said Moonsinger, and lifted up a thin, black wafer from a platter of yellow quartz.

"And what is that? It looks like dried pond algae. Which I have never cared for."

The eunuch chuckled and looked at her with a warm concern as he handed her the wafer.

"Brother, I don't think she should!" Nuvao said, trying to tear the wafer away. Moonsinger blocked Nuvao's arm and then offered the queen the wafer again.

"Everyone should have one of these, Queen Trellana," said Moonsinger. "It's the ladder to the gods, the means of entering into their most lovely world. And after you leave their world, you might be able to accept this one."

Trellana was shocked and sat up. "I know what that is! That's the Holy Mildew!" She glared at Nuvao. "And ingesting it like this—sharing it with someone other than a priest—it's sacrilege!"

"Who knew sacrilege could be so wonderful," said Nuvao. "The Britasytes, one of which you are wed to, have been ingesting the Mildew for centuries. The Sand has not crumbled nor has the sky fallen."

"I'd like to be sacrilegious every day," said Moonsinger. "But I might laugh my lungs out." As the two men were possessed by laughter again, Moonsinger dropped the wafer, which floated this way then that before it landed near Trellana's hand. She picked it up and looked through its dark translucence.

"Don't eat that, Trelly," said Nuvao, recovering from laugher. "In your state, you may not react well." He turned to the servants. "Go to the kitchen and get the queen some kwondle tea, please."

"I don't want tea," said Trellana as she folded the wafer into a wad she could fit in her mouth.

"You should have some *tea* before the surprise gets here."

"I thought the eunuch was the surprise," she said as she stuffed the wad in her mouth and chewed. It was bitter, and as it dampened, it became tar-like and stuck to her teeth.

"I do have your best interests in mind, Trellana," Nuvao said, looking over his shoulder as he heard footsteps. "Though I don't know that ingesting the Mildew was the best idea right before receiving your visitor. Please stand and welcome her."

Barhosa entered the dining chamber and behind her was a woman in fine, thick dress and small but stylish antennae. "Announcing Her Majesty, Queen Omathaza of Shishto."

All rose to their feet. "Aunt Omathaza! This *is* a surprise!" said Trellana, wobbling. "What brings you to the edge of the Dustlands?"

"You do, honey-crystal." said Omathaza. "I have heard you are in need of some company."

Trellana sobbed out of relief. "You have heard correctly," she said between sniffles. "Please . . . let's find a seat for my aunt."

"Good evening, Omathaza," said Nuvao. "Very kind of you to visit."

"Very kind of you to receive me," she said, and Trellana watched as her aunt took in her brother from head to toe, with her eyes slitting in suspicion or contempt, or both. "I was a young queen once and sent to live at a strange mound. I know some of what our benighted little blossom must be going through here at Palzhad—Palzhad, which has always been such a peculiar mound. I have come to offer her a bosom she can cry on, since her own mother is so very *busy* in Cajoria."

"She is," said Nuvao. "And Mother has no plans to rest until the very end of her days. Such is her devotion to the new nation. Would that we were all so dedicated to such high ideals."

"High ideals, indeed," said Omathaza. "Your description of her intentions is so very . . . generous."

"Forgive me, Auntie," Nuvao said. "Allow me to present Brother Moonsinger of Mound Loobosh."

"We are already acquainted," said Moonsinger

as he bowed. "I was a history tutor to the queen's youngest some time ago. Prince Bahadoor."

A pained look came over Omathaza's face as she took in the face powder that hid his darker color. "My little flea-slayer," she said. "I'm afraid the Hulkrish invasion was his first and last battle."

"I am sure he fought most bravely," Trellana said. "I heard he was quite handsome."

"He was indeed—the very image of my husband in his youthful glory, the both of them with widely spaced eyes of a piercing green. Little Bahmi would have been the most beautiful consort to a general's daughter or perhaps some lovely princess."

"Prince Bahadoor was a . . . a *good* pupil," said Brother Moonsinger, though his face indicated that he thought otherwise. Omathaza remained lost in some precious memory when Trellana, feeling energized, beckoned to her maidservants.

"Good servants, let's not have my aunt sitting and eating on the floor like the working people on a hot summer's day. Please, let's bring everything over to a proper table with chairs that will suit a queen."

"Actually, child, I think that we would be more comfortable in your own chambers. And these jolly, uh, *individuals* here would be so bored by women's talk. Might we bring some food and drink back to your own dining table?"

"Certainly, Auntie. We could . . ."

"That would not be a good idea," said Nuvao. "Not now. Trellana should stay with us for the evening."

"I am sorry," Omathaza asked. "Was this not a good time for a visit?"

"It is a brilliant time for a visit," said Trellana. She was feeling a bright and pleasurable energy in her bowels that radiated through her limbs and made her skin tingle. "Brother, I will have my ladies nearby in case of any emergency. We can have them fill some platters and bring over some drink. I feel as if I am the one who has interrupted your pleasures."

Nuvao glared at her. "Some unfermented drink," he said. "Promise? The both of you?"

"I swear it by Mantis," said Trellana,

"I give my word as a queen," said Omathaza.

The servants gathered up some food as the queens drifted out to the hall in a leisurely way to make small talk about the journey south. After they settled at Trellana's dining table, Omathaza spoke in a whisper. "I have very interesting news for you, Trelly."

Trellana gasped. "Is it true? Is he . . ."

"Alive? Yes."

Maleps is alive! she wanted to scream.

"How do you know?"

"Since the Partition, we have been able to pass messages at Venaris. They have reopened and extended one of the ants' tunnels that goes deep into the East and intersects with a tunnel of Mound Fecklebretz; we are going back and forth. We know now that the Slope is *not* about to fall to the Beetle Riders. They have been pushed back! At the moment, we have a truce."

"A truce? How?"

"Our men have learned something from the Dranverite—about fighting on foot behind shields soaked with repellants instead of riding on ants. And on the fringes of the Dustlands, they have found different and more powerful weapons that were left behind by the Hulkrites. The missiles from these massive crossbows destroyed the Britasytes' roaches. And they can penetrate the Carpenters' war beetles."

"The Dranverite," said Trellana. She felt a sadness plummet through her.

"Do not worry about him, little sugar moth. He has his own troubles. We have heard he may be lost forever among the Seed Eaters. If Maleps is indeed alive, you are still married to a Slopeish king. Your union to that insidious interloper will be annulled."

"But I carry his children in my belly."

"Exactly. *His* children." Omathaza was quiet as her grin turned to a toothy smile. "You must come to Venaris," she whispered. "For a wedding! One to be attended by the queens and princesses of all the eastern mounds in the Lost Country."

"Who is marrying?"

"Not a marriage so much as a commitment ceremony. Our distant cousin, the Princess Tajette of Habach, will be the new Nun Queen of Venaris. At the next new moon she is taking the Yellow Veil as a bride of Grasshopper. She has invited you and all royal women to her celebration. Tajette is celibate, of course, and no men are allowed—except his Ultimate Pious Dolgeeno, who will conduct the rite."

"They're allowing Dolgeeno to return to Venaris?"

"The dispensation was approved by the Dranverite and your mother. They're busy with other things, want us out of their way." Omathaza paused, then smiled and leaned in. "Trellana, this ceremony is an opportunity for us, for we royal women to convene and take charge of our destiny, to speak with one voice and make some decisions. As the Dranverite's wife and the mother of his children, we are looking to you to join us, to help us take back what is ours."

Trellana's heart was pumping hard and fast. She felt the beginnings of an uncontainable ecstasy. The flood of feelings was springing from some extraordinary news, but the effect of this Mildew had multiplied her joy a hundredfold. Everything, even the dark emptiness of her chambers, had a strange and colorful sweetness. She looked up at the ceiling and it dissolved before her and opened to a gorgeous view of the gods in their palace at the Tree Top of Ganilta. They smiled fondly on her as they sang her name. "Trellana, Trellana, glorious Trellana," sang Grasshopper. She was chortling, eager for life again, and feeling a rock-hard sense of hope and power.

"Auntie, let's not eat yet," said Trellana, turning

away from her vision. "Let's summon a tamer to rouse a carrying ant and take us down to the cathedral! I have yet to see it here at Palzhad."

"The cathedral? Really? Are you feeling devotional?"

"I am feeling more than that . . . I am being touched by the gods! Their warm, gentle hands are guiding me to visit them. I know something now, as I know my own name. I must offer my life to their service. Tonight I must visit their altar and leave them some of my blood to drink."

"*You* want to serve the gods? Are you all right, little caterpillar? I *do* know what you might have eaten before my arrival, and I am just the slightest bit shocked."

"I couldn't possibly feel better. No one, until now, has ever been this happy. I must know how our gods will use me, for our cause as royal women. It can only increase my inner mounting joy!"

Omathaza looked at her, unsure, but smiling.

Some time later, the niece and aunt were seated atop a slow but steady riding ant as it was lured by a reluctant and sleepy ant-tamer who had been summoned from his bed to don a turban of *finding-scent*. Trellana had brought her chamber torch and the tamer had brought one as well, but their dim lights were drowned in the darkness of the unlit stair spiral. As they made their way down and deeper, Trellana relished the blackness and felt it as warm and loving.

The sound of ant and human steps played in her ears as an intricate music. When they reached the ornate wall ring of the cathedral's entrance, the tamer tied the ant to a post, then held back the slit of the diaphragm to allow the queens to pull themselves and their heavy gowns inside the sanctuary.

"I've got to sit down," said Omathaza, who felt in the blackness for a bench at the back of the cathedral. "That ride through the darkness was most unsettling."

"Please do take a seat, Auntie," said Trellana as she heard her name repeated by a thousand whisperers. "They are calling me! Can you hear it?"

"I cannot."

Holding her torch before her, Trellana raised her chin and felt a rush of pride pour through her as she approached the altar and its clustered idols, her faint light revealing their faces. As she got closer to the deities, the cathedral filled with the yellow sunlight of day. The ceiling turned a bright and heavenly blue, and under its vault was a southward migration of milkweed butterflies with bright orange wings that sang sweet melodies as they flapped. The idols stood as stiff, painted carvings until Ant Queen and Mantis rattled and rolled. They came to life to walk upright and knock aside Locust and Cricket, then trampled over the toppled carving of the Roach Demon to stand before Trellana.

"The time has come," said Ant Queen as Her golden antennae probed Trellana for kin-scent. "You,

Queen Trellana, must fulfill your mission as my most favored descendent."

"Your will be done," said Trellana, and curtsied. Next, Mantis probed the queen and cocked Her triangular head with its great bulging eyes. She grabbed Trellana's hand with Her right fore-claw and pierced the palm for a drop of blood, which She brought to her mouth to lick.

"Trellana, Queen of All Slopeites," said Mantis as She crawled to the idol of Cricket and chewed off its head. "You and Omathaza must send messages to all the Slopeish queens and princesses who live in disgrace in the unholy East. Tell them it is their duty to come to Venaris for the wedding of Princess Tajette. They must attend."

Ant Queen stepped forward and lifted the idol of the Roach Demon with Her mandibles and then ripped its body into pieces with Her six claws. "Then you must tell all your aunts and cousins, all my lovely daughters, what they must do to restore the Great and Holy Slope," said Ant Queen as Her halo brightened to a blinding white.

Trellana's eyes burned in the brilliant light but she kept them focused as a gorgeous vision unfolded of the mission her goddesses had given to her.

their young children stood before the window, staring. Behind them stood the family's servants in their loose, pleated robes and the outlandish bonnets that obscured their faces and even their sex. Twin boys with shaved heads and single side-locks of orange hair turned to their mother to make a request, and she smiled and nodded her consent. A bonneted servant stepped forward, opened her robe, and produced curly sticks of a sweet from one of a hundred pockets in her robe's lining. As the children sucked on their candy, the family was joined by others who pointed at Anand and Daveena and discussed their appearance.

"Should we return the favor?" Anand asked, pointing at the husbands.

"Yes, let them wonder what cruel comments we're making about *their* physical appearance," said Daveena as she pointed at the wives and then at each of their children.

"Look at me and smirk," said Anand. "And then we'll break out in laughter."

Daveena did as Anand asked, and they watched as the families took offense. They moved on, but were replaced by new gawkers who munched on treats from leaf bags as they stared. Hungry harvester ants approached the gawkers and antennated them, opening their mandibles and then their mouths in hopes of being passed some digested food. "The harvester ants are hungry. And so am I," said Daveena.

"And it's getting hot in here and my mouth is dry,"

said Anand. "How do they expect us to put on a show if we aren't properly fed and watered?"

"Let's lie on the floor and clutch our stomachs and maybe they'll figure out we need some refreshments."

The two were lying with faces to the back of the room when its walls were pulled open by strongmen yanking on ropes. The High Priest of the Moon stood at the back of the men, chin tilted up and clutching his staff, surrounded by some other holy men and a priestess. He shouted to Daveena.

"We have been invited to the second breakfast of His Divinity, the Emperor Volokop," she translated for Anand. The priest gestured to them to walk out of the cell and into the vast chamber where an indoor sled awaited them. To Anand, the sled looked like a giant hairbrush, with a thickness of bristles on its underside instead of scale runners. They walked up the short flight of steps at its back, then followed the priest onto its platform, where they took seats on a divan shaped like the crescent moon. The hauling boys in their golden armor dragged them over the empty expanse of the palace floors, where occasional courtiers stopped to stare or stepped aside. The sled entered a tunnel in the wall cut in the shape of a katydid in profile, then emerged into the emperor's reception chamber. It was a vast, ovoid room with a cone-shaped ceiling and filled with a rich orange light from its walls of amber panels.

The emperor was wearing another extraordinary robe that was a replica of his palace, but this version was a pale violet. He had not worn his crown, but his bright ginger hair had been sculpted with beeswax into the shape of a mantis with upright claws. He was seated, or maybe standing, at the top of a star-shaped structure with graduating levels, and each level was covered with platters, jars, and bowls of prepared foods and drinks. A bonneted attendant was atop a ladder feeding the emperor with a small, pronged shovel that carried bits of chopped food to his mouth. On the other side of his mouth was an attendant whose broad spoon offered drops of a black liquid from a keg worn around his neck. This attendant used his sleeve to wipe the emperor's mouth just before he spoke.

"He wants to know if we were comfortable last night," said Daveena.

Anand nodded his head and heard Daveena say, *"Dagh, shpeebo."* Yes, thanks. He felt something behind his legs, and realized they had been brought chairs. A table in some loose cloud shape was pushed before them; it was covered with splat-shaped platters bearing roasted seeds steeped in different juices to dye them all the colors of the rainbow. The emperor shouted down at them.

"We are commanded to eat and drink," said Daveena. "For he wants us alive and well."

"Dagh, shpeebo," Anand said, and the emperor

almost smiled. As he spoke, Anand took in the details of his costume and felt unsteady.

"He wants to know if Dranveria is going to give him any more trouble," said Daveena.

"What trouble have they had?"

For the first time, Anand saw that the emperor had hands when he lifted up some spangled sleeves from the folds of the garment. One hand was enormous and clubby looking, with fused fingers, and the other was thin and skeletal. He made a motion of waves.

"'Dranveria has never warred on the Holy Barley Lands because they are protected by the Great Freshwater Lake. But lately I have reports of more and more Dranverites in their floating wooden houses coming closer to my shore. Are these houses full of soldiers?'"

"No. They are called *ships* in Dranverish—large boats—and they are full of lake harvesters—the men and women who gather the treasures of the waters to sell and eat."

The emperor raised his abnormally high eyebrow even higher as the translation was completed.

"'The Dranverites have conquered the Mushroom Eaters and the Stink Ant people. When are they planning on conquering us?'"

"The Dranverites have not conquered the Slope, nor the Stink Ant people," Anand said. "And they will not conquer you."

The emperor cocked his head, looked with suspicion on Anand.

"'You told me yourself that a Dranverite sits on the throne of Cajoria. And the Dranverites have tested us recently. When we retook our mound of Glixict from the Stink Ant people of the Sycamore Stands, the Dranverites invaded our reacquired territory and polluted it with their red hunter ants. They evicted my subjects after infecting them with a sleeping potion and then dumped them like trash at the old border. One of my subjects is missing.'"

"Your Highness, the people of the Dranverite Collective Nations did no such thing. The Stink Ant people of Glixict were forced into Dranverish lands. The Dranverites evicted your people so that the Stink Ant refugees could return to their homes. I assure you, the Dranverites offer peace to your great nation and the chance to be friends. That is a message that your missing subject will return with in the next year."

"'Offers of peace do not come without a demand. Now that the Dranverites have conquered the Slope, they will use it as a bridge to circumvent the lake and steal my empire.'"

"No, Your Highness. Dranveria did not conquer the Slope. They will not take your nation."

"'You mean my empire!'"

"Yes, your empire."

Volokop blinked in the silence and cocked his

head as he gathered his thoughts. His next words were quieter.

"He asks if you know their king," Daveena said, more quietly.

"Dranveria is not ruled by a king. They are not ruled at all. They are *governed* by an elected council. Their current head is a woman known as the People's Agent."

Anand heard Daveena use the Britasyte words for *govern*, *agent*, and *elected*. Volokop grumbled.

"He does not know these words—I do not know how to translate them," Daveena said to Anand.

"The People's Agent is the voice of all the people; she represents them, speaks for them, but does not rule them. They chose her as their leader. She leads them, relying on their wishes."

Volokop laughed in a slow, deep way as Daveena finished her translation.

"'Do you know this she-voice?'"

"I have met her, yes."

The emperor looked at his priest and the both of them shook their heads in disgust.

"'This notion of letting people rule themselves is a dangerous one, bad for them, like giving a baby a blade of razor-grass as a toy. You, Dranverite, will take a message to this People's Agent. Tell her we have slaughtered the Hulkrites. Tell them the Slope is ours, and that they must abandon all aspirations to it. Tell them they must withdraw this Dranverite they have placed on the throne of Cajoria or we will send them his bones in a bag. Tell the Dranverites to stay in the lands beyond my lake, or we will drive them and their red ants over the Edge of the World to fall for eternity.'"

Daveena paused in her translation. "Be careful, what you say next," she added in her own voice. "Find some agreement with him."

"Majesty, yes," said Anand, forcing a shallow bow. "I will relay your message on my immediate return to Bee-Jor. But I speak the fullest truth: the Dranverites have not conquered the Slope. And they will not conquer your Barley Lands."

The emperor shook his head before speaking, looking at Anand as if he was little more than a mischievous brat. Daveena was breathing hard as she relayed his words, her eyes wide with panic.

"'No, little roach-eater. You will not return to Bee-Jor. You will take my message to Dranveria *now*.'"

Anand was silent. He nodded his head in subservience.

"I will bring your message to the Dranverites, Your Majesty. As soon as I return my wife to our families in Bee-Jor."

"'Impossible. We are preparing for war. Your wife will be safe here, with us, as my guest. You will go to Dranveria now. And if the Dranverites are concerned for the lives of the Mushrooms Eaters, they can host them once we drive them out.'"

The emperor's head disappeared, dropping below his collar. Anand and Daveena watched as a slit in the garment opened to reveal an old and almost naked man, who hobbled towards them wearing nothing more than a vast loincloth around his body, which was a complete mass of deformities. His arms were both swollen and atrophied. One side of his chest was puffed and lumpy while the other revealed his rib cage. His legs were the strangest thing of all, huge trunks of bulbous, ropy flesh with calves that looked pregnant with adults. The voluminous garment he had left was more of a shell for his body than a tent. He came closer in his heavy waddle, towards Anand, who tried and failed not to react to his jarring appearance. The emperor grinned with his lopsided mouth, delighting in the shock he had produced and laughing in a slow way that made his deformities jiggle. When he turned towards Daveena, he bent his head and got too close to her. She turned her face away from him, having felt and smelled his breath as he spoke.

"He says, 'Do not worry about this big, beautiful girl with her skin like the night while you are gone. I will take very good care of her . . . and the little one who lives inside her.'"

The emperor shouted to the bonneted attendants lining the wall. They threw back their hats, then raised their swords from out of their robes. Anand reached for his blowgun when he felt a sword piercing his back.

"He says to drop it," Daveena said, then gave with a cry of pain when the tip of a blade pricked her own back.

The emperor was standing before Anand now, his skeletal hand extended.

"He says, 'I know exactly what that is. And I thank you for bringing us one,'" said Daveena as she panted in fear. Anand breathed hard and looked into the dark green of the soldiers' eyes surrounding him. He took the blowgun from around his neck and handed it to Volokop, who stared at it, amused, as he considered its function. Anand felt something damp and heavy fall over him. The soldiers had thrown a wet blanket over his head that reeked with the poisonous stink of the harvester ant's war spray. He was sick and dizzy in an instant. When he fell to the floor, his limp body was picked up and stuffed in a box with holes in its lid.

"Daveena," he tried to shout, and felt his lips move, but no sound came from his throat. The last thing he heard was her shrieking his name as she fell on the box and grasped at its lid.

The emperor's guards had their blades in Daveena's back as her shrieking turned to sobbing. "Where are you taking him?"

"I have told you. He is on his way to Dranveria."

Lord Madricanth, no! The Seed Eaters will trample over Bee-Jor without Anand in command.

"But you can't! It's unwise! He's not safe there!"

"Madame Roach Rider, I can do anything I want. Never tell me otherwise. I am the emperor," said Volokop. "Do not worry, Sweet Darkling. Once he has passed my message, he can return. Part of my message will be that if he is killed or wounded, they will be inviting their own destruction. Let me show you your home while you are our guest here."

Volokop signaled to one of the servants who waited nearby with a simpler garment for him, a floor-length robe of shimmering orange cloth that Daveena recognized as a Britasyte product. His body trudged up the short staircase of the palace sled with a series of thumps. He invited Daveena to sit next to him, patting the divan's cushion with something like a polite smile, as if she were his wife or daughter. The sled veered around the throne to another tunnel with an entry shaped like a worm squirming from a star. The tunnel turned dark before the sled entered a chamber that had been divided with a wall of bars. Bonneted guards stood on the far sides of what Daveena realized was a cage for a hundred people.

She looked through the bars and saw the silhouettes of men and women who were pacing and muttering prayers against the amber light of a large quartz window—they were also on display to the public. The prisoners came to the bars and looked at Daveena and the emperor with a mix of fear and curiosity. As she got closer she could see the prisoners' skin and clothes and recognized them as Slopeites. All had yellow-white skin and were wearing expensive if greasy-looking garments. The women were the high-born wives of officers and royalty, and the men, from their purple robes, were priests. As her eyes adjusted, she saw that all of them had scabby, nubby patches where they should have had right ears. The smell of putrefying flesh assaulted her nose, and she looked at the left of the cage to see a pile of corpses in neatly stacked piles. The dead were still dressed in their finery, but rotting and stinking.

"These are my guests from the mounds they call Dinth and Habach in the Slopeites' tongue," said Volokop. "I await their ransom, but have received no message from the Mushroom Eaters. I really can't afford to feed them anymore," he said, followed by a phlegmy laugh that sounded like choking. "We sent a message to Venaris through your roach people that we held these prisoners. We were hoping to negotiate their return, but it seems that message was not delivered."

"If you paid to send this message through the Britasytes, then they delivered it," said Daveena, who was shaken, breathing hard. "I am sure these people have been forgotten, with all that has happened on the Slope . . . rather, on what used to be the Slope."

Volokop sighed in an exaggerated way. "So. My prisoners no longer have value. They look important, but perhaps they are little more than garbage. Maybe

I should just toss them in a pit with some moon roaches as a bit of entertainment for my subjects."

"I don't speak much Slopeish but I will make some inquiries," said Daveena as the guards pulled out something like a drawer at the bottom of the cage and pointed to it.

"If it please you," said the emperor. Daveena realized she was to lie at the bottom of the drawer to be pushed through a slot. She complied and stepped out of the drawer on the other side of the bars. The Slopeites looked at her with a silent hatred, then just as soon turned away to ponder their own misery. She looked to her right, at the pile of corpses, and wondered how they had died.

Will I die here too? How long will I wait?

"You will be well taken care of while I am gone," said Volokop. "When I get back we can chat again."

"Your Majesty," Daveena shouted at him as he climbed his sled. He turned very slowly to look at her.

"May I ask . . . where are you going?"

"To prepare for war, of course. To squash the Mushroom Eaters and exterminate their yellow ants."

"If you destroy the Slopeites and kill all their ants, there will be no more Slopeish cloths and clay vessels and mushrooms. And no more of the . . . *procheskya brezen*."

Volokop froze. "The seers' slime? What do the Slopeites have to do with the slime?"

"It comes from inside their mounds—scraped

the pits he saw erections of the wood-and-straw idols of their moon/war god, mounted on a night-blue mantis. The camps were crowded with laborers but had few soldiers. As Anand had told him, these were all feints. One of them would swell to become the real point of attack, but he had yet to see which one.

Hesitant to fly further east, he knew he must when he picked up the sweaty scent of Seed Eater men. It was a stink like rotting onions, a smell he knew too well from his days in the midden. He looked over his shoulder at the squadron that followed him. Most of the twenty locusts and their pilots were dutifully flying behind him, but one had been lost to the locust's fatigue or hunger. The squadron veered around Xixict, the mound Anand had returned to Emperor Volokop. He saw but a few harvester ants crawling from under the mound's rain shield. The ants and humans had just established their colony and were likely low in both numbers. The ants he saw were small, and they struggled with the corpses of dead leaf-cutters, which they ported to their outdoor midden.

The smell of men got stronger, and mixed with that of the Great Freshwater Lake with its essence of algae and mud. Just south of the lake, Terraclon saw a growing human presence over a grassless clearing. He promptly signaled for the squadron to fly up to avoid detection. As his nose had told him, the real army was here, a mass of hundreds of thousands, with just as many ants waiting inside an uncountable sprawl of cages. The Seed Eaters' plan, so obvious from above, was to draw the Bee-Jorites to multiple feints near the South, while their real attack would be on the North. Terraclon felt something like a sharp punch to the stomach when he realized the enemy's true intention: they were going to take Cajoria. *They've figured out where our capital is! Chop off the centipede's head and kill the rest of the body!*

He signaled a return to Mound Shishto with a slow turn of his palm. The flight back was an easy but anxious one, and the bright sun of the Southwest stabbed at his eyes. As the mound came into view, he prayed to Cricket that Anand and his caravan had returned, at last, from their foolish mission. *It's less than half a moon before the Barley people attack. And Anand, my brother, you are still out there!*

He felt his back and arms tensing with a new wave of worries, something that passed into the locust when her flight went awry. She dove, then rose, then tilted and jerked. He gritted his teeth, then relaxed both his jaw and his grip, righting the locust with short strokes of the antennae, which steadied the speed of her wings. Just as she settled on a smooth current, his eye was drawn to distant sparkles. *My prayers have been answered!* he thought when he sighted a chain of brown crawlers, and behind them, jewel-crusted sand-sleds making their way west.

"Anand! Thank Cricket!" he said, and smiled for

the first time in days. He raised his fingers and made a circling motion to signal the squadron to spiral and land. As the locusts circled lower and made crawling stops, the border guards of Shishto rode out to meet them.

"Quegdoth and the roach people are returning!" Terraclon screeched after landing, and just as soon, he regretted using such a high and excited voice. "Dismantle the wall!" he shouted, forcing a deeper and more commanding tone.

The guards looked at him in silence and then away in shame.

"Quegdoth is returning!" Terraclon shouted. "The wall must be opened!"

"Who are you?" one of them asked, a dark-skinned man whose face had been a scowl all its life.

"Oh. Good Shishites, forgive me, as . . . I forgive you. I am your . . . Ultimate Pious Terraclon," he said, unconvinced of it himself and trying to look imperious. He remembered he was in a pilot's simple garb and was without so much as a cape. "I, uh, yes . . . this," he muttered as he reached into his tunic and pulled out the amethyst medallion that marked his office. "Blessings of all gods upon the people of Shishto. *Karikshus al quikshi-bya Shishto-teela*," he added, making up some words that sounded like the holy tongue. This triggered bows of the head and set the guards to action. Commands were passed in the words of working men's Slopeish as the pilots led the locusts to the nearby crowding cages for rest and wet straw.

As a section of the wall was torn open, Terraclon resisted pacing and tried not to look impatient. He reminded himself to stand in imitation of Anand with his shoulders back, his chin up, and his feet held solidly apart, as if daring someone to push him. From the corner of his eye, he looked east and saw war widows in their grimy whites returning from a trip to the weeds. Terraclon assumed they had been out for an idle pleasure ride, but he could see their saddles were hung with stuffed foraging sacks and they rode sturdy carrying ants instead of the smaller obstacle and speed riders. *The widows are gathering their own food now, instead of expecting its delivery. This is progress!* Turning briefly to smile and wave, he was reminded of his dark skin when none of them returned his gesture or even acknowledged his presence.

The roach caravan was traveling at a good clip, but it could not arrive fast enough. At its head, Terraclon saw a bright orange blur and then realized it was the tunic of a young driver whose face looked all too grim as the sleds got closer. Alarmed, Terraclon ran to the driver as the sled made its crunching scrape over the loose sand of the wall's break.

"Where's Anand? Where's Daveena? What's happened?" he shouted.

The driver's face fell and he looked both ashamed and panicked.

"No much Slopeish words," he said, and then pointed back at the Barley Lands. "At Worxict. With emperor."

"Flea-piss!" Terraclon cursed, feeling his heart bashing around his rib cage. "Who speaks Slopeish in your caravan?"

The boy shook his head.

Should I fly to Anand? What would I do if I found him? I can't even talk to these roach people! Wait, there are Slopeish speakers among the Britasytes in Cajoria— the ones who escorted the bee people.

"Cajoria!" Terraclon shouted. "You're going back to Cajoria," he shouted at the boy. "Fly him back with us, now!" he commanded a female pilot in the process of docking her locust. She nodded, remounted, and offered her hand to the young driver, who took it as he climbed the spikes of the insect's leg to sit behind her on her saddle. Terraclon remounted his own locust, prodding it with long strokes of its left antennae to dissuade it from finishing a trough of finger grass.

On the flight to Cajoria, Terraclon looked down at the familiar landmarks to guide him home, but everything looked dry, sun-bleached, and unfamiliar. For a moment he was sure he was lost . . . that chain of rocks, that star-shaped patch of sand, that cluster of drying poppy pods didn't look right. After these were the great patches of datura, that lovely but deadliest of plants, with its enormous moonflowers and its thorn-covered fruit. The smell from the flowers reached his nose, which was pleasant at first and then made him faintly dizzy, then mildly ill. He was painfully reminded of the time he had wandered up to a datura, so taken with its massive blossoms that he crawled on its leaves to touch its bright white sepals that fused into a single tube. Sometime later, he remembered, he woke up ill and with blurred vision. For days, he was stuck in a waking daymare where he argued and wrestled and punched at a larger version of himself. During all of it, he endured an endless thirst and a constant need to piss that left him aching with a thousand inner itches he could never scratch. When the effects finally subsided, he found himself lying in Anand's shelter. "I had to drag you out from under that plant and clean the pollen from your face," Anand had said with a loving anger. "You fought with me, punched me in the eye, and made my nose bleed. I had to knock you out before I could carry you back to the midden. Your own mother wouldn't care for you so I dragged you up here." He had looked over at Corra kneeling next to him, and realized she had been forcing aphid syrup and lymph water down his throat and had been changing rags about his middle . . . the most humiliating thing of all. "Nothing I haven't seen before," she had said as she brought him some proper food. "Mine's bigger," Anand had said with that smile that radiated like the morning sun.

Terraclon felt haunted by that smile now and ached to see it again.

Anand. How many times have we rescued each other? And where are you now, my brother? If the Seed Eaters have harmed you in any way, they will all suffer and die. As Terraclon stared below at the windblown weeds, he imagined the Seed Eater soldiers were already under them, crawling by the tens of thousands on their bearded, poison-spewing ants.

He was lost in his thinking when the locust made a sudden dive over the datura patch. "No!" he screamed out loud when the insect landed on one of the massive flowers and began to eat it from the inside out. Terraclon pinched his nose, held his breath, and jumped off the saddle. He ran under the plant to a clearing where he could be sighted, and waved his arms at his squadron until one of them spiraled and landed. Terraclon ran to his rescuer and climbed onto his saddle, and released his breath once they were in the air. Just as he gripped the pilot's waist, he felt a touch of the datura's madness, like a blackness bubbling over him as they leapt into the sky. Sometime later, he woke from an addled sleep to see Cajoria coming into view.

Maybe Anand is a hostage of the Seed Eaters. What would they want from us to give him back? I hope Polexima can help.

Polexima was seated with Pious Frinbo in her quiet, sun-warmed chamber as he supervised her attempts at what he called "record keeping" and what Anand called *writing*. She watched as he scratched the figures into the roll of coated paper before handing her the stylus, this firm sliver of hard wood with an embedded amethyst tip. His intricate figures, which stood for her name, were compact and neatly rendered; but when she tried to re-create them, she could not help but make large and crooked scrawls. She sighed.

"Like any skill, Your Majesty, writing takes practice," Frinbo said. "And I'm not sure it's something a woman could ever do that well."

"You should be very unsure, Pious. Quegdoth says half the *scholars* in Dranveria—their name for the very learned—are women. And it was a *female* commander who soundly defeated the pioneers of Cajoria before they could reach for their arrows. And Quegdoth says it is a *woman* who presides over their collective nations of hundreds of millions—who serves in the same capacity as a king."

"The gods created women to bear and raise children," said Frinbo. "And this is a great honor. It is what makes women happiest—if they embrace that duty. Would not Your Majesty rather be spending some time with your grandchildren instead of wasting it on record keeping? That has been *our* job since the Sand was created—what the gods call on holy men to do."

Polexima, worried about her most recent children in the care of Dneepers in the Grasslands, had completely forgotten her grandchildren. One of them was named Sahdrin the 87th or 88th, she was not sure. They were looked after by her husband and his concubines, she assumed; and then she realized she did not know. *Perhaps I should check up on them—in case Sahdrin is dipping their sugar tits in spirits to keep them from crying.*

Her worries were interrupted when she saw a dark and sinewy man pull himself through the flaps of the wall opening. Following him in was a Britasyte boy with great masses of curly black hair that were split into three cricket-tails.

"Majesty," said the man, and she realized it was Terraclon in the tight clothes of a locust pilot. "I need to speak with you. And just you."

"Oh, Pious Terraclon! I did not recognize you. Pious Frinbo, can you allow us some privacy?"

"Right," said Terraclon. "I should have asked . . . can we . . . *may* we have some privacy please, Pious Frinbo."

Frinbo looked annoyed as his eyes darted between Polexima and Terraclon and the young roach rider he had brought with him. She realized Frinbo objected to leaving her with an outcaste, whose clipped ear was all too visible under his wind-tangled hair, regardless of his promotion to head of the clergy. And Frinbo didn't like the young companion of the Usurper's Priest either, whose bare legs were smeared with roach grease under his smelly cape.

"Pious Frinbo, would you be so kind as to visit

the king and check on my grandchildren?" asked Polexima, smiling at Frinbo's frown. "Could you make sure that they are well and comfortable? I was just on my way to visit them."

"As you wish, Majesty."

Frinbo pulled his hood over his head, reset his antennae, and fluttered off in the rustle of his long-jacket. Once he was gone, Terraclon doubled over, clutching his stomach as sobbing shook his body. "Anand's lost in the Barley Lands," he blurted out.

"What?"

"His mission has failed. He's dead . . . or a prisoner of Volokop. And so is Daveena. The Seed Eaters are gathering their forces, masses of them, and they're coming for Cajoria—in half a moon or less!"

Polexima was quiet as she absorbed the news. She told herself to take deep breaths, then looked at Terraclon's companion, a boy who did not speak Slopeish but joined with Terraclon in his crying. She looked into Terraclon's tear-filled eyes as they broke from her gaze. *He's ashamed. His tears reveal his love for Anand.*

"We must fight without Anand," she said, gripping her staff and standing her tallest. "We must ask ourselves what he would do, what he learned from the Hulkrites. In this case he would *not* wait for the enemy to invade, to draw them in. He would throw the first punch."

Terraclon gave her a ghost of a smile. "You're right,

Polly. But these are not Hulkrites," he said. "Anand knew the Hulkrites. And I fought them. But the only Seed Eaters I ever knew were corpses at the midden. I only know how they smell . . . not how they fight."

She managed a chuckle. "I know someone who does. Let's hope he's not too smelly to receive us."

"As our Holy Slope expanded north, it was the barley dwellers' ants more than their soldiers that stopped us from taking the lands we needed," said Sahdrin with smiling eyes. Polexima saw he was flattered by her visit and the chance to advise her. "The harvester ants have an insidious poison that they shake from their abdomens when at war. It made us weak and dizzy and blind for days. We became easy targets for the Seed Eaters' spears and arrows, as well as the attacks of their ants. We could not defeat them until my ancestor, Lakjin the 93rd, adopted the silk-layered breathing masks of the weed worker caste of Culzhwitta."

"Why did the weed workers wear breathing masks?" Terraclon asked.

"They wore them when they removed the deadly datura plants."

"Daturas!" said Terraclon.

"Yes," said the king. "It is the worst of weeds. Just the slightest exposure can induce insanity, and a small ingestion means death. I have smelled it recently on my pleasure rides—those maddening flowers—and meant to order its removal. Of course no one listens to me now."

Terraclon was struck with the start of an idea. *Datura! The locusts eat datura! They are immune to it!*

"Later, we added the goggles worn by the hunting castes in their pursuit of the stink-spewing darkling and blister beetles." the king continued. "Once we were equipped with these, the harvester ants posed less of a threat. We took the lands our gods had granted us and pushed the Seed Eaters east."

"One has to wonder if the Seed Eaters' god is telling them to take back those same lands," said Terraclon, falling into a royal accent as he reached for more of a kiln-steamed fruit fly in a black sauce of nightshade berries. He passed the platter to the Britasyte driver at his side, who had barely eaten a thing and spent the dinner nervously taking in the opulence of the royal chamber.

"Why, after two hundred years, did the Seed Eaters start winning again?" asked Polexima.

"For the same reason that anyone wins a war: they had more men than us," said Sahdrin. "The Slope's armies had been divided in two, with half in the West to fight the Carpenter nation. The barley dwellers were aware of that—alerted to it, no doubt, by those slimy roach people who play all sides for the right price."

"Do you have proof of what you're saying about

the roach people?" asked Terraclon as he dropped the platter with a clank and glanced at the boy next to him. "If you don't, then you are violating the sixth law of Bee-Jor . . . lying about others to cause them harm."

"No proof," said Sahdrin. "But strong suspicions, since roach people have betrayed us in the past. Their loyalty is to their own."

"As your loyalty is to *your* own," said Polexima.

Terraclon squinted and his mouth tightened. "Tell us, Majesty . . . if you would, please . . . just how do the Seed Eaters fight?"

Sahdrin shrugged and looked upward with his good eye as if that was a stupid question.

"Much the way we do—on the backs of their insects. The harvester ants have their poisons, but our leaf-cutters are inured to it. Our ants are faster, have thicker chitin, and their longer mandibles are the sharpest of any insect on the Sand. Harvester ants have large and heavy seed-chewing heads that slow their crawl. And they are low to the ground and thin-shelled—vulnerable to punctures from above."

"What advantages would the Seed Eaters have in the next battle?" asked Polexima.

"As I said—more men. Likely *many* more men, now that our noble army has been devoured by ghost ants. The Seed Eaters' royals will send thousands of waste-soldiers on antback as the first wave. These men are sacrificed—the fodder-pawns—to waste our ammunition and draw us out."

Polexima and Terraclon looked at each other, appalled.

"Yes, waste-soldiers," said the king. "We've always fought atop their corpses against the second wave, the highborn warriors who are better armored and mounted on mature soldier-ants. The last wave are the tower-ants, on stilts. These have a driver and a bowman on their saddles, to aim down with venom-dipped arrows. And always among their forces are the under-wave, those stealthy, stinging ants that are too small to ride. Just a few of them can overwhelm the mightiest leaf-cutter by clamping on to them to inject their poison. And just one of those little buggers can kill a man if they can sting through his armor or find open skin."

The king signaled his servant for more liquor, a too-red drink with the cheap, sweet smell of blood flowers. Polexima used her staff to block the servant. "Thank you, kind servant, but the king has had quite enough to drink at the moment," she said.

"Oh, Polly," Sahdrin said as the servant rolled the barrel away. "You have always underestimated me."

"We must remind all our soldiers that water and kwondle tea are the only good drinks before a battle," said Polexima to Terraclon.

"Yes, Majesty," said Terraclon. "Fermentation only

makes us *feel* smart." He turned to Sahdrin. "Your Highness, I saw the stilted ants in the war with the Hulkrites. Their riders were up high and very difficult to shoot at with arrows or blow-darts."

"You don't aim at the riders. You aim at the ant," said the king. "Kill the ant and you topple the riders. Once they've fallen, plunge at them with a sword or shoot them with an arrow. You can also rush the tower-ants on foot with a shield over your head. Hack at their stilts with a battle-axe, and then attack the riders once they have fallen."

"That is *not* a good idea," said Polexima, on the verge of losing her temper.

"And how would *you* know, Polly?" asked the king. "What battle did you fight in?"

"I know that a long time ago, a certain young prince attacked the stilts of one of these tower-ants with his new amethyst battle-axe, a weapon he was all too anxious to try out. And I know that the tower-ants' riders toppled, then rose up on their legs to chop off those of the same young prince . . . . and take one of his eyes."

Sahdrin was quiet, hung his head. "Who told you that? Some long-ago rival? Or some gossipy hairdresser?"

"I had heard it before I ever met you. Everyone has heard it."

A silence passed that was embarrassing for all of them. She was searching for something to say when Terraclon spoke up.

"King Sahdrin, what can you tell us about how the Beetle people defeated the Slopeites?"

Sahdrin looked at Terraclon with what Polexima thought was some grudging respect, meeting his eyes as he spoke.

"They used a cowardly trick. Their only victory against us in centuries was the digging of traps—deep trenches at the back of the usual battlefield. They hid these trenches with a canvas disguised with pine needles. Our ants and soldiers fell into these traps and were attacked by soldiers embedded in the trenches' walls. The soldiers that crawled out were picked off by crews of Beetle Riders with their leashed tridents, a cruel and crude weapon that yanks out hearts and rib cages."

Terraclon was quiet and turned to Polexima. "Why don't we have trenches on all sides of our nation?" he asked.

"Deep, wide trenches," she said. "And why don't we use tridents on retractable leashes?"

"And why would the two sides fight each other at the usual places of battle . . . as if they had agreed to meet there?"

"I do not know," said the queen. "It seems foolish to . . ."

"It was honorable!" said Sahdrin, interrupting. "Or it was. We had a code once."

"Assuming a code of honor in an enemy is stupid," said Polexima. "The Hulkrites built a vast empire in a matter of decades because they had no honor whatsoever."

The king winced, then looked annoyed with his wife. "You will have to fight in the old way. If you are planning some kind of preemptive attack on the East, then I should lead it."

"What?" gasped Polexima.

"Who else will do it? I am one of the few remaining kings in this land. And the only one qualified to lead an army."

Polexima glared at her husband as her lips drew tight. She held her breath, but before she could stop herself she laughed out loud, in a sharp, coarse way that embarrassed her. "Excuse me," she said. "I meant no offense. But thank you, Sahdrin, for the kind offer. So very brave of you," she said, and then burst out laughing again.

"Are you telling me *you* are going to lead this?" he asked. "A lame *woman* who has never been to battle?"

"She has not been to war, but I have," said Terraclon. "And our Laborers' Army defeated the Hulkrites and *ended their empire*. Something the Slopeites failed to do."

"The Slopeites did not have night wasps at their disposal," said the king. "Nor do you Bee-Jorites at the present moment. And you have little of the potions your Dranverite commander used, which depleted our priests' stores. We have barely enough kin-scent to last through the fall."

"We will figure this out together," said Polexima, looking fondly at Terraclon, who was warmed by her gaze and by the hand she placed on his arm. She looked at the roach-boy next to him, who had been mystified by the entire conversation; but something had changed which allowed him to relax, finally, and eat his meal.

"A warrior-queen and a warrior-priest are going to need new clothes," said Terraclon. "I've no time to sew, so we'll just borrow a few things from the barracks' wardrobes and make some adjustments."

"I've always envied men their clothing," said Polexima. "Women's clothing is a cage made of cloth."

"I've always envied women *their* clothing," said Terraclon. "You get to wear such vivid colors."

"So can you . . . now that you're a priest. You know, in Hulkren even the Termite clerics got to wear something like women's dress. I wonder if the Seed Eaters' priests wear something like a lady's frock."

Sahdrin kept his face down, but made a strange upward stare. He shook his head before he raised it, glaring at Terraclon with open hatred. "I'll have more liquor now!" he bellowed to his servant, who smiled nervously, nodded his head, and rolled over the clay barrel.

"No," said Polexima, rising up and staring at Sahdrin.

"I am having a drink!" he shouted, and used his

crutch to push her back. "If I am going to tolerate the presence of such low and perverted company, I will be allowed my own comforts!"

"We are not finished speaking!" she shouted when the barrel came within Sahdrin's reach. He dropped out of his chair, his false legs falling away from him, as he used his hand to scoop up a drop. Just as he was about to slurp, Polexima smashed his hand with the end of her staff and sent the liquor spraying. Sahdrin grabbed her staff and used it to climb towards her, his legless body swinging from it. "I'll bite your fucking lips off, you flea-cunt!" he shouted when his weight pulled the staff out of her trembling hands. Sahdrin fell to the floor near the toppled barrel and stuck his head inside it to lick at the liquid that clung to its insides.

Terraclon stroked his chin as he looked at the tar-colored sauce coagulating on the fruit-fly roast, then poked at it with the little spear that royals used to eat with. He looked to the quartz-slice windows of the walls of the chamber and then up at the arching buttresses of wood that supported the ceiling. The servants ran over with a push broom and a pan to sweep up the broken shards. In his head, these elements fused into a clear and sudden vision.

"I can see it!" Terraclon said. "How we can stop them! But we've got to start digging. And building."

"Creet-creet," someone called from outside the portal. A messenger appeared and addressed Polexima after bowing. "The Plep clan of roach people have arrived per your request, Majesty, and await you on the riding course. They have their own urgent news."

Polexima, Terraclon, and this young roach driver—whose name she had learned was Punshu—were staring at a frightened young woman convalescing on a cocoon mattress at the back of the Two Spirit's sled. "Her people were already residing in the oak," said Zedral through a two-tongued woman. The jewel-encrusted cabin was lit with a fungus torch held in the sixth hand of an idol of Madricanth.

"The *oak*?" asked Polexima.

"Oh, what you call a bortshu, after your tree god," said the translator. "We call it an oak—the evergreen giver of acorns."

Polexima looked back at the invalid who had fallen from the tree of New Bulkoko. The queen was fascinated by the woman's tightly curly hair, which was like a yellowish globe that wrapped around her head. Polexima had never seen anyone who looked like this, not even in Hulkren. Terraclon was taken with the girl's clothing, which was a fine bark cloth printed with dye stamps, as well as her neck and wrist adornments, fashioned from the black and red shell of the black-widow spider.

"She was attacked by the bee people?" Polexima asked.

"They were all attacked, then hurled," said Zedral. "She is one of the few to survive. They must have been well hidden in the tree, a small number of them, at its top. We have seen others like her in the northern outland—but usually as old corpses, dropped to the ground in leaf wrappings in some funeral rite."

The young woman pleaded faintly in her language, which had a resemblance to a rain shower, with soft plopping sounds as her tongue tapped at the roof of her mouth.

"And no one speaks her language?" asked Polexima.

"We have some words in common," said the interpreter. "But few. Your Majesty. Chieftain Zedral invites you to the second supper."

"We will join you, thank you."

Outside the cabin, Polexima saw boys and men posting torches in the circular clearing between the sand-sleds, while girls and women unrolled human-hair rugs with their elaborate pictures and patterns. One of the boys posting torches had lighter skin and orange hair, and when he saw the queen, his jaw fell and he stared.

"Who is that?" Polexima asked the interpreter.

"Forgive Odwaznee for staring at you. We told him the Queen of Cajoria, the most famous captive of the Hulkrite's prophet, might be among our guests tonight."

"He's a Seed Eater," said Terraclon.

"He was," said the interpreter, Zedral's third and

youngest wife, who wore a deep black roach cape that blended with the night. "When we found him he was a Hulkrite, guarding the Bulkokans. He's just recovered from their attack on him."

"Perhaps he could be of use to us," said Polexima to Terraclon.

"Perhaps," said Terraclon. "Majesty, I think it's time you tell the Pleps."

Polexima nodded gravely, and turned to Zedral as platters with the evening's last meal arrived.

"Beautiful wanderers," she said, using a little of the Britasyte that Anand had taught her. "I don't come with good news. Your divided Entrevean clan has returned safely from the Barley Lands—all of them but our commander and his wife. They are lost to us at a time in which I must ask you, all of you, to help us in a coming battle."

The Britasytes dropped their heads and mumbled prayers.

"We pledge our help," said Zedral. "Bee-Jor is our nation too."

Polexima tried to speak again, then stopped. She felt a wave of the deep and unmovable sadness that had plagued her for so many moons. *So much carnage in these last years*, she thought. *And so much more to come.* Her grave expression triggered silence and knit brows as the gathered considered the agonies of another war.

Terraclon looked just as worried, hanging his head

to hide his watering eyes, but then he looked up to admire the gem-encrusted carvings of the Britasytes' sleds. He looked around at the sad faces and began speaking in a quiet way. "I have to admit something," he said. "Every time I've been in a roach camp, I feel like a Britasyte trapped in the body of a Slopeite."

A quiet chuckling followed. Polexima laughed quietly as she wiped away a tear. *Better days could be ahead,* she thought. *And I will fight for every one of them.*

CHAPTER 38

SEPARATE TRAVELS

"**Y**ou look rather excited," Nuvao said as Trellana closed the lids, all by herself, on only three modest traveling trunks. Barhosa and the chambermaids stood nearby with very little to do.

"Of course I'm excited," said Trellana, smiling in a way that was unfamiliar to him and which he found to be surprisingly pleasant. In all his own worries, he was strangely happy for his sister, and even envied her.

"I didn't know you were so close to the nun-princess," he said. "You are happy for her."

"I am ecstatic for her! Once my children are raised and my widowhood is proven beyond all doubt, I just might want to become a bride to Grasshopper myself."

"But not a sister to Cricket," he said, and for the first time, the usual frown soured her face.

"No, not a Cricket sister, certainly not. That is an altogether noisy devotion, and I do like day better than night."

"Well, that's because you don't have to work. Not very much anyway."

She glared at him, all her sweetness vanished.

"But when you do work," he said, struggling for words. "Well, it is very much appreciated by ants and Palzhanites alike."

"Very kind of you to mention it," she said, her good humor returning.

"Speaking of which, you have been . . ."

"Yes, yes, yes. Eating my wafers."

"And you visited the ant queen today and left your essence? I have been distracted, I have to ask."

"Most certainly," she said while batting her eyes, looking at him as if she were flirting, something he knew that she knew made him very uncomfortable.

"I had to ask," he said. "Since I am going away and you are going away."

"Palzhad is quite safe from the Yellow Mold," she said. "For at least a fortnight."

"We have to be absolutely sure. There are still hundreds of thousands of refugees out there, and for the next half-moon our only defense against them will be our ants."

"The ants will be well and healthy. And I have not forgotten the refugees," she said with a precious little frown and a wrinkle of her nose. "I pray for them every day."

"You know, Trellana," he said, smiling, "you've made some stunning progress. If things go well it may be time to send for your sons—and have them raised here in Palzhad."

"Oh," she said, and looked startled.

"I thought that would make you happy."

"The idea of reuniting with my sons makes me very happy. I cannot say I imagined them growing up here as Palzhanites." She reset a garment in a trunk that was sticking through the lid, and then pushed it shut. Her eyes ran up and down Nuvao's clothing, which was plain and tight and covered with random splotches of green. "I've forgotten, Nuvao. Just where is it that *you* are going?"

"To war!" he said. "We're gathering in Cajoria. Remember?"

"Oh, yes, war," she said through a snigger. "I'd almost forgotten. That's why Mother was here at the stadium a few days ago. That was quite a long speech she gave, dressed in one of Father's old uniforms and looking absolutely dreadful. Just what are *you* going to do in a war?"

"I suppose I might have to fight in it."

"Well, isn't that just adorable," she finally said, and laughed. He searched his mind for a cutting insult, then decided against it.

"Blessings of Cricket for a safe journey," he finally said.

"And the very same to you," she responded. Her eyes squinted at him as he was joined by the company of some similarly dressed pilots. They were a mix of light and dark faces, some being defectors from the upper castes who had taken up the Dranverites' cause. Nuvao put his arm around the shoulder of one of them, a tall and muscular youth with thick hair as pale as summer straw and a chin as strong as stone. Nuvao looked over his shoulder to see that Trellana was staring at them, her face tightening with envy. *That girl just can't conceal her emotions*, he thought as he smiled all too broadly, then gave her just one more wave good-bye before he lowered his arm to the youth's waist.

Trellana shrugged off her brother's attempt to rile her. *I've got my own fine soldier*, she thought. The Palzhanite royal sand-sled arrived and though it was somewhat small and creaked when it moved, she was delighted with it, as well as with its modestly draped hauling ants. Even its old and slovenly drivers seemed charming in their worn-out uniforms. "What a lovely little sled," she said as the maidservants loaded their queen's trunks into its storage area, then added their own modest luggage. Barhosa, arriving with a provisions basket, looked at the queen with concern as she readied to take the stairs to the cabin.

"Blessings for a safe trip, Majesty."

"Thank you, Barhosa. And I do thank you for all your excellent service."

"My service?"

"Yes, just thought I should mention it now."

"I look forward to continuing it . . . for many years to come," said Barhosa, taken aback, as she handed the basket to the servants.

"For many years to come, yes."

"Your Highness . . . forgive me for bringing it up, but I . . . I found these. Under your dining table."

Barhosa reached into the pouch of her skirts and produced broken pieces of flower-shaped wafers, with dark flecks of fruit as their stigmas. Trellana frowned, then smiled.

"Oh, Barhosa, I've eaten all too many of those over the last moon, and they don't always agree with me while I'm pregnant. You are quite welcome to them."

"But these wafers have been consecrated by the priests. They are never permitted to any other than . . ."

"I permit you to eat them. I am the queen here. The Dranverite has said this is the New Way—privileges for everyone and all of that." She forced a smile she knew was not convincing. "Enjoy them."

"Yes, then. Thank you, Majesty," Barhosa said, and bowed before departing in the old way, not turning her back until she was ten paces away.

The trip's beginning was a slow one. The route was thick with men and, strangely, a few women who were marching on foot in the same sand-colored clothes her brother was wearing. The marchers' quivers were stuffed full of arrows and their blowguns swung left and right from their necks. Hanging over their backs were the crude shields of thickly bound straw they would interlock to make a moving wall. The hauling ants of the royal sled would not take to the route in the presence of these soldiers, and attempted to return to the mound. Trellana was not sure why until she identified the pungent, musty odor.

"Sorry, Your Majesty," said the sled's lead driver. "We'll have to wait before we can proceed north. The ants don't like the smell of these marchers."

"Neither do I. That's roach-scent splashed all over their shields. But it is a fine morning, driver, and we can enjoy it while we wait."

"You *are* in a good mood," said Bavakoof, and Trellana noticed a chain of smiles among her servants.

"I am indeed."

"Aren't you worried about the war, Majesty? We have heard the Seed Eaters greatly outnumber us."

"We'll be quite safe in Venaris—so very far from this little border conflict."

When the route was cleared of marchers, the driver regained control of the ants. "It's all going to go beautifully well," Trellana said as the sled righted and turned north. Soon, it picked up speed. The runners' scales slid over fine, well-traveled sand for a smooth and pleasant ride.

"What yummy delights has Barhosa packed for us?" Trellana asked as she opened the basket to find decorated dainties of honeyed barley wafers and pickled chunks of a blue death-feigning beetle.

Blind, thirsty, and hungry, Anand couldn't guess how long he had been traveling. Lately, the air was not sweet and clean but dank and sour, and he never felt any warmth or sunshine. *I must be traveling in a tunnel again,* he thought. His head was aching less but his legs and back were a mass of rolling pains from the rattle and scrape of the crude sled. The worst of it was the tedium—nothing to look at, little to hear, and all too much time to imagine the worst. Panic and rage were his closest companions as he worried about Daveena. *My wife is the pregnant prisoner of a diseased man inflicting his madness on the world.* And then, there was Bee-Jor. *My helpless infant of a country, recovering from one war and poorly prepared for the next.*

Traveling in darkness sent Anand's mind back to his greatest suffering: the Living Death. At least in this cage he could move his limbs, sit a little, and toss and turn. He lusted for books—something to occupy his mind—and he remembered that ecstatic moment in which the little bits of ink on paper became words he realized he could read. *What was that first book? It was a children's story! Where the moon and sun were a brother and sister who argued over who would occupy the sky before their mother, the Sand, ordered them to share it.* Anand was struggling to remember the rest of the narrative when he felt a shift upward, and the darkness turned into a soft gray light. The smell of a lakeshore filled his nose, and the lapping of its waves was sweet in his ears. His cage's door was unlatched and then his captor yelled at him as he was yanked out and left on some slimy sand. He did not understand much of it, but he heard the word *Dranveria* and the words Volokop had used for ship—*plabuchy dahm*—that Daveena had translated to "floating house."

Anand rubbed his eyes as his captor drove off. The diffuse gray light was filling with blurry sights. The warmth on his head signaled him to look up; the brightness of the indistinct sun hurt his eyes and filled his head with orbiting stars. He turned to the sounds of the lake, and saw a blurry stretch of what had to be water with foggy sparkles. Stepping to the left towards a broad object, he found the sides of a large container, and realized when he reached into it that it was a boat. He probed around its sides and found the bench he could sit on and then a pole. It was not a flimsy boat that rocked when he stepped into it, but something safer with a deep bottom and some ballast to keep it from capsizing. After seating himself, he dipped his fingers in the water to taste it, and it was fresh, not brackish, and he knew he was in the North. He sucked down some more of the water, which had a dirty aftertaste. He stood, picked up the pole, and stabbed down at the water's bottom to push off in the direction he believed would take him north to Dranveria's distant shores. As the boat went further into the lake, he saw the towering shadows of what might be punk weeds, and heard the splashes of what he hoped were boats or ships. "Hello! Help me!" he called in Dranverish. "I'm blind! I need your help!"

No one answered. At one point, the pole no longer touched the lake's bottom. Anand felt a light wind and hoped it was pushing the boat north. Was that voices he heard in the distance, or just the murmur of water?

Terraclon and a squad of flyers surveyed the decimated weeds outside Palzhad's borders. The refugees from Hulkren had stopped growing, but they were still an innumerable mass. Perhaps some had died, perhaps some had gone back to Hulkren, but the hundreds of thousands that remained had to be hungry and suffering. Their camps had become a strange patchwork of tiny nations surrounded by makeshift fences. He sighed. *Nothing we can do for them now.*

The squad turned east to make aerial inspections of each of the Bee-Jorites' border positions, where they had established counterfeints to the Seed Eaters' feints. The counterfeint armies had raised new and impressive watchtowers, and paraded decorated sentry ants atop the border walls. The Bee-Jorite patrolmen flaunted the gaudy ceremonial armor of the old Slopeish army, as well as their ant-shaped banners from a pole attached to the saddle. As they had been instructed, Terraclon heard the defenders shout-singing war prayers to Mantis near the border walls, a revival of a Slopeish intimidation tradition. Some of the bravest or most foolish Bee-Jorites dressed in sand-and-leaf camouflage to venture as sham-scouts into the Barley Lands, and then scamper back home in an obvious way.

On the way back to Cajoria, the squad flew over the fields of daturas, which had been turned from lush plants into skeletal twigs. Nearby, in the star-shaped clearing of open sand, Terraclon saw sun-kilns and masked and goggled workers as they roasted and dried the daturas' flowers and leaves. Next to these were sturdy, windowless huts where the poisonous weed was powdered with mortars and pestles and sifted into containers of baked and hollowed aphid corpses. As they got closer to Cajoria, he was heartened to see the vast spread of defenders from all over Bee-Jor who had heeded Polexima's call to arms.

The squad approached what had been Cajoria's royal riding field. Set between the old course obstacles were countless cages that were stacked and crowded. Their inhabitants had been deprived of water, to transform the green grasshopper nymphs into flyable blue locusts. Beyond these cages, new pilots were practicing circular flights. Further south, the Entrevean and Plep clans had combined in a single camp, where they had been gorging their roaches with piles of amaranth. Inside the roach pens, women were at work with rags to extract the roaches' grease. The Britasyte men set to the making and repairing of bows and arrows and blowguns.

We just might be ready, Terraclon thought as he circled back and signaled his squad to land.

After returning his locust to a cage attendant, he walked with his pilots past an area in the riding fields where new defenders from Cajoria were being trained in the shield-locking technique, as well as the use of a blowgun through a slit in the shield. Among those aiming at targets were Keel, Tal, and the rest of his lunky sons. Terraclon halted and stared at them as they filled a straw dummy with the darts, skillfully pulling the loaded cartridge through the blowguns' chamber for repeated shootings; they were good at it. When they were out of darts, they turned to each other, dizzy from exhaling, and laughed in the guttural way of their family. Tal noticed Terraclon was studying them, and he lowered his gun and sneered. "Your Worshipfulness," he said, and curtsied. Terraclon felt a faint shock, and then an old fear of the boy who had made his life so miserable.

"Well," Terraclon said, puffing his chest and clasping his arms behind him to display what had been Sahdrin's armor. "I'm surprised," he said, using the voice of his new authority.

"By what?" asked Tal.

"That you've joined the war effort."

"Not our first time," said Tal, returning to his harsher tones. "Like we was trying to tell you a while back. We're good Bee-Jorites. Willing to sacrifice our lives, we are."

"Indeedy, yes, Your Piety," said Keel as his thick body curtsied. "We wants our own house above the flats. We'll kill as many Seed Eaters as it takes to do it. And don't you look just terrifying in your darling little war get-up."

Terraclon felt as if he had just woken from a bad dream on a frozen morning; he was at a loss for words, and wanted to shout something crude about cutting off their balls to hang from their noses. *Say nothing to them now,* he thought while turning his back. *I'll ask their squad leader to keep an eye on them. Who knows what they're up to.*

When the pilots reached the main artery, they

caught an ant train up to the palace. Its conductor and its other riders smiled and saluted Terraclon with a slap to the heart and a bow of the head, but he was still fixated on his treatment by Keel and Tal. *They've mocked me as they've always mocked me—still trying to keep me in place!* A blinding anger overwhelmed him, and he gritted his teeth and clenched his fists. He imagined coming upon them in the midden, their backs turned to him. He would shout, "Hey!" before they faced him to have their fat cheeks filled with venom darts, to send them falling and squirming on the ground. Then while they had no use of their limbs, he would kick them in the ears to deafen them with their own blood. He would keep on kicking until their neck bones snapped and their ugly, lipless faces went very, very still.

Terraclon noticed the other pilots were staring at him sideways as he got lost in his rage. He shook himself out of his imaginings and realized they were halfway to the palaces. The Cajorites of all castes were coming out of their shelters to see him, and they stood at the edge of the route with reverent faces. He watched as they clasped their hands and bowed to him before raising palms to the sky as an appeal for the gods' protection. All of it felt like a dream—like someone else's dream—to go from being mocked one moment and worshipped in the next. *All I ever hoped for was a chance to sew,* he thought. *And now I'm a warrior-priest—in charge of a flying army.*

He entered the ballroom and found it cleared of all furniture. Defenders from all over Bee-Jor stood and talked among themselves. They quieted when Terraclon passed, and pulled aside with slaps to the heart and bows of the head. He reminded himself to walk in an erect way, as he felt the thick pads he had placed inside his boots to make himself even taller. Polexima and Nuvao were at the end of the ballroom, standing atop a platform where they discussed their plans while drawing in a dust-box. Behind them, on a stilted board, was a map of northern Bee-Jor and what was known of the Barley Lands to its east. On the left and right of the platform were altars that featured Cricket, Locust, and Madricanth. Polexima looked up at Terraclon, smiled in relief, and clasped his hands.

"Thank Cricket you're here," she said.

"Majesty," he said, and bowed. He turned to Pious Nuvao. "Pious, all blessings upon you. How was your trip north?"

"A blessing," he said, and smiled to reveal his even teeth, as white and lustrous as a daisy's petal. "Which is to say it was uneventful."

Terraclon had a hard time looking away from Nuvao. He possessed the easy confidence of the uppermost caste, and the man was just too pretty. His face was that spellbinding mix of high cheekbones, a prominent and dimpled jaw, and then the small, fine nose and long-lashed eyes of a beautiful girl. Terraclon had to remind himself to look away from Nuvao every so often as he spoke. That was impossible to do when he smiled, something he did too frequently, and it was just too beautiful not to be looked at. To distract himself, Terraclon looked out at the gathered defenders.

Each of Bee-Jor's fifty mounds had been asked to send four men who were celebrated veterans of the Hulkrish war, leaders who were "smart, brave, and capable with the traits of a good foreman." A good number of the leaders looked like Nuvao, with light skin and fair hair. They were young men who had broken from their castes to follow Anand and help him defeat the Hulkrites. Other leaders looked to be people of mixed blood from the castes of common merchants and craftsmen. The darker-skinned representatives were men of imposing physical size who were working-caste foremen.

Polexima struck the floor with her staff three times. The room came to order, with all taking seats on the floor so that everyone could see the presentation. Terraclon raised his chin, and reminded himself to push out his rib cage to look more authoritative. Polexima's Cricket priestesses walked in with their great false legs rising and falling behind them, to set platters of mushrooms, sweets, and cut grass before the altars as they chanted "*Creet-creet*" to summon the goddess.

"Defender of Peace," Polexima shouted to the ceiling. "Queen of the Night. Bless this gathering and offer Your guidance, so that this war may end as soon as it begins. Hail Cricket."

"Hail Cricket," shouted the crowd in turn. Polexima nodded towards Terraclon. He took several deep breaths to steady his nerves, then stepped forward to speak.

"Brave and loyal Bee-Jorites," he shouted as his voice reverberated around the crystal walls of the ballroom. "From above we have sighted the Seed Eaters completing the excavation of their pits, which they will fill with human beings as sacrifices to their bloodthirsty war god. They will attack our nation on the morning following this gruesome ritual. That day is near, so we . . ."

From the back of the ballroom, Terraclon saw several palace servants squeezing through the cloth flap. The women made their way through the crowd, stepping over or through the defenders, heading towards Polexima with crying bundles in their hands. One of them carried a small nutshell chest, and another held the hand of a crying toddler dressed in a garment of woven straw.

Polexima jolted, coming to the edge of the platform.

"What's this about?" she shouted, staring at the toddler.

"Excuse us, Majesty," said an old servant with a great overbite of cracked teeth. "Some locust riders with yellow skin and a funny way of speaking dropped these off for you. They said they was fulfilling a promise and it was time for you to fulfill yours."

Polexima burst into tears. "Pareesha!" she said, and fell off the platform as she ran to meet the daughter she had left in Dneep. Terraclon and Nuvao looked at each other. The babies in bundles were handed to Nuvao and the little nut chest was handed to Terraclon. He lifted up its lid it to see a tiny skeleton inside, glued to the bottom to retain its shape. The sight was disturbing and saddening, and set off new worries as the words *"it was time for you to fulfill yours"* echoed in his head.

"Don't look in here," he said to Polexima as he closed the lid. "We'll say good-bye to this little one later."

CHAPTER 39

THE PROPHETESS OF PALZHAD

Trellana beamed to find a richness of lights as she entered the Grand Cathedral of Venaris. A torch was set in the hand of each of the arm-shaped sconces, to illuminate the chapels of the eastern and western walls, with their altars to the minor gods. At the main altar, kettles of fungus lights tilted upward to shine on the deities. This night they had a glittering, dizzying beauty, as they had been smothered in gold chains, ropes, and cables that obscured all but their faces and hands. At the idols' feet were puddles and piles of earrings, nose rings, bangles, and jewels.

She had to look away from the altars' beauty, which hurt her in a pleasant way, like the jiggling of a loose tooth. She thrust her hands into the spacious pockets of her gown and looked up at the dangling lighting fixtures. These held fresh fungus torches that revealed the ceiling's elaborate frescoes, which had their own penetrating beauty. On the ceiling's south side was a richly painted rendering of the day sky in turquoise blue. Crawling over the swirls of the bright white clouds were cunning depictions of leaf-cutter ants holding little mushrooms in their mandibles, or multicolored leaf chards. At the center of the clouds was a portrait of the fierce Sun God, extending His thousand arms of light atop His mount, Yellow Flower Spider.

Trellana looked for relief from the beauty, and wandered under the ceiling's north side to take in the fresco of the night sky, which was darker but no less gorgeous. In the middle of the indigo vault was the Sun God's grandmother, Glowing Mushroom, in Her full aspect, with pockmarks and wrinkles and a halo of a hundred spinning powder moths. Surrounding Her were the constellations of Sprouting Acorn, Lightning Split Tree, and Double Boots, as well as Scorpion and his prey, Long Worm, who squirmed between Great Brush and Little Brush. At the very end of the ceiling was a painting of her favorite constellation and her namesake, Trellana of Calladeck. She was the beautiful mortal princess murdered by Ant Queen in a jealous rage and transformed by her lover, the grieving Grasshopper, into a cluster of stars to sparkle in eternal beauty. Trellana sighed in awe and resumed her duties. Why hadn't she ever thrilled to the beauty of a cathedral before? *The gods have opened my eyes,* she thought.

Before approaching the main altar, Trellana visited each of the chapels of the cathedral's east side. She prayed before each of the altars dedicated to lesser gods, like Mite, Gnat, and Green Treehopper, as well as the elemental deities of Rain, Dew, and the puff-cheeked Goddesses of the Four Winds. Each of these deities, no matter how small, received some blood from her pricked thumb as an offering. She scraped her thumb to leave a smudge of red on the edge of the sacrificial bowls, then reset them before the idols' feet.

As she made her sacrifices, the cathedral filled with the princesses and queens of the eastern country—or that place her fallen mother and the Dranverite called "Bee-Jor," in all their arrogance. As each of these royal women entered, they searched for Trellana, then greeted her with a true reverence. The attention thrilled her and she understood that *this* was what had always been missing from her life. The smile that stretched her face felt unfamiliar, but she knew it was the thing that had finally completed her, that had remedied the flaws of her beauty. Some who knew her as a close relative gave her warm hugs she could really feel, as they had all dressed, like her, in a single gown of dark gossamer that allowed their skins to touch. When her aunt Omathaza entered the cathedral, the two almost ran to each other—something they could do in the plain and comfortable walking boots they had worn for the occasion.

"Darling Trellana," said Omathaza, trembling as she tucked her niece's undone hair behind her ears. "It is a most happy night."

"And the beginning of happier days," said Trellana. As the two embraced, she rested her head on the comforting warmth of her aunt's full bosom and felt a blissful peace, as if she were a baby rocking in her nurse's arms.

"Shall we make a sacrifice together, Auntie?"

"We shall, dear."

The two walked up the stairs to the main altar and stood before Grasshopper and Ant Queen. Jutting from the gold chains that drowned Them were the idols' fifth and sixth hands, in the open position for the bestowing of boons. Trellana removed a thorn pin from her gown's shoulder strap and pricked her aunt's thumb before the two knelt and scraped their blood on the sacrificial bowl of carved amber that floated atop the loose jewels. When the aunt and niece completed their offering, they turned to see the cathedral's pews had filled to capacity with their fellow royal women. All of them glowed with piety and excitement.

The entry opened again, and princesses holding drumming clubs and plectrums went to the orchestra pit before the main altar. Those with plectrums took seats behind gourd instruments strung with human intestines, while those with clubs went to carillons of differently sized human leg bones. A few of the musicians with thicker clubs stood at upright drums of stitched human leather and began their somber beating. A choir entered, and dance-walked down the aisle to join the orchestra and commence the first of the Ant Queen hymns, *"Praise Her Odors,"* followed by *"Tireless Is Her Womb."* Next were some sacred songs to Grasshopper including *"The Jumper's Blessings Fall Like Rain"* and *"Nourishing Are His Sons and Daughters."*

The flaps of the cathedral were pulled open, and the first and only male entered, His Ultimate Holy Pious Dolgeeno. He wore a simple pocketed cassock and loose trousers of the same dark gossamer as the women. His only real adornment was his blue miter, which featured a gold rendering of Grasshopper and Ant Queen as the Eternal Couple afloat in the sky. The priest looked thinner, and strolled up the aisle with a sprightliness Trellana had never seen. He easily took the steps up the altar, and bowed to the deities before turning to greet the gathered women with a raising of his left hand.

The flaps of the entry opened again, and four male carriers entered with the palanquin of the Infertile Princess of Venaris on their shoulders. She had brought a hundred little grooming ants that swarmed over the palanquin's roof and the cloth that pushed out its windows. The carriers look around furtively, and were shamed by the stares and silence of the female congregation, and departed quickly. Once the males were gone, the palanquin's door opened and a mass of dark cloth pushed out. The Infertile Princess rose up from out of the cloth and shed it to reveal a pocketed gown. She walked not to the altar, but to a pew in the back. Her grooming ants worked their way out of the cloth, and crawled over the laps and heads of the other royals to gather on the Infertile's head and dress. Some of them crawled over her hair and to the ends of her antennae, where they dropped into her lap to repeat the cycle. The music came to an end when Dolgeeno held up his right palm, dusted with golden pyrite.

"Welcome, Queens and Princesses of the Lost Country," sang-shouted Pious Dolgeeno. "The gods bless this gathering and thank you for your bravery in traveling to Venaris." He nodded towards Trellana, and stepped back as she stepped forward. In silence, she turned her new and irrepressible smile on the crowd, beaming it from east to west like the day's journey of the Sun. It ignited a thousand other smiles, and she opened her arms as if she might embrace them all.

"Daughters of Ant Queen," she began, feeling a godly strength that rose from her bowels through her lungs and then her throat as her voice filled the cathedral. "We come here tonight, not to observe the ritual marriage of the Infertile Princess of Venaris to Grasshopper. That will wait for another time. At this time we have an even higher purpose." Trellana nodded to Omathaza, who stepped forward and locked her arm in her niece's.

"Trellana has been granted a prophecy," shouted Queen Omathaza. "A vision confirmed by Pious Dolgeeno in his own conversation with the gods."

Dolgeeno stepped forward and, looking upwards, threw up his arms. "Rise up, righteous women of the Holy Slope," he shouted. "Rise up and take what is ours: the gold shed by Sun, the jewels dropped by Grasshopper. Take them, all you can, and wrap them around your arms, your legs, your neck, and your heads. Pin them to your ears and nostrils! Slip them onto your fingers! Work them into your hair! And stuff them into your pockets!"

Dolgeeno shut his eyes and chanted quietly in the holy tongue as he bobbed his head while retreating into the clutter of the idols. Trellana and Omathaza bowed with palms pressed together to Grasshopper and Ant Queen. Afterwards, they stood on tiptoes to relieve the idols of their swaddling of jewelry. The chains and ropes of true gold were transferred to their own necks and arms and ankles until they could bear no more. The loose jewels and bangles were stuffed into the pockets of their gowns.

The rest of the women solemnly went to the other idols as well as those of the chapels. They bowed before each of the 113 deities and then quietly transferred their treasures to themselves. When all the idols were shorn of their treasures, the women did not return to the pews, but stood in the aisles and waited. They linked each other's arms, clattering with jewelry, as Dolgeeno pushed aside the idols of Grasshopper and Ant Queen to reveal a passage.

"Holy sisters and mothers," shouted Trellana. "We love our country, our ants, and our people. Our gods have set us at the center of the Sand to manifest Their glory and fulfill Their perfect order. We have displeased our gods, broken that order, and created the chaos that plagues us. *I* have seen the way out. *I* have seen what we must do to strengthen and please our gods. *I know* what we must do to restore our country."

Trellana looked out at the women whose heads were raised as their jewel-bedecked bodies swayed in unison. They were sobbing in ecstasy as they looked upwards, their hands raised, catching rays of hope and grace.

"The restoration of the Holy Slope begins with the destruction of Bee-Jor!" shouted Trellana as hatred sharpened her booming voice. "Let Bee-Jor fall into foreign hands and be trampled under foreign boots! Let its sands be overturned and polluted by unholy ants! Let its infidels fall to the bearded harvesters to be stung and poisoned! Let Bee-Jorite hearts be shredded by Seed Eaters' arrows and their throats slit open with Seed Eater swords!"

Dolgeeno took Trellana's hand as she looked to the ceiling, left and right, her eyes flashing as she saw her visions. "Let the ants of Bee-Jor suffer and succumb to the Yellow Mold! Let the mounds of Bee-Jor rot and implode!" she shouted. "Let every last insurgent die! And when they are dead, we will be ready to destroy the Seed Eaters, retake the East, and reunite the United Queendoms of the Great and Holy Slope!"

The joyous sobbing of the women increased. They sounded on the edge of climax as their bodies shook with the divine spirit that had entered them.

"Are you ready, daughters of Ant Queen?" Trellana shouted.

"Yes! Yes! Yes!" shouted the women as they raised their jeweled fists and gasped and spasmed in a collective release of cries and laughter.

Dolgeeno took several torches from the hands of the idols. "Rise, take a torch, and walk with me, Holy Sorceresses!" he shouted. "The blessings of your urine must leave this darkened land." He handed Trellana and Omathaza a torch, then raising his own, he turned his back and walked up the corridor of idols until his dark garment blended into the blackness. Omathaza and Trellana turned their backs, raised their lights, and walked after him. The rest of the women took torches from the sconces and quietly walked up the altar's steps to follow.

Dolgeeno reached a yellow curtain at the altar's back, and rolled it up with a drawstring to reveal a dark portal. He entered it, his torch dimming as it bobbed. Trellana followed after him, and felt she had stepped into the sweetest dream. The torch showed her the walls of a rough tunnel, and a rougher floor she knew would tire her legs and twist her ankles. But she was eager to march, no matter the distance, even as she was swelling with the babies of an outcaste. The gods would guide her, as much as her torch, to her husband—her true husband—who would join her side and fight to reclaim everything that was theirs.

bobbed, Trellana followed after him, and felt she had
stepped into the sweetest dream. The torch showed
her the walls of a rough tunnel, and a rougher floor
she knew would tire her legs and twist her ankles. But
she was eager to march, no matter the distance, even
The gods would guide her, as much as her torch, to

CHAPTER 40

THE LATECOMERS

Pleckoo was alive to see another sunrise lighting
up the dew beads on his cage. He remained tied
to the cage's bars above the floor, wrapped inside
the rope cocoon, and expecting the moment the
guards would enter and force a tube of glop down
his throat. He would open his lips and allow them to
do so, determined that they would never again jam
the tube into what had been his nose and empty its
contents down his windpipe. That had plunged him
into a choking panic that was the worst thing he had
ever suffered . . . and lately he had suffered so much.

The feeding/watering was late, but so much else

was different that morning. Through the bars he could see the Cajorites heading east in loose formations. They carried swords at their sides, blowguns around their necks, and had rectangular shields of stained straw on their backs. Ants that neared the soldiers skirted away, repelled by the scent. Interspersed with the marchers were women and boys hauling cargo-sleds full of food and beverage containers, as well as more mysterious contents—pods, bladders, and barrels, as well as darts and arrows. *They are off to war in the East. But why?*

As he thought about it, a war made sense. The Seed Eaters knew this new nation of Bee-Jor was depleted and barely under rule; but looking at these marchers, they were eager to get to the border and hungry to fight. *And why wouldn't they fight for what they've won? They could never go back to the old way—any more than I could.* Then it occurred to Pleckoo that the Bee-Jorites *had* to fight. The Seed Eaters did not want slaves or converts to their religion; they wanted land where they could relieve themselves of their masses, and soil to grow more seeds.

From their clothing and skin color, he saw that the Cajorite soldiers marching east were bands of mixed castes and both sexes. *Women fighting in wars!* The last of them, as usual, were middenites, but this time it was not because they were forced to the back of the queue. They were last because they were marching from the distant midden. Pleckoo knew most of their faces, and saw that they were the first of the soldiers that looked scared. *These little shit-scrapers stayed home for the last war, but now they want some glory—some glory that might win them a dwelling up the mound.*

It was strangely quiet, but for a breeze that rustled the nearby tar weeds, with their chunky yellow flowers that bloomed through autumn and had the sharp sweet stink of the Tar Marsh. Pleckoo's thirst was growing as bad as his hunger, when finally Butterfly Goiter stepped out of the supply shack and reconstituted some powdered lymph with the morning's dew. He spat in the drink before he filled the bladder, then winked at Pleckoo. "Suck it all down, Prophet," he said after entering the cage and climbing the ladder to feed him. "Suck it like it was the prick of your Termite god—all you can take. We don't know when we'll be back to feed you."

Pleckoo believed him. *I'll drink whatever they bring me and more,* he thought, and gulped it down until the bladder was shriveled. His stomach bloated and chafed anew against the fibrous ropes that trapped him, and he struggled to keep down the meal. The Cajorite guards who kept a constant vigil around him were more active that morning, as they tested their blowguns and the sharpness of their swords, and tightened the bindings of their shields. Always there had been ten guards, day and night, but by late morning all had left for the war but one—a boy with barely some whiskers on his chin. He was the one they called Stubby for his short, deformed arm; the boy whose usual task was to bring them food and drink.

When the breezes ended, Cajoria got even quieter. The brightening sun was unseasonably warm, and Pleckoo feared it would dry him out and scald the skin of his face. *What if these Bee-Jorites lose and don't come back?* he wondered. *What if the Seed Eaters find me and learn who I am? What kind of tortures do they practice?*

From his bed in the palace, Yormu looked through the window at soldiers in loose groupings as they marched down the artery. Some of the men wore scavenged pieces of what had been the armor of the old military caste. They had also appropriated their handsome bows and ornate quivers as well as their swords with hilts of amber. Some had taken Slopeish shields and covered their carvings with a wash of red. *They're going to war! War against the Seed Eaters!*

The veterans of the Laborers' Army may have appropriated the old military's regal trappings, but they weren't riding ants into battle. The ants themselves were nowhere to be seen; were they hiding from all of the roach-scent? There were just a few midden ants heading downward that morning, with trash from inside the mound. Yormu guessed that Terraclon and Polexima had planned a surprise offensive; if ants were included in their forces, the enemies' harvester ants would smell them coming and alert the Seed Eaters to an imminent attack.

Yormu was struck with a powerful memory, one that was painful as he recalled its details. As a boy in the distant border weeds, he had seen harvester ants incited to war. They spiraled frantically as they gathered their numbers in a dense circle that sprayed a poison that had almost killed him as he worked in the weeds that day. For the next moon, he felt as if he had no lungs, just a raw hurt inside when he breathed.

Aching from this memory, Yormu could not lie still. He got out of bed and rubbed all the bony places on his back and legs that were sore from lying too long. He was still aching on his right side, from where his ribs had been broken, but it felt good to stretch and walk a bit. A palace servant entered to bring him a breakfast of morning dew and a sweet porridge of the moistened gratings of a dried evergreen berry. The servant, Mulga, had yellow skin and thousands of splotchy freckles. She was annoyed to see him out of bed.

"Good Worker," she said, then corrected herself. "Honored Defender Yormu—you are not supposed to leave your cushion. By order of Commander Quegdoth."

He sighed and attempted to mouth words she

might be able to lip-read. *No, I can't lie there another moment,* he wanted to say as his arms flew. *I'm needed!*

"Back in bed!" shouted Mulga, raising a finger like a truncheon. He shook his head, shrugged his shoulders, and pointed out the window at the marching soldiers. Women and older boys and girls were following after the soldiers, hauling the supply sleds.

"They're off to fight the Seed Eaters," she said. "All of them, even Queen Polexima and that dark-as-night Terraclon, that one who used to sew and prance around in priests' robes before he got obsessed with weapons and locust-flying."

Yormu attempted to say his son's name but he had no tongue to tap the roof of his mouth for the "en" and "deh" sounds.

"Oh," said Mulga. "Anand, as you call him. No. Quegdoth's not back yet. I believe he's why they're going to war. Rumor is that he's dead and so's his roachy wife. They say the Seed Eaters' Emperor Volokop put them in a big round cage for his entertainment—a cage loaded with velvet ants. This Volokop is some deformed monster who watched the cage roll around until your Anand and his woman were exhausted, then stung to death. We heard their bodies were thrown in a pit after that, with seeds tucked into their arms."

Yormu blinked at Mulga, then grimaced. He wanted to slap her across one cheek, then backhand the other. He grabbed the top of her arms and shook her as he tried to shout. *You are lying about my son! My beautiful son!* But all he emitted were shrieks and gasps—what sounded like a baby's attempt at words. Mulga was frightened and recoiled from the pollution of his grip. "Keep your hands off me!" she screamed as she dropped to the floor and twisted away to break his hold. "All I'm telling you is what I heard!" He was angrily sobbing, pacing, and for a moment she looked at him with pity, then backed away and rushed from the room—probably to a scenting tub, he guessed. He looked at what she had brought him.

I must eat to get strong! he thought. *I am going to this war!*

He sucked up the thick, white bulge of the porridge from its bowl, then looked around the chamber for his boots, tunic, and antennae. *My weapons are at home, in the midden,* he remembered as he dressed. As he limped through the palace's halls and empty chambers, his anger built on itself as the ache in his side flared. The palace was disturbingly quiet as he wandered its halls in search of an exit. He passed but a few servants, most of them older, or women, and didn't see a single guard or messenger. *Everyone's left for the war!*

When he found the servants' portal to the outside ring, it was agonizing to squeeze through its cloth diaphragm as it pressed against his ribs. Once he was out, he staggered to the trail of the midden ants and had to wait for one. He turned and antennated one of the few, which had a scraggly clump of spent soil in her mandibles. She dropped her load to open her mouth and feed him. As a bubble of regurgitated mushrooms grew from her crop, he climbed up her legs, then carefully mounted her between the dangerous thorns of her thorax. He held tightly to the tallest thorn at the front to anchor himself, and pressed his lower back to the base of the thorn behind him. The ant resumed her load and Yormu rocked and strained to hold tight as she took him to the midden.

No one, not even an emperor, can hurt my son! he thought as the pain sharpened on his side.

Pleckoo looked through the bars at the occasional old woman who arrived at the dew station, then left in disappointment after seeing the morning's water had been taken to the eastern border. The occasional midden ant passed his cage on its way to dump some invasive fungus, or the corpse of an insect intruder. Stubby, the little guard, was bored and humming to himself as he paced in a circle around the cage. Later, he practiced his archery with a bow designed for his shorter arm, on a straw target he set barely six paces from himself. Even then he had trouble hitting the target, much less landing an arrow at its center. He grew bored with his bow and arrows, and by noon he sat on a pebble bench outside the twig hut, after retrieving some chopped gnats rolled into fruit leather from the shed. After eating his lunch, he yawned, then leaned his bow and arrows against the bench. He napped with his longer arm over his face to block the sun from his eyes.

Pleckoo was envying Stubby's ability to lie down when an ant came near with a face like a bearded man. As the ant got closer, Pleckoo saw that the beard was just a piece of spent and shaggy substrate from a mushroom farm. Riding on the ant was a man without a saddle or a means to steer it. Pleckoo heard a painful cry as the man slipped from the ant and fell to the sand, gasping as he crawled into the tar weeds. Pleckoo, barely able to move his head, strained for sight of the fallen stranger but he had disappeared. Was he someone come to taunt or torture him, now that the cage was barely guarded? From the cage's other side, he heard voices and the footsteps of a group of men. He strained his neck to turn it slightly and shifted his eyes to see them.

Eight or nine men came into his peripheral view, though perhaps some of the shorter ones were boys. All had a lumbering gait and large, thick arms that swung like clubs at their sides. They had crude swords tucked in their belts and blowguns around their necks. Strangely, all of them wore pointy sacks of egg-cloth over their faces, with roughly cut eyeholes. "Good morning, Pleckoo," shouted the largest of them. Pleckoo, recognizing the voice, broke out in a sweat as heat flashed through his body. *It's Keel! Keel*

and Tal and his other sons! They've come for me now that
everyone's left!

"Can I help you, Good Bee-Jorite?" asked Stubby
as he rose up from his bench, addressing Keel and
squinting from the sun as he fumbled for his bow and
an arrow. "No one is to talk to the prisoner." Stubby
frowned, then froze when he saw the men's faces
were covered with hoods. "Why do you hide your
faces?" he asked, and loaded his bow and aimed.

"What a precious little bow," said one of the
others, and Pleckoo recognized Tal's voice. "Made for
a precious little freak with a precious little arm." Tal
looked up into the cage and came forward. "Hello,
Pleckoo. How's your homecoming been?"

"Get away from the prisoner," said Stubby, stretching his bowstring tighter.

"Or what?" said Tal. "You're going to beat me with
your stumpy little arm?"

"Or I'll split your face with this arrow. What do
you want?" Stubby asked.

"Nothing. Just wanted to say hello to our cousin
from the midden before we head to the war."

"Then you best be moving on," said Stubby.
"You're late as it is."

Tal and Keel looked at each other.

"Move!" shouted Stubby as Tal raised his hood
with one hand, and then raised his blowgun with the
other. The arrow flew. Tal arched backwards and fell
on his backside. "Oww! You mangled little prick!" he

screamed. He yanked the arrow out of the right of his forehead where it had jammed between his skull and scalp. Blood soaked the hood and turned it red. Tal pulled it off to reveal his face as blood beaded over his brow, then rolled down his cheek. "I'm gonna rip your little arm off and stuff it down your throat," he shouted as he stood up, then lunged. Stubby scrambled for another arrow and was reloading when he fell to the ground and twitched. Keel and his other sons had targeted the little guard with their blowguns. The boy was rolling on the sand, foaming at the mouth, as piss soaked his tunic.

"We gotta kill him now," whispered Keel, looking around for witnesses.

"Be glad to, Dad, but why?" asked Tal.

"Because he saw your face, stupid," said Keel. "He'll talk."

As Stubby twitched, he tried to regain control of himself, shouting broken words. Tal stepped on the boy's chest and plunged into it with his boot until he heard it crunch. "Hold still," Tal whispered, then kicked at Stubby's cheeks until teeth flew from his bloody mouth. He kicked the side of Stubby's head, harder and harder, until he heard a crack in his neck. The boy's body went still and then his eyes rolled up in his head.

"C'mon, boys, let's push this thing over and make it quick," Keel said. His sons gathered on one side of the cage and pushed it towards Stubby's body to trip it for the fall. Pleckoo's heart pummeled his lungs as the cage fell and his back slammed against the sand. *Save me, Hulkro*, he tried to say aloud as his body was stunned with the impact. Keel and his sons, making the sounds of ravenous termites, cut up the ropes that bound the cage's gate, then tore it off. The sons poured into the cage, surrounded Pleckoo, and made the sign of the Termite by curling their fingers into little antennae while squeezing their eyes shut. They snickered quietly as they sawed at his ropes with the teeth of their daggers. Pleckoo's eyes filled with tears as they freed him from his confines, but he was too shocked to move his limbs.

The sharp stench of the shit-soaked ropes was stifling. "Lord Termite, you stink!" Tal shouted. "Like your mother's rotten hole, you do!" Tal hauled up Pleckoo's limp body by his neck and pushed him up and out of the cage's opening. Keel jerked him up, then tossed him onto the sand. Pleckoo felt blood returning to his limbs, both agonizing and a relief. He got to all fours, slowly, then stood and wobbled. He tried to back away as Keel and his sons surrounded him in a circle. They scowled at him through the eyeholes of their hoods and he heard their snickers.

"Look at him," said Tal. "He's got pocky skin!"

Pleckoo looked at the skin of his arms and legs, which bore their impressions of the ropes and made him look like a basket. Much of his chest and stomach were covered in scabs and wet scrapes. An intense nausea overwhelmed him and he fell. *Kill me! Make it quick!* Pleckoo tried to say, but all he could do was wheeze as Keel and his sons pressed in.

"What's that?" said Keel. "You want us to kill you? End your misery here and start it anew in the Netherworld?"

Pleckoo knew Keel would not be merciful but would protract his torture, keep him just a step from death to extend his pleasure. The two looked in each other's eyes, glaring. How would he do it? With one final whipping, stretched over a pebble until he bled to death? Or would they fill his naked skin with darts to watch him twitch until he succumbed to their poisons? As Keel stared in his eyes in silence, Pleckoo heard his own breathing and soon it seemed as loud as a windstorm. Keel reached for Pleckoo's wrist and jerked him to his feet.

"Go," Keel said, pointing his chin to the North.

What? Pleckoo mouthed.

"I said *go!* Before anybody sees you."

Pleckoo's legs felt as brittle as straw when Keel released his grip. Pleckoo was struggling not to black out and fall when Keel pushed him.

"Get out of here, Pleckoo! Before I change my mind."

Pleckoo scrambled away with the world wobbling around him. As he limped as quickly as he could, he looked south over his shoulder, sure that at any moment darts or arrows would be filling his back and this cruel game would come to an end. But Keel and his sons just stood there, looking right to left from inside their hooded heads, worried that someone had seen them.   As Pleckoo stumbled north, the strength of his legs returned and his arms started swinging. He squeezed through drying weeds and yellowing grass, veering around the midden's shelters where old women or children might sight him. As he got further north, he could dimly see the bortshu forest beyond Cajoria's borders and he could smell the dankness of the Freshwater Lake. Strangely elated, he imagined reaching the border wall and climbing up it to slide down its other side—to the place, he had been told, "where priestly magic ends."

Whatever was beyond that wall, it had to be safer than Bee-Jor. At the very least, it was a better place to die.

Yormu lay under the tar weeds, having to breathe their difficult reek. "All right, sons, let's hurry off to war," he heard Keel say. "Let's see if we can't kill a few Seed Eaters and win us a nice house up on the mound."

"If not our own palace. I like that one Anand was living in," said Tal to his brothers' laughter.

Yormu muffled his breathing as he waited for them to leave. The pain in his side was throbbing again, but a worse ache was in his head, like mallets banging from the inside. *They let Pleckoo go! They freed him just to torture my son!* He muffled his breathing with his hands and thought back to those days after the war, when Anand had set the new order. Yormu remembered shaking his head when Anand told him that, for now, the foreman of every caste should remain in his position to provide a "smooth transition," and later there would be something called an "election." If Yormu had his way, he would have hung Keel and Tal by their ankles in the center of the midden to be gnawed on by moon roaches until they were nothing but stinking bones.

Yormu took deep breaths to calm himself, then realized he had to find somebody to try and report what happened. He crawled from under the tar weeds and dragged himself to the fallen cage. He was using its bars to stand when a group of boys ran into the dew station. The tallest and oldest of them with a fuzzy mustache came at Yormu, his hand near his dagger holster. "Who are you?" he shouted, rage in his face. Yormu shook his head, weakly, and leaned against the cage.

"You released him! You released Pleckoo!" the boy shouted when Yormu staggered and fell. His opened mouth revealed his missing teeth and tongue as he cried out in pain and clutched his broken ribs, furiously shaking his head no as his tears flew. His left hand pointed weakly to the East where Keel and family were on their way to war. His right hand

CHAPTER 41

REALITIES

Brother Moonsinger was hopeful as he wandered through the empty southern palace of Palzhad to survey its chambers. It had been abandoned for centuries, but as his three-toothed sandals stirred up clouds of dust in its corridors, he saw its potential as a place of higher learning. Old Pious Feegalo of Palzhad followed him dutifully, his tattered long-coat making little rolls of the floor's thick and fibrous dirt as it dragged. They entered a vast hall with a domed ceiling, and Moonsinger recognized it as a hall of assembly where priests, officers, and royalty of all the mounds had planned their battles and celebrated their victories. On its northern wall was a faint mosaic of

Mantis with Her six weapons and the bleeding Moth god clutched in Her mouth. *I'm not sure about restoring that!* he thought.

The hall had been a sunny place—ideal for the writing and reading of scrolls—but the great quartz windows were pocked and cracked from windblown sand, and they were stained with a stubborn grime. He walked towards one window with a break in its quartz, when he smelled something both sour and musty and wondered where it came from.

"Do you smell that?" he asked the priest.

"I'm afraid I haven't much sense of smell left," said Pious Feegalo, whose tiny nose had just slits for nostrils. "All I can smell here is neglect."

Moonsinger lowered his head to sniff through the window's break and was astonished by what he saw. Stretching to the southern horizon were the refugees from Hulkren. He had known they were there, but the weeds that had hidden their numbers were gone— and now their numbers were staggering! The last time he had looked from the palace to the Dustlands, the refugee camps had been further away, and there was a buffer of weeds between them and the border wall. Now, that buffer was gone, and the refugees had divided into hundreds of factions and were camped in a patchwork of flimsy fences, filled with flimsier shelters. *They've destroyed all the weeds! A good storm could shift everything and throw them into chaos!*

On top of the border wall, he could make out a

skeleton crew of Bee-Jorite border guards mounted atop their patrol ants. The ants weaved slowly and clumsily through each other as they paced east and west. Among them were unmounted sentry ants, looking almost as sluggish. Moonsinger looked over to the stadium's arena, where the markets had been suspended, and he saw a spread of ants that were listlessly crawling, and a few that were dead. The Hulkrish war had diminished Palzhad's modest number of ants, but in the last moon they had recovered, were almost flourishing. Why weren't they off in a parade to gather leaves? Why hadn't the dead ones been dragged to the midden? *It's too soon to be slowing down for the winter rest!*

He heard, faintly, what might have been the shouts of refugees from below the wall, then watched as an unmounted patrol ant raised its gaster in the attack mode and quickly disappeared. *She looks like she's been yanked!* he thought. He heard cheers, and realized the ant had been caught and killed. A short time later, the ant's rustlers appeared, hauling her corpse behind them as they returned to their camp. The Bee-Jorite patrolmen were threatening arrows, but Moonsinger saw they were few in number. New bands of rustlers came towards the wall to capture their own ants, emboldened by the success of the others. *These people are risking their lives just to feed themselves!*

His heart stopped for a moment, and he held his breath when he realized there was a much greater problem. "I need to visit the ant queen," he blurted out.

"Brother Moonsinger . . . you are not a priest," said Pious Feegalo with a haughty chuckle. "Only a priest may visit the egg-layer in her chambers."

"Pious Feegalo, may I kindly remind you that King Nuvao ordered you to show me every part of this mound that I wish to see," he said, sniffing the air again. "And it is urgent that we check on the ant queen."

The priest had a strange little smirk that made his nose look even smaller. "As you wish, Brother. I need to visit her myself."

Sebetay and his men were on their hands and knees at the northern edge of the camps, examining and repairing their noose. It was at the end of a rope they had fashioned from tightly twisted rags of their own clothing. They stood, nearly naked, holding shields made of acorn husks with their left hands and gripping assorted weapons with their right. Sebetay was not sure if the rope was strong enough to capture an ant, and worried that if it landed on the thorn of one's back that it might shred and snap. Then he worried that he was not strong enough to hurl the noose at all.

The journey to the wall had been both exhausting and contentious as they negotiated, pushed, and squirmed their way through different, dangerous camps. Many refugees would not let them pass until the Ledackis raised their weapons and threats were shouted. A skirmish with some Stink Ant people had resulted in a wound to his leg. The Stink Ant men filed their teeth into sharp points, and one of them had bitten into Sebetay's calf and tried to tear it off. He had to jab at the biter's neck with his spear until he finally severed the man's spine. The beads of blood that had dried on Sebetay's calf were an itchy reminder of the gruesome encounter, and he fought the urge to scratch at them.

He saw the rumors about the sentry ants were true—they were fewer in number, smaller, and seemed slow and clumsy as they paced atop the border wall. Only a few of them were mounted by patrolmen. As the patrolmen shouted threats in their strange tongue, he realized from the pitch of their voices that they were boys—boys who looked new to their weapons and lost inside their oversized armor. Sebetay turned to his men and pointed at the sky as a signal for prayer.

"Great Meat Ant," he prayed aloud. "Help us feed Your people. Bless us with abundant meat so we may serve You better." After his men lined up behind him, he strutted forward, raised the noose, and twirled it with one arm as his shield bobbed in his left. A sentry ant at the top of the wall turned in his direction when she caught his scent. She raised her gaster and then her antennae before she raced down the wall with her mandibles parted. A patrol boy was on the ant's back, having lost control of it, unable to aim an arrow as he shouted his threats.

Sebetay looked up into the ant's growing face when he hurled the noose, sure he had thrown it too soon. It flew over the antennae and dropped on her node. "Pull!" he shouted, and the men yanked on the rope and cinched the noose. An arrow bounced against Sebetay's shield when the ant was jerked forward and off its legs. The patrol boy's threats turned to tearful crying when he lost his seat and fell. He turned and struggled up the wall, slipping in its loose bits of sand, until a woman, perhaps his mother, pulled him to safety.

The ant was not theirs yet, but Sebetay could almost taste its blood, and he grinned. He used the loop on his shield to hang it from his neck and protect his back before joining his men on the rope. They hauled the ant south but when they reached the edge of the camps, they saw a wall of men who looked like living skeletons. They were a mix of different tribes, but all of them were weak and staggered as they stood. They did not beg as the men and their carcass came forward, but stood in a disturbing silence with their hands outstretched, their mouths agape.

"Halt!" Sebetay shouted to his men, realizing they could never drag the ant corpse through this camp, much less the hundred after it, without it being ravaged. "Cut it into three and shave it!" he commanded. The men set to work at shearing off the ant's legs and antennae, and then chopped through the node and petiole. Afterwards they used their random blades to scrape the sharp bristles off the divided parts until they were smooth enough to carry on their shoulders.

"Before we go back, we'll eat some," said Sebetay. "We'll need our strength."

The living skeletons watched in silence as Sebetay scooped out a handful of lymph from the opened end of the ant's head and scraped it onto his men's palms. They licked and sucked and gasped in relief to taste food and feel it in their stomachs. When all had eaten, they squirmed under the divided ant to raise its pieces. "One . . . two . . . three!" Sebetay shouted, and the Ledackis rose with their burdens and marched. *We'll avoid the Stink Ant camp,* Sebetay thought. But he knew other, perhaps worse, obstacles were all along the way.

The army of skeletons had multiplied and were standing ten-deep, unmoving except for their blinking eyes. "Step aside!" Sebetay shouted, threatening with his spear in his free hand. "Step aside or be killed!"

The rest of his men kept pace with him, their teeth bared and their brows furrowed, as they brandished pikes and swords and screeched and roared. But the army of skeletons did not part. The Ledackis pushed forward, their pikes piercing chests and their swords slicing limbs and heads. As the first wall of the starving fell away, they were replaced by fifty more. These living skeletons pressed together in a tighter wall, blocking the Ledackis and their precious cargo, weakly reaching for the ant meat. The Ledackis attempted to push through but were having a hard time breathing in the density of humans; the air was poisoned and stank with the bitter breath of famine.

Sebetay looked behind him to see the living skeletons were pressing on their rear. Hundreds had surrounded his men, a barrier of skin and bones that left them no room to fight. Before Sebetay knew it, the ant head on their shoulders was drifting away from them, as if it were a leaf fallen on a stream. He looked right, then left to see the abdomen and thorax floating away atop a sea of spindly arms. Soon after, he heard the crack of chitin as the pieces were broken open, then screams and shouting as the starving fought over every drop of lymph.

"That's our food!" Sebetay shouted inside the mob. "We caught that ant! Return it—or we'll cut open your stomachs to take back what you stole!"

No one heeded his threats. Unable to use their blades, Sebetay and his men pulled to the center, pushing and shoving the living skeletons to prevent themselves from being crushed and smothered. Once the ant carcass was consumed, the horde fell away. The Ledackis were grateful for the space and air, and caught their breath. Sebetay looked around and saw a mass of trampled corpses on the sand, and the bits of the ant's chitin. A few of the trampled were alive and struggling to crawl or rise. From out of a nearby camp, he saw what looked like spiders rolled in broken straw, then realized they were men in a frightening covering of grass bits glued with human blood.

"Raise your weapons!" Sebetay shouted to his men, sure this was a new threat; but the straw men were scavengers, not predators. They crawled onto the corpses to claim them, hissing and snarling at the Ledackis before dragging the dead through an opening in the wall of their camp. The wall was quickly rebuilt before the straw men gathered in a circle to butcher the corpses with hand axes of shattered sand grains.

Sebetay was in shock as he stared at these men—if they were men—then fainted from holding his breath too long. He dropped his head to fill it with blood, then raised it to hear the gruesomely wet ripping sounds of the scavenger-cannibals flaying the corpses. When he stared too hard, they stood to hiss at him, and threatened him with the bloody ends of their tools. When he didn't move, they hurled bits of the butchered humans. He snapped out of his shock when an ear, then a pair of testicles, landed on his face, then slid down his chest.

"South," he said, turning to his men, whose faces

mirrored his horror. *And once we get there, then what? What do I tell my princess Jakhuma?*

Moonsinger had traveled farther than he expected into Palzhad's depths. His arm was tired from carrying a torch by the time they had arrived at the ant queen's chamber. "We have traveled very far," he said to Feegalo.

"Yes, Brother," said the priest with a touch of condescension. "I would have thought you knew our ant queen and her brood chambers are down deeper than all the other mounds on the Slope—or rather, of Bee-Jor *and* the Slope if you will. It is the oldest and largest of all our mounds."

"I did know that, but I had never experienced it," said Moonsinger as they dismounted from the carrier ant. "But I might add that the ant also seems slow. *All* the ants seem slow."

They stepped off the spiral platform to the short tunnel leading to the ant queen's chamber, and found just a little ant traffic. The ant queen was smaller than Moonsinger had expected, and she still used her legs, shifting back and forth as her attendant ants groomed and fed her. "The egg-layer is rather small," he said to Feegalo as he watched the nursing ants crawl to a chain of freshly laid eggs, then take each one to the hatching chambers.

"She has not been our ant queen for long," Feegalo

said as he removed a prayer cloth to reveal a delicate container of Trellana's urine. "She will grow much larger if . . . if . . ."

"If what?" asked Moonsinger.

"If Goddess Ant Queen wills it," Feegalo said. Again, Moonsinger saw what he thought was a smirk on the priest's face in the combined light of their torches. *He knows something he's not telling me.*

"And you have set some of Trellana's urine before her since her departure?"

"Of course I have. I'm offended by the question. Excuse me while I conduct the ritual."

Feegalo raised the container to the ant queen as she probed his shoulders with his antennae. He muttered in the Holy Tongue and then smashed the jar into pieces. The liquid within it sprayed in little beads that were caught on the claws of visiting ants, where they would spread it throughout the mound. As Feegalo bent to pick up the pieces of the jar, Moonsinger bent to help him.

"No need for that, Brother. This is my duty."

"I do not mind at all," said Moonsinger as he used his sleeve to mop up a bead.

"You should not, Brother. Only a priest may handle a Vessel of Sacred Urine, even after it has been broken."

Moonsinger nodded and handed Feegalo the pieces, which he set inside his handbasket, then fussily rearranged.

The two of them were returning on the ant up the spiral when Moonsinger sniffed, his nose detecting that musty and acrid smell again as they neared one of the mushroom chambers. *Is that odor coming from there?*

"I have never seen a Palzhanite mushroom farm," he said to the priest.

"They are little different here than the ones at Loobosh," said Feegalo, ending his sentence with his pompous little laugh. "Or at any other mound."

"Well, I should like to see one. For one thing, I'm hungry."

Before Feegalo could stop him, Moonsinger slid off the riding couch and approached the farm's entry, his torch before him. The odor—stronger now—was sharply sour. He held up his torch, and saw that across the chamber's outside wall was a faint coating of bright velvet. He stepped through the rough opening and saw the chamber had no human tending to it and, frighteningly, its mushrooms were dead or dying. They were withered or liquifying under clumps and tendrils of a bright yellow mold.

"Mold!" Moonsinger whispered, and felt sick in two ways. "Yellow Mold! Pious Feegalo!" he screamed towards the entry. Moonsinger felt his skin rising up and trying to crawl off his body. An ache in his skull was throbbing and turning into an ear-pounding. Bright, painful lights flashed in his eyes. He felt his lungs shrivel, and ran from the chambers as he coughed, knowing he should not inhale. When he was out in the tunnel, he inhaled the better air, then took the sleeve he had moistened with urine and rubbed it over the velvety mold. The mold should have disappeared in an instant; but it remained and seemed to grow before him.

"Good gods!" he said, staggering before he collapsed. As he looked around in the dark, he realized Feegalo and the carrier ant had left without him. *And he's likely fleeing this mound!*

Princess Jakhuma ate the last of her stash of acorn shreds, sharing the final bits with Kula and some other mothers with babies at their breasts. A woman of her country, staring into their circle, came towards the princess humbly, with large, pleading eyes. Her cheekbones were all too prominent in her face. She extended her thin arms and bony fingers in the fashion of praying as she bowed her head. "Please, Princess. I am your loyal subject Tsepalang. If you have any more food to share, I have been without it for days now."

"I am sorry, Tsepalang," said Jakhuma. "I eat what little remains, not to nourish myself, but to feed the babies who can only suckle for food. We have, all of us, lived some years. These babies may die before they see one summer."

The woman, looking shamed, dropped her head.

"Yes, Princess. Your heart is as great as your wisdom." The woman bowed again, but was too weak to raise her head and stumbled before she fell.

"Sit," Jakhuma commanded her, then reached into her garment for a last bit of acorn. "Take this," she said, and pressed it into the woman's mouth. "Our men are returning soon and I know they will bring us food." Tsepalang, touched by the princess's compassion, wiped at her eyes as she chewed the bit.

Jakhuma looked to the sky, and saw a few clouds as the sun touched the western horizon and its bottom melted and blurred. She was praying to her rain goddess when she heard a clamor in the other camps. Sebetay and his men were returning from the border wall. She saw their weapons stained with human blood, not insect, and her heart sank. The men's expressions were fierce as they pushed through the Spit Witch's camp to reenter the safety of their own. Spit Witch and the others in their camp paid the returning Ledackis little attention, too weak from their own hunger to make any threats. Jakhuma braced herself, and set her face to hide her disappointment.

Sebetay struggled to reach her, exhausted and out of breath. His legs and arms were covered with deep scratches and his shoulder was bloody with a knife wound. She looked at the other men behind him as they collapsed to their knees, a heaving mass of fright and fatigue.

"I am sorry, Princess," said Sebetay as he tried

not to sniffle and look weak. "We captured a big, fat leaf-cutter, but . . ."

She watched as he lost control of himself, bending in half to clasp his knees with his hands. He was hiding his wet eyes from her, biting his fist to quiet himself, but his shame and his suffering had erupted in convulsive gasps as his body trembled. Her own tears came and she looked down at him, across the sinews of his bloodied back, and was stirred by a whirlwind of different emotions. Beyond her despair, she realized there was a darkly sweet ache at the center of her misery. He had been a common soldier in their old country. Now, she knew, she loved him.

"You bring honor to our nation," she said, and touched his shoulder and felt the warmth of his skin. "All of you fine Ledacki men have risked your lives to try and save ours. Your mission was not possible."

Sebetay stood, gritting his teeth to steady himself, and looked in her eyes. He had become, once again, her valiant protector. "I must be truthful," he said.

"Speak your truth."

"Princess, there is no future for what remains of our Meat Ant people beyond that wall."

She was quiet, aware that everyone around them was listening.

"But there is no future for us *here*," she said.

"I do not disagree. But the people of that nearby country are not letting us in. And if they were to let us in tomorrow, we would be sharing it with all . . ."

"With all of *those* people," Jakhuma said, jerking her head to the other camps.

"And worse. Far worse," he said, lowering his eyes.

She looked at the baby, who pulled away from her breast and had something like a smile on her little face.

"Where would we go?" she asked Sebetay.

"Away from here," he said.

"Ledack . . . or whatever it has become . . . could not be worse than here."

"No place could be worse than here."

The two were quiet, looking into each other's eyes, silently relaying their fear of returning to the South and their greater fear of staying in the camp.

"We'll leave in the morning," she said, raising her voice, knowing that all had been listening. "I command no one to follow," she said, turning to those around her. "Though all of you may join us."

"We're going on a journey," said Kula as she patted the back of No Name, who was draped across her shoulder. "But I think it's time we named you before we go. I'm going to call you Hopeful. Would you like that?"

The baby burped. Jakhuma smiled . . . and so did the rest of her people.

CHAPTER 42

A FINE DAY OF RECKONING

Polexima was not comfortable wearing armor. She could not imagine anyone ever was, as her body plates banged against those of the driver in the saddle they shared. Punshu had prodded their roach south, near the shores of the Great Freshwater Lake and he spat every so often as he chewed a plug of kwondle bark. In the lustrous chitin of the roach she saw the pink and orange of the dawn as the sun edged up and painted the mountainous clouds with blood and fire. It had been a long night of travel, but at last they reached the corner of the lake, where they were to turn east and cross into enemy territory, the direction marked by a twig tower with a bloodred arrow at its top.

"Left," she said to Punshu, who adjusted his grips along the roach's antennae. It felt like a strange and unnatural thing to do, but she raised up the sword at her side—a sword she had never swung—and tilted its end towards the Barley Lands. From behind her she heard the tapping of claws on the sand. As her arm grew tired, she wondered how long she could hold up the sword, this light, little thing made for a child to train with. *Here I am, a lame woman riding a roach into war. And people are following me, ready to fight, because they believe in me as their queen.*

I wish I believed it myself.

They passed under a drying chamise shrub, with thick clusters of tubular flowers that fell and drifted over the roaches like sleepy little ghosts. Ahead in a clearing was a locust cage, where pilots stood at its front, awaiting the queen's arrival. She waved her sword and they bowed, entered the cage, then cut the rope that released its back panel. The first locust that emerged flew north to Cajoria to confirm her arrival. The second flew east to the Barley Lands. The third pair circled in a wide arc above them.

The procession picked up speed when the roaches' smaller antennae lashed and snapped, drawn by the scent of other roaches. After weaving under a canopy of mallows, the procession emerged to find the sleds of the Britasytes sparkling in the newborn sun. Just beyond them, men of the Plep clan completed the dismantling of the border wall to allow for a crossing. The sight was frightening to Polexima and made her stomach flip. Here it was: this entry point to war, to danger, to certain carnage. "Mother Cricket," she prayed aloud, "I ask for Your protections and seek Your guidance." Breathing deeply, she felt herself sinking below her fear to find her resolution, and within a few breaths the trembling ended. Punshu, sensing her confidence, turned and looked at her, smiling to reveal the bright white teeth that come with youth. She envied those teeth, so large and straight and shining in his dark and beautiful face. Anand had told her that Britasytes only married strong, bright, or beautiful outsiders in order to improve their race, and she wondered if Punshu wasn't an expression of all three. He halted their roach as Zedral rode out on his own to greet them.

"Are we ready, Chieftain?" she asked as their roaches' antennae made a thwarted attempt to probe each other.

"We are . . . Your Majesty," he said with a faint, brief smile that failed to mask his apprehensions. "Once our banner is lowered, proceed quickly."

"Understood."

Polexima watched as he rode back to the caravan, then tethered his riding roach to the chain of them at its tail. After climbing the ladder of the last sled, he shouted, "Hoist!" through its voice-cone. The first sled raised the long, unfolding pole with its banner of Madricanth. They waited for what seemed too long before a pole in the East rose with the green and orange banner of Katydid.

"Permission has been granted to the roach people to enter," said Polexima under her breath. *Though it may be the last time they ever do.* The Britasyte sleds lurched forward, followed by the reserve of loose roaches.

"Forward," Polexima shouted, raising her sword, and Punshu slackened the antennae. The queen and her driver rocked in their saddle as their roach crawled over the break in the wall, to follow the Pleps into the Barley Lands. Polexima looked over her shoulder. She exhaled in relief to see that thousands more mounted roaches were, yes, still following. Ahead of her, she saw Seed Eater laborers dismantling their crude, loose wall of sand and ant droppings to allow for their entry.

The queen knew her mind should be focused on the war effort and alert to attackers, but she felt a strange satisfaction as, at last, she entered this foreign country. All her life she had wondered what it was like in this place that was so close, yet so forbidden. She had seen harvester ants and Seed Eater soldiers as corpses, and sometimes as captives at assemblies. But here they were, brown ants in their own country, retreating from the roaches to the tops of weeds and barley stalks to wag their gasters and shoot their poisons before they abandoned their territory.

The queen and Punshu pulled up their goggles and breathing masks from around their necks before the poison could reach their lungs and eyes. To their right she saw the first of the pebble mounds and the scrawny, tawny-skinned villagers who had cleared the wall. They had the slow gait of the weak and hungry, and seemed unafraid; but they tensed when the Britasyte's sand-sleds pulled to the side of the route to let the parade continue—a continuation of armored warriors on riding roaches. Polexima watched as the villagers whispered, pointed, then quietly went east. She turned over her shoulder to see them all running, as best as they could, to a fresh release of Bee-Jorite acorns.

She looked to the pebble tower, where an armored sentry was all too stiff as he stared at her from under his orange helmet beneath the Katydid banner. The sentry was stunned, slow to realize that he was witnessing an invasion. He reached for the knotted end of a rope to sound his wooden warning bell when an arrow cut through his wrist and severed his hand. A broad arrow found his neck and sliced through his throat. His head tumbled out of the tower and landed before the queen's roach, which would not proceed until it had licked it, then eaten it.

We can kill each one we pass, but they'll know we're

here soon enough, thought Polexima as she looked into the sky. The locust scouts circled above her, signaling that the Bee-Jorites were safe from attack—for the moment. She took the bow from around her back, loaded its string, and pretended she could aim it as she searched through the weeds. Her arm tired quickly. "You are an old lady," she muttered to herself.

Emperor Volokop was seated on his raised throne at the edge of the sacrificial pit as his high priest and Mantis priestess completed the morning prayers to Lumm Korol and His mount, Night Mantis, as they disappeared with the stars. The clerics sang the ancient words as their cenobites counted severed right ears in piles of twenty-eight. The prayers came to a halt when it was certified that three hundred and sixty-four ears had been counted and piled into the ceremonial turquoise basins. One was set under Night Mantis's triangular head, and the second was set on top of it so that Lumm could enjoy their blood and aroma. It annoyed Volokop that the laborers who were refilling the pit were wailing and sniffling when they had been warned against it. He summoned the moon priest and whispered in his ear.

"Blessed subjects of His Divine Emperor Volokop," shouted the priest. "Do not desecrate this offering to the gods with your sniveling. Be joyful that your loved ones have been relieved of this life and honored to enter the Land of Ever Young, where they are drinking and eating at the Endless Feast, seated under the shade of Goddess Katydid. Be happy, be relieved, and know . . . they wait for you to join them."

When the last of the sand and soil was tamped down, the high priest and the Mantis priestess circled around its rough surface, then up the throne's platform to transfer the string of skull-shaped moonstones from the idol to the emperor. The beads were slipped over his crown's antennae, but they caught on the protruding lumps and thick folds of his deformities. The emperor tugged the string down to what had once been his neck.

"Lumm Korol accepts your offering and offers His grace, Your Imperial Majesty," said the high priest.

"Night Mantis wishes you the quickest victory," said the priestess.

Volokop looked to his brothers, sons, cousins, and nephews, standing to the right of his throne in their gleaming armor of golden beetle chitin. "Noble princes and princelings, Moon has blessed this war. We honor Him by retaking what He granted to His chosen people at the center of the Sand." The emperor rose from his throne, and unsheathed his sword as he joined the clerics at the bottom of the platform, slowly shifting the bulk of his legs as the princes and princelings lined up to kneel before the three. Each was tapped on the shoulder by the emperor's sword, slapped in the face by the priest, then kissed on the cheek by the priestess. When all were blessed, the emperor raised the curved end of his sword. "To war!" he shouted in the Four Directions, and the message was repeated to the ends of the vast camp. Hundreds of thousands of common soldiers raised their swords, then filed to the cages to release their ants and ride them on the sand route leading west. As the first of their divisions rode out, the imperial elite fighters went to their corral and uncaged the largest and strongest of the war ants to follow after the fodder soldiers. Further away, the princes and princelings rode to their corral, where they climbed up two-sided ladders to mount the stilted ants to be the last to arrive at the invasion and prepare for the emperor's entry.

How long I have waited—how long my people have waited—to solve this Slopeish problem, Volokop thought as his own mount and its driver were brought to him, a gorged and sturdy war ant that could support his weight. Little stinger ants were crawling over and under its massive abdomen that rose to reveal its end beading with poison. The emperor's bonneted servants helped him up a gilded ramp to reach the saddle-throne that had been customized to fit his immensely swollen legs and buttocks. As he looked into the sky to check for rain clouds, he noticed a pair of blue insects winging in a strange pairing in the distance.

The blue mantises again! The ones who appeared over the sacrifice yesterday. This is a good omen!

But a moment later, the sight struck him as odd. *What message is Lumm sending me with mantises that fly in pairs? And during the light of morning? That our victory is won in two days? Or two moons?*

The insects turned west and disappeared.

In any event, it is a fine day for riding, and a finer day for reckoning.

Terraclon stood on Cajoria's ant riding field, trying not to pace, as the sun neared the noon position. He looked to the midden in the South, where enormous piles of locust and roach moltings made rustling sounds as they were picked up and shifted in the wind. He turned his eyes to the sky, as much to the gods in prayer as it was in hopes of seeing his messenger pilot. The first had come by early morning with news that the Seed Eaters were indeed on the march after burying their human sacrifice. He stroked the amethyst pendant that dangled between his breathing filter and his blowgun, and listened to the flutter of the locusts inside their cages. They were as anxious for freedom as he was anxious for war.

His pilots, standing in loose formations, also looked to the sky, but turned every so often to look at Terraclon, he thought, in admiration as much as for direction. As much he should have been thinking about war, he was satisfied to know that his alterations of Sahdrin's uniform had been effective. He had darkened the armor from the inside out by stuffing it with tar-soaked cladding, a practical innovation he had suggested that all the defenders adopt. On top of his helmet were short and practical antennae, extending from a low crown of hammered gold he had taken from Sahdrin's dressing shelf. To complete it all, the quilted gambeson wrapped around his chest plate featured a cunning rendering of Locust the Sky God in rare blue thread. Terraclon wondered if the pilots would respect him as much if they had seen him late in the night, frantically completing his embroidery under the fading light of a fungus torch as he mouthed a prayer with every stitch.

At last, from above, they heard a faint buzz and then sighted it: the returning locust, leaving an identifying trail of red powder before its approach. "Give him some room," Terraclon shouted, and the pilots stepped back to make a clearing. The locust went into a landing spiral, but its rotation was too short and it fell on its side with a thump. It lay on the sand as a brown liquid bubbled from its mouth, through jittering mandibles. The pilot rolled off, and was helped to his feet as the locust was righted and inspected for punctures and wing damage. "Speak!" said Terraclon, mildly surprising himself with his increasing comfort at giving commands.

"Pious Terraclon, the roach brigade has succeeded at following the Britasyte caravan into the Barley Lands. They are stretching along the Southeast

Weedlands of Xixict and are nearing their sand route leading west."

"To your mounts! Inspect and adjust your loads before flying!" shouted Terraclon. "And may Locust be with you!"

"Locust! Locust! Locust!" shouted the pilots as they ran to the stacks of cages, climbed their ladders, and entered to mount the thousands of mottled blue flyers. Terraclon went to his own locust, freshly painted with white stripes, and hitched to a pole in the open. He examined the chains of filled egg- and aphid-shell capsules that lined the locust's belly, and checked the twine that bound them. "Are you ready, Defender Mikexa?" he asked the muscular, yellow-skinned pilot who sat in their saddle, patting the locust's head.

"Ready, Pious," she answered in a voice deeper than Terraclon's own, before she handed him a thorn horn. He blew it three times, then counted sixty breaths before blowing one long blast. The cages' doors fell open in a great clatter, and released their locusts, which united in a rising spiral.

"Up!" Terraclon commanded his pilot, and they leapt into flight and joined the swarm. The drone of thousands of wings was deafening, and made his armor vibrate; but as the locust whirled in the vortex of this flying army—*his* army—he had never felt more elated, more determined, more deliciously powerful.

"North and east!" he shouted into Mikexa's ear, and their locust broke out of the spiral. He looked in back of him at his pilots and bowmen atop their mounts, and was sure that he had never seen anything more beautiful. They winged over the Freshwater Lake as it reflected the blue of the sky and its white clouds and the flickering undersides of their locusts. When the lake ended, they continued north over the sea of barley grass, and flew high enough to avoid the arrows of the hungry hunters within it.

Unsure of how far to go, Terraclon was worried he had already overshot his mark, and was nearing Stink Ant country when he sighted a beetle-drawn convoy heading southwest along a sand artery. He pushed his feet further into his stirrups. "Veer west!" he commanded, and the pilot lowered her head, shifted her grips. The locust tilted to the right for a turnaround, and the swarm swung towards Xixict.

I'll find this Emperor Volokop, Terraclon thought. *This Great Deformity who hides like a coward at the tail of his army. And once I capture him, I'll rip his abundant body apart . . . until they bring me Anand!*

Polexima lost sight of the flying locust guides when a strong wind blew them south and rustled the long stretch of marsh marigolds that hid her roach brigade. The roach's smaller antennae were waving in a blur as Punshu held tight to the longer pair to keep their mount from crawling forward. "Hungry," he said in Slopeish. "Roach hungry smell good thing."

"Yes," said Polexima when she heard the unexpected sound of crickets chirping out of synchrony during the day. Several of them crawled from under the marigolds, disturbed from their sleep, to jump away. *I will take that as a sign,* she thought as Punshu regained control. She looked through the weeds to the near distance and saw what might have been the tops of the punk weeds growing on the lake's edge. The guiding locusts were back in view, circling sunwise, to signal to the roach brigade they had come as close as they needed and should remain where they were, hidden, at the edge of a loamy clearing.

"They're coming, hold position!" she shouted as she set the flat of her sword just above her helmet. She looked to her left and right and saw the riders pass her signal by setting their own swords just above their heads. Breathing hard, she felt like she might vomit if her stomach held any contents. Glancing at the sky, the locust guides were still circling. The roach brigade waited to advance when she heard the faint clacking of a chain of wooden bells from behind them in the South.

"Attackers from the South! Hold positions! Bowmen, pivot!" she shouted with a full rotation of her sword. Though it pained her, Polexima turned in her saddle, her back to Punshu, to face the southern threat. She saw flickers and shadows of what had to be Seed Eater sentries from the nearby villages filtering through the weeds on foot.

"Arrows first, blowguns second!" she commanded, and heard her words repeated north and south.

Jakhuma, Kula, and the other women with small children and babies in their arms were at the center of the slow-moving huddle of Ledackis, heading south through the camps. The Ledacki men were on the outside of the huddle, holding shields to make a walking wall while keeping weapons at the ready. Most of the refugees they approached let them tramp through their camps until they reached a clan of Mosquito Hunters. "Give us your food and we'll let you pass," said their leader, a man whose fuzzy hair was caked with red swamp mud. His hand gripped a blade in his waist strap.

"We are in *search* of food," Sebetay shouted, leading the huddle.

"Then leave us a baby . . . or one of your children."

"I will give you the sharp end of my sword," said Sebetay. "So your children can eat *you!*"

Each time they trudged through a camp, the Ledackis halted until the men at the back could reset the wall they had broken through, and the men at the front could negotiate the next part of the journey. They had halted again and were waiting in the brightening sun when Jakhuma turned to Kula Priya.

"Can you bear me if sit on your shoulders?" Jakhuma asked.

"Not for long, Princess," said Kula. "Why?"

"To see how much farther it is to the end of the camps."

The women passed their babies to Tsepalang to hold. Kula knelt, and let Jakhuma climb on her back to her shoulders. With the help of the other women, Kula stood and let Jakhuma peer over the lake of humans to the distance.

"What do you see, Princess?"

Jakhuma could only see a great stretch of humans; but somewhere at the horizon, she thought she saw movement. "I'm not sure. Maybe others leaving. Or maybe more arriving." As she stared she saw a faint rising of dust and heard a distant commotion. Sweat burst out on her upper lip as she felt her heart pump.

"Set me down," she said, as if she had been punched in the stomach. "Sebetay!"

"Yes, Princess?" he shouted to her from the front.

"We must hurry! Faster! Something is coming!"

"Then we should stay here. Wait for it to pass."

"No! Forward! Before it gets here!"

Each time they trudged through a camp, the beetles halted until the men at the back could rest.

"**T**his kind of work is worse than cleaning shit pots," said Keel. "This suit's been scratching me raw."

"Me too," said Tal. "First they sets us to excavating days and nights, and then this sticky-mucky business. If this is war, then I fucking hate war."

Keel and his sons dumped some heavily caked

trowels in a pile, then stood in a line, waiting to be stripped of the head-to-toe wrappers of tightly woven straw they had labored in since before sunrise. Tal reached one of several young women from the cloth-maker caste of Shishto who was dressed in a wrapper that revealed just enough of a pretty face with sensuous lips. She pulled the blackened mittens from Tal's hands, then used a quartz dagger to cut the suit off and peel it away from his oiled skin. He lingered before her, excited to be naked in the open, and looked for some sign that she was interested in what was growing.

"Next!" she called, looking around him.

"Not yet," he said. "What's your name?"

"They call me Prick Cutter,'" she said, raising her knife. "Care to find out why?"

Tal's face tightened, and he drew his arm back to smack her when Keel grabbed his wrist. "Let's not lose our pricks, son," said Keel as he pushed Tal towards his other boys, who stood naked, warming themselves in the sunshine as their bodies glistened with seed oil. Tal sniffed his arm. "I think there's roach grease mixed into this oil."

"Yeah. That's what's been making me sick all morning," said Keel. As they waited for the rest of their division to be stripped of their wrappers, they turned and looked at the wall they had helped to build. Men from inside the structure were crawling out of holes spaced through its top to complete some inspection. The wall was darker in color, its sand grains adhered with tar, and the side facing them had rows of window-like holes, which were also being inspected. At the bottom of the wall were some large slits.

"I'd say that wall's at least ten times taller than before," said Keel.

"And it ought to hold in a rain since it's been glued together," said Tal. "Except for all them holes."

A thorn horn blew and the divisions' captain appeared, recently promoted, wearing armor stolen from a dead Slopeite. He stood in the weeds a few hundred paces west. "Defenders!" Captain Klonpak shouted through a sound-cone. "The Seed Eaters are near! Use the spans, quickly, but one at a time! Resume your weapons and your position and check your ground ropes!"

Keel and sons waited their turn to trot along one of several beam-and-rung structures just above what looked like a ground covered with fallen leaves. At the end of the span, the captain reached into a sack and offered each defender a grateful smile and a sugared mite. Keel took his mite and noticed the captain's right earlobe was clipped.

"Did you see?" he whispered to Tal as they bit into their meal while walking to their assigned position. "Our Captain Klonpak is a shit worker like we is."

"And not even a foreman, like you, Dad. Who's he to be ordering us about?"

"I guess he killed himself a few Hulkrites," said Keel as he checked the tautness of the red ground rope that stretched to distant stakes ahead and behind them. He turned and spoke to his sons as they dressed and set breathing masks and goggles around their necks. "Boys, let's see who can kill the most Seed Eaters. The winner gets a prize. The loser gets his ass beat."

Volokop was annoyed when the march stopped again. The stilted ants were wobbling as they were forced to wait. "Find out why we're slowing!" he shouted to the messenger on a speed ant at his side.

The parade picked up and continued but at a slower, maddening pace. The messenger returned. "Your Imperial Majesty, the ants are slowing as they reach the stretch near some marsh marigolds, where they become difficult to control."

"Why?"

"We are not sure. Perhaps roaches."

"Roaches? Britasyte roaches in the Northwest outland?"

"Perhaps, Majesty. If not wild ones."

"If there are Britasytes nearby with roaches, find them and threaten them with their lives. Have any leaf-cutter ants crossed our border yet?"

"None reported, sir. No conflicts."

The messenger touched his chest and rode off, his ant weaving under the stilted ants, then crawling over and through the war ants of the elite forces to relay the emperor's command.

Why aren't any leaf-cutter ants attacking us yet if we're at their borders? Volokop wondered as the parade continued. *They would have smelled us by now. Did the Slope lose all their ants to the Hulkrites?*

Perhaps this is going to be easier than I imagined.

Polexima's thumping heart quieted as she looked over her arrow dipped in spider venom. Shadowed figures were coming towards the line of roaches from the South. She saw their orange helmets, bobbing like lightning flies in the shadows, as they got closer. *Village sentries,* she realized. *From the watch towers.* Arrows flew, one over her shoulder, making a *fwish* sound. She aimed her own at a shadow beneath a dandelion, waiting for someone to appear. *Fwish, fwish, fwish!* She felt Punshu's breath on her neck as he turned his head in concern. An orange helmet in the shadows came forward, and Polexima released and missed. She heard her arrow skid over the loam, and reached for the next in her quiver.

A sentry came close enough for her to see that he closed one eye as he aimed at her face. Their arrows were pointed at each other when she released. She heard the arrows slide against each other in the air, then felt a sharp pain in her shoulder. An arrow had pierced her armor but stuck in the cladding with its tip, making a shallow puncture. She heard herself scream, not in pain but in rage, and loaded her bow again. The sentry howled at her, running forward as she struggled to pull back the drawstring. She could see the spaces in his teeth when he stopped to aim. He fell on his back as he released his arrow, sending it upwards as he writhed on the ground, his back arched over the ground. Polexima turned, saw Punshu over her shoulder, his blowgun at his mouth, having saved her. He had released the antennae and their roach was crawling forward. He scrambled to regain control as the insect's antennae whipped and whirled.

Polexima raised her blowgun and steadied the soft magazine as the next sentry advanced. She missed, pulled the magazine one slot, then aimed again, this time piercing the sentry's chest armor and sending him falling and foaming at the mouth. She looked to her left and her right, and saw that the brigade was keeping their positions, but some riders and their drivers had fallen. One roach was wandering north with a corpse slouching in its saddle, as its unpracticed driver struggled to turn it back.

"Tethers!" Polexima shouted left and right. As the command was passed down the column, Punshu took the hooked ropes from under the saddle and threw their weighted ends to the nearest roaches. The drivers or the bowmen caught the ropes, and linked them to their saddles to hold the roaches in a steady barrier. Once his roach was stabilized, Punshu stood on the saddle behind the queen, targeting the attackers from the South with his blowgun. *"Pancha, shava. saata,"* she heard him counting. He aimed at a sentry running up when the roach lurched forward, then snapped back in the tether to send Punshu falling. He conked his head on a jutting sand grain and groaned.

The attacker, a young man with a sparse red beard, shouted in rage as he took in his fallen fellows. Reaching into his quiver, he found it was empty and dropped his bow. He yanked out his quartz sword and ran towards Punshu, leaping over the corpses to lunge at him. Punshu struggled to stand, and reached for his own sword. The sentry jumped up and his arm came down. The sword shattered the shoulder plate of Punshu's armor, and he stumbled, then dropped to his knees. The sentry, his nostrils quivering and his beard wet with sweat, raised his sword to swing out, and then down through Punshu's neck.

Polexima threw herself from the saddle and onto the sentry, knocking his chest to the ground. The sentry screamed and rolled up from under her, bashing her nose with his forehead, stunning her and drawing blood that welled inside her nostrils. He pushed her off, then stood to jam his blade through her neck when Punshu grabbed the sentry's wrist. He clamped his teeth on the sentry's fingers, biting deeper, until he dropped his sword. Punshu snatched the sword and threatened its end as he anchored himself. The sentry spun around him, attempting to tear his hand from the teeth.

Punshu's face screwed tighter and his skull bulged through his skin, when the sentry fell to the ground, screaming, it had to be, for mercy. Polexima sat up. She felt lost, half-conscious, consumed by the pain in her shattered face, and having to breathe through her mouth. She saw the sentry grasping for her sword with his free hand, dragging Punshu with him in order to reach its hilt. Rage exploded through her, and a scream ripped out of her throat that deafened her own ears. She stood on her weak legs, grabbed her sword, and hacked off the sentry's hand at the wrist, with the blade breaking on the pebble beneath them. The shock of the impact stiffened her arm and made the puncture in her shoulder pulse in agony. Punshu got off his knees, stood, and spat out severed fingers. A moment later, he spat out his bloody front teeth before he hacked through the sentry's neck.

In the quiet they heard the scampering of what remained of the sentries in retreat—for now. Polexima looked above her. The locust scouts were flying widdershins, signaling that the Seed Eater parade was near.

"Majesty, look!" shouted the Slopeish roach rider at her side as he pointed north. Polexima and Punshu turned to see crickets, katydids, and grasshoppers leaping up and out of the weeds, jumping towards them. The marsh marigolds across from them were shaking. Punshu seated himself on the roach and offered his hand to Polexima. She hesitated, then grabbed the sentry's quartz sword before ascending to the saddle. After refilling her quiver from the saddle's box, she loaded her bow, then looked to the sky and awaited the signal.

The Ledackis neared the mouth of the Petiole to find refugees running and screaming as they abandoned their camps. Thousands had fled east, and were struggling through the mud of the Tar Marsh or wading in its shallows, unable to go any farther without risking drowning. Thousands more were struggling to climb up to and through the rough rock piles of the West, with their jagged edges and cramped spaces.

The Ledackis' huddle came apart. The men stood before the Petiole, shields before them, weapons at the ready, to defend their women and children. The crying of the children was drowned in the screams and panic of the masses behind them. Princess Jakhuma stepped forward with the nameless baby and looked at the approaching forces, and knew they had no chance. *Who are they? Hulkrites?* she wondered. *Have they gathered to attack on some other ant?* A long arrow hit Sebetay's shield and broke it in two. Other arrows shrieked overhead.

"Sebetay, to the right!" Jakhuma shouted. "Into the marsh!"

"To the marsh!" Sebetay shouted, and the Ledackis scrambled down the low incline.

"Get away!" shouted the refugees in the marsh, packed tightly at its edges and threatening weapons. All along the marsh, the refugees struggled to stay close to the boggy edge, and were both slipping and stuck in its mud. Panicked screams came from those who had been pushed into the water and were thrashing and drowning. More of them were backed into the water as the Ledackis pressed in.

"I said stay back!" shouted a brown-skinned woman who aimed her spear's tip at Jakhuma's throat. She looked at the woman's face, bumpy with ritual scars, and knew the marsh as a refuge was pointless.

"Ledackis—to the West," she shouted.

"West!" she heard Sebetay repeat as he yanked Kula and Tsepalang from out of the grip of the mud. As they crossed to the piles of pebbles and rocks, Jakhuma could see what was coming.

Roaches. Grass roaches, from their dark color.

The men helped the women and children to the treacherous piles of rocks leading to the Great Jag. They were pushing the children up to climb when refugees from above pelted them with sand and poked them with pikes. A rough pebble came tumbling down and knocked Kula and Hopeful to the ground. She clutched the baby tighter in her arms after she landed on her back.

"Get away!" shouted a yellow-skinned youth from above as he pushed a pebble to the edge. "We've no room here for black Ledackis!" The rest of his clan attacked the Ledackis as they tried to climb by stomping and stabbing at their hands, or kicking their chins until they fell to scrape down the rocks.

The Ledackis clustered together, the women wailing, and looked north, behind them, to see tens of thousands of refugees milling as a panicked, screaming barrier as the roaches came closer. All of them wondered, as Jakhuma did, what to do next.

No going back, she realized.

"Weapons!" Sebetay shouted as the army on roaches came near. "If we can't live, we will die fighting!" Jakhuma stood behind him and spoke in his ear as she tried to comfort the baby in her arms.

"Thank you, Sebetay," she said. "If I never get to tell you, I bestow the honor of Whapenzee Sebetay upon you, for you are one of my beloved."

He barely nodded his head. The roaches came close enough that they could see their riders. At their head was an older, yellow-skinned man with the close-set eyes and grass-yellow hair of a Dneeper. On the roach next to him was a younger man, who might have been his son. The younger man raised up a cone and spoke something that sounded like Hulkrish.

"You occupy promised land of Dneep people," he shouted. "Leave. Now. Or die."

"How can we leave?" Jakhuma shouted. The older man, a king, she gathered from the spangled straw miter on his head, gave a command. Archers from the back of the roaches shot arrows that arced above the Ledackis, then fell on the refugees behind them. As the arrows hit random marks, they incited new screams of grief and panic.

"Back! To Palzhad!" commanded the Dneepish young man as the roaches pushed forward in a slow, steady crawl.

Sebetay and Jakhuma looked at each other.

"North! To Palzhad!" she shouted to her people, and to those behind her, not of her tribe. "North to Palzhad, to save your lives!"

"North!" shouted Sebetay. "To Palzhad!"

The Ledackis turned their backs on the roach people of Dneep and took tiny steps. The slow, churning mass of hundreds of thousands trudged, stumbled, and crawled to the North as the men on roaches herded them. Jakhuma burst into tears when she stepped over the corpse of Tsepalang, an arrow in her slender back.

Jakhuma clutched the baby girl in her arms tighter.

Darling infant, you will see another day. You will have another chance.

"Chance," she said out loud to the girl. "I'm going to call you Chance."

Brother Moonsinger looked around his chambers and was haunted by its quiet. Everyone was at Shishto or Cajoria, awaiting a battle. Perhaps it was under way. Here in Palzhad, in this empty palace, he had no one to talk to, no one to perform for, and very little to do as he waited for Nuvao to return. The brother had already eaten, already bathed, and already dressed. And he had already made his request, futilely, for a messenger to relay the urgent news that the Yellow Mold had appeared. *This mound will never become a learning center. It's about to implode, and the priests knew it—wherever they are.*

Shame and regrets were gathering over him like a storm cloud. *I should have gone to Cajoria and insisted on joining the defenders—even if I am nothing more than an old eunuch who talks too much. I'm not any safer here. And what will happen, gods forbid, if the Seed Eaters prevail? The only way they welcome me in the West is as a big, fat sacrifice to Mantis.*

He sighed. *I have to leave. I must tell someone—anyone—what I've seen here. And if a dying ant can't take me to Mound Smax, I'll walk.*

Though his stomach was full, Moonsinger ate the rest of some fermented buckwheat and mealworm cakes, then changed into practical clothing and walking boots. The servant entered after calling, *"Creet-creet"*; she had a dozen deep ridges in her brow, and was muttering inaudibly as she shook her head.

"Anything else we can bring you, Brother?" she asked as she picked up his tray and muttered some more.

"Yes, Barhosa. I'll need a water bladder and some travel food, please."

"Yes, Brother," she said. "Though I don't know about traveling."

"Why not?"

"You might want to take a look at the South."

Moonsinger rushed from the bedchamber to the hall, then to the nearest exit. He squeezed out to the uppermost ring, empty of ants and people, and trotted south to view what had been the border weeds. The refugees were still spread to the far East and far West, and from what he could see, they looked to be just as dense in the South. Something caught his eye and he gasped to see a couple of refugees making their way over the border wall and through the sentry ants. The ants had gathered all their diminished numbers at the wall, but they seemed to be greeting the intruders instead of destroying them. These cheeky intruders were easily dodging the ants' attacks as they zigzagged under and through them. The intruders seemed even less intimidated by the last of the human sentries who rode atop the ants.

More refugees crawled up the wall—a hundred of them, loosening the barrier as it flattened under their feet to brandish their weapons. The human sentries jumped from their saddles and ran north to take shelter. Once these had left, the refugees attacked the ants.

They were clubbed, pierced, and ripped into pieces. The ant killers swarmed north, taking their pieces with them to the stadium, where they found privacy and space to sit and lick their lymph. Thousands more refugees were rushing over what had been the wall. A moment later, no ants, not even dead ones, were visible in Palzhad's southern clearings. Moonsinger bit his fist as he looked down at the flood of human beings splitting east and west to the housing rings on the north side.

Soon enough, they will occupy every abandoned shelter! Then challenge the occupants of those which are not! How soon before they are up here? Inside this palace?

Keel and his sons were bored and yawning. "May as well tug out some spunk and take a nap," said Tal as he lay in the hollow of a sand grain and pulled his shield over his body. "Wake me when the Seed Eaters gets here, if you'd be so kind." Keel and his sons were laughing as they watched Tal's shield bobbing above him, when Keel noticed the defenders to the left and right were giving them the sideways glare.

"Get up, Tal," Keel said. "Everyone's giving us the shit-eyes."

"All right," said Tal as he stood and pulled down his tunic. "Not really in the mood for a wank anyway. I'm just bored enough to drink my own piss. Anyone got any kwondle?"

Keel was reaching into his tunic when a scout in sand camouflage slid down from the wall's top to a voice-cone. "Alert! Alert! Invaders sighted!" he repeated. Scouts all along the wall passed the message from the lakeshore to Shishto.

"Goggles up, filters up, shields up!" the captain shouted. Keel and his sons raised their eye and nose protection, then set their shields before their toes and looked out the slits at their tops. In back of them, they heard the second line of bowmen draw arrows from their quivers.

A moment later, Keel heard the harvester ants arrive in what had been predicted as the first wave. His heart raced—*I get to be in a war!* The invaders were shouting, *"Za yatchmin, za Volokop,"* as the first of them nosed up the top of the wall. In the distance, Keel thought he could see their bowmen standing in their stirrups behind their drivers and shooting. A few arrows fell just before their division, far short of their marks, and they scattered and rolled like little sticks.

They must be wondering why they don't see any ants, Keel thought. *And where are our ants?* He felt something like an explosion in his gut—*fear*—when the harvester ants were abruptly thrust above the wall. Pikes were ramming up through the top holes to pierce both ants and riders. When the pikes were retracted, they left human and ant corpses to tumble down the wall. The ants and men that made it past the pikes were just as soon skewered by pikes that punched through holes in the wall's face.

Keel and his sons watched the carnage with mouths open, stunned at first, then laughing as the Seed Eaters kept coming and the pikes kept jabbing, again and again, to kill them by the hundreds. The corpses were shoved into a pile with long-handled push brooms from slits at the wall's bottom. A rising barrier of dead ants and soldiers was building before Keel's eyes, nearly as tall as the wall. When the corpses clogged the wall and the pikes could thrust no more, the enemy poured in. Keel could hear the muffled sounds of the Seed Eaters' army as they continued their advance by climbing up the second wall of their dead.

"Hold positions!" shouted Klonpak. Atop the corpse wall, Keel saw the first antennae and the beards of the brown ants, and then the soldiers mounted on them. With this swell of soldiers came the smaller stinger ants that darted around their larger sisters. The ants spilled down the rough, steep hill of corpses to right themselves and advance.

"Hold positions!" shouted the captain again.

Keel watched as the advancing ants came to a slow halt. Their bowmen were jerked out of their stirrups, and some were thrown from the saddles. The drivers panicked, unable to goad the ants forward or stop them from turning around. The ants wanted to go back. Some climbed up the wall of the dead only to be crushed under the mass of more of their arriving army.

It's this roach grease that keeps them back, Keel realized as he sniffed his arm. He felt humbled and embarrassed for a moment and had an annoying reminder of Anand. As the Seed Eaters' army was turned into a tangled mass of confusion, Keel saw they had no choice but to abandon their ants. By the hundreds, they fell or jumped from their saddles to march on foot after raising up shields, and nocking arrows.

Keel and his sons looked at each other, grinning in anticipation, even as arrows whizzed past their ears or landed in their shields. One of the Seed Eaters yelled, *"Za yamiche! Bravajnay!"* Their front line shot their arrows before they ran in the hundreds, swords flashing above them.

All at once they stopped. The Seed Eaters jerked forward, their feet caught, to fall facedown in tar. Keel and his sons guffawed, watching as the Seed Eaters suffocated in a hopeless attempt to pull their faces from the black glue. A few fell back in the tar, their hands and bottoms getting stuck as they were crowded and trampled by the soldiers behind them.

"Bowmen, forward!" shouted Klonpak from behind the defenders. Keel and his sons turned to the side to allow the bowmen to step through and aim at the helpless targets.

"Shield bearers! Two hundred paces back," was

the captain's next command, and as they had practiced, Keel and his sons and their division marched
backwards. Through the slits, Keel could see the Seed
Eaters' ants were coming forward again, harvesters
of all sizes. They crawled over the men trapped in the
tar until they got stuck themselves. The ants struggled, then ripped out their own legs to let their bodies
fall to the glue. Their riders attempted to escape by
leaping from ant to ant but most of them slipped and
fell and were caught. When the tar trap was full, the
ants and men who struggled in it were thick enough
to be a passageway for the next swell of the army. The
Seed Eaters kept coming, riding over the trapped ants
and the men screaming for mercy.

Keel was dizzied and delighted as he watched the
Barley people march to their own demise. *But how
many more have they got?* he wondered. He looked
with his sons at the next wave of mounted ants;
these ants were larger and their soldiers were better
armed and armored. The ants came closer and then
halted again, repelled by the roach-scent. The ants
were turning back again, but these soldiers had expected it—they jumped from the saddles to make a
tight formation, shields before them, to march on
foot. A line of bowmen was in the back of them,
shooting thick arrows high from powerful bows to
fall in a lethal rain. Keel was looking up, in fear of
the arrows, when he heard a piercing scream. He
turned to see an arrow had burst through Tal's gog-

gles and jammed in his eye socket. Tal collapsed on his back, shrieking in agony and unable to pull the arrow out of his skull. Gatherers of the wounded ran up from behind him to drag Tal off in a travois. Keel wanted to run forward and attack, to protect the rest of his sons. He would target every last Seed Eater with his blowgun, then gut them once they had fallen.

"Hold positions!" shouted the captain a third time, and when Keel turned to look, he saw Klonpak was commanding him in particular. When Keel looked back to the Seed Eaters, their foot army had multiplied by hundreds, and he could hear their boots as they marched.

"Ropes!" shouted the captain. Keel and his sons hesitated—they wanted to lower their breathing masks and shoot darts.

"Ropes now!" shouted the captain. "Do not disobey me!"

The defenders hung the top loop of their shields around their necks as a barrage of arrows whistled through them. Keel and his sons reached to the ground to raise up one of the bright red ropes spaced along the front.

"Pull!" shouted the captain, just as an arrow pierced his arm. "Pull, pull, pull!" he screamed in pain. Keel trudged backwards, yanking the rope, when he felt a violent pang in the left of his face. An arrow had lodged between his teeth and his cheek.

His blood sprayed as he screamed before fainting. His sons dropped the rope.

"Pull that rope!" commanded Klonpak as he ran up to replace Keel. The Seed Eaters marched closer.

Messages were filtering back to Volokop as his ant fought the driver's commands. "We have penetrated, deep into Slopeish territory, half our forces," was the latest word. But there had been no messages from inside the Slope. *Or Bee-Jor, or whatever these Mushroom Eaters under the boot of Dranverites want to call their country.*

Volokop was imagining his army, valiantly fighting, preparing the way for the final blows, when his ant shifted off the sand route. The stilted ants were weaving off it as well. *We must be nearing these accursed roaches! If it was Britasytes who brought roaches near a battlefield they will have to be punished—kill a few, then a tax of some kind, a complete emptying of their sleds.*

The emperor's thoughts were interrupted when the imperial ant turned in the opposite direction. The driver struggled to right it, but the ant was determined to reach a gray mudwort and climbed up its stalk. "Take control of this ant!" he commanded the driver.

"Majesty, I can't, it's . . .".

The ant righted itself on a leaf, which bent under the weight and bounced. To his right, the emperor had a view of the lake. From below he heard shouting and saw that the stilted ants had stumbled to the lakeshore, pushed by the invisible repellant of nearby roaches. The ants' riders were wobbling as their ants' stilts slipped in the mud and tripped through clumps of hair sedge, until half of the stilted fell in the water. The princes and princelings struggled in the lake, unable to swim in their heavy armor. They screamed for help to those on the shore, who cut down punk weeds and extended their fluffy cylinders as floats to pull them in.

Volokop, enraged, could not see any messengers from atop the plant—he looked through the weeds to see his army and their ants clustered along the lakeshore's edge, slipping in its mud or climbing its marsh plants. *How unbecoming of the Sand's greatest military power! How long must we wait here?*

Polexima looked to the locusts above her which were flying north and south in a narrow oval. "Masks and goggles!" she commanded, and she and Punshu raised their own to their faces. He lifted his mask briefly, to spit out blood, and stuffed some cloth ripped from his clothing into the raw gap in his teeth.

"Northeast!" she shouted, raising her sword and pointing. The roaches followed her single file, their riders calling to each other as they traversed low, rounded rocks, moist soil, and a thicket of gray-green marsh salvia. When she reached the sand route and saw fresh ant droppings, she knew that Volokop and the tail of his army had passed and were not so far ahead. She could smell the lake just beyond, and heard the rippling of its surface when the wind blew. Punshu pointed to the sky, and she saw the locust scouts had joined in a pair again, confirming her position was correct and that the roaches were aligned from north to south. One of the locusts spiraled down and landed before her.

"Just in time, Majesty," said the pilot, who had blue paint on his face. "This locust was about to give out." As the locust crawled off to drink at the shore, Polexima turned to look in the sky behind her, searching its clouds, when an arrow flew past her, its fletching grazing her face.

"Bowmen, reverse!" she shouted, then struggled to turn in her saddle and face an attack from the East.

Keel was furious and pushed away some boys who tried to roll his bulk into a travois and haul him from the battle. "Fuck off," he shouted at them, then stood to rejoin his sons to pull their rope. As it tautened, they felt the stake give in the distance. A leaf-spattered tarp peeled back to reveal the chasm they had excavated from Shishto to the lakeshore. Some Seed Eaters were caught in the tarp and were folded into it. Others were skidding to the chasm's edge, failing to stop and falling in. Most of the enemy reached the chasm, then stepped back. A moment later, they turned and ran.

Ants erupted by the hundreds of thousands.

Leaf-cutters crawled over and up and through each other to catch and dismember the invading soldiers. Keel placed a hand to the bloody gash in his cheek, and watched the commotion of ants and listened to the screaming within it. The Seed Eaters had their limbs sheared off and their torsos cut in two. Some of the ants had already picked up the shredded bits of the bodies and headed back to dump them in the middens of the border mounds. One poor Seed Eater was sheared of all four limbs, but still had his head. He was alive and screaming as his torso was held high, clutched atop the mandibles of a leaf-cutter who marched him past Keel and his sons. They laughed until they were breathless. The Seed Eaters captured in the tarp were squirming within it, looking for an exit, when the defenders ran over to stab them through the canvass.

The leaf-cutters continued as a dark yellow flood that swarmed over the wall to destroy the Seed Eater soldiers and their ants in their own lands. When the last of the leaf-cutters left the chasm, it seemed, finally, the invasion was over.

"Shit, boys," said Keel from the right side of his mouth. "We didn't get to kill a single Seed Eater. But I bet we gets to deal with their stinky corpses."

Volokop was uncomfortable. The saddle-throne's restraining straps gouged into his flesh as his ant climbed down the mugwort. *The roaches must have moved on,* he decided as his driver regained control and veered the ant back to the sand route. The stilted ant riders had salvaged half their mounts and were speeding along, catching up with the elite force. The emperor looked up to the sky and saw the sun at its zenith, and figured the first wave might be at Cajoria by late noon and he would arrive by early evening. *I hope the Cajorites have had the good sense to abandon their mound by now. We'll need some place to sleep tonight.*

A messenger ant reached him, but the boy on his back would not meet the emperor's eyes.

"Imperial Majesty . . . we . . . we . . ."

"Yes?"

The messenger opened his mouth and the emperor heard something like words but they got lost on a passing breeze. The sun seemed to dim and the emperor had a feeling of shrinking inside himself, as if he were nothing but a poppy seed inside a rattle.

"I await your response, Majesty," said the messenger.

"Repeat the message."

"The captain of the Thirty-ninth Division informs you that an uncountable number of leaf-cutter ants have invaded and are advancing and have destroyed the Fortieth through Ninetieth Divisions.

The captain urges an immediate retreat of our remaining forces."

The emperor coughed.

"Your message . . . Majesty."

"Where are the First through Thirty-eighth?"

"Unaccounted for."

The emperor kept coughing, unable to speak, as convulsions rippled through his deformities. He finally tapped the driver on his shoulder. "Turn our ant around and quickly. We are going back to Worxict."

The attackers coming from the East towards the roach brigade were not skulking, but out in the open. As they came closer, Polexima saw that they were common villagers, whose only weapons were shard daggers and crude pikes that were nothing more than sharpened barley stalks. The look on their faces was more terrified than terrifying. Goading them from behind were sentries, shouting commands and kicking them in their withered behinds.

I couldn't possibly shoot at these pathetic people, she thought, until a serious arrow lodged in her chest plate. She felt dizzy again, getting too little air through the filter over her blood-filled nose. As the sentries aimed arrows, the villagers rushed the roaches and tried to climb the sharp, greasy bristles of their legs. Others made human pyramids to reach the riders and those who got to the top attempted to stab them.

Punshu cut off their heads from their skinny necks as he danced around the saddle in his grip boots. One attacker was up and lunging towards Polexima when she took her new sword and thrust it into his meager chest. After he fell, she looked around her and saw hundreds more coming, distracting her and the other riders as distant bowmen shot their arrows. The roaches were pivoting now, panicked, and crawling out of position as the villagers converged on them, attacking their legs with pebble mallets.

Polexima was stuck in the saddle, struggling to rise in it, when she heard a buzzing from overhead. "Thank Cricket," she said inside her breathing mask, then wiped sweat off her goggles. Eggshells fell and exploded, releasing fine powders. Soon, the ragged villagers' army was coughing, then seizing, then shouting, then weeping. They wandered in blindness, colliding and attacking each other, shouting at themselves and using their fists to bang their skulls until they fell on the ground to bang some more. Some were rolling around, violently wrestling with invisible partners, or each other. Others screamed at the heavens, then down at the ground as they tried to peel their own skin off with their nails or daggers. Some bumped around, screaming in panic from sudden deafness and hoping to hear their own voices as they tore at their ears. One man was licking the air, over and over, while another man stopped yanking out his own hair to yank out someone else's.

Datura madness. May I never know this agony, Polexima thought.

Unable to shout her commands or risk breathing
the powder, Polexima raised the flat of her sword over
her helmet. The tethers were thrown and hooked, and
the roaches held their position in a field of screaming
madmen that were madness making.

She looked up to the sky, in search of Terraclon,
who was on one of these locusts overhead. She both
resented and admired him for what he had wrought.
I will never underestimate that one again.

Terraclon looked down at the roach brigade, assured
of their safety and their position after swooping low
enough to see that the powders had taken effect on
the unexpected attackers. "Bring us up!" he shouted
within his filter, and the swarm followed his lead and
flew west above the sand route until they saw the
head of the Seed Eaters' procession. They were racing
east in retreat to Worxict.

Or somewhat racing. At the head of the parade
was a grandly decorated and cumbersome ant that
the procession was too respectful to overcome.

*I can guess who that is. He leads from the back during
the attack, but races at the front during the retreat.*

"Spiral and follow," Terraclon commanded. The
swarm circled above the head of the procession as it
continued east.

Volokop looked up at and gasped when he saw a swarm of blue mantises spiraling above him like some great sky flower. He wondered if Night Mantis had sent them as a protective escort to surround him. The ant was slowing again—for no reason—and so were the ants behind him.

"What's wrong?" he asked the driver.

"I don't know, Majesty. Maybe hidden roaches again."

Volokop turned to see the procession bunching up behind them, crowding the sand route. His ant came to a halt, and those behind him could not go further either. He looked up as the mantises lowered and re-alized they were locusts—with human riders on their backs.

So it's true—they fly on locusts. He felt his heart drop and splatter.

"Arrows!" he shouted. "Aim at those locusts."

"Spiral lower," Terraclon commanded his pilot, and his locust lowered until he could see an enormous man seated on a throne strapped to his ant's thorax. *Volokop!* And he had seen them—Bee-Jorites mounted on locusts—as he was jostled in the crush of his forces piling up from behind.

"Spiral up," Terraclon shouted as they aimed their arrows. He punctured a thigh pod on both its sides until it emptied its orange powder as his drop signal. He slit the rope behind his saddle, which snapped to unload the chains of aphid shells. They landed and exploded around Volokop, and through the stilted ants behind him and the divisions after them. The swarm continued their flight above the sand route to drop the rest of its bombs on the forces behind them.

"Turnaround! East!" Terraclon shouted, and looked below as both harvester ants and Seed Eaters trembled with palsy. The riders slumped or fell from their saddles and the ants twitched and pivoted in place. The massive ant that carried the emperor had fallen off its legs and to its side. Volokop, in some massive orange garment, was jiggling like an algae pudding. The stilted ants crashed around him, and their riders fell from saddles to wander in madness, walking and jumping, it seemed, with arms outstretched, as if trying to catch their own heads floating away from them.

"Land," Terraclon shouted, and the locust circled to a halt and was guided to Volokop. He looked down at this man, this emperor, strapped into his fallen throne, and was astonished by the mass of his deformities. "You're coming with us," he said, "and when you've regained your sanity, you'll arrange to return our Commander General, Vof Quegdoth of Cajoria of Bee-Jor—also known as Anand of the Britasytes."

Terraclon gritted his teeth—he ached to hurt this man, to use his sword and slash at his bountiful flesh.

The emperor was deep into madness, his eyes

rolling, and Terraclon knew he had not been seen nor heard by him. He watched as the emperor gurgled a stream of words and then tore at his garment, covered in fish scale sequins, as if it were a spider attacking him. When the garment was undone, Terraclon saw that the man's legs, like his chest and part of his neck, were a swollen mass of folds, clumps, and ropy growths. His testicles were each the size of a baby. He weighed as much as six other people, and could never fit on a locust saddle.

"Pious," said the pilot, pointing up. The locusts above them were releasing a yellow warning powder. *The rest of their army is returning from the West, will be here soon.* He looked over at one of the fallen riders of the stilted ants, a young and refined-looking man in beautiful armor of golden beetle chitin. He was shaking, sobbing, talking to himself in his madness. Terraclon felt pity for him and, strangely, affection.

"Him!" he said. "We'll take him! He'll tell us how to get back our commander."

The pilot threw Terraclon a coil of soft rope and he tied the young man's hands behind him, then his ankles, before raising him up to the pilot to set in the cinching cradle behind their saddle. Terraclon was not sure what to shout as his next command.

"Home!" he finally said, and they flew up and into the swarm. He looked west to see the last of the Seed Eater army, retreating by the tens of thousands from a swarm of leaf-cutters chasing them east. As the locusts flew west, the roach brigade crawled under them and all made their way to . . . Bee-Jor. "To Bee-Jor!" he shouted.

Yes, Bee-Jor lives another day. But what about its founder?

the locusts flew west, the roach brigade crawled
under them and all made their way to . . . Bee-for.

Yes, Bee-for lives another day. But what about its

CHAPTER 43

THE PLACE WHERE PRIESTLY
MAGIC ENDS

Pleckoo spent his first day beyond the northern wall
in the center of a fuzzy mint plant. After squeezing
through its dried and bristly outer stalks, he collapsed
in delight in its lush center. It was glorious to be free
of the ropes, to move his arms and legs again, and lie
down, even in the confines of the plant. He plucked
one of the green leaves and chewed on it, to quench
his thirst and fill his stomach even as it numbed his
tongue. The mint's aroma made the plant a safer
place to hide since it repelled most insects but he was
frightened when there was a sudden shade. A milkweed butterfly had alighted on the plant's top to flirt

with its faded flowers. She found no nectar and resumed migration to her winter home in the South.

Pleckoo plucked more leaves to make a bed of them and then lay down to luxuriate in the downy softness of their tops. Stretching and napping, he stared up at the blue sky with a pleasantly empty head, as the clouds performed a slow dance to the music of the wind. *I'm staying here all the rest of my life,* he thought. *Why do I need other humans?* When the sun neared the West, he stood and used the veiny underside of the leaves to scrub and scrape his body clean. It was then that he noticed his arms and legs had atrophied. *I'll get strong again—stronger than I've ever been,* he thought. As he felt his head and chin, he was heartened to know his hair and beard were returning.

The coming darkness brought a chill that ended his idyll and reminded him of his plight. *I need clothes! I need weapons! I don't even have a knife!* He stacked several mint leaves atop each other as a layered blanket and nestled under them, but he could not get very warm. Looking up through the sprigs, he could see the eastern rise of the orange moon reflecting the rays of the bloodied sun. The sight did not fill him with hope or comfort. As the moon rose higher and whiter and the night got colder, Termite stood like an old and stern grandfather over him, ready to swat him with a withered hand. *Hulkro, You are a cruel god,* he thought, *if You are even a god at all.*

Tree crickets, numerous in the autumn, slowed

their chirping as the chill deepened but they were no less annoying as they screeched in unison. Pleckoo shivered inside his leaves, and stuffed his ears with bits of them in hopes of finding quiet. Slipping into a shallow sleep, he dreamed one of those dreams where he was aware he was dreaming . . .

He dreamed of that beautiful time on a warm evening when he had commanded hundreds of thousands of Termite warriors—men who looked at him with both fear and admiration. They had herded uncountable ghost ants to the Slope to devour its idolators and purify its sand with green and crimson blood. Pleckoo, riding a gorged and magnificent ghost ant, reached the watchtower, where the Roach Boy had commanded his pathetic defense. Pleckoo's laugh had tickled the stars and made them squirm, when he could see his cousin on the tower's platform tearing out his beard and howling in defeat. The men were chanting the round of Hulkro's names as they chopped at the tower's legs, then clapped and stomped when it toppled and crashed into flying pieces. Pleckoo dismounted from his ant as his captains reached into the wreck and drew out the body of the one who had called himself Vof Quegdoth. Now it was Little Cousin Anand who slumped in his captors' arms, half-alive, with his head bent and his hair covering his face as he was dragged before Pleckoo.

"Look at me," Pleckoo commanded, but Anand refused to raise his head. "Look at me, Roach Boy!"

he shouted. Slowly, Anand lifted his face, which had taken on a heavenly brilliance. The light of his skin lit up the red of his garments and the faces of the men who held him.

"Look upon *Me!*" shouted the glowing figure as He flipped the men who held Him into the sky with flicks of His fingers. He grew in size and increased in brilliance as He sprouted termite wings from His back.

"I heard what you thought! You thought Me cruel and doubted my existence!"

"Forgive me, Termite, I . . ."

"I have *delivered* you. Instead of thanking Me you have *insulted* Me."

Pleckoo looked around him as the night turned black as tar. All had vanished except himself and Hulkro, who was winging into the night sky to perch on his lapis throne. Pleckoo tried to fall to his knees and beg for forgiveness, but there was nothing to fall onto. He was floating in space in complete silence, watching as his hands, his arms, and the rest of his body crumbled and dissolved. *This is it,* he thought, terrified that all that was left of him were words. *Hulkro tests the faithful,* Pleckoo heard, as if it was whispered by the wind . . .

He felt a cold, wet kiss on his ear that woke him from his sleep. Stumbling out of the leaf blankets, he felt his heart pound to the point of exploding; but he knew he had not died. He burst into tears and wept and felt ashamed, imagining that he looked like some sad little child. Tiny beads of dew had grown on the sprigs of the mint stalks, and glinted with bits of moonlight. Afraid at first, he braced himself, then dared to look at the moon in its western descent. "Your will be done," he said. Clouds floating over the moon stretched into arrows with their heads pointing north. "North," he said aloud.

Sleep was pointless after that. *May as well start now,* he thought, and pushed his way out of the mint's dead stalks as their prickles scraped at his skin. Naked, bootless, and shaking with cold, he searched the sky for Big Brush, then found Little Brush and with it the Northernmost Star. *One foot down and then the other,* he thought as he took a step towards the deepening blackness of the northern oak forest.

For days, Pleckoo had stuck to terrain that was drenched in sun as he made his way to somewhere— perhaps this Dranveria, where his god had *some* mission in mind. He skirted the shade of trees and their moist soil in fear of cannibals from above and lair spiders from below. Traveling through sunlit patches meant weaving through grasses and weeds, but before him now was a route so clogged with wild barley he would have to crawl on top of it, bending with each dip of the grass to pull himself onto the next clump. The stalks were dry and when they broke they had sharp and dangerous points. Worst of all, there were no florets with any edible seeds. His stomach grumbled.

He had been filling his stomach with grass shoots as well as dandelion and mallow leaves; but always, within moments of eating, he was famished again. *I'm meat hungry,* he thought, feeling as if his inside was feeding on itself. Only a seed or some fungus or an insect could end the headache that dulled his senses and weakened his limbs. Squirming up the tallest, sturdiest barley stalk he could find, he saw how far the thicket of grass stretched. Its end looked too far away on a day when he was feeling weak and all alone. He looked to his left at the sky-scraping oak tree, which had been in his sights for the last two days. *I'll risk hiking under its shade if it's dropped any acorns. But even if I found one, how could I open it?*

The shaded ground of the oak was covered in thick layers of its brown and spiny leaves. They would have been a wealth to leaf-cutter ants if they were safe to forage in this place. . . but they weren't. Some human presence hunted, and likely ate, any foraging scouts before they could return home and leave a trail of *leaf-find.* Pushing through the spread of leaves, Pleckoo looked for acorns but there were none—only the caps that once held them. *Humans have already been here,* he thought, *and harvested them all.* In fear, he looked up in search of branch dwellings and rope bridges and at the tree's trunk to be sure he didn't see a spiral-ladder climbing up its bark. He remembered the old crib tales that spoke of long ropes that fell from branches to the ground—ropes used to swing down and kill men with spine-breaking jabs from foot daggers. Pleckoo looked up in the branches and saw none of that. *You worry like a woman*, he scolded himself. Resuming his trek, he sighted something dark and glistening at the edge of the shade. From a distance, it looked like a dead tree cricket, but it was fresh and shining, untouched by scavengers.

Food!

Pleckoo ran carefully over the leaves with his bare feet, avoiding the pricks on their edges but falling when they slipped from under him and flew up. At one point he sank into a shallow pit of leaves, and was suffocating until he figured his way up, almost swimming through them before he got to his feet. As he got closer to the cricket, a faint thump in his gut made him halt before he stepped any further.

The cricket wasn't real. It was something carved and painted. *What is it? Some idol fallen from a tree altar?* He looked up to the branches again for signs of a tree village, when he heard a rustle of leaves, then felt a rope cinch tight around his ankles. Rising up from under the leaves were tree cannibals, their skins covered in leaf camouflage. Screaming and cackling, they yanked hard on their rope's noose, felling Pleckoo and dragging him towards them as they gnashed their teeth. He tore at the rope around his ankles when a second loop lashed around his arms and bound them to his sides. The cannibals rolled him over, his face on the ground. His wrists were gouged as they were tied together and his arms were stretched from their sockets. A third rope was looped under his armpits and chafed them as it tightened.

Unable to breathe, unable to scream, he was dragged over the ground with his face ploughing up leaves and scraping over sand. What was left of his nose was being rubbed off and bloodied and filled with dirt. He bent his head forward for space to breathe when the dragging stopped and he heard one rope being lashed to another. His head was raised, and then his chest as he was hoisted up. When his toes left the ground, his body started spinning. The cannibals gnashed and chanted while pulling on the rope that raised him to his slaughtering.

Strangely, Pleckoo felt little. It was just one more agony, and now he was dizzy—a discomfort that was almost a pleasure. The sacrifice of his blood and body to a tree cannibal's god seemed as good a way to die as any. And once he was dead, what would he care if his thighs and calves were eaten by savages and his skull was turned into a drinking-cup? *I'll be dead. So what*.

His body was slowing in its rotations; he seemed stuck. He looked down to see that some of his captors had fallen. In the next rotation, it looked as if they were twitching on the ground. The cannibals had been attacked! But by whom? Other cannibals? One of them looked to be getting away, running and slipping through the leaves, when he slumped and fell. The rope that held Pleckoo lost its tension, and he dropped slowly to the ground, next to a cannibal whose limbs popped up and made jerking circles before they went still.

The last two cannibals grunted at each other before they dropped to the ground, grabbed the rope around Pleckoo's ankles, and burrowed under the leaves to drag him away. Darts were pouring down when the slinking cannibals abandoned Pleckoo and made their escape, slipping through the leaves. Pleckoo felt a puncture in his thigh, then a heaviness in his limbs that was much too familiar. He could not raise his head but at the bottom of his sight he saw a dart in his flesh. He tried to squirm out of his ropes but could not move arms, nor toes, nor fingers. He tried to blink and could not do that.

The Living Death!

He wanted to scream but had no voice. He needed his arms to rip his own head off and forever end his life. A moment later, he heard the scurry of insects crawling towards him, then the voices of their riders. Sleek red ants painted with blue and white stripes ran their antennae over his body. The ants' mandibles were bound with ropes and their stingers were covered with a protective cloth. The ants' riders wore an extravagant armor made from their ants' red chitin; it was too fine, too intricate, too beautiful, to be real. The riders' faces were hidden by a mask with a grille that was attached to the undersides of their helmets.

Are these Dranverites? Were they expecting me? Did Anand send them?

The tree cannibals' limp bodies were rearranged with their faces up. Once the riders remounted their ants, they blew on thorn horns—as if to call the attention of the cannibals' clan to retrieve them. Pleckoo was picked up and bent over the shoulder of a tall, strong Dranverite who handed him, carefully, up to the arms of an ant rider who was just as strong. The rider, a woman, it seemed, from her voice as she spoke to him in an unknown tongue, set Pleckoo into a large, padded cradle at the back of her saddle, where she secured him with straps to prevent his falling out. She pulled a green dart out of a pouch at her side and peeled a wrapper off its end before she stuck it in Pleckoo's arm. He felt a mild sting, then quick relief from the thousand pains that wracked his body and the latest mutilation of his face.

The relief turned to joy. He was looking at the back of the woman's armor, so fascinatingly beautiful, when he felt a sweet, swirling sensation. The world around him was slowly spinning, turning into a blur of brilliant colors before he lost his sight.

Sight returned. He looked around him and saw an astonishing meadow of flowering plants. The sweet smell of evening primrose was in his nose. He was lying in a hammock of fine, dyed silk stretched between the stems of blooming velvet blue curls. On one side of him, he heard the deep melody of a slow-moving stream and turned to see it gushed with berry-wine. On his other side was a concert shell, where an orchestra of incomparably beautiful women awaited his permission to play. He nodded his head and the opening notes sent a shiver down his spine. A red hunter ant decorated with chains of jewels arrived at his side. An unbearably beautiful girl was kneeling on the ant's head and offering a tray. She was naked, perfectly formed, with a tiny waist and high, round breasts. Her thick and glistening nipples had tiny beads of milk at their ends. As she descended from the ant, her flawless skin changed colors—black, brown, tawny, yellow, pink, and white. As she came closer to Pleckoo, her eyes shifted colors and sparkled with the depth of gemstones—amber at first, then rose quartz, followed by turquoise, amethyst, and then opals with their rainbow iridescence. Her hair was like a thick and shining fall of sun rays that swept the ground behind her.

Pleckoo was aroused and looked down to realize he was naked. His endowment had been enhanced—he wasn't sure it was his, and grabbed it to make sure. The woman looked at him in deep admiration as she set the tray on a table and pressed a sweet in his mouth. Its outside melted, and a honey infused with endless flavors released in a long and delicious chain as she pressed her warm, full lips to his and her tongue danced with his own. She broke away to raise up a drinking bag of berry-wine. She held its nipple to his mouth and squeezed, and after he drank, a warmth in his stomach spread through his chest and tingled in his fingers and toes.

"Where am I?" he asked as he giggled like a child.

"In Bee-Jor," she said, and her voice was like the warmth of the womb.

Before he could speak another word, she climbed into the hammock with him, knelt on his sides, and lowered herself to take him inside her. The sensation was intense, and made him sob with ecstasy as she rocked atop him, pulling up to his end and then plunging back down. "Stop!" he shouted, anxious that it would end too soon. She smiled and leaned forward, offering him her breast. When he took it in his mouth, he licked around her nipple before sucking it to drink a stream of sweet milk that filled him with an even deeper bliss. When he could drink no more, he pulled away to look at her when her skin, her hair, and her eyes turned a deep, poppy red. The flowers, the trees, and the sky above all emptied into red. The redness darkened and gave way to a celestial blueness, and a profound and peaceful sleep. Within that state, Pleckoo's spirit rose from out of itself and looked down on his own reclining body. He felt a pure, ever-growing rapture as it became his own guardian and protected his sleep.

Days and nights passed until a rip opened within the ceiling of his sleep to allow in the light of waking. The spirit of Pleckoo felt a deep and irresistible pull as his body yanked at him with invisible hands to draw him back inside. *I don't want to wake!* he thought. *I'm staying right here!* But he felt again the weight of his head and the feel of a cushion pushing up on his back. This was followed by the shock of a damp cloth being wiped over his head and over the gap that had been his nose. The moisture it left had a sparkling irritation that faded and left a bitter stink. The wet cloth was scrubbing over his right ear, then inside it, producing a loud rubbing noise as it twisted inside his ear canal. The cloth went to his left ear and pulled on the edge of what had been his lobe before it had been amputated so very long ago. *Why can't I see?* he wondered, then felt something like shallow cups set over his eyes to blind him. He tried to grab them in order to see who was perpetrating this strange mischief, but his arms had no power—he was still caught inside the Living Death.

Something like a moist stick with a liquid on its end moved over his forehead. He heard voices and then a strange language, and realized that several people were there—wherever there was. A room? The outdoors? And what were they doing to his face? The pounding of his heart was in his ears as he realized something.

These are Dranverites! They're going to eat me! These

are the real cannibals! They'll stuff my face and my stomach with onion, then bake me alive in a sun-kiln!

To confirm his suspicions, something sharp, like a fine and tiny knife, was pressed to the outside of his ear to make a shallow incision. He felt the skin of his ear being separated and peeled apart and then the slicing and removal of cartilage. *What kind of torture is this?* he wondered as pain radiated through the left side of his face. It worsened when he felt something like a needle pulling thread through the incision, and then he felt some burning liquid. Soon after, the knife went to the top of his face, between his eyes, and made an incision that cut to his hairline. The knife cut a shape he imagined was like a long-stalked mushroom. The blinding white light of pure pain was burning in his skull when he felt this flap of skin being lifted and stretched. Inside his skull were a thousand screams echoing within each other and pushing out his eyeballs as they flowed with tears.

The tormentors stopped whispering among each other and were shouting now in anger and panic. Some of their words sounded like the Slopeish for "awake" and "eye-water." He felt a prick in the side of his arm again and then . . . that same euphoria that had sent him to Bee-Jor.

How quickly the pain subsided. The Land of Endless Honey was coming back into view, lovelier than the first time, its flowers beaded from a warm rain shower. And there, just above those golden lantern flowers, was that gorgeous girl with her skin that changed colors. Her breasts were bobbing as she flew towards him on the back of a black cloak butterfly . . .

Pleckoo was waking again once more from a sleep inside the Living Death. How much time had passed? He remembered there had been another prick to his arm, and the injection of some potion that sent him into ecstasy, than plunged him into some deep and silent sleep that lasted for days . . . or a moon. He heard footsteps coming towards him and hoped they had brought another of these darts to jam in his flesh.

The oiled cloth they set over his eyes was removed. Pleckoo saw the face of a curious-looking man. He had a trimmed purple beard that contrasted with the yellow-orange paint on his face and the natural green of his smiling eyes. The man wore a pink-striped jacket with padded shoulders over a pair of bloodred leggings. He squeezed open Pleckoo's mouth with a gentle pinch of his fingers and smelled his breath. Around the man's neck was a pendant of a flat, round crystal that he picked up and peered through as he examined Pleckoo's nose, eyes, and ears.

Pleckoo felt an itching at the center of his face, one he could not scratch. The itch was growing worse when he sneezed. His head lifted up and fell back into a pillow and then he saw a flash of darkness. He had blinked! The man before him grinned, ran off,

Pleckoo was sure, to summon others. Pleckoo's finger-tips were curling and he could bend his thumbs. He could waggle his toes and, a short time later, he could turn his feet up.

When Purple Beard returned, he was in the company of others with skins painted in the colors of meadow flowers. All of them wore red clothing. They watched Pleckoo as he pulled his legs off the cushion of his raised bed and let them dangle over its side as he sat up. His arms had come back to life. Slowly he reached towards his face, to the insuffer-able itch in its middle. He made a claw of his fingers to scratch himself when the strangers gasped. Purple Beard gently grabbed his wrist.

"*Rara, rara,*" the man said, shaking his head. He took a hand mirror of black obsidian from the top of a tall chest and held it up to Pleckoo's face. Hating mirrors, Pleckoo turned away; but Purple Beard was insistent, and forced him to look.

Pleckoo blinked and stared at what he saw, then grabbed at the mirror to stare some more. His body shook uncontrollably as he laughed and cried in disbe-lief. His face and his ear were filled with scary, black stitches, but they held in place a restored earlobe and something else so miraculous he had to touch it to make sure it was real. He raised a finger to his face, then collapsed in tears when he felt a warm tip at the end of his very own nose.

ACKNOWLEDGMENTS

Thank you to Matt Goodman and Robert Rodi for the careful reading of the early drafts—I'm still getting *lay* and *lie* right and, damn, those commas. And thanks always to Mike Dobson and Polly Grose for their ever-loving support.

ABOUT THE AUTHOR

CLARK THOMAS CARLTON is an award-winning novelist, playwright, journalist, screen and television writer, and a producer of reality TV. He was born in the South, grew up in the East, went to school in the North, and lives with his family in the West. As a child he spent hours observing ants and their wars and pondered their similarity to human societies.

Discover great authors, exclusive offers, and more at hc.com.